The *Flight* of the *Deer*

The Flight of the Deer

GILBERT VELIZ

Dec 7 2015

Gilbert Veliz

TATE PUBLISHING
AND ENTERPRISES, LLC

Published by Tate Publishing & Enterprises, LLC
127 E. Trade Center Terrace | Mustang, Oklahoma 73064 USA
1.888.361.9473 | www.tatepublishing.com

Tate Publishing is committed to excellence in the publishing industry. The company reflects the philosophy established by the founders, based on Psalm 68:11,
"The Lord gave the word and great was the company of those who published it."

Book design copyright © 2015 by Tate Publishing, LLC. All rights reserved.
Cover design by Maria Louella Mancao
Interior design by Gram Telen

Published in the United States of America

ISBN: 978-1-63449-967-5
1. Fiction / Cultural Heritage
2. Fiction / Hispanic & Latino
15.08.07

Acknowledgments

Some have said that Juan Guadalupe Posada's work helped to promote revolution in Mexico. Before his death in 1913, he produced vivid illustrations for the penny news sheets that sold on street corners and outdoor *mercados* (markets) of Mexico City. Later, muralists Jose Clemente Orozco and Diego Rivera, in the '20s, painted the story of the revolution and claimed Posada as one of their own. Posada used fleshless *calaveras* (skeletons) to depict the collective soul of the Mexican people. They were living in a place whose social structure was shifting beneath their feet. Newly arriving *campesinos* (rural people) came to a giant city where little was stable and enduring, except the traditions of the rural and timeless Mexico that they brought with them.

In the spirit of Posada and the Mexican muralists, graphic artist Eric Favela made skeletal *calavera* drawings for each section of the book, and muralist David Tineo, whose murals have decorated many Tucson spaces, painted the mural for the front and back cover of the book.

Both are Mexican-American artists who live in Tucson, Arizona.

Contents

Los Yaquis bailan

The night of the Yaqui ceremony at Pascua Village, a conglomeration of the devout and the curious were there to observe. It was obvious that the commencement of the activities was based upon something other than the clock.

The dance was to take place in the three-sided ramada with the dirt floor. The dancers were from Sonora, Mexico, from Torim, one of the eight Yaqui towns. It was the one that had undergone the least changes caused by the massive agribusiness in the Yaqui Valley.

There were three dancers: two pascolas, who depicted hunters, and the *maaso*, who portrayed the deer. The dance was to be accompanied by musical instruments of both old and, in Yaqui's eyes, modern types.

On the right, near the opening to the ramada, where the observers stood, was the man who played a battered violin. To his left, a boy stood with a native instrument made of a dried half gourd that he struck with a stick or used as a resonator for the rasping sound made by rubbing two notched sticks together. Another strummed a small harp also of native manufacture, which had about twenty strings and was held in a horizontal position as he played.

Virgilio Valenzuela was the old man of the fiesta and, it was said, the best dancer. He had long white hair to the shoulder, tied at the neck with a red ribbon like a pony's tail. The dancers' costumes were scanty, nothing above the waist. Each pascola wore a small but heavy-looking wooden mask of a human face grotesquely painted, with slits in the wood for eyebrows, where there was placed the bristly fur of some wild animal. The masks were pushed to one side of the face when the pascolas were not dancing, and under the light of the mesquite blaze gave the eerie appearance that they had two faces.

Another musician was tuning his drum by carefully holding it over a bed of hot coals, tightening its skin. The dancers casually talked to each other in a language that I didn't recognize and waited patiently until everything was perfect before they would start.

Each dancer wore a special rattle made of the cocoons of the giant silkworm. Each cocoon contained within it a few pebbles that made a dry crackling sound as the performers moved. The cocoons were sewn together in strings of about six feet long and were wound around the legs below the knee. They were called teneroim and were very old and above any valuation in money. All three dancers were barefooted. Around the waist, they wore leather belts where tiny brass bells hung, which softly jangled as they paced in preparation.

When I looked carefully at Virgilio, who continued to murmur to the others as they waited, it was obvious that he was well into his sixties, maybe seventies. The muscles in his shoulders and arms appeared weak and slack in his slim brown body. He didn't appear as if he could dance much, much less be the best.

After meticulous preparation and adjustment of instruments and costumes by the performers, when everything was perfect, the musicians started with a steady, even rhythm, and first, the Pascolas danced. The transformation of Virgilio was wondrous. Every slowly spinning movement of his body, head, arms, and legs, flowed naturally and somehow correctly, in an aesthetic way, with the other.

His precise movements were not displays of strength or agility but of virtuosity, the virtuosity of the spirit, the still passionate virtuosity of age and spirit that overshadows mere technical brilliance.

The deer dancer was a much younger and suppler individual. A white shawl was tightly wound on the top of his head, where a deer head was placed. It was made of deer hide and antlers adorned with red ribbons. In each hand, he had a rattle made of a gourd and a wooden handle. Only the shrill whistle of a wooden flute and the hollow thump of a drum, which were played simultaneously by a seated individual, accompanied the part of the pageant when the maaso and pascolas danced together in the prehistoric ritual.

By focusing in that light on the head of the deer, the impression of a desperate animal in flight from the hunters was overwhelming. It has been said that when a deer dancer is good, he moves with the grace and presence of a bullfighter. The performance that night in that dusty shed, with only a handful observing, was worthy of any sunny Sunday afternoon in Mexico City, in the Plaza de Toros, or of the sacred rituals conducted by the ordained in a towering cathedral. That night, in the weak yellow light of a bare bulb, the pascolas and maaso did their ancient dance, for God.

Two blocks away, oblivious to all this, could be heard the revving up of engines and the penetrating sound of amplified rap as the multiplex theater disgorged their occupants. Almost unobserved in Tucson, in the middle of the Sonoran Desert's metropolis, an ancient ritual, older than the beginning of agriculture and older by far than the two-thousand-year-old religion of which it has become a part, the Yaquis worshiped and prayed for the success of their hunt, and of their survival.

Part 1
Los de ayer

Padrecito

A man with a battered guitar sang softly as four others, each with the end of a rope placed under the pine coffin, slowly lowered it into the yawning brown earth.

> Mexico lindo y querido si muero lejos di ti,
> Que digan que estoy dormido y que me traigan aqui,
> Mexico lindo y querido si muero lejos di ti.

The small cemetery outside of Naco, Sonora, was peppered with ancient wooden crosses, one or two now bending sideways; others appeared to bow to the visitors. Here and there, remnants of what had been cement borders around graves pointed now in unexpected directions as the soft ground that had supported them had long ago given way.

The handful of people who had heard about Padre Reyes's death with sufficient time to travel from nearby towns were clothed in black; the women, with *pañoletas* covering their worn heads and faces in the old way. These were the ones who had accompanied him for years—no, decades—as he led them every Sunday night in the rosary, the Mexican's prayer to the Virgin de Guadalupe. Now, only the very old or those attending a wake ever participated in the ageless ritual.

It was perhaps nostalgia or perhaps some other subconscious reason that had drawn me to this dusty sad place. For I had known Padre Reyes only through the eyes of a child as he ministered to my grandparents and parents—all long gone now—and to the other mining families of the Mexican community in Bisbee, Arizona.

As a child, I had overheard talk by my parents about his having arrived from Mexico in the clothes of a common laborer, seeking work in the copper mines. It was with the intercession of the bishop of the diocese of the region that the ecclesiastical black suit and Roman collar were soon provided. As was a small hall located in the middle of the barrio where the *mineros* and their *familias* lived that, with a few modifications, became the church where they worshipped. For the next sixty years, as the Bisbee copper mines boomed and finally ran their course, Padre Reyes was to be the spiritual center of that Mexican community's world.

⁂

The road north from Naco rises slowly in elevation for seven miles into the Mule Mountains in its approach into Bisbee. My young niece Vanessa, who had accompanied me to the funeral, drove her Honda Civic up the winding road toward our destination. She, like many Mexican-Americans of her generation, had been struggling, mostly successfully, to learn Spanish. She asked me to interpret the words of the haunting melody that had accompanied the simple ceremony. And with limited poetic ability, I said, "My beautiful and beloved Mexico, if I die away from thee, say that I am but asleep and bring me back to thee. My beautiful and beloved Mexico, if I die away from thee."

"We never spoke Spanish at home, except when my parents wanted to keep something secret from me, then they would exchange such a flood of words that I could only pick up about every sixth one. They wanted an American daughter, not one who spoke pocho English and pocho Spanish," she said.

"They did the right thing, *hija* (dear). When I was in grade school, it wasn't my folks, who themselves were carrying on their own battle with the new language, at Saint Pat's, we just got a rap on the knuckles with a ruler. The nuns claimed that any Spanish words they didn't understand, and they didn't understand any, having arrived from the convents in Boston or Chicago, must be a curse word or something obscene or disrespectful. At that time, I thought it was no big loss."

"Different strokes for different folks." She laughed.

"It all came to the same thing. Strange how things work out. Here you are making trips all over Southern Arizona, trying to recruit folklorico dancers for Pima College from the high schools, and I make a living by taking photographs of things Mexican for travel mags and luxury liners selling the Mexican Riviera. But in the future, *sin duda* (without doubt), all our lives lie with computers and science and not to south—"

"*Sí, Tío*" (Yes, Uncle), she answered quietly, and I didn't know if she agreed with me or just was avoiding a touchy subject.

※

It is always a visual shock to see the gigantic expanse of Lavender Pit, whose copper ore for so many years filled the coffers of the Phelps Dodge Corporation and that, at the same time, placed food on the tables of thousands of men and their families. Men, like ants, scrambled up and down its steep sides in pursuit of their daily bread.

A road had been cut into the pit's side, and it had permitted monstrously sized trucks to descend in a slow spiral to the depths of the hole. Now, because of abandonment and neglect, the road had eroded back to more natural slopes in many places as the earth healed itself with weather and time. At the very bottom of the pit was a small pond of milky-black-and-turquoise-colored liquid.

Before this unearthly vision could be reconciled with reality, the highway pushed through a short canyon between two hills, and before me was old Bisbee. On the right side is the red hill that is still scarred with horizontal red rock foundations, where houses, high up its steep side, once stood. Interspersed among the carefully cemented red rocks, there are concrete stairs that extend like fingers hundreds of steps up from the bottom of the canyon and now lead to nowhere. This had been the Bisbee barrio of many Mexicanos. For many years, it has been called Chihuahua Hill.

Once past this area, you find yourself in a space in which a person, if magically transformed to the present from the 1920s or '30s, would recognize and be comfortable. So few are the changes that only the vehicles are now of modern vintage. For the nostalgic, this town had the good fortune of having been very well built of concrete and stone when the mines were awash in money. When the copper gave out, there were no new enterprises needing to tear the old buildings down and build anew as the long-haired and artistic fled their suburbs. The town appeared to have remained frozen in time, leaving remnants of its vibrant past everywhere.

⁊

David Molina had, for the last years of Padre Reyes's life, been his eyes and his strength as he drove him to the various small communities in Southern Arizona so that the ancient priest could officiate at the important milestones, usually weddings and funerals, of his scattered flock's lives. Don David, as he was referred to by the parishioners, had invited a small group to lunch after the funeral, at the Copper Queen, a once-elegant hotel that now showed the well-worn patina of its age. I also called him Don when I addressed him publically, as though he was my social superior, which he was, at least in age.

This was not as it was normally done, but David did not have an appropriate residence for this function, and anyway, there were just a very few who would attend. Father Reyes had outlived almost all those who had shared and framed his life.

Around the luncheon table, the windows decorated with lace curtains and tables graced with bone-white tablecloths, conversation turned to the strange requests Padre Reyes made on his death bed. One was that he be buried in Mexico, and the other that, that song be sung at his interment.

It was known by the padre's friends that, after he left Mexico over sixty years ago, he had never again set foot on that land. He had lived on the Mexican border all that time and, with a five-minute deviation, when he went to give communion to his homebound parishioners in Naco, Arizona, could have easily been in Mexico. Whatever had been the cause of his estrangement from the country of his birth died with him.

What seemed stranger was the request for the popular folksong. Here was a priest who was so tradition bound that he wouldn't or couldn't follow the modern changes of Catholic rituals. It was now required that the priest face those attending the mass and interact by repeating the sacred words in English or in Spanish instead of Latin, as had been so for a thousand years in ten thousand places.

Over the years, he became a well-known and discussed figure in the Southern Arizona mining towns as he struggled to climb the hills and steps in his scuffed black shoes and his worn black pants and shirt, to visit his flock. For it was known that Padre Reyes continued to say the Mass like it had been for so many years, his attention focused only on the altar and in Latin.

In his daily renewal of the ancient ritual, there was to be none of the imposed fellowship which now required, at certain times in the Mass, that members of the congregation turn toward and greet and hug each other. Nor did they join hands, in chainlike unity, when they recited the Lord's Prayer. His breathy renditions of the centuries-old Gregorian chants were never to be replaced in his Mass by a mariachi band singing its version of a sacred hymn.

To his eyes, all these adaptations directed by Rome and the bishops were politically correct attempts by a church trying to recapture its relevance for its lonely parishioners who were living the isolation of modern life. But by changing the focus of the mass to the people and the community instead of the communion with Christ, he thought they had succeeded in substituting the mundane for the sublime. In his gentle way, he displayed a stubbornness of steel, and he would have none of it.

He hadn't wanted to disobey his superiors for he was not a renegade or a rebel. It was that his religion had been instilled into his very bones, and who of us can change our bones? So why was there not a Te Deum or a "panis angelicus" as his body was deposited into the earth? For this mystery, nobody in the small gathering had an answer.

David's association with Padre Reyes had begun many years before. Shortly after his young wife's unexpected death, he had sought the solace of the church and of Father Reyes. Over a period of time, and because of Father Reyes's compassion and understanding when he suddenly lost the love of his life, David began to spend all his evening after his shift at the mine; and his Sundays, at the parish rectory. He did whatever had to be done to keep the padre and the church functioning smoothly. He cooked and took care of the priest's quarters and the maintenance of the small church.

For decades, sure as clockwork, the two would attend whatever athletic event the local high school team had against those of the surrounding communities. In those innocent days before radio or television, football, basketball, and baseball, or whatever competition the local young men—the Pumas—participated in, took up an inordinate amount of attention and importance in that isolated mining community. The aging miner with his frayed red baseball hat with the gray *B* and the priest were no different. They all identified with the latest crop of "stars," whether they came from the elegant stone houses surrounded by lawns in Warren, from the shacks perched on red shale of Chihuahua Hill, or from Brewery gulch. Everybody knew that, after the seasons of glory, there would be time enough for all to assume their preordained posts in the mine and the community.

Father Reyes, to avoid gossip in the small community, refused the help of the parish's women in any household tasks although they were infinitely more qualified than David in those matters. Since the priest was sought by many and could not always be available, it sometimes fell to David to assist some women who came to the rectory in times of crises or depression. Some sought help with simple home repairs that required a man's strength; others needed someone who was discrete to commiserate about personal problems. The handsome young widower was talented in these endeavors. His greatest talent over the years, it turned out, was keeping the fact of them all only to himself.

In this way, the two men grew old together. The dedicated priest accompanied by his more-worldly assistant. But there was more to the old miner's dedication to the priest and the small church. David was silently atoning for what he suspected—no, knew—had occurred when he was a young boy in Mexico, in La Colorada, Sonora.

He was about eight years old when, very early one morning, there had been a great uproar in his home, with much shouting by his mother and cursing by his father. His father and older brother took the family's ancient single-shot pistol from its hiding place and rushed out of the house. They were gone for months. He later learned that they had pursued the young priest who had impregnated two of his young sisters, across the American border all the way to Oregon. When the men returned, there already was a new family member and one more shortly expected. They said they had found the errant young priest. He had been so afraid when found and confronted by the two that "he died of fright before our very eyes." David's mother crossed herself when she heard the story.

Because of the shame of the fatherless infants, all of the family drifted across the border, where they were not known but where they knew work could be found in the copper mines. David thought that there was no greater sin in the eyes of God than killing a priest no matter what the justification. When he met the almost-saintly Father Reyes after the unexpected death of his wife, he dedicated himself to the path of atonement for the curse, he believed, had fallen on him and his family because of his father and brother's crime.

⚬

As the group was breaking up, David pulled me aside and asked if I still traveled often into the interior of Mexico. I told him that it was my intention to again go to Guadalajara in October to observe their month-long fiestas. That extravaganza of art, music, and dance when the Tapatios annually reward themselves for having had the good sense or good luck to live in that beautiful city.

"More and more, I find that I am drawn back south. The old cliché that 'you can take a Mexicano out of Mexico, but not so easily take Mexico out of a Mexicano,' in my case at least, is proving to be true."

And then somebody suddenly said, "*Arriba para* (Raise your glasses) Padre Reyes and all the Mexicanos in Arizona's mines to whom he showed the right path." We all raised our glasses in a final toast.

David said that he had a few personal things that belonged to Father Reyes, which the priest, in his delirium shortly before his death, had asked be delivered to his sister, Maria Luisa Castañeda, who lived in Guadalajara.

Two weeks later, Federal Express delivered a package. The small box contained a tattered prayer book, a rosary whose round beads had been worn oblong from thousands of times that devout fingers circuitously moved from one bead to the next. A worn grey envelope contained a faded photograph of a seated man and a standing woman both in formal clothes; she had her hand on his shoulder, a familiar wedding pose in the old days. There was also sepia-colored photograph of a girl who was just beginning to blossom into the beauty of young womanhood. The photographs had been carefully wrapped in yellow waxed paper. I smiled to myself. Father Reyes, at least in this way, had been constant to the end; no plastic or Saran Wrap for him. Finally, there was an address in David's scrawl.

312 Avenida Lazaro Cardenas
Guadalajara, Jalisco, Mexico.

It was precious little to pass on after a lifetime of toil, at least according to our conventional wisdom.

Maria Luisa

It was a taxi ride of teeth-clenching dimensions as the happy-go-lucky driver, right arm lazily thrown back on the front seat, conversed with the "Americano" about whatever came into his stream of consciousness. He steered absentmindedly with his left arm through the murderously threatening traffic and the "eighteen-wheelers" on the *periferico* (freeway), turning constantly to assess my reaction to his latest statement. Not a moment too soon, darting dangerously in front of other tourist-carrying taxis, he stopped at the Plaza de Tlaquepaque. I, grateful to be alive, handed him a wad of pesos and, without waiting for change, tumbled out while he pointed me in the general direction of Calle Lazaro Cardenas.

The plaza, like so many other public spaces in Mexico, is dominated by a church. To the left between the church and the kiosk was a sidewalk. It once had been a narrow street appropriate for burros or horse-drawn carts. Now on both sides of the walk, shops full of wondrous objects of blown glass, ceramics, leather, wood, textiles, and silver were for sale. As always, I was struck by the fact that Mexico is a land of artisans. Everything here was made by hand and thus imparted that different kind of quality that only a human's touch gives to an object, imperfect through the object may be. My mind flashed back to the infinitely accurate microchip with its cold and inhuman precision and to the plastic perfection of the other machine-made products that surround our lives to the north.

My eyes were drawn to a table where an ancient, shriveled Indian woman displayed for sale collections of tiny clay skeletons no larger than my little finger. Among them, there was a bony couple in formal wedding garments, their skulls thrown back in a grimacing amorous embrace. In another scene, a grinning black-robed skeleton priest with a rosary hanging from his neck sat in a tiny square confessional. He appeared to be listening to the sins of a kneeling penitent, whose skull was reverentially bowed over bony hands with interlocking digits.

There was a depiction of the joyous movement of life, or of death, by a group of colorfully dressed skeletons dancing to the music of macabre mariachis complete with tiny instruments and matching charro outfits. And in the most prominent display on her table, a group of skeleton mourners, arranged in a circle, peered into a grave while the skeleton in the coffin looked back at them with a knowing grin of what too awaited them all.

I knew this type of folk art is a not-too-subtle view of the indios' belief of the inseparability of life and death, a humorous acceptance and celebration of the mortality of us all.

The toothless *viejita* (old lady) who was selling these wares said, as if to no one in particular but which I knew was directed at me, "Skulls and *esqueletos* (skeletons) have an important role *en las religiones de Mexico's indigenos* (religions of Mexico's Indians), and this has been long before the arrival of the *Españoles* (Spaniards).

"*En el Dia de los Muertos, familias enteras* (On the day of the dead, entire families) spend the day and the night in a fiesta with their dead relatives and amigos at the *panteon* (graveyard), and outside the cemetery's fence is set up a market of food and flowers. Crowds of indios squeeze in between the headstones and wooden crosses to be with their loved ones. Cempasuschitl, which you Norte Americanos call marigolds, and little skulls made out of sugar, are seen everywhere. Because we don't forget so easy. In all the years I worked in El Norte, never did I see, after the day of the parade of black cadillacs on buriel day, a return visit by the family.

"*Es que la creencia de los Aztecas* (The belief of the Aztecs) was that souls did not die but resided in Mictlan, somewhere southeast of what we now know of as Mexico City.

"*En ese dia magico* (On that magic day), the souls leave Mictlan and travel through the mountains, *desiertos y barrancas* (deserts and ravines), to their home, wherever their bones lay buried. To help lead them back, their *amigos y familias* (friends and families) light candles throughout the night. Flowers are strewn in the paths to the cemeteries so that their scent foretells the feast of food and drink that has been prepared by the living for the souls' yearly return.

"When the spirits arrive, we can feel their presence, and in the flickering yellow light, some lucky ones even see them. Throughout the night, surrounded by candles, incense and the favorite food and drink of the returning visitor, the living, in a solemn but joyful mood, share old memories and tell of new experiences to their visiting loved ones," she said in an aged tremulous voice.

I knew that this tradition of celebrating the inseparability of life and death was so deeply rooted in the Aztecas that, after the conquest, the Spanish missionaries were not able to stamp the practice out and, instead, assimilated it into the Catholic rituals of All Saint's Day and All Soul's Day, which in turn became our Halloween fantasies.

Seeing that I was not going to buy anything and had just been pumping her for information, the wrinkled one, apparently having, in the past, picked up bits and pieces from her gringo customers' and from her travels in El Norte said sarcastically, "You foreign photographers, you who await the judgment day and the resurrection of the dead, or who await at any moment being whisked away into the presence of God in—*como se dice* (how do you call it)—the rapture, you focus and shoot away with your fancy cameras, and more than once, I've heard comments on the 'innocent quaintness' of the *indio descalsado*'s (shoeless Indians) belief of the spirit migration. But what are the words to describe your beliefs?

"What you don't hear while you crowd among the stone and wooden crosses, and the statutes of the Virgin, with the indios with sandals with soles cut out of abandoned tires, as they look up into the clicking cameras, they mutter and wonder among themselves about the strangeness of the annual visitation by the Norte Americanos who seem intent on recording on film the indios' yearly family reunions."

~

Shortly, I arrived at numero 312. The very old rectangular one-story masonry and rock building was built to the edge of the sidewalk. It abutted on either side buildings of almost identical height and appearance, except for the colors of their walls: vivid pink, purple, and canary yellow. I thought about how those walls had, for generations, kept unwanted things out and precious things in. Against these walls, countless dogs, after having determined who had preceded them, left their own calling card for the next canine visitor to consider. Abuelas, having grown old, sat with a grandchild in their arms on straight-backed wooden chairs propped up against the wall and enjoyed the sun's warmth or the cool of the shade, depending on the season and the height of the sun.

For many years, lime whitewash had been tinted with colors obtained from natural sources and boiled with the juice of nopales before applying it to the walls. This was supposed to improve the durability and adherence of the wash. No matter the effort, the watery concoction, after a time, would flake off. This permitted imaginative new colors to be applied by the owners over the old. On some walls, depending on their exposure to weather and sun, flakes of the several coats deteriorated at different times. This left an unexpected history of color. It was like an expressionist painting left by weathering and time, and not an artist. All the varied muted colors hinted that each heavy wooden door opened up into a different world.

An old man looked up from watering a pomegranate tree, greeted me gruffly, and then shuffled out, grumbling as he went, apparently to announce my arrival. Passing through a short corridor, I escaped the heat and clamor of the street. The house opened up into a sunny square patio that was surrounded on all four sides by deeply shaded porches. Their roofs were supported by columns of rock and masonry and by wooden beams. Each porch was topped off with gracefully slanted tile roofs.

The porch felt naturally airy and cool, perhaps because of its considerable height and the open design of the building. Here and there, in the open space in the center of the patio, there were splashes of vividly colored flowers and luxuriant plants in massive containers. The containers had been intricately carved by hand out of soft stone. Space had been reserved among the thick flagstone, which otherwise covered the patio's entire floor, for plantings. In these openings, the roots of fragrant bushes and of the small pomegranate tree were visible as they reached downward into the earth. At the center was a small fountain that gave off a small cooling sound.

Against the inner wall of the corridor opposite the door I had entered, there were philodendrons planted in a hedge. They had been placed in square stonework whose sides were decorated with rows of white tile, each with blue hummingbirds facing first one way then the other so that their beaks almost touched. Underneath the row of birds, there was another row of tiles with a Spanish-Moorish design in the same white-and-blue colors, followed below by another identical row of birds. Behind the white, blue, and green colors of the tiles and plants, there was a watermelon-colored wall. It was all a creative fusion of Iberian,

Islamic, and Mexican-Indian concepts of beauty, depicting a vibrant tranquility with color and design.

I sat down in the old carved wooden chair that was pushed up against a table and waited. The tabletop was adorned with a beautiful geometric design made of hundreds of tiny embedded pieces of mosaic tile, and felt cool to the touch. I had the impression of being in a place of unusual serenity. Light and shadow, cool and warmth, silence and sound—all in constant variation with each other—seemed to heighten the awareness of my senses.

One of the doors that led from the interior of the house to the patio opened, and a tall, slightly stooped woman, elegantly attired in gray and black, entered. Her black hair was generously interspersed with white so as to give it a gray metal sheen. The still-thick mane was severely pulled back from her face into a very tight bun. Perhaps because of this, her cheekbones appeared unusually high for a woman of her obvious age. Her features were fine, with a slightly aquiline nose, above which peered startling blue green eyes.

In an elegant and refined Spanish, she introduced herself as Maria Luisa Castañeda. She asked the old man to bring us café con leche and empanaditas, and then in perfectly accented English, she said, "I understand that you are from the United States."

"Yes, this is the third time I've been to the Fiestas de Octubre, and I've brought a few personal effects of Padre Reyes's, which, before his death, he asked to be delivered to you."

Her face blanched, as if all of the blood had been drained from it.

"I had not seen or heard from Antonio for over sixty years," she said in a flat voice, which didn't reveal anything that she was feeling.

With startling-white smooth hands, she opened the small box and removed the few objects. As she touched his tattered prayer book and worn rosary, it seemed to me that she noticeably was restraining herself from any too-obvious display of emotion.

"And where was it in the United States that Antonio lived?" she asked.

"In Arizona, along the Mexican border, in the mining camps, mostly in Bisbee. Bisbee is seven miles north from the frontera, at Naco, Sonora."

"Is that near Agua Prieta?" she asked.

"Agua Prieta is just a few miles away, also on the border. Douglas is on the American side. Bisbee and Douglas were once referred to as copper's twin cities. In the old days, copper was mined in Bisbee, and then the ore was trained to be smelted and refined in Douglas. But all that is finished," I said.

"I suppose that because of modern technology and your missiles, the demand for copper casing for bullets has diminished," she suggested.

Startled by the sophistication of her comment, I answered, "No, it's not that complicated. It's just that the copper ore deposits in that region were exhausted, or so they say. Before the mining boom, this area on both sides of the border had all been part of the great expanse of the Apaches. In fact, years later, after what was left of them had been moved by the US Army to where they could commit no further mischief, the county where these two towns are located was named for their great chief Cochise."

I noticed that her hands suddenly were trembling excessively, almost as if she had a neurological condition. She stopped our short conversation suddenly by stating, "And I am exhausted from the shock of emotions that your delivery of Antonio's possessions has provoked." Her cup made a clattering sound as she clumsily tried to replace it on her saucer.

"Since you are here for the fiestas, perhaps you can return another day for I am most anxious to hear about Antonio's life in the United States. Please forgive me for not having asked you, but what is it that you do?"

"I am a freelance photographer, but unlike many, I choose to photograph things that I find beautiful, and not the hideous and shocking that seems to be so much in vogue today. That's why I've returned to the fiestas, again. As a hobby, I also like to study other's photographs and try to get into the photographer's mind to see what he or she saw when the photograph was taken. It is so common to just casually look at an image but not really look. I try to really look, if the photograph interests me."

"I suppose that, in a matter of speaking, beautiful things can be found here in Mexico," she said and, after a short pause, continued. "It would please me greatly if you came on Thursday at about the same time. I have something that I want to show you."

The old man suddenly appeared as if by magic and, in a sullen and irritated manner, escorted me to the front of the house and slammed and latched the door.

That evening, in the Teatro Degollado, among many foreign tourists and those Mexicanos who could afford the price of a ticket, I photographed the wonderful colors and shapes of the dancers of Mexico's many different regions and knew that I had come to the right place.

Revista Ilustrada

A small table with immaculate linen had been prepared in the patio, near a blossoming crimson bougainvillea. Two chairs made of the traditional-woven cedar strip foundation covered with drum-tight-stretched pig skin had been positioned to provide comfortable access to the silver coffee urn and pan dulce. My hostess immediately appeared and, after some superficial conversation about my activities in Guadalajara, said, "I see you are admiring the equipal. People from the north find it surprising that the Tapatios can make such comfortable and durable objects from so little and all by hand with just the crudest of tools. It is part of the genius that we get from the indios." She then opened a leather case and pulled out a Mexican periodical that was obviously very old, the paper fibers starting to come apart. It was held together in a thin plastic wrapping.

"I am a bit of a historian and, over the years, have collected materials of interest to me. This magazine, which was published shortly after the actual event took place, has a description of the battle of Agua Prieta. It has a photograph of the victors—Alvaro Obregon, Plutarco Elias Calles, and Lazaro Cardenas—together after the battle with Pancho Villa. Considering subsequent historical events, I found it extraordinary that they would all be there together. Don't you agree?" she asked.

My quizzical and uncomprehending look must have told it all because she suddenly, in an obviously irritated manner, said,

"You Norte Americanos are truly monumentally self-absorbed. I thought that, because you are from that region, you would have some appreciation for this!"

When she regained her composure, she added softly, "You would think that one hundred million people across a two-thousand-mile border would arouse some, curiosity. But we might as well be part of the Ming Dynasty."

Defensively, I mentioned my budding interest in Mexico and its historical photographs and the courses in Mexican history that I had taken at the university. But the Battle of Agua Prieta had not been mentioned in any significant way. That, I would have remembered because the site was almost in my backyard, figuratively speaking.

In a further attempt to excuse my ignorance, I said, "There was something else. The thread of the history of Mexico in those times seemed all jumbled up. The story, as presented in our classes, was replete with names and dates but seemed absent any logic as to the reasons for all the momentous events. It appeared to me that one general would rise to power to be put down by another, and then the process would be repeated and repeated."

I looked at the old woman to see if my comments had upset her further. She silently pushed the old magazine that she had placed on the table in my direction. I picked it up and started to leaf through its pages. Before I could finish my examination, she said, "The whole story is not there, as we were to find out later."

There was a long silence as I waited for her to explain. Her eyes glazed over with thoughts that were far from that shaded patio. I returned the magazine to her. She carefully placed it on the table and smoothed out its pages. Trying to find some common ground, I said, "I have a collection of photographs of those times that I've gathered from books and other sources. I like to examine them now and then, but it's true. They haven't cleared up a lot of my questions."

In front of her sat a man in his early fifties. On his craggy face, he had a receding hairline; gray sideburns; and a large mustache, like an inverted *U*, extended beyond the outer edge of his lips. Its color matched his brown eyes and hair. His still-solid body, thick hands and scarred knuckles hinted that he once had swung a sledge hammer underground before his new life of pursuing images on paper. He, unexpectedly benefiting from the civil rights turmoil of the '60s by late admission into the University of Arizona, had been almost thirty-five when he was handed the parchment that stated, "Master of Fine Arts." That long-awaited day had almost faded from his memory. The memory of the nightly shock of the crisp, perfumed desert air when he came out of the stale, dank mine, where he labored to pay for his schooling, had not.

At the time, he had felt a little conflicted for taking advantage of his new status as a member of a minority, a so-called deprived minority to boot. This was something that he had never sought. He had been mightily influenced by his parents, who were born in Mexico and spoke only broken English. On his birth certificate, he was named after his father, Ricardo, but they gave him the name of Richard and named him a junior. His name was to be in English no matter that his father's was in Spanish. From his birth, they gave notice to the world and to him that their little boy was 100 percent American. In his formative years, his parents assured that there was no hint in their home that they were poor or deprived or different from anybody else in that mining community, where everyone knew his role and followed the rules with deadly seriousness. Never in his young life did he ask himself, "Why are things the way they are?" Up to then, he felt so blessed that he didn't even know the question existed. Many of those malignant things that he was to become aware of later were hidden from his young eyes.

The national civil rights movement in the late '50s and early '60s came as an unexpected shock to him, and he had been a little embarrassed to take advantage of that rebellious solidarity. Embarrassed because he had been so thoroughly indoctrinated in those innocent days that he had never considered himself discriminated upon or deprived or, in any way, lesser than any other person. The blinders had been tightly fastened, and if he noticed that they lived in the barrio only with other Mexicanos and that there were no Mexicanos who were teachers or police officers or anything else but miners, well, that was just how things were.

Now, as a middle-aged man, he saw that being a Mexicano was not a misfortune of birth, nor was it an achievement to brag on. It was just a reality that couldn't be erased. Being Mexicano issued from being himself as did his being an American, both as fundamentally joined together as his arteries and heart.

She slowly stirred her coffee with a tiny silver spoon and then continued pensively, "Perhaps I'm being unfair, because in those terrible confusing days of the revolution, the opposing factions kept forming and reforming, forming and reforming, until it was difficult to tell who stood with whom and what it all meant.

"The victors, as always, wrote the history. Afterwards, Mexico's budding communists and fascists twisted events to their advantage. Spin—I believe you call it now—and superimposed upon all this, representing all their varied interests, was the American eagle and its newspapers, with its wings widespread. It's really no wonder that the events of those days are so murky.

"It was not until years later, when Antonio tried to open my eyes and explain the contradictions which had developed, that I started to seek out answers and tried to understand those things that I had observed as a child, uncomprehendingly."

Calmly, trying to control her shaking hands, she refilled my cup with the dark steaming liquid and looked up with a quick glance at Don Miguel, who said, "Todo esta listo."

She responded, "Gracias, Miguel." Then turning to me, she added, "The cocido for the afternoon meal is simmering. It still needs a few minutes more. It's just vegetables and a little meat cooked in broth. Will you have some with us?"

A little surprised by her change in attitude toward me, I answered, "In the early morning, I ventured out from the hotel for a breakfast of birria, beans, and corn tortillas. That will do me until the evening. But I thank you for your generosity."

"If you had looked a little further, I'm sure you could have found a McDonalds." She glanced at me with an amused look.

I made a face indicating displeasure. She laughed softly then said, "Let's us Mexicanos keep that birria secret to ourselves."

A muffled "ha" came from Don Miguel's direction when she included me as a Mexican.

For a second, her face had been transformed into a shadow of earlier beauty. Meanwhile, surprisingly agile and quiet in his movements, Don Miguel placed a purple straw mat before her on the table's circular dark leather top. Then from a tray, he followed it with a thick pewter dish covered with a cloth napkin to keep the corn tortillas warm. He ladled a clear broth into a yellow Talavera soup bowl that, at its center, had a large hand-painted blue flower. She delicately unfolded an embroidered napkin on her lap and picked up the silver soup spoon. She then continued, "At first, it was relatively simple to understand. The senile old octogenarian Don Porfirio Diaz ran to Paris after the revolution first erupted. Finally, after almost forty years of having had the heel of his boot on Mexico's throat, he was gone."

I recalled having seen a photograph of Diaz as he rode through the streets of Mexico City. He was in an open black carriage pulled by a team of four prancing black horses. It was a public appearance similar to those used by European monarchs when they showed themselves to their subjects. Seated next to him was a high-ranking military officer. They both had white plumed hats with chest medals and shoulder epaulets. Above each of Diaz's white-gloved hands could be seen the bottom of his coat sleeve, which was adorned with three gold stripes. In perfect formation, six mounted and matched escorts rode in front of the carriage, their elaborate white hats kept in place with a leather strap under their chins. The cavalry made space for the carriage as it pushed through the crowd. High in the carriage's front seat sat two men who maneuvered the team of horses. They wore black coats buttoned at the throat and formal top hats. On the mirrorlike finish of the carriage door could be seen the image of a ragged young boy running alongside, trying to keep up; he was shoeless.

❧

"How the American and European oligarchy had loved that man and the privileges and concessions he granted. Oil, gas, mines, the choicest of cattle ranches, and railroads. New railroads crisscrossed the country so that the booty wrenched from our earth could be removed to the north and across the sea. The Mexican Central Railroad extended north from Mexico City to Ciudad Juarez and the United States, and also southeast to Vera Cruz and the rest of the world.

"Was it any wonder that those people called him one of the great men of the world? His justification for all this, if he was to be believed, was Mexico's need for industrial development and its need for American and European capital.

"During those times, Mexico City looked to Paris and New York for its style and fashion. The privileged women on the Paseo de la Reforma could not be distinguished from those on Fifth Avenue. Diaz was photographed riding with an English saddle and riding clothes in Chapultepec Park, indistinguishable from any European Monarch."

Surprised that she had referred to Padre Reyes's interest in the political issues of that time, I said, "Obviously, it was your closeness to Padre Reyes that opened him up to these discussions because the priest we all knew never disclosed anything about his thoughts or opinions or, as you now know, about his past."

"How little words mean, promises like dead leaves rattling in the wind soon disappear."

She played her spoon on the inside of her cup for a long while,

"But searching in the trunk of memories, to glance backward, is necessary sometimes."

She dropped her eyes and appeared to be looking at the back of her hands. Light blue veins could be seen through her tissue-thin, mottled skin. After a while, she raised her eyes, "As a young priest, he was very political. In those days, he didn't have any hesitation in expressing his views on any, subject. He was a firebrand from the pulpit, but a person's life has a way of changing us all," she said.

I again detected the beginning of a small tremor in her hand as she brought her cup up to her lips. Don Miguel unexpectedly entered with a tray of sweets and placed it on the table. She, impatient at having had her thoughts interrupted, waved him off brusquely and then, with a much more courteous gesture, offered me some caheta. I tasted a bit and said, "Excellent."

"Made from quince, my mother's secret recipe. Even after more than fifty years, prodigal daughters have their mothers deep within them somewhere." She continued, "The person around whom the revolutionary movement coalesced was Franciso Madero from the northern state of Coahuila, which, as you know, abuts Texas.

"As heir to one of the five richest families in Mexico, educated in Europe and Berkeley, California, he seemed unlikely to attract the likes of Francisco Villa. But Villa turned out to be his hammer in the north. South of Mexico City, Emiliano Zapata sought return of the indios' lands in the State of Morelos. Together, they began to threaten Mexico City's ruling elite."

⌀

My mind kept flashing back to the historical photographs that I had seen over the years. I thought of the prim, fussy-looking lawyer who appeared more appropriate for the courts or the house of deputies than the battlefield. His demeanor and appearance reflected an affluent family. In fact, his family connections in Northern Mexico numbered over 150 prominent males, an extended family that had huge land holdings and owned large interests in cattle, cotton, lumber, mines, smelters, and alcohol distilleries. The high point of Madero's tragic revolutionary and political career occurred after his election when he was photographed—the presidential sash visible under his coat—with the vice president. They were in exactly the same spot in the presidential palace where Porfirio Diaz and his cabinet had been photographed not too long before. Behind the new president and vice president, resplendent in their formal attire, a number of uniformed military officers ominously look on with cold and expressionless faces. In contrast, the eyes and expression of the new president was hopeful, benevolent, and unwary.

✤

"Madero's promises were simple and understood by even the lowest *campesino*, return of the land to the villages and Indian communities that had been taken during Diaz's regime, and political liberty for all. His simple slogan, 'Valid voting, no reelection,' was crystal clear to those who had lived close to forty years under the dictatorship of Diaz."

For the first time, I noticed a small rooster and a hen, both with extraordinary coloring and which she enticed with little crumbs that she carefully broke off from her empanada. As they pecked around her on the flagstone, it was obvious that they were her pets, treated like how we would treat a cat. There were always these subtle differences between the two cultures, which would suddenly startle me. She noticed my interest and said, "They were given to me for, *dios mio, my cumple años* (my god, my birthday). I suppose one must celebrate, at my age, having survived another year. Nobody would guess it, but their bloodlines are of extraordinary courage and fierceness. I particularly enjoy the rooster. With all that pride and swagger, he must think he is the ruler of the continent, at least of Jalisco."

I thought about the hundreds of Mexican prize fighters that, for decades, had crossed their northern border to fight in our boxing arenas and Vegas casinos. By aficionados, they were known as "old school." The best were athletic, fluid, tough, and vicious. These small pure warriors were known for their courage and fighting spirit. Qualities that we, here in the north, have come to take for granted and expect from them. I was about to mention these characteristics that Mexicans, as a people, seemed so much to admire and try to emulate when she smiled and, looking appraisingly at me, said, "You are a strange Americano, Ricardo."

"How do you mean?" I responded, a little grateful to be on my own turf at last.

"Digging into the past that doesn't involve Abraham Lincoln or Ellis Island, or even the Alamo, into a past that nobody cares about."

"I care."

"You do? *Por Dios* (My God), I can't see why. You should leave it all in the dust bin of the forgotten."

"I can't," I said, not really understanding why I felt so strongly about it. "Societies are like people. We forget things, sometimes important things." She nodded and, for a few moments, appeared to be deep in thought. I noticed, not far from the fighting birds, a peacock in full display of its glorious plumage. Without further comment on what I'd said, without skipping a beat, she resumed where she had left off.

"Madero was a dreamer, an idealist. He was an appeaser, not really a revolutionary. After his election, he surrounded himself with the same gang that had been patiently crouched in the corner waiting for Diaz, the old fool, to die."

"But what about Madero's supporters, those that had helped bring Diaz down?"

"Almost all of them were somewhere up north, in Chihuahua, Sonora, and Coahuila, or south in Morelos. They still had plenty of trouble in their regions to deal with. What they hadn't planned for was those Diiztas still entrenched in Mexico City. Madero thought the problem had been the man, but it was an entire class of that society who were the predators. Madero, in an effort to appease the military establishment, appointed one of them, Victoriano Huerta, as major general of the federal forces."

She paused for a few moments before she continued, "But before you close a wound, you have to clean out the rot, and the rot was Huerta. One night, after having been taken prisoner by Huerta and while being moved from his place of confinement, it was said that as he stepped out of a limousine, Francisco Madero, Mexico's elected president was executed and, soon thereafter, so was his vice president.

"This horrible crime awoke the jaguars who had been asleep throughout the land, and the jaguars didn't sleep again for twenty years."

She paused for such a long time, as if she was giving me an opportunity to grasp the horror of the nation's supreme military commander murdering his president and the vice president in a civilized country.

"Antonio used to say that this was Mexico's first lesson in this kind of violence and that with all the similar lessons she would be given in the following years, Mexico could have graduated from the *universidad* (university)!"

Before I could ask her to explain the strange comment, she continued to speak in a torrent, as if my understanding was very important to her and she feared losing my attention before she was through.

"Huerta had calculated that an election to those who had no experience with one for forty years, if ever, meant next to nothing.

He knew that Madero had not been a military man like Diaz and he, and that Madero personally commanded no troops. Madero, with his small slight stature, goatee, and intellectual manner, was a subject of derision amongst an officer corps infected with machismo."

❧

Huerta, before his ascension to the highest office, showed himself to be a wiry, compact, brown-skinned general, his skin tone contrasting sharply with his snow-white mustache. He wore a *no-nonsense* tan uniform with a matching small-brimmed military officer's hat. There were no medals or extraneous adornments to divert attention from his taut tough face and determined jaw. Highly polished leather boots matched the small carrying case at his hip. A leather strap to which the case was attached crossed his chest diagonally from neck to hip. Inside the small case, he carried no weapon, instead perhaps a small pair of binoculars, more likely some smokes—perfect attire for the Mexico City of those days where the danger was political and not physical.

In another photograph taken not too long afterward, the same closed-cropped head stares into the camera. Now in a top hat and rimless spectacles, riding in an elegant carriage like the one favored by Diaz, he had the presidential sash diagonally across his chest—from neck to hip—over his elegant formal wear. His lips are thin and tight; his eyes have the expression of a fish.

❧

"Huerta often stated that Diaz had lost control of the reins of power because he was old, and senile. Not because of the military strength of Villa and Zapata, whose bases of power were separated from each other by more than a thousand miles, while he sat in Mexico City between them. Huerta's troops controlled all the major cities and the railroads so he could move his men quickly anywhere in the country, if the occasion required.

"Huerta thought, now that he had grabbed the reins, that Diaz let drop, that all of Diaz's former national and international support would flock to him. His strategy was simplicity itself. First, he would finish one rebel and then turn on the other. He openly joked that Villa was an illiterate bandit and Zapata an insignificant tribal chieftain."

Suddenly, out of the corner of my eye, I saw Don Miguel, who had apparently been watching and listening without my noticing.

"Senora, your medicine," he said.

"What a lack of courtesy to interrupt a lady," she snapped at him.

Don Miguel nervously pulled at and, with an open hand, smoothed out his snow-white mustache and goatee in consternation.

"Miguel, you shouldn't worry so much. Before too long, I will lie down forever, and the generous earth of Mexico will open it's arms to give me shelter, and you, Miguelito, will finally be able to say, 'Requiesat en pace (Rest in peace).'"

"God will call us all to his bosom, señora," he said.

"His voice for me, Miguel, was silenced for good long ago."

"As for me," he responded, "I'm not afraid of death. As long as I'm not there when he appears." He smiled wickedly in my direction.

"Señora please, you are overtiring yourself. You must be careful." This time he looked at me with undisguised impatience as he shook his head.

For the first time, I noticed the gray pallor of her face and what appeared to be extreme fatigue. Her lower lip now constantly trembled as when a child is about to start to cry and is fighting to avoid it. Since she wasn't speaking about anything that I thought was personal, I guessed it might be the early stages of Parkinson's. For a few moments, she closed her eyes. Ever so slightly, she rocked back and forth. That and the continued movement of her lower lip confirmed it.

"Miguel, please let me finish. You know the past with Antonio is all I have left," she croaked.

I suddenly realized that it wasn't interest in the historical past that was so important to her. Instead, the past, as she was describing it, was somehow related to the intense emotional bond she once had with her brother and lost. All this was a thread of something that they once had shared.

From the kitchen, Don Miguel reentered. He poured a glass of water from a pewter pitcher, mixed a blue powder into the liquid, and stirred it. He handed it to her. "Is it time?" Maria Luisa asked, barely above a whisper. She took the glass, and he stood by and watched as she drank it down.

"Ay, Miguel, Miguel, whatever am I going to do about you?" she said.

The old man fluffed up the pillow that supported her back. "Nobody's perfect, señora," he answered her sweetly.

After a long pause to reorganize her thoughts and to have the medicine begin to take effect, she continued in a diminished quiet voice, "During his short tenure as president, Madero appointed Venustiano Carranza as governor of Madero's native state of Coahuila, not surprisingly, a man of the same social class as he. But before Madero's assassination, Carranza anticipated the counter-revolution that he thought would surely arise against Madero. So Venustiano made alliances with the other northern governors, those appointed by Madero, from Chihuahua and Sonora.

"Within a month after Madero's assassination, Carranza declared himself as Madero's rightful successor and the leader of the constitutionalist forces against Huerta whom everybody was now calling the 'murderous usurper.'"

*

The photograph is of the tall bony man on a magnificent black horse. He has adopted the campaign hat, above-the-knee leather boots, and multi-buttoned coat—fastened to the throat—of the elegant generals of the confederacy during our civil war. The hands on the reins are protected by kid gloves and between his saddle and horse, a saddle blanket made of a spotted leopard skin. Obviously, Carranza has taken great care in how his appearance would be judged by those whom he sought to lead.

My mind jumped to what would occur long afterward to Carranza and the photographs that have been engraved into my mind.

Above the head of the casket that was covered with a black cloth and flooded with bouquets of flowers, a group of men stand. In respect for the occasion, they all have shirts buttoned at the collar; some with coats and ties. They are in semicircular rows around the coffin, each row on an ascending step. Each row of the onlookers diminished in number as they stood higher on the steps until, at the top, only a couple of men stand. In the photograph, it appears as if the head of the dead man is being crowned with the outline made up by the faces of the men who had scrambled for a chance to be part of the history that was being preserved.

The eyes on the face of the corpse are swollen shut. The impressions of round coins, having been jammed into his sockets after his death to avoid the ghastly sightless stare of the dead, are perceptible. In each nostril, pieces of white cloth have been inserted to avoid any leakage. Around the closed lips and jaw is the dead man's identifying symbol, a chest-length white beard and wavy mustache. The sideburns, cheeks, and jowls are cleanly shaved.

~

She suddenly became aware of herself and how she was reacting; her eyes then focused on the concerned face of Don Miguel. She changed the subject and her tone and gestured toward him.

"He acts as if he is my servant, my mozo, but for over half a century, he has been my only family and friend, my anchor to the past. I call him Miguelito, but only when we are alone. We have gone through so very much together."

He didn't react with a smile or a nod; it was as if she hadn't spoken. I felt an emotional tension that I didn't understand. Having made amends with him, she went back to what she had been describing.

"Now for the first time, the Sonorenses, Alvaro Obregon, and Plutarco Elias Calles entered the stage that they would dominate militarily and politically for so many years and who, years later, were to have such a profound effect on so many, including Antonio and myself. Do you know Guaymas? And the territory between the Mayo and Yaqui rivers in Sonora?" she asked me.

"Yes, I used to spend weekends and vacations at the beach at Algodones, outside of Guaymas, before it became a Club Med, and I've passed through Ciudad Obregon several times on trips back and forth to Guadalajara."

"Then you know the area where Calles, the part-time teacher, part-time bartender, and Obregon, the grower of garbanzo, came from."

She then touched the old magazine, Revista Illustrada, which she had placed on the table on the prior occasion and had brought once again.

"I don't know where Antonio found this old magazine, probably in some old secondhand bookstore. It was at least ten years old when he gave it to me. He thought it was of interest because of the description of the Battle of Agua Prieta, which was to have such significance in Mexico and, indirectly, on the United States. There were the two generals, Obregon and Calles, both from the barely civilized state of Sonora, who were photographed there together after the battle. Both were to be future presidents of Mexico. Antonio was also born in Sonora, as you probably know. Because of future events, the subjects of this magazine article, who were thrown together in that northern

Mexican outpost, were to be placed in the absolute center of the political life of Mexico."

She opened the magazine and showed the grainy photograph and continued. "I thought that you might also have an interest because the third person in that photograph depicting the victors of the battle was a colonel, a boy probably just out of his teens. Much later, after Antonio had disappeared, he too would become president, the famous or infamous, depending on your point of view, Lazaro Cardenas. In fact, this street is named in his honor."

She reflected for a moment and said, "I'm sure Antonio would have loved the foresight of the magazine article, of those three 'then relatively obscure' persons being photographed together on that dusty battlefield adjacent to Douglas, Arizona, after they had clashed with Francisco Villa and his Division del Norte. It was a capsule of those that would make Mexican history for the next twenty-five years."

Before I could even start to unscramble that statement, she carefully closed the magazine and placed it in the plastic cover and sighed.

"Huerta now faced a three front uprising. In the north and central region, there was Villa. In Sonora and the northwest, along the Pacific coast, Obregon. And in the south, Zapata. The three fighting a common enemy together under the direction of Carranza."

She suddenly jumped up and, wringing her hands, began pacing frantically back and forth. "You see, Ricardo, I know that life is short and not to be wasted, yet in that short time, I've managed to lose everything, everything!" She suddenly collapsed on her chair before I could move a muscle from my seated position to help her.

"Por favor, señor, I must insist," Don Miguel addressed me, almost pleadingly, as he tried to sit her up. "You must not take advantage of her hospitality."

I noticed that bringing up the subject of Obregon and Calles had been what so visibly had upset her. She offered no objection as I quickly excused myself.

Plaza Tapatia

The beautiful melody of "El Condor Pasa" was being played by a Quechuan quartet from Cuzco, Peru. The music seemed to mesmerize the Mexican audience. The outdoor space behind the Teatro Degollado was framed on four sides by buildings, and in this plaza, people sat with other Tapatios on hundreds of temporary wooden folding chairs. For those Tapatios who couldn't get into the formal performances inside the theater because of space or cost, every evening in the month of October, free open-air performances of different types were given in the Plaza Tapatia. On this night, two musicians with wooden pan flutes were being accompanied by a third with a drum. The fourth played a small four-stringed instrument that was similar in shape to a guitar but of obvious Indian construction. They were playing the simple and immediately identifiable music of the Andean people.

These descendants of the Incas, who live in the highest mountain range in the Western Hemisphere, were very different in their culture and environment from the ancestors of many in the audience, whose partial lineage traced back to the Aztecas or Mayas. Yet the audience, judging from their response, seemed to feel an indescribable prehistoric connection.

That night, after the concert, I treated myself to a carriage ride around the Plaza Tapatia. The clip-clop of hoofs on cobblestones of the huge colonial-style plaza was muffled by sounds of splashing water from the many fountains. Here and there, small gatherings of families and friends were out quietly enjoying each other and the evening air—away from television, computers, or fast cars.

Elderly couples leisurely strolled arm in arm. Teenagers, who may have been their grandchildren, slowly circled the fountain; the girls going clockwise, the boys in the opposite direction. Meanwhile, seated middle-aged women kept a sharp eye on their flirtatious charges as they walked past each other. In the air, there was a faint smell of roses; in this, the City of Roses. I wondered, as I looked for photographic opportunities, how long Mexico would be able to hold on to its past.

On another evening at the same outdoor stage, the tango from the most European of the countries in the New World was featured. It was a dance of embrace, but with the partners barely acknowledging each other. A dance, born in the brothels of Buenos Aires, that draws a distinction between sex and love. The dancers, accompanied only by an accordion, amazed the audience with gliding steps, intricate footwork with unpredictable hesitations and dramatic dips. All the while, they held a rigid torso and profile, absent any possibility of independence. Reputedly, this dance was wildly popular with the Italian upper-class fascists in the thirties. The performers hinted at this political heritage as their locked knees became like goose steps, a subtle comment on their recent history and culture. The European-appearing Argentines seemed to reflect much more accurately the not-too-distant life and culture of Spain and Italy than that of the mestizos in the audience.

There was an intermission so that the dancers could clear the stage of their instruments and scenery and another group could take its place. I walked through the festive people who crowded around the main fountain. The balloon vendors sold their spheres and latex airplanes that were in a medley of bright florescent colors. A line formed in front of a girl who smeared melted butter and grated cheese on roasted ears of corn. Others sold fruit flavored ice paletas and homemade candy.

Off in the distance, around an ironwork band shell, an ensemble of musicians played traditional melodies from the south of Mexico on their marimbas. Under the canopy of sound, little groups of people sat on lovely, intricate, ironwork benches, whose design matched the band shell's, and quietly talked.

Later on that evening, it was flamenco, from Spain, the European mother country. The well-known dance form was stylized and passionate. The dancers were accompanied in their bursts of heel stomping by a lone guitarist, who displayed stupefying technical virtuosity. Only the heels and castanets of the dancers provided accent and counter-rhythm as his fingers flew in intricate runs up and down his guitar's frets. Either because of the shared recollection and resentment of four hundred years of domination or perhaps because of the difficulty of following the melody or lyrics of each wailing song, which to my ears had more than a hint of Muslim North Africa, the mestizo audience seemed polite but ambivalent.

It was still early evening when I headed back toward the hotel. Three blocks away from the outer edge of the peaceful Plaza Tapatia, a profusion of small Nissans and old Volkswagons sped down a one-way arterial street in a wild scramble from one red light to another. The air was saturated with the heat and smell of their exhausts.

On the sidewalk, a middle-aged woman in a housedress and slippers bumped into scurrying pedestrians as she sang a familiar song with a sweet, sweet voice. The lights of the cars illuminated her face and her eyes, which had no irises. Men and women rapidly slipped by her on one side or the other as she stood there singing with an extended cupped hand.

A block or so further, in the shadows, her back propped up against a building, a tiny Indian woman with an infant suckling at her breast sprawled on the sidewalk. She sat quietly, waiting for somebody to take notice and to take pity.

When the cars stopped at the red light, a platoon of young boys poured out among the still-moving cars. They voluntarily sprayed and cleaned the windshields with the hope of receiving a pittance for their work from the irritated drivers.

Then a man with a ghastly tanned face pirouetted among the stopped vehicles, and every few seconds, a flame spewed from his mouth like a torch. He squeezed between the stopped cars, waiting for somebody, anybody, to reward his bizarre performance.

I thought back to Maria Luisa's statement that she "supposed" beautiful things could be found in Mexico, and lest, I became carried away by any romantic notion; the opposite was true also.

The last performance I saw before my planned return to the United States was the exposition, through dance, of the most complete blend in the new world of European and indigenous cultures, the Mexican folklorico. The performers made full use of the complete panoply of European and Indian musical instruments and costumes. The variety and the scope of the dances reflected the cultural diversity of this sprawling country. There were dances from the northern section of the country with whom a person from present-day rural southern Texas—with their boots, cowboy hat, and accordion-accompanied Tex-Mex corridos—would be completely comfortable.

Another region's dances included multicolored, feathered, exotic attire similar to what Cortez must have observed when a European first looked at the inhabitants of the Valley of Mexico. The Spaniards then had looked upon a city that was—at that time, some say—the biggest one on earth. The dances and costumes the conquistadores observed were similar to those still to be found and worn daily in the hills and jungles of Chiapas and Oaxaca. Yet the dancers were now accompanied in part by European musical instruments adopted by the tribes long ago.

Then there were the elegantly attired women from the coastal regions of Vera Cruz in white floor-length dresses decorated with yards of white lace. The dresses are reminiscent of those seen in a Velasquez painting of some royal Spanish personage of the sixteenth century and now displayed in the El Prado in Madrid. Their male partners were attired in all white: pants, shirt, shoes, and hat—a costume found in the most tropical of hot and humid zones. They were accompanied by harps or marimbas made of the New World jungle's resonant exotic woods, with which the Jarochos played their intricate heart-stirring music.

Perhaps because we were in Guadalajara, the culmination of the evening's concert were the *sones* from Jalisco played by a fourteen-piece mariachi composed of trumpets, violins, guitars, and a guitaron. The women wore trajes de gala from Jalisco. Brown-skinned women in layered multicolored explosions of whirling fabric were accompanied by their charros, whose tightly fitted earth-colored suits have more than traces of the Spanish-Andalusian plain, except for the enormous Mexican hats.

Without a doubt, one of the objects of the fiestas had been to contrast with other countries and to celebrate the blending in Mexico of two culturally powerful civilizations; one symbolized by the cross, the other the pyramid. As I clicked away with my camera, trying to record this extraordinary congruence, I couldn't help but think of the sterile barren reservations of the north, where we had virtually imprisoned the native North Americans in remote areas, apparently in part, to foreclose any possibility of cross-cultural infection.

La Capital, Entonces

Shortly before I was to return to the United States, I received an unexpected telephone call from Don Miguel saying he wanted to see me. He was nervously waiting outside the house when I arrived.

"Apparently, your delivery of Padre Reyes's things has resurrected memories and emotions which Maria Luisa had not buried permanently in her past." He looked at me with the same smirk, shaking his head.

"I believe she has a real need to talk to someone about them, even if it is with one that speaks in a confusing mishmash of Castilian English or Spanglish or whatever that is that comes out of your mouth."

My ears felt hot as they do when I am in a flush of embarrassment. I was well aware of my Spanish limitations and of Maria Luisa's exquisite command of both languages. When he saw how strongly I had physically reacted to his rebuke, his tone softened.

"Ricardo, I know this is not of your doing, but sometimes I forget. I've been her mozo since we were children and lived in her father's hacienda. You should know that, as a young boy, her father commissioned me to watch over her, and I have for all these years, except for a few unavoidable periods. But speaking to me is, for her, I fear, like speaking to a wall. Probably because of your knowing Padre Reyes, she seems to have an affinity towards you. Anyway, she asked that you visit again. She still hasn't been told all about his life in Arizona. But please, señor, be careful and consider her condition, and the situation."

I said I would, not knowing what condition and situation he meant and not wanting to be thought intrusive by asking.

This time, she was seated awaiting my arrival and asked me to sit down at the massive colonial-style-carved wooden table. She said she had been preparing a surprise for me. While Don Miguel busied himself setting the Talavera dinnerware and silver utensils, she asked if I had any new impressions of Mexico as a result of this most-recent trip. I commented that the pace of change in Mexico seemed so much slower than in the north.

She said, "It is that change in the United States is driven by technology. Every year, we read of something new—computers, the internet, DNA, digital communications…Any one of these and the other marvels available to the people can transform a society in five or ten years. Since these are not available here, except to a very few, change is brought about the same way it has been for centuries, by the church and the government and the family. But many times, I fear, they seem to be satisfied with the status quo. With them, change occurs, if ever, over a period of generations. I look to the north, and it is as if there are multicolored shooting stars constantly exploding and bathing all those underneath them with new beauty and promise, while here, we are caught as in a swamp." She rearranged the plate in front of her and was silent for a minute.

Then she said, "There are some things from the past, Ricardo, that are unsurpassed, even among today's marvels." Don Miguel was busy setting some steaming serving dishes on the table.

"As a young girl, my parents sent me to a convent in Mexico City to study. The convent, in those days, was basically unchanged from those that had existed in Mexico City and the provincial capitals since colonial times. The daughters and unwed sisters of the aristocrats and hacendados were sent to the nuns so they could educate them and, of course, to protect them from worldly dangers and temptations. There, as always, Indian women and girls did the work not appropriate for girls of our, so-called, social class. Kitchen work was some of what was deemed not appropriate for young ladies. Thanks be to God. I say that not because I am adverse to cleaning frijoles or peeling a chile, but as a result of the Indian servants in the convent's kitchens, over a period of time, there was an experimental blending of Spanish cuisine and indigenous ingredients unknown to European palates. Chiles ancho, mulato, chipotle, and other local varieties were simmered with tomatillo, anise, clove, and other exotic local spices. It was all blended with peanut and almond butter and ground raisins and prunes. Then the ingredient that had been unknown even to European royalty, chocolate containing cinnamon, was added. After careful blending and cooking, the resulting thick mole was ladled over pheasant boiled in aromatic water and then sprinkled with sesame seeds. The myriad of contrasting ingredients were served with frijoles de la olla and freshly made corn tortillas. The result was a medley of pungent and aromatic flavors and sensuous textures unknown to European cuisine.

"When the bishop was invited by the mother superior after Sunday services for lunch, mole, in one of its great varieties, was invariably served. Some say that it was in the colonial city of Puebla where mole was first concocted. Thanks to the presence of convents throughout Mexico and visiting prelates not wanting to be thought backward after they had experienced mole's delicious flavors and textures, the recipe spread, and Indian kitchen helpers took what they had learned in the convents for their own tables for the less illustrious—of course, substituting pollo for pheasant.

"I, with the help of Miguelito, have prepared mole for our lunch, it has been quite some time since we last prepared it, but this is a special occasion."

Maria Luisa proceeded to serve both of us a chicken breast, which she flooded with a generous portion of the aromatic mole and frijoles from a clay pot, and corn tortillas. After a few mouthfuls of the deliciously unique food she continued, "As I said, while just a young girl, my parents sent me to a convent in Mexico City to study. From a second-story balcony, I witnessed some extraordinary things. At that time, I didn't understand. I didn't understand what the reason for the parade of the thousands of strange-looking people in a column that seemed to stretch out for miles was. Some were on horseback, some not, as they passed below our windows. Much later, as a young woman, I told Antonio about that experience as a child at the convent in Mexico City. He explained in his patient way what I had witnessed and everything that had preceded it.

"Mexico City, at that time, was a city poised between its past and what was to be its chaotic future. At most, it was one-twentieth of its present size. The city was centered around where the colonial capital had been and before that, the island occupied by the Aztecas for centuries.

"Street cars drawn by teams of horses led back and forth from the zocalo, the city's central plaza, to a number of nineteenth-century colonial towns. Towns like Tacuba, Coyoacan, and Tacubaya, which was next to Chapultepec Park. The roads leading to these *colonias* were like spokes on a wheel, the hub being the Zocalo.

"The cathedral was at one end of the gigantic plaza, and all important governmental buildings also bordered the plaza. It was a place where modernization had not yet intruded. Instead, it was a place that had a direct relationship to the past, all the way back to the Aztecas. The life of the small towns and villages was to be seen everywhere, without self-consciousness or embarrassment.

"Our mother superior and the other nuns would take us to Chapultepec after Sunday mass. We would catch the trolley on Avenida Juarez, not far from the cathedral. It turned on the grand Paseo de la Reforma. That broad boulevard led us into the middle of the huge park. The park was a gathering place for all classes of people, some only passing through on the way to the Foreign Club or the Country Club at Chapultepec Heights.

"We would sit under the shade of a tree, our dresses modestly arranged around our legs so as to cover every part except our high-top shoes. They were never to be highly polished, lest the reflection might lead a weak-willed observer to sin, in his mind.

"We would laugh at the racket made by the little black cars with nervous little men, trying to appear nonchalant, driving, and their women holding their sun bonnets with both hands down by their ears. The people in the carriages would curse them when they passed as they tried to get control of their frightened horses. I personally preferred the noise and not the steaming deposits that the horses left." She laughed at her little joke.

"Under the canopy of trees, I remember little groups gathering everywhere, men with three-piece suits and hats and lighted cigarettes in their hands. Women with small children running around in every direction tried, unsuccessfully mostly, to get control of their situation. They all appeared to me to be standing as if in a lake of ivy and flowers that covered everything below their knees. The foliage was that profuse. Only the top half of the children was visible to me as they squirmed here and there. Years later, I saw a painting by Diego Rivera of an Indian woman on her knees surrounded by lilies. I swear I saw her first, kneeling on the flowers at Chapultepec, a colorful mantilla covered her head, as she talked gaily to her customers. To her left there was a basket and a pineapple with gracefully curving foliage just like in his painting.

"I loved those Sundays when we would march after mass in two rows down the busy sidewalk to where we could board the trolley. The streets were where much of life's drama was being enacted. With the buildings having been built up to the edge of the sidewalks, the doorways and storefronts were used both as living rooms and playgrounds. The people lived out their lives in public, on front stoops, and sidewalk curbs.

"Small businesses thrived on the sidewalks. All a man needed was a wooden stool, a cloth to keep the hair out of the collar, scissors, a leather strap to sharpen his razor, and he was in business. Of course, it helped if he could talk and entertain with opinions and stories. Other Indians silently waited, leaning against the crumbling walls or seated on wooden crates. Perhaps they were customers. Perhaps not. It didn't seem to matter much.

"There was one who needed even less for his business. On his head, he wore several hats, one on top of the other. Each was exactly the same as the other, an elegant charcoal-gray color with a contrasting dark band where a fashionable tiny feather was inserted. He always kept one hand in his pocket to protect the proceeds of any sale. With the other, he would twirl a hat like a juggler and constantly chatter and whistle like a bird to draw attention to himself.

"But our favorite was the tambourine man. With one hand, he would keep time by striking the tambourine on his chest. In the other hand, he held a thin wooden reed that he raised above his head when he wanted his four little dogs to dance on their hind legs. When he lowered it, they would resume their normal position with all four feet on the ground and dash madly around him. This was when he would pass the hat. He never failed to have fifteen or twenty, mostly children, seated on the curb, gleefully watching. Sometimes, somebody gave a few heavy copper coins; mostly, not.

"There was one corner that we always avoided by crossing to the other side of the street. There, people slept on the sidewalk outside of a building with swinging doors. It was not unusual at all to see people sleeping on the streets or living on the streets. But this corner was different. I could see that those lying on the sidewalk had only one leg or maybe no legs. There was one woman who always seemed to be leaning against a light post and stared ahead. She used her hands to guide herself if she had to move. There was a man who would shout and curse at nobody that I could see.

"Whenever we passed that place, it seemed that someone we had seen before would be gone and another one, or maybe two, had taken their place. Of all the people that I saw there, I never saw one that had on any shoes, even in the winter."

Francisco Villa

After a long pause, her eyes misty as she relived those days in her mind, she continued, "Carranza assumed power of the revolutionaries in early 1913, and it was in late August before Mexicans in the capital first became aware of an extraordinary force that was arising in the north. First, Pancho Villa and his ragtag combination of vaqueros, drifters, and muleteers routed the *Federales* at San Andres and captured some locomotives and their boxcars as booty. Suddenly, as Antonio used to say, 'the scorpion began to sprout wings.'"

✐

My mind flashed on a photograph of the leaders of Madero's revolution, taken outdoors before an adobe wall somewhere in one of the northern states in 1911. Madero, as the focal point, is seated in the middle. Seated on his extreme left is Carranza; next to Madero on his immediate left is the governor of San Luis Potosi. On Madero's right, the governor of Chihuahua, followed by the governor of Sonora. On the extreme right of the front row is Pascual Orozco, the rebel's field general. All of them had been appointed to their positions by Madero. They all wear three-piece suits, watch chains, and derby hats, except Orozco, who sports a Texas type Stetson at a jaunty angle and the unbuttoned coat of a two-piece suit. They obviously have not been chosen as the representatives of the poor and downtrodden. In the second row are Madero's father and brother, similarly nattily attired. There is also a number of unknowns; two with straw hats with small round flat brims and top, as worn by the urban dandies who followed the styles set in New York and Paris. At the extreme left, almost out of the picture in insignificance, is Colonel Francisco Villa with a large-brimmed uncreased practical hat usable out in the elements. He wears it guilelessly on the back of his head so that his entire face and forehead are exposed. With unmatched pants and a jacket buttoned at the throat, he is the only one without a tie and seems out of place in the illustrious congregation of rich men and politicians.

Disappearing into the horizon, two columns of mounted armed men can be seen. One column is approaching diagonally from the left of the photograph; the other, diagonally from the right. The columns reform into a larger one and intersect immediately behind Francisco Villa, the Centaur of the North. He and his black horse dominate the photograph as he rides toward the camera. To his left can be seen the wheels of a cannon as the mules drag it up the scrubby dry valley. He wears his uncreased large-brimmed hat on the back of his head. His face and expression, a study of fearlessness and determination

Only three years later, there is the famous photograph of Pancho Villa in Mexico City, seated on the extravagantly carved and gilded presidential chair in the nation's governmental palace; and Emiliano Zapata, darkly handsome and charismatic, seated at his side, looking menacingly. Both look as if their presence there, away from their *muchachos*, is some kind of colossal farce. Neither remained there much longer than the time required to take the photograph. These men were of a different breed than those shown so prominently in the first photograph.

♂

"In October, Villa's Division del Norte, as it came to be known, captured Torreon, one of the most important and wealthiest cities in Mexico and the hub of the railroad-transport system in the north of Mexico.

"In November, Villa captured Juarez, thereby assuring a source of military resupplies from the American arms dealers. He now had a door to the American market for the cattle and other spoils he obtained from property seized from Huerta's rich supporters in the northern states. After these victories, the American merchants along the border started to accept Villa's printed money at discounted prices in anticipation of their value increasing substantially when the constitutionalists triumphed.

"Antonio joked that Villa's printing presses were the only thing busier than Villa's amorous activities. At that battle, he also captured three thousand prisoners. The officers were immediately shot! When he was criticized by the American newspapers for this barbarity, he asked, 'What would have happened if I or my generals had been captured?' As was his custom, the common soldiers were given an opportunity to join the Division del Norte. Many of them did.

"After Juarez, it was as if a dam had broken. Thousands of the poor crowded the train terminals and tracks, wanting to be part of Villa's army. A week later, he captured Tierra Blanca. In December, Chihuahua City fell, then Ojinaga, and then Saltillo. The illiterate bandit had suddenly caught not only the attention of the Americanos but also of Hollywood, who rushed their primitive cameras to Mexico to try to capture Villa's actions on celluloid. Representatives of American and European periodicals clamored to be permitted to accompany him in his campaign and report what they found to the curious world.

❦

Ojinaga struck a chord. A photograph has captured the image of a Mexican woman covered from head to toe, like a Bedouin, standing at the Rio Grande's edge, waiting to cross to safety. With two small children, she has all her possessions in straw bags and blankets tied with twine. She was one of more than five thousand refugees who fled across the river to Texas after that battle. Soon, they all were moved to Fort Bliss, where they were surrounded by barbed wire and area lights like criminals. Already, even then, there were some complaints of them being unhygienic and indigent and becoming public charges of the good citizens of Texas. Of course, the wealthy Mexican families were taken in with open arms by El Paso's elite society. But most thought, if newspaper reports are to be believed, that these people would be a source of prosperity and not a menace to be feared.

It had become a spectator sport for the Americans. Ten freight cars, lined up one behind the other, have every inch of available space on their roofs occupied by sitting or standing men and boys trying to get a view of the fighting across the river. While another photograph taken along the Rio Grande shows women with long dresses and parasols easing up to its edge with their gentlemen to try and catch a view of the excitement. Across the river can be seen multitudes of people, men, women, and children, at the water's edge, looking anxiously north.

∽

"There had never been an army like this one. He now had at his disposal fifty or sixty locomotives, with hundreds of boxcars to carry the bizarre cargo."

She laughed softly to herself, apparently enjoying the spectacle she was describing and which she had undoubtedly shared with her brother.

"Hollywood, in its infancy, made moving pictures of hundreds and hundreds of horses being loaded onto the boxcars with the use of long wooden ramps. Villa accommodated the moviemakers by charging repeatedly on his stallion, Siete Leguas, toward crude cameras as they tried to record the event.

"After the horses were loaded, the soldiers, their wives, girlfriends, even children, would climb on top of the boxcars, singing and laughing and waving their rifles in the air as they moved toward a battle. Villa recruited many young boys thirteen, fourteen, fifteen, sixteen years old from among the poor. Most of his soldiers had nothing of value, except what they brought with them."

⚶

Seven stand rigidly in a line in what must have been "attention." None of their hands can be seen as they are either in their pockets or underneath their skimpy coats for warmth. Each of the first five, all different in age and height, wear a hat of different design and fabric, mostly of straw. They are not armed, nor do they have any facial hair on their adolescent dirt-encrusted faces, except one. He is cultivating what appears to be a wisp of hair on his upper lip. The last two are older, in their late teens or early twenties, and are in tan military uniforms with matching hats and haircuts. They are Federales who were given an opportunity and joined Villa after they were defeated.

⚶

"The women, at first, helped in scavenging for and preparing meals for their men. As the war progressed and many men were killed, sometimes the fiercest of the women participated in, and even led men into battles, the famous 'soldaderas,' scandalous in the Federales' eyes.

"How Antonio laughed at this revolutionary version of proper feminine conduct. I, who had spent years with the nuns in Mexico City and Guadalajara, at first didn't know how to react to his joke, but I too was to learn.

"By bringing their family with them, his soldiers didn't mind fighting far from their homes for the trains had become their home. This gave the Division del Norte a mobility and a scope of operation that Zapata never had.

"Because of what happened later, Villa was depicted as a buffoon and a bandit both in the United States and Mexico. It was important to Antonio that I understood the critical part that Villa played in the success of the revolution. Zapata, who always remained loyal and allied to Villa, has been depicted by some as the major revolutionary force in the defeat of Huerta while Villa's reputation was dragged through the gutter.

"Zapata was so conciliatory of the opinions and needs of the others in his army that it was not unusual for his army to dissipate and disappear into the hills of Morelos when planting season arrived. His soldiers fought for the most part in the state of Morelos. Their reason for fighting was to obtain the return of their expropriated land, not the other matters that concerned their revolutionary allies from all across the country."

Maria Luisa asked if I wanted more coffee, and when I declined, she served herself a bit more, swallowed the tepid liquid, and made a disapproving face. She continued before I could make any comment, obviously relishing in my rapt attention.

"There was another major difference between the two revolutionary armies. Perhaps because of colonial Spain's fear of a huge horse-mounted Indian population in Southern Mexico or perhaps because of a farming economy, it was not common for the poor indios in the south to have mounts or to have much experience with horses.

"In the north, it was in many areas, a life based on ranching and mining. Even the poor grew up with horses and mules. As a consequence, the Zapatistas were infanteria, the Villistas caballeria. Even without a horse, a Villista was considered by his general to be a dismounted cavalryman in their battle tactics. And this was to be to their great misfortune in the later stages of the revolution.

"But it was the proximity of Morelos to Mexico City that made the Zapatistas so dangerous to and feared by Huerta and the people of Mexico City."

⌒

On the cattle car, through the wooden side slats, can be seen the dark images of rumps and legs and heads of horses. Men are hurriedly scrambling up the iron ladders attached to the cars at one end. Already on top are women with black shawls and their small children. They are all seated and surrounded by stuffed cardboard boxes and straw baskets and blankets. The lucky ones also have open umbrellas to provide a little protection from the sun and wind. Others have used a pole and blanket and made a crude tent under which to crawl. Most of the men wear enormous floppy straw hats, protection also against the elements. Only one or two rifles are visible in the hands of the soldiers who already have found a place on the roof, but they all have a cartridge belt over their shoulders and diagonally across their chests. The passengers are all seated with their backs toward the middle of the car. They brace themselves with their feet on the metal two by four that traverses the length of both side edges of the cattle car as the rickety train hissing through its teeth starts to move.

The maize is mature and ready for harvesting. The six-foot-high plants provide a lush background that extends deeply into the field. In the distance, over the top of the field, can be seen the dome and side structure of a church. In the foreground, on a path shielded from observation by the vegetation, march a detachment of fifty men. The Zapatistas are clothed in white cotton pants and long-sleeved white shirts and leather sandals. With a rifle slung so that the muzzle extends behind their heads, they all have a cartridge belt around one shoulder and a rolled-up *zarape* around the other that cross each other on their chests. Women in long peasant dresses walk alongside, carrying lumpy burlap bags of cooking utensils. Both men and women wear large straw hats that provide each with shade as they move toward another battle.

⌒

Don Miguel, who seemed to know her every thought, struck a match and lit the candle that had gone out at the base of the silver urn that was supposed to keep the black liquid warm. After a few moments to let it reheat, she resumed the role of a gracious hostess and refilled my coffee cup without asking my permission and then hers. I reflected that the life of a person in this tranquil setting had probably not changed in any material way since the days she was describing. Why this lack of change seemed completely acceptable and even gracious in Mexico but unacceptably old-fashioned and inefficient to the north, where we all anxiously await next year's model and unhesitatingly discard the past, left me perplexed.

"The courage and ferocity of Villa's cavalry charges became legendary," she continued. "Five, ten, fifteen charges in the face of withering fire were not uncommon. They did not stop their attacks until the defender's nerves broke and they ran in terror. Villa was starting to be seen as invincible!

"Yet despite all the carnage, he developed a reputation for taking care of his wounded. Villa had a train with specially equipped hospital cars and a system of ferrying back the wounded as they were removed from the bloody fields.

"He also paid his soldiers regularly to prevent them from looting the areas that they defeated so as not to antagonize the people from whom he would later try to recruit into his army.

"Antonio laughed when he said that Villa permitted looting for three minutes after a battle. Antonio said, 'Even Pancho had to acknowledge human nature to that degree.' But after that, anybody caught looting would be shot, and he meant it. From property confiscated from the 'enemies of the revolution,' as he called them, he paid his soldiers. But this property was to be confiscated in a disciplined way, and he controlled from whom it was taken.

"If the train tracks were ripped out by the Federales so as to stop the juggernaut from approaching, Villa had a repair train with several crews who would tirelessly work day and night to re-lay the track as the troop trains patiently waited and then lumbered forward. There were a couple of trains, which, in addition to the boxcars carrying the soldiers, were armed with three-inch cannons mounted on flatbed cars. The cannons, as Mexicans love to do, were given nicknames 'La Niña' and 'La Jesusita.' Antonio swore that the flatbed car carrying 'Jesusita' gave birth to a lively corrido popular to this day, 'Jesusita en Chihuahua.' I said the song was the reason the cannon was given that name, and back and forth we went."

She smiled, recalling the joke between them and continued, "Anyway, the three-inch cannons provided long-distance cover from the federal forces as the repair crews did their work on the tracks." She then returned to the theme that she had already touched on

"No matter what the eventual winners said or say about all this, it was Villa and his Division del Norte that defeated Huerta. Carranza knew it, and all Mexico knew it.

"Carranza did everything possible—he even denied Villa coal for his locomotives—to stop him from capturing Mexico City. He feared the military and political power that this 'illiterate' would then represent. Desperately, he even attempted to divide the Division del Norte in two by assigning part of it to another general. An order that Villa ignored. So at the very moment of their triumph, the revolutionary coalition was starting to develop some substantial cracks."

Suddenly, as if she had just remembered something, she stood up and walked toward a multi-drawer wooden cabinet and opened the top door. Inside was a phonograph player with an ancient-metal–plated trumpet speaker. She picked up an old 78-rpm record from several that were stored on their edges in a slot on the side of the player. She carefully slipped off the dusty paper cover and turned the player on. The old woman then delicately, with almost loving care, placed the needle on the rapidly spinning disc.

"Do you remember that waltz?" she commented to no one in particular. Underneath the scratching of the needle, I could faintly hear a string orchestra playing unfamiliar music.

"I think it is 'El Club Verde,'" she murmured to herself. Then she looked at me and said,

"As a young girl, I remember the beautiful waltzes that were played by orchestras in the plazas of Mexico City. On Sunday afternoons, before the start of evening devotions, our mother superior would herd us all to the outdoor concerts. We would sit together on blankets spread out on the grass, surrounded by the soft climate and the leaf-filtered light. The beauty of the music and of the ambiance permeated our innocent, young girls' dreams.

"Our mother superior, Dolores de los Angeles was her name, used to say it was as if Mexico City was becoming Vienna as the music of Mexican composers was played interspersed with that of Strauss."

The needle hit an imperfection on the record, and the same two notes repeated over and over. The arm of the phonograph didn't return to the starting position, and close to half a minute passed before she moved. With the unhurried patience of the very old, she picked up the arm with the needle and then turned the knob that shut the record player off. I hadn't wanted to interrupt whatever had quieted my storyteller from the intensity of her silence.

"So much of all that elegance was quietly wiped out in the years after the revolution, without our even being aware. Now, only an old woman listens to these scratchy relics and remembers. That music became as irrelevant to ordinary Mexicanos as Don Porfirio Diaz."

She resumed her chair and rearranged her elegant floor-length skirt. "Ricardo, it isn't only the history that the victors write, and it's not that there was a coarsening of the public's art. I say public because, in those days, music was experienced with all classes and ages mixed together. It was played in the open in the bandstands and pavilions of the plazas and parks. There, casual listeners conversed. Some consumed food purchased from vendors, and youngsters flirted, all accompanied in the background by music they would never otherwise hear. And the musicians? They seemed to play. Not for money or the audience, but for themselves, to make something of beauty.

"Now, persons holed up in their living rooms and bedrooms play whatever is being sold to them that week on radio or television in Mexico City or in the United States by those interested only in their money. And out in public? Most orchestras gave up trying to compete with mariachis and their trumpets, and the accordions of the norteño bands singing their narco ballads as they move among the crowds, trying to pick up a few pesos here and there.

"After the revolution, a new type of genius bubbled up from even the lowliest of the Mexican people, not from the centuries-old traditions and studied formulas from across the sea, and new art was born. But, por dios, I still miss what was lost. A result I suppose, you might say, of my withered state.

Obregon y sus Yaquis

And just as suddenly, she returned to the theme that she had been relating to me before her mind had been distracted by her memories.

"And it was the entry into Mexico City of the troops of these vastly different armies, representing such different interests that I observed from that balcony at the convent, and much later discussed with Antonio.

"For there were three, and I have yet to describe Obregon and his army. His was the first and, in many ways, the strangest that arrived in the capital.

"It was in the middle of August when Obregon and his troops entered Mexico City. He had approached the capital from the west along the coast and, as I was to learn later, by taking Guaymas, Mazatlan, Tepic, and then Orendain near Guadalajara, where it was said eight thousand dead littered the ground.

"At the head of the eighteen thousand men that entered Mexico City, first there were ranchers and miners and people on horseback, apparently from the cities and villages of Sonora. They were followed, most strikingly, by thousands of Yaquis on foot.

"Dressed in their native clothes, cotton pants, embroidered shirts, their long flowing hair tied back with ribbons. Almost all still carried bows, quivers, and rock slings. Some wore earrings, and I even saw one with a golden nose ring. They spoke in a combination of Spanish and what sounded to me like guttural sounds.

"To this native attire, some added huge hats, and all also carried .30-30 Winchester rifles—the caliber and make, I was told later by Antonio. They also carried very well-stocked cartridge belts, and they marched to the beat of native drums.

⚬∽

In my mind flashed the photograph of two lean Yaquis with shoulder-length hair. They are hidden in a sandy arroyo that was serving as their cover. Both are facing away so that we see only their backs, and they are aiming bolt-action rifles at some unseen enemy. The one on one knee is wearing moccasins; the crouching one is barefooted. Strikingly, both wear only a loin cloth. Between them, a white man with knee-high leather boots with his pant legs stuffed into them is aiming a large black camera in the same direction as the Yaquis. His hand is on the camera's turn handle as he records the action. He wears a sturdy-looking long-sleeved shirt with leather elbow patches and a campaign hat. On his belt, he carries a holstered pistol. Since this was not the Yaqui's conventional military garb, I wondered if the photographer had posed the men like that so as to grab the imagination of some newspaper editor up north. Perhaps the photographer wanted to confirm his vision of the combatants—modern man meets the savages. What had the sister said, "The American Eagle with its press, its wings widespread," had created a new reality. And who was it that photographed the photographer anyway?

⚬∽

"Antonio, having spent a substantial period of time in Guaymas, Sonora, knew a great deal about Obregon's background. Obregon had lived as a young man among the Mayo and their cousins, the Yaquis, in southern Sonora. With his resourceful intelligence and winning way, he devised a way to recruit these legendary warriors who had kept the Mexican army at bay for decades. He also developed tactics that complimented their military skills.

"Increasingly in the last ten years of Porfirio Diaz's rule, the land in Southern Sonora, south of the Rio Yaqui, which was almost perfect for irrigation, had been dammed and taken with the government's acquiescence by rich Mexicanos and foreign speculators.

"Unfortunately for the Yaquis, one of the most fertile regions on this continent was the land, the Yaquis believed, God had given to them. Obregon only had to promise its return, and Yaqui leaders provided thousands of men from their eight towns to fight for him.

"Using completely different tactics than Villa, Obregon never ordered headlong charges. Instead of the naked bravery that Villa called for from his cavalry, Obregon's tactics involved guile and psychology. From entrenched positions, each defender would dig his small foxhole. Obregon would then lure enemy troops into reckless charges. After they exhausted themselves with fruitless attacks, Obregon would then encircle the exhausted enemy and destroy them. The disciplined, brave Yaquis would face these foolhardy charges and never flinch or withdraw.

"Antonio said that the Yaquis had always excelled in what you would now describe as guerrilla warfare. They would use ambushes, attack lines of communication, and lines of supply, stretch out the enemy in fruitless pursuits, and when the enemies' resolve had weakened, only then would any major battle take place.

"I remember that before their arrival, the residents of Mexico City, including our mother superior, had given thanks to God that Obregon, a white man, would arrive first and not the brown hordes of Zapata.

"But we didn't know that part of the reward permitted Obregon's army was the right to loot the supporters, or the supposed supporters, of those that were defeated.

"Soon after they entered, everybody in Mexico City became terrified because his soldiers went into homes indiscriminately and stole chickens, pigs, food, clothing—anything of value. Obregon believed that the foreign residents of the city, the well-to-do and the Catholic clergy had all supported Huerta in his revolt against Madero. And for this treachery, they were all going to be very heavily taxed and their property confiscated during his occupation of Mexico City.

"To our horror, his soldiers entered the churches and, with impunity, stole the sacred vestments and dressed themselves and their horses in them. They pulled down the images of the saints from inside the ancient churches with ropes, looking for gold. It was common for the troops to use the churches as their camps for all kinds of activities—cooking, sleeping, urinating, and other unmentionable things. After they left, my schoolmates and I went into a church and saw the havoc they had left. Antonio told me that this was the first symptom of what was to become a raging epidemic."

~

Inside the church, between two of the roof's supporting columns, a pew with a slatted wooden back serves as a repository for scattered items. Closest to the lens, leaning against one of the columns, there is an ornate gold-plated candelabra. Underneath the pew where somebody dropped it, can be seen part of a leather saddle and a large Mexican hat of the type commonly used by the revolutionary soldiers while out in the elements. Toward the middle of the pew, there is a monstrance, a gold-plated receptacle in the shape of a sunburst with a clear glass center. That center is where priests place the consecrated host so that it can be shown to and adored by the believers after ordinary bread has been turned into the body of Christ according to Catholic dogma. Leaning against the monstrance is a wooden frame with a half-hidden painting of the Sacred Heart or perhaps of the Virgin de Guadalupe or of a saint. Also piled on the pew can be seen a crucifix and a statue of the blessed mother. Scattered all over the floor, there are papers that could be sheet music for the pipe organ or perhaps parts of a ripped catechism. Leaning on the saddle, there is a golden chalice. This is the vessel where the priest carries the consecrated hosts so that he can place them on the tongues of the kneeling men and women as they partake of communion. All this booty awaits somebody to collect it and haul it away.

⚘

For the first time, I noticed that Don Miguel had been standing by one of the columns, partially hidden by the shadows, listening to her.

"Carranza did not want Obregon to remain in Mexico City when Villa and Zapata arrived. Since he considered the city to be of symbolic and not strategic value, he instructed Obregon to vacate Mexico City.

"Once again, this time in December 1914, I observed troops, this time belonging to Zapata and Villa, enter into Mexico City. They had waited for each other's arrival so that they could ride together as they entered. The city's population, after their experience with Obregon's army, shook in anticipation of the arrival of the 'brown hordes' from the south. Thousands of Zapata's men entered in a dramatic procession, all dressed in the campesino's garb of coarse white cotton shirts and pants, sandals copied from the Franciscan monks, enormous straw hats, cartridge belts crossed on their chests, and each with a machete. On their hats were pinned small images of the Virgen de Guadalupe or their village's patron saint. Here and there, instead of flags, some carried standards with a depiction of the *virgen*.

"Politely, they knocked on doors asking for food or water. These were the people of rural Southern Mexico, completely out of place in the great city. Zapata—with his dark skin, slim face, and slender frame in a resplendent charro outfit complete with a huge sombrero and a beautiful white horse—seemed the antithesis of a military leader.

☞

"Just like a papal visit, the great plaza had been photographed from on high, perhaps from the cathedral's bell tower. Off to the side, a multitude has engulfed a street car, reminiscent of San Francisco's cable cars, on all sides so that only its windows and roof are visible. One hundred or more deep on each curb, the spectators on the street part and crane their necks to catch a glimpse of three men on horseback, one completely in black, except for silver adornments on the outside seam of his pants. The three are entering a strangely empty plaza. While the background is completely saturated with people squeezed against each other, the foreground is a large empty open area. Strange only until along the open space, men in enormous hats and white peasant garb with rifles and cartridge belts are spotted in strategic locations keeping the crowd back. Behind the three mounted men can be seen a column of white hats and the top half of white peasant shirts all with cartridge belts around a shoulder as they push through the crowd and prepare to march into the Zocalo. To one side of the empty space surrounded by an armed honor guard in the same peasant garb, two men wait in three-piece suits and matching felt hats. They are there to officially greet the new power in Mexico City.

☞

"In contrast, Villa and his Division del Norte entered Mexico City with thousands of mounted, well-armed, and provisioned men, including amongst them the famous Dorados, his elite fighting unit of five hundred men, all in yellow outfits. It was said that only if and after a soldier distinguished himself in a battle would he be allowed to join them. Mules dragged numerous pieces of artillery behind them through the streets.

"Villa, with a florid complexion, wearing a pith helmet, sweater, khaki trousers, leggings, and riding shoes, and riding the biggest horse I had ever seen, waved at the crowd as he led his *compañeritos* into the ancient home of the Aztecas; and I witnessed all of this with a child's comprehension."

I sat transfixed as she related her story so vivid in her description as if she had seen it yesterday.

"Finally, it was clear to everybody the strangle hold that Diaz and Huerta had on the Mexican people was gone.

"That is when the unthinkable happened, and the whole thing began to unravel."

Convencionistas y los Constitucionalistas

"Carranza thought that as the 'primer jefe' of the Constitutionalists, he was the legitimate power of the new revolutionary Mexican state and that the military leaders were subject to his control.

"At the same time, Villa and Zapata had observed Carranza's self-serving and arbitrary actions directed against them in the Mexico City campaign against Huerta. They knew that Carranza was allied, by birth and social station, to some of Mexico's wealthiest landowners in the north. They also believed his commitment to the redistribution of land and other social reforms was questionable.

"'Shouldn't those who did the fighting choose the new direction of the country?' they asked. 'That bewhiskered white-haired *viejo* who rode his horse like he was seated on an easy chair and who was mainly concerned about his image, hiding his eyes behind his smoke-colored glasses, contributed precious little to our victory.'

"Ever the resourceful character that he was—and that's what Antonio called him, a character—Villa called for a convention of the generals who fought and won the war. It was to be held at Aguascalientes, north of Mexico City. One hundred and fifty generals attended. The only qualification was to be that each represented at least one thousand soldiers. Who and how that count was kept was never disclosed. Villa and Zapata were represented at the convention. Obregon was there to observe for Carranza and, of course, in his own interest."

❧

Aguascalientes was the conference where the conflicts between Carranza, Villa, and Zapata were supposed to be worked out. In the photograph, General Alvaro Obregon from Sonora is entering the conference hall without fanfare and is not accompanied by any kind of escort. He is dressed in an unostentatious military uniform and cap. He holds a rolled-up paper in his right hand. It is still a few months before his mutilation. Others in civilian suits and hats are also unobtrusively filing into the building. He is the Trojan horse. As an agent representing Carranza's interests, he quietly participated for over a month. During which time, he was able to observe and assess his future enemies that would include Villa, Zapata, and Carranza. From his non-adversarial position, he was able to calculate their strengths, weaknesses, and probable future actions. With an eye toward future alliances, he impressed others with his remarkable intelligence and amiability.

❧

"Antonio explained that there developed a clear understanding that Carranza was insisting on a strong central government and he was to be the 'primer jefe.' It was Carranza's belief that the greatest threat to Mexican sovereignty had always been the Colossus to the North and that only a centralized and powerful Mexican state would permit its development into a modern capitalist nation to counterbalance the historical threat to the north.

"'How would this be any different from Porfirio Diaz?' asked the generals with Villa and Zapata, most of whom were there because they were chosen by the men as the bravest and fiercest, and not because of any political abilities or knowledge.

"Villa, on the other hand, had no national ambitions. He had always had good relations with the Americanos, and he had no intention of imposing the system he had established in his northern region on the other regions or other leaders of Mexico. Villa proposed to leave the control of the other states and regions to their state and local leaders."

Maria looked up, and her eyes twinkled with amusement. "Antonio said that the greatest source of Villa's power was his ability to communicate, be it in a crude way so that even the lowliest campesino could understand."

She said that Antonio gave her an example of this ability which, even if he was physically threatened, Villa had no fear of proposing.

"Among the negotiations that occurred between the contending parties, somebody suggested that both Carranza and Villa resign jointly so that new leadership, absent of past frictions, could be chosen. A question was asked that if both resigned and then one reneged on his resignation, wouldn't that be a way of getting rid of the rival? Villa proposed an immensely practical solution. Immediately upon their joint resignation, he and Carranza were to be taken outside, forcibly stood up before a wall, and shot! 'That way,' he said, 'it is guaranteed there will be no *chingaderas* (bulls——t).' Carranza, ashen faced, declined the invitation." She had blushed at Villa's words.

"Antonio roared as he imagined how the common soldiers must have admired and laughed at el general's solution and el primer jefe's reaction.

"The net effect of the convention at Aguascalientes was that there was now a new and distinct claim for leadership of the revolution and the Mexican state. The Conventionalists now opposed the Constitutionalists.

"War was inevitable and soon declared by Villa when Carranza attempted to impose his authority upon him. Obregon sided with Carranza, Zapata with Villa. The victors of the revolution now faced off against each other."

Sorpresa

The dignified old lady seemed energized and suddenly animated for having guided me through the maze.

"You will have to excuse me for having dominated our conversation. It's as if a dam of memories broke when you brought me Antonio's things. I want you to tell me more about Antonio's life in Arizona. After he left on the train in 1929, I didn't know if he was alive or dead or in prison. For all I knew, he had been caught and hanged or shot by the federal authorities.

"Perhaps he thought that if he communicated with me, I would be placed in jeopardy. Perhaps he had other reasons. You can't imagine the shock when you told me that he had been alive and spent his life in an American town close to Agua Prieta. But on the other hand, now it starts to make perfect sense."

Her statement completely perplexed me. What could the old priest that had been such a quiet reassuring fixture in the community of my youth have done to merit such possible punishment? My recollections of him when I was a child were of his saying the daily mass, hearing confessions on Fridays, baptizing the newly born, or officiating in the last rites of those who were about to meet their maker—doing all the tasks that simple rural priests have done for centuries. Why would she have been in danger if he had communicated with her? And why did his having ended up in Bisbee, close to the Mexican border, make perfect sense to her?

I started to carefully probe, trying not to offend but seeking to get some answers to these questions. So I focused on the objects I had delivered to her and thought they were a safe subject.

"May I ask if that picture of the young woman is you?"

"Yes, that is me, but you'll agree that it seems to come from another life," she said pleasantly.

"And the wedding picture of the couple, is that your and Father Reyes's parents?" I asked amiably.

She seemed to be taken aback. Her demeanor immediately changed, and her complexion turned ashen as she looked at me with shocked comprehension.

"What do you mean 'our' parents?"

"Your and Antonio's parents," I said.

She immediately stood, knocking over her coffee cup. "But how could you possibly think that? I am light skinned with light eyes. He was dark with black eyes. His mother was Yaqui. His name was Reyes. Mine is Castañeda!"

In embarrassed panic, my erroneous assumptions that Castañeda was her married name and that the difference in her and Padre Reyes's skin color was because he had spent sixty years in the Southern Arizona sun, now left me speechless. With a voice pleading for understanding, I said, "But Padre Reyes told David to deliver his things to his sister Maria Luisa Castañeda."

"I am, or was at one time, Sister Maria Luisa Castañeda, a *monja*, a nun!"

With that, she fled from the room in a spasm of embarrassment and anger and perhaps other hidden emotions.

I never saw her again although I later contacted Don Miguel and asked that, at least, I be given the opportunity to excuse my stupidity in person. She wouldn't see me. Some time later, on another trip to Guadalajara, I called her number and was told that she had died and that Don Miguel had returned to the family hacienda somewhere in rural Jalisco.

Part 2
La batalla

Cosas de que no se habla

When I returned to Tucson, I often thought about my last meeting with Maria Luisa, although I didn't know if I should refer to her as Sister Maria Luisa. No matter how much I thought about what she had told me, I didn't have a clue as to the questions that our last conversation had raised.

The next summer in late June, I returned to Bisbee to try to capture in photographs the sudden appearance of the thick cumulus clouds, which announce the arrival of the monsoon in the high desert, over the red hills that surround the town.

Since the town is in a deep valley between steep hills, the approach of the storms cannot be seen developing off on the horizon. They appear as a welcome surprise. Rapidly, the blue above is blocked as if by a constantly changing white-and-gray curtain.

Very shortly thereafter, huge raindrops pelt the tin roofs of what used to be the miners' homes in a wild syncopation of cooling relief. I thought to myself that to capture that feeling in the two dimensions of a photograph would be the trick.

David met me at the Copper Queen restaurant, greeting me with the usual formal pleasantries of Mexicans of his generation. Since we hadn't spoken since the funeral, I told him about my conversations with Maria Luisa. We animatedly bantered back and forth as to whether to refer to her as Sister. We concluded that in respect to Father Reyes's belief at the time of his death, she should remain a sister, at least in our conversations. When and why she had decided not to refer to herself as a nun, I thought I was never to determine. The tone and content of her conversations had left, at least in my mind, a suspicion.

David was as astonished as I had been by the revelation by Sister Maria Luisa that Father Reyes had been sought by the Mexican authorities for something that could have merited his execution.

"There is one thing that doesn't surprise me now that I put it all together. That is, Sister Maria Luisa saying that his mother was Yaqui," David said. "During the time that I knew him and drove him here and there, we would always go during the Easter season to Old Pascua Village in Tucson."

He paused for a minute as he gathered his thoughts.

"I thought it was Father Reyes just being the good shepherd as was his nature. I knew that that Yaqui community didn't have a priest to preside at their very unique religious ceremonies. I thought he had just assumed the responsibility.

"In fact, I remember also having taken him to Guadalupe in Phoenix, and even to Eskatel, a community of Yaquis in, believe it or not, what is now Scottsdale.

"Phoenix was well beyond the areas of Southern Arizona that he regularly visited, so the connection must not have been geographical but tribal."

"Is there anything else that you remember? Did he ever mention anything about the Yaquis?" I asked.

"Come to think about it, he once said that his mother told him that when Mexican soldiers captured Yaqui women or children in their pueblos, that they would take them far from their homes and make them household servants for the well-to-do. He said that this was just another failed attempt to exterminate the tribe by separating the male and female populations. But even if they had Mexican fathers, most of the children still considered themselves to be Yaquis.

"Other than that, he was so closed mouthed about himself and, in fact, about everybody that there never was a time that I remember when I heard him speak about himself or about anybody else. In our trips in the old Dodge, his conversation was always about what was to be done or what we had just completed."

"A perfect priest for the confessional," I joked.

"There was an old Yaqui holy man, I guess you'd call him, at Pascua, with whom he seemed to have a special friendship," he said.

After a silence of several minutes when he seemed deep in thought, he told me he had just returned from the monthly maintenance of the grave where his nephew, Robertito, the son of the murdered priest, was buried.

"Many years ago, when Robertito was a very young man and sensitive to other's malicious talk, it was said in our family that he accidentally hung himself while playing a game."

There was a long pause, as if he hesitated to go on.

"I started to have my doubts about that story when I discovered that he was buried in unconsecrated ground, among others who had refused to be baptized or those that had killed themselves—the killing of a person that, by the nature of the act, had to be unrepented. It leads to damnation, at least in the eyes of the Church."

His eyes became moist with tears.

"Later, I put a marker, a cross made of three pipes that I welded together. I had the mound of the grave covered with little round river rock that I gathered from the San Pedro and encased it all in cement so that it would not get all weeded up. Little by little, that area of the cemetery has been squeezed on three sides by the mountain of waste rock that has been dumped there by the copper company, until only a small clear patch of ground remains. I still go there often to keep the grave cleared of rocks so that the past doesn't completely give way to the sightless present. But after I'm gone, it's hopeless. Everything, even the memories, will be gone."

I, without comment, marveled at the character of this man who loyally served Father Reyes for all those years to atone for the murder of the priest committed by his father and brother. At the same time, he had made a shrine to the memory of one that had indirectly been a victim of the same murdered priest.

There was a certain perverse symmetry to all this. It had started in Mexico, with the love of the two innocent young sisters for the predatory priest. Now after the priest's murder and the suicide by the priest's ridiculed son, the boy without a father, because of his grandfather and uncle's revenge, Don David was bracketing this quiet tragedy with his love.

At the end of a silent ten minutes, he rose to his feet and said, "There is another grave besides my wife's that I also visit. Perhaps my time should also come soon. It seems that my thoughts are more in the graveyard than with the living. Juanito is also buried in the Mexican section of the cemetery, not too far from where the boy is. He was my *compadre* and my partner underground. We worked together for years with a pick and shovel, swallowing dust and shitting in pails of sawdust deep underground. We were the fodder of the mines, the lowest of the low, the Mexicano muckers who could be pissed on.

"One nightshift, it was on Easter Week, Holy Thursday, we were working the eight-hundred-foot level of the mine, in a stope. Like a lightning bolt, some rotting timbers gave way, and it all collapsed around us. I crawled through the shattered timbers and boulders and tried to breathe in the choking dust. My fingernails bled from frantic scratching and digging as I looked for a way out. I found my tin waterproof container with matches and ignited one after the other. I called and called for Juan, who had walked down the tunnel to get some blasting powder. From under a huge boulder the size of a coffin, I saw a dark red billow of ooze spreading out in the dirt. The same thought kept pounding in my brain until I thought I would go crazy. 'All his life, he dug his grave. All his life, he dug his grave.'

"The next day, I went to the little barrio in Naco, Sonora, where they lived. It was I who told my comadre Olga while little Martita played on the linoleum floor with the faded blue flowers and their infant boy slept in their bed.

"I never went down in the mine again. The company found something for me to do on the surface. Payment, I suppose, for having spent those hours waiting for the rescue team to punch through and for keeping my mouth shut. It wasn't fear. We all have to die. Out of every ten of us, ten will die. I just couldn't stand the thought that someday, somebody would say the same about me as I laid buried somewhere in the bowels of the earth. 'All his life, he dug his grave.'

"Life is hard, and we who are permitted to live have to do our penance. Juanito's little family did very hard penance. In those days, before the unions, they received just a few pennies for his life. He was just another dead Mexicano, and there was a long line of desperate men waiting to take his place. I did what I could to try and help. It wasn't nearly enough. By Christmas, when I took the children some little trinkets, the little family had disappeared. I never heard of them again."

His face was expressionless, and no one could have guessed the raw emotions and resentments he carried within him.

Later, I was to learn about David's other demons, those that he didn't mention that afternoon. It had happened in La Colorada shortly after his father and brother had disappeared for a few months in their search for justice and revenge, when David was just a boy of four or five. It was a few minutes before noon on a beautiful spring day in 1909. The shrill sound of the company whistle pierced every inch of the town; and every heart, like a high-powered bullet. The deafening wail came from the Gran Central, La Colorada's principal mine. Frantic men, women, and children rushed to look for sons, fathers, brothers, and husbands where the steel triangular tower lowered the cage into the ground. A steel cable wound around the huge wheel as the cage surfaced empty amidst a cloud of dust. The cage was lowered again and again to the level where the disaster had occurred and raised again and again, and no one appeared. There had been an enormous cave-in, and the entire shift of over one hundred miners was entombed, trapped in the lowest section of the mine in the porous soil. A rumor spread like a hideous stench that the pumps would not be adequate to remove the water that was pouring into the collapsed section. The company officials had decided that no attempt was to be made to rescue the miners because of the limited equipment available to them and the dangerous soil. In their pursuit of increasing the daily production of ore, company officials were familiar with the occasional death of a worker. Didn't their mayordomos speak glowingly to the workers about the legendary El Caballo Ortiz (the Horse) who, they said, made the daily wages of three or four miners? After the face of a rise was blasted, in the midst of the swirling smoke and dust, El Caballo would cover his head and shoulders with an empty wooden dynamite box to protect against falling rock and enter the blasted space. Then, they said, he would immediately start to poke overhead with an iron bar to collapse around him anything still hanging from the ceiling. New holes in the rock face had to be hand drilled for more rolls of tightly packed dynamite. Meanwhile, his mucker, in candlelight, crushed the collapsed boulders loosened by the explosion with his sledgehammer and then scooped up the rock ore into little steel railcars for the profitable journey to the surface. But the scope of this disaster was different. That knowledge swept the hysterical families who waited outside like an electrical jolt.

The entire town was devastated as every person lost at least one relative or friend. In that small intertwined community, most of them had lost much more. From that point, the town never really recovered. Some of the survivors moved to Hermosillo to try to forget the mines forever. Others, little by little, moved to the mining camps of Southern Arizona, where it was said miners didn't die.

Pascua

Old Pascua Village is squeezed into a few square blocks and is approximately a mile and a half from the center of Downtown Tucson.

On its west side, the barrio is bordered by the railroad tracks; and then further west, by the Interstate Highway. On the other three sides, there are major business streets. A multiscreen theater adjacent to Pascua spills out its exiting customers nightly onto its narrow streets.

Adjacent to the theater, the garish lights of a Sonic drive-in light up the night skies. Encroaching on all other sides of the small tribal area are businesses of the diesel repair, pest control, and storage rental variety. The residents of this community—it seems obvious—had no clout with the local zoning authorities.

As I drove through the barrio, I noticed tiny adobe homes built years ago and, here and there, a sprinkling of newer small block and brick homes.

A municipal sign notifies drivers of an approaching park. This city park is the size of a medium-sized backyard, but it has the locally mandated sign "Park Closes at 10:30 p.m." What there is to close escapes my observation. There are no trees, basketball hoops, barbecue grills, benches, or fences, just a patch of unkempt grass, a jungle gym and a plastic slide.

At the T-intersection of Calle Matus and Calle Central is the plaza and the Church of San Ignacio. This is the center of the community. It becomes immediately apparent that this is not like the Mexican-style plazas that dot the towns and villages all over Mexico. There are no trees or plants of any kind in this plaza, nor are there sidewalks or a kiosk or other structures in its center for concerts or other public performances. The central area of the plaza is the size of a large basketball court, except that its floor is completely of dirt.

Here and there, as I drove through the village, I observed white wooden crosses erected in different places in the streets and front yards of the barrio homes in what appeared to be random fashion. Several of these crosses were in the plaza. Later on, I would learn that these are the stops for the Roman Catholic ritual of the fourteen Stations of the Cross that commemorate the path Christ took to his crucifixion.

Piles of heavy mesquite firewood were stacked at different places around the plaza's edge. There was a covered three-walled adobe ramada, with the open end of the ramada facing the plaza. The floor inside the ramada was dirt. Opposite this structure was the church.

The Church of San Ignacio is the dominant building in the plaza and the village. But it is different from other churches. Its entire front, facing the plaza, is open. It has no wall or solid doors. Instead, there is a metal door across its entire front that opens and closes like a huge accordion when the church is not in use. From that side, the church is open to the outside elements.

Two spires on the sides of the white structure each housed a single large bell. On the altar, which is clearly visible from the outside front, there is a profusion of crosses and images of Jesus and of the brown-skinned Virgen de Guadalupe. Most of these objects of faith have been constructed or painted by hand and placed there by believers. Suddenly, it dawned on me that the central area of the plaza was not intended for public use as a park or gathering place but was instead an outdoor extension of the church. Its primary function was for sacred, religious ceremonies.

On a wall on an adjacent building, there is a large mural of a map depicting that part of Sonora where the Rio Yaqui drains into the Gulf of California. Like beads of a necklace, the names and locations of the eight Yaqui towns along the river were printed on the image with the Bacatete Mountains to the west. A hornless deer observing a man with the head and horns of a deer on his head as he dances completed the center part of the painting. The Tineo mural is decorated with saguaros and the other plants and animals of the Sonoran desert and of the Sierra Madres, the mountain range that is the source of the waters of the Rio Yaqui. Above this panorama, with arms outstretched, is a drawing of Christ.

I was greeted by a wiry Yaqui with an enormous mustache, which had started to sprout wild gray hairs. With a long needle, he inserted a waxed string first through one flat piece of leather then through another. Both leather pieces were on the opposite sides of a wooden cylinder.

"What are you doing?" I asked.

He looked at me to see if I was joking, and when he saw instead that it was sincere ignorance, he said, "Making a drum."

He seemed friendly but was not talkative. As he continued his work, I asked, "There are ceremonies that are to be conducted for San Ignacio?"

I had heard that the Pascua Yaquis have a festival on the weekend closest to July 31 to honor St. Ignatius of Loyola, who founded the order that first brought Christianity to the Yaquis in Southern Sonora.

"Every year," he responded.

"Will there be deer dancers?" I asked.

"Only one." He looked at the camera that hung from my neck and said, "Photographs are not permitted."

"Did you know Padre Reyes, who used to come to the Pascua and San Ignacio festivals?" I asked and was surprised by his response.

"I am Yaqui, born here in Tucson. There are many more Yaquis born in Mexico. Just like there are Mexicanos born here that can't speak Spanish, I'm just learning about my Yaqui customs."

Before I could respond, a boy of fourteen or fifteen who was walking by, dressed in baggy Adidas apparel, stopped when the man said, "Ask him. He knows more. He is being trained to be one of our dancers."

The boy told me that he had seen a Catholic priest participate at some of the ceremonies but not for a few years.

"But people that knew him will be here on Friday night. The ceremonies for San Ignacio will start at nine in the evening, or later, with the appearance of the Pascolas and the deer dancer."

Viaje ha Sonora

To one side of the ramada where the deer dance had just been performed, a line of those who had been observing formed in front of a blazing mesquite fire. There over a shallow pit, a large iron pot was boiling. To one side of the cauldron was a square, card-table–sized cast iron griddle with stacked bricks supporting each corner. Occasionally, chunks of mesquite were shoved into the glowing embers with a long pole so as to maintain its heat.

A stout middle-aged Yaqui woman who claimed the space in front of the improvised stove was handed a thick dinner-plate–sized tortilla by a pretty Yaqui teenager. The girl—her face and arms dusted with flour—had used a rolling pin to stretch out one of a number of large balls of masa, which lined the wooden table where she worked. The older woman used the tortilla to bridge the space between her flour-coated forearms and then started a process using her fingers, wrists, and forearms, gently, carefully stretching the oval—first by moving one forearm then the other like paddles. She used her fingers and wrists to adjust, align, and repair the growing tortilla until it was of a circumference the size of a man fully extending his arms and touching his index fingers to each other, and until it was opaquely thin. With a strong snap of her head and neck, a welder's mask, which in the flickering light of the fire I had thought was a hat, dropped over her face and eyes to protect them, and she proceeded to bend way over the superheated cast iron while she gingerly placed the tortilla on the griddle to cook. As soon as bubbles appeared on its surface, she grasped a corner and gracefully turned the tortilla over, all the while deftly avoiding scorching her arms and hands. After a few seconds, it was done and folded in half. With a toss of her head, the mask was back on the top of her skull, and the girl handed her another fat-dinner-plate–sized tortilla, and the process started again.

As an honored guest of the fiesta, Virgilio, the ancient Pascola, his face and body still glistening from his effort in the deer dance, was moved to the front of the line, where a huge bowl was provided and filled with the bubbling soup of hominy and cow's stomach, which had been cut into bite-sized squares. Nobody seemed to notice that he still had on the regalia, except for the wooden mask, used in the deer dance.

"Deme patita, por favor," (Give me a little foot please) he said, and a partially dissolved but still recognizable boiled remnant of a pig's foot was plopped into his bowl. He stepped over to some wooden boxes covered with oil cloth and, from some plastic containers, added spoonfuls of cilantro and chopped green onions and squeezed over the gelatinous menudo, the juice of a quarter lemon. From an old coke bottle, he measured into his palm three dried chiltepines into a paper napkin where he carefully crushed the pea-sized "diablitos" without touching them with his fingers and then sprinkled them into his soup.

The next Yaqui in line, making the sign of the cross, said loudly, "Virgilio helps to take care of our *espiritu* (spirit), but la Chepa takes care of the body *que nos dio Dios* (that God gave us)." The Yaqui woman laboring over the fire smiled beneath her mask without looking up.

Between slurping scalding spoonfuls of menudo and tearing chunks off his tortilla, Virgilio listened attentively with an impassive face to my inquiries about Father Reyes. Finally, he said, "Si, I knew Antonio well. For many years, he helped us in the ceremonies. Some of the sacred words are spoken in Spanish, some in Yaqui, and some in Latin. There are some words that should be spoken only by an ordained priest. And he kept all of the sacred words in his memory. Since we have no priest now, we have a maestro read those portions that can be read by one of us without he being ordained."

He pointed and said, "The maestro is the man that you see using the flashlight to illuminate the book. The prayers are still in Yaqui, Spanish, and Latin, but it is not of the same quality as before. They have not been memorized."

When I told him that I'd known Padre Reyes as a child growing up in Bisbee, Virgilio stated, "That was another thing. Antonio used to talk with Anselmo Martinez about Bisbee, about the past. Anselmo, for years, came to Pascua from Mexico also to participate, first, as the maaso and, later on, as one of the Pascola's. Finally, when stiff ankles and knees didn't permit him to dance anymore, he was the maestro. Anselmo read from the book that Antonio gave him.

"Later on, after Antonio completely took over the spoken parts of the ceremony, Anselmo still came every year, sometimes twice a year. Only in the last six or seven years did he stop coming. I've been told he still attends the ceremonies but only in the Yaqui pueblos in Mexico. He is very old."

I thought about the very limited financial resources of these people and wondered out loud how they could afford the four-hundred-mile one-way journey to Pascua village in Tucson.

"Just the same as when the Yaquis first came to Pascua. Inside boxcars from Empalme. First on the Ferrocaril del Pacifico (Pacific Railroad) to Nogales and then on the Southern Pacific from there, like when the Yaquis first went to Yoem and to Guadalupe in Phoenix." He shook his head in exasperation at my obvious lack of basic information.

"And what was it about Bisbee that Anselmo and Father Reyes talked about?" I asked.

"Oh, it wasn't about Bisbee specifically, but I overheard more than once a discussion about the Battle of Agua Prieta and its consequences. Anselmo, as a boy, had been with Pancho Villa's Division del Norte. He has traveled and experienced much. Even now, he is greatly respected by the Yaquis for his knowledge. He is one of the wise men."

I used my work as a freelance photographer as an excuse for my next trip. This time, it was to Southern Sonora, the Yaqui River Valley. I had never seen photographs of the Yaqui towns that were identified in the Pascua Mural. If I couldn't sell any of the photographs I took there, at least the expenses of the trip, I had learned, could be deducted for tax purposes as an unproductive business endeavor, and who knows maybe there would be something unusual there that would catch my eye. My prime purpose, of course, was to follow the intriguing lead Virgilio had given me.

As I drove the modern highway south into Ciudad Obregon, I noticed that there was a dizzying profusion of eighteen wheelers fully loaded with fruits and vegetables going north. This was the harvest of the Yaqui River Valley headed for Los Angeles, Seattle, or maybe even the East Coast.

The city itself is modern and cosmopolitan and has very broad streets and avenues. A result of having been built after the second decade of the last century when it had become clear to city planners that the automobile and not the horse would dominate the urban environment. Water is abundant as modern irrigation canals transport it to distant lush fields. The city landscape is dotted with mansions that lie hidden behind high walls, but all this is south of the river.

The Yaqui towns lie north and west of the river. Their towns are poor and dusty and quiet. In one area, there was an open sewer close to Yaqui homes. Untreated sewage flowed toward the bay, carrying the discharge from the homes of affluent city dwellers.

Anselmo lived in Potam, which, owing to its location, is one of the Yaqui towns that have undergone the fewest changes after the agricultural explosion. The town is dominated by what can be best described as a fortress church.

If it wasn't for the arched openings left for the placement of stained glass windows, the building would look like a prison or a fort. The massive scale of the building, in comparison to the Yaquis' simple structures and its heavy unadorned stone walls, was obviously intended to impress the Yaquis with the power of Christianity.

Anselmo

As I passed the cemetery, I noticed a profusion of crosses of the exact color, dimension, and construction on the small burial mounds as those scattered at Pascua Village for the Stations of the Cross. I asked a young girl if she knew Anselmo and where he lived. She laughed and said that he was well-known to everybody, and then she directed me to Anselmo's small adobe house. She said to look for him in the backyard because it was very difficult for him to walk. I walked through the wooden gate that gave passage through a tight fence of blooming ocotillo. Each stalk of the fence was so close to the other that its thorns would keep rattle snakes out. He was seated under a mesquite tree, carving a wooden flute.

I've heard that as we age, the gelatinous discs in our spines dry, and as a consequence, we become shorter. Anselmo appeared to me to be the shortest man I had ever seen who was not a dwarf or a midget. His face was nut brown in color with deep ravine-like wrinkles crisscrossing it in every direction.

He had a shock of shoulder-length white hair that fell naturally over his ears and neck. Two darting eyes—one of which was partially clouded by a large cataract—looked at me appraisingly, and it became immediately apparent why Virgilio said he was known among his people as a wise man. Before I could say a word, he dropped his gaze and said in a voice that was strangely resonant coming from that tiny body, "You are not Mexicano."

"I am Mexican-American, but both of my parents were born in Mexico," I answered almost apologetically.

"And the huge black snake, that even now threatens the Yaquis and that we were warned about by the talking tree, brought you." Then muttering to himself he said, "Even if they speak perfect Spanish and wear clothes made in Mexico, I can always tell."

In a louder voice to ensure that I heard, he continued, "There is something. Maybe it is because they are as full of pride as a cow is of wind."

Taken a little aback, I said, "I am from Tucson, but I grew up in Bisbee. Father Antonio Reyes was the priest there since I can remember."

He nodded in recognition of Father Reyes's name. While he continued to busy himself with his carving, I proceeded to tell him about Padre Reyes's death and about my meetings in Guadalajara with Sister Maria Luisa and with Virgilio in Pascua.

"And now you come to me to hear about Villa, about Agua Prieta, before it is too late," he said, smiling to himself with self-awareness of his great age.

He then continued without any further prodding, "I was just a boy then. But after a few weeks of chasing chickens or pigeons for food, they discovered I could slither along the ground at night, like a snake, without making a sound. Just like when we hunted the deer."

He smiled toothlessly and very slowly moved his arms and legs like in slow motion and said, "I moved so slowly that weeds would grow over me. I could get so close to the Carranzistas that I could hear their muffled conversations and smell their corn tortillas as they cooked them."

"I am confused," I said. "I thought that the Yaquis were with Obregon and not with Villa?"

He pulled out a filthy rag and loudly blew his nose and looked at me as if he couldn't believe what he had just heard.

"Many, many were with Obregon, but there were some Yaquis with Villa. At one time, we were all on the same side. In my case, when Porfirio Diaz and his Rurales first started taking Yaqui land and damming the river, some Yaquis were killed outright. Others, like my mother and brothers and sisters, we all were shipped to the south to work on the henequen and sisal haciendas in Yucatan. Indians always provide cheap labor, as you know."

I didn't know if this was a statement or an accusation or perhaps a ploy to see my reaction. I didn't respond. After continuing to shave the piece of wood with a special two-handled knife, which he drew toward his body as he carved, he continued.

"When in Yucatan, when we first heard that the Federales had been defeated and that Huerta had fled the country, it was said that Obregon and his army of Yaquis was going to occupy Mexico City. But by the time we—there were a number of us Yaqui men and boys—were able to find our way north to Mexico City to join him, they were gone. Instead, Pancho Villa and Emiliano Zapata and their troops were there. It was easy to join the Division del Norte. All I had to do was climb on top of a boxcar with everybody else, heading north toward my home, and I was a Villista! Ahoooaa!

"Like the *dicho* (proverb) says, 'Every one to his own taste,' as he kissed the sheep. Aha-ha-ha." His face turned serious again. "But it would seem like a very long time before I returned here to my *pueblito*."

He dipped into an earth-colored olla with a gourd and took a sip, which spilled all over his chin. He offered me a drink of water from the same gourd, which I didn't dare refuse. He carefully watched me drink then continued.

"Some of what I remember now is what I experienced. Some is what was made clear years later, when I talked to Padre Reyes. It is all jumbled up now. Maybe because I was only twelve years old then. Maybe it's because of my age now. I'm getting as useless as a .30-30 shell in a shotgun."

He roughly took the gourd from my hand and dipped it into the olla for another sip of water.

"After we left Mexico City, after I joined the *bola* (bunch), Villa began to lose his reputation for invincibility—first in the battles of Celaya. The battle site, which Obregon chose, was crisscrossed by irrigation ditches. Villa was so full of himself and flushed with all his victories that he didn't consider these natural obstacles. He had no respect for Obregon and referred to him laughingly as 'El Perfumado' (the Perfumed One), a dandy, a sissy."

Obregon, the only white man in the photograph, stands in the middle of several rows of his Yaqui troops. The troops are all in new clothes, sturdy shoes, and hats—greatly different in appearance from the ragged army that had entered Mexico City. The troops exude satisfaction and confidence that their general will keep his promises to them. Juxtaposed are photographs of Obregon taken during the same time period with men in ill-fitting coats and ties. They are urban workers who do not appear to be comfortable in the unfamiliar garb but who posed for the camera because of the solemnity of the occasion. During the three-month period after Obregon entered Mexico City with his Yaqui troops and before the city was abandoned to Zapata and Villa, Obregon had recruited the organized urban workers, the International Congress of Workers, to the Constitutionalist's side. They were all to present a unified front against the "reactionary" Villistas and Zapatistas, as he described them. To seal his promises to the labor movement, he gave the workers, for their meetings and offices, a convent and other school facilities, which had been seized from the Catholic Church. With the foundation of the Red Battalions, Obregon was seeking supporters and allies in a way much different than Villa's haphazard invitation to join the melee. All the while, Obregon had acted without approval of Carranza, who did not trust the "proletariat."

"Obregon's infantry, mostly Yaquis, didn't even have to dig trenches! They used the irrigation ditches to hide and wait for Villa's massive cavalry attacks. Obregon had studied the war raging in Europe. He knew that with barbed wire to funnel Villa's charging *caballeria* (cavalry) and with machine guns firing from each side of the funnel's opening and with the horses having been slowed by minefields and the machine gun's crossing fire, that cavalry charges were obsolete, useless, murderous of so many *hombres bravos* (brave men). Obregon read newspapers. He sought the opinion of others.

"Villa was a macho. He would never back down from anybody—*anybody*. He thought he had learned well, and he *knew*," he spat with disgust, "what wins battles. He didn't need other's advice. But this time, he was as surprised as a dog when he attacks his first puma."

From Anselmo's vivid descriptions, I realized why Father Reyes, an educated man, had sought him out for conversations. Here was a man whose formal education, if any, ended well before he was twelve years old but whose intelligence and narrative ability were easily Father Reyes's equal.

"Those defeats were followed by the siege at Leon. Finally, Villa's advisers convinced him that massive cavalry attacks were no longer irresistible, even if the attack was led by Francisco Villa.

"For over forty days, our troops were entrenched along a twenty-kilometer line facing Obregon's waiting troops. It was said that it was just like the European war that was killing men by the thousands. But Villa's strength had always been brute force and attack and attack and attack—not the delays and discomforts and cowardice, which he thought were the result of trench warfare.

"The stench of unburied bodies between the lines and the rats and flies and lice are things that I particularly remember as we waited for I don't know *what* in those trenches.

"Finally, as could have been predicted, it was Villa who attacked first. With his reserves, he attacked the rear of Obregon's entrenchments, but his cavalry was stopped again and again and again in the bloody charges.

"For a second time, we suffered huge casualties. I climbed to the top of a little hill, and I saw floods of people moving away from the battlefield, leaving many abandoned pieces of artillery. We had smelt up the wrong hound's butt for a second time.

"Up to this time, I had been an observer, a helper, a person who, like a woman, scrounged around for food and water for the soldiers. As of yet, there had been no use found for my... special talents.

"Again, we clamored on the boxcars, and the trains moved what was left of the Division del Norte northward toward Chihuahua. Villa was everywhere. He didn't remain in the small caboose, making plans with the other generales and his old compadres.

"He was talking, joking, saying it was the lack of ammunition in Celaya that had caused the retreat. At Leon, he shouldn't have followed the advice of those who said the way to fight Obregon was like rats burrowing in the dirt and waiting and *waiting*! We had not fought like the machos of the Division del Norte! He told us, '*Muchachos* (Boys), when a man straddles a fence, he is going to get some sore *huevos* (testicles).' Aha-ha-ha." Anselmo slapped his knee, then he whispered, "He didn't look like a general. He was dressed in an old wrinkled khaki uniform without a collar and with buttons missing. His hair had not been brushed in days, and he had stubble for lack of a shave.

"He walked slightly pigeon-toed among the soldiers, with both his hands in his pants' front pockets, and would nod here and there when he saw somebody he recognized. Sometimes, he reached out to touch a *compadre* or *compañerito* (pal or partner), as he liked to call us. I heard him say laughingly, 'The sun doesn't shine on the same mule's *nalga* (butt) every day, muchachos.' Aha-ha-ha! I knew at that moment, that I would die for that man."

La batalla de Agua Prieta

"We retreated toward Chihuahua and, this time, turned the tables on any possible pursuers. Mile after mile of the steel tracks behind us were pulled up from the ground and twisted out of shape so they couldn't be used again. Men would attach cables to the track and after the Division, with all its boxcars and locomotives, had passed, the last locomotive would pull the tracks out and twist them around a tree so that they couldn't be reused.

"Although he didn't take advice from the others, when we arrived at Nuevo Casas Grandes, Villa was generous in disclosing to us all what his new strategy would be. Chihuahua and Durango, his *partes fuertes* (strongholds), had been cleaned out by extensive fighting, and their resources, exhausted. He had taken cattle and everything of value from the rich hacendados and used their wealth to pay his soldiers and to buy ammunition.

"'Now compañeros, we will head west toward Sonora. There has been no fighting of any consequence there. There aren't a large number of Carranzista troops occupying that state, so we can live off the land. There are plenty of resources there—cattle and copper and silver mines—that can be tapped and their products sold in the United States to buy arms and ammunition. And when we are ready, we move south and join up with Zapata,' Villa told us.

"'And I,' I thought to myself, 'will be home.'

"'In case of any unexpected attack by the enemy, our backs will be against the United States' border to avoid encirclement. General Pershing has always been sympathetic to me,' he added.

"His explanation made so much sense and sounded so easy to do when he talked about it that we all were reenergized and ready to start immediately on this new adventure.

"But he failed to tell us"—Anselmo seemed to stare at me with his clouded white eye—"that there were no railroad lines that connected Chihuahua and Sonora. So for the first time, the Division del Norte would have to ride their horses or walk to a battle. There were to be no troop trains, no special cars for officers, no la niña or la jesusita. Even the hospital train was left behind, as were the women and familias.

"There was so little water along the barren roads, and hauling the artillery pieces through the mountain passes was brutal— only Villa in his dusty and sweat-stained uniform urging his *compañeros* (partners)—and even the *mulas* (mules), to pull harder, could have inspired the soldados to go through all that. Along the way, the trees were so small and far between because of a lack of water that even our dogs didn't bother to lift a leg. Aha-ha-ha.

"But we entered Sonora a strong and intact army!" His good eye became a little black reservoir of energy and determination as he remembered it all.

I stood up from where I had been squatting, and both of my knees popped. There was a dull ache in my lower back, the result of my years underground and of the long cramped ride from the border. For just a moment, Anselmo's face had gone out of and then back into focus. The tiny man who, notwithstanding his great age, was still extraordinarily vigilant of everything around him, carefully watched me and, satisfying himself that I was all right and would not fall on my face, continued with his fantastic recollections.

"That's when I was told what my role in the attack on the garrison of Agua Prieta would be. As we approached Agua Prieta,

Villa received what he said was 'excellent' information, that there was only between 1200 and 1500 Constitutionalist soldiers there and that they were positioned with their backs to the United States border to avoid encirclement.

"Villa was going back to his earliest tactics. The ones he used when he didn't have masses of men and horses and artillery. We would attack at night.

"He knew that this garrison would again be protected by entrenchments and barbed wire placed so that any attacks would be funneled into areas which were covered by overlapping machine gun fire and mines.

"But this time, there would be a number of us, mostly Yaquis and a few Mayo, who were used to hunting at night, who could creep up to the barbed-wire entanglements and cut them with wire cutters. In doing this, we were to move as shadowy and silently as a thief who has just witnessed the execution of the *cuate* (buddy) who helped him skin the patron's cow.

"In this way, instead of having to go through the deadly areas which would be swept by thousands of bullets spit out by the machine guns, the attack would go through the unprotected areas. Of course, the defenders were to be distracted from what we were up to by a false attack, where it normally would have been expected.

"That night, carriages with the cannons and caissons were brought up and positioned in several clearings. Their canvas covers were removed in preparation to fire. The telescopic sights and range finders were not set up because they are useless at night. But their shots were only intended to hide our real intentions and didn't have to be accurate.

"Very soon a huge sound started to erupt from them. Shock, shock, shock, shock."

A dribble of spittle ran down his chin in his imitation of the cannon.

"Riflemen with Springfields and heavy Mausers began to pepper their defensive positions. Our riflemen would take a few shots and then move so that the defenders who remained stationary in their dug outs couldn't get an accurate bead on them.

"All around me, I heard the crackling of our rifles. The riflemen had been instructed not to fire in a way in which a round could enter the United States. Villa didn't want to provoke the Americanos in any way.

"Because we expected to fight face-to-face with the Carranzistas, we were told to pin our hats up in front so we could identify each other in the dark.

"I heard one of the artillery officers curse that the shells were not detonating again as his crew tried to empty an unexploded round from the red hot tube. 'God damned homemade *cagada* (sh——t),' he yelled frantically as they took their lives into their hands trying to unload the cannon.

"The men with the Mausers were shooting at the elevated water tower, where it was thought some of the defender's sharpshooters were hiding.

"While both sides vomited noise, we crept silently toward the barbed wire with our cutters.

"Since the success of the attack depended on surprise and speed, hundreds of Villa's cavalry moved up very close under the cover of the darkness, inching up toward the paths they intended to take that we were preparing. The only thing that disclosed that anybody was there was the soft 'ching, ching' of their spurs. But this sound was masked by all the other noise.

"There were at least thirty of us who crawled up to the wire, and we were given fifteen minutes to do our work. All around, I could hear 'snip, snip' as the cutters did their job.

"Then at the time specified, a terrifying blast of bugles shrilled behind me and the piercing cry of 'Viva Villa! Viva Villa!' announced the start of the charge down the paths we had cleared.

"*Chinge su madre!* (Son of a b——ch!) All of a sudden, I was blinded when *torrientes* (torrents) of light from several huge spotlights in front of me lit up the entire battlefield, where we all were. When I recovered from the blindness, I could see our massed *cavalleria* (cavalry) right behind me, all in exposed positions. Our artillery tubes were out in the OPEN! The gunners had thought that they could move out of range before daylight.

"A deafening roar of machine guns and rifles exploded in front of me. There seemed to be thousands of different flash points. Even my direct front, where we thought only the wire provided protection for the defenders, was ablaze with the flashes of hundreds and hundreds of weapons. They had gotten a bead on all of us before even a *pulga* (flea) could have hopped out of danger.

"Then I heard the muffled 'shock shock' from their artillery. In the silver gray of the light, they could see well enough to adjust and correct the aim of their cannons to hit any exposed targets near pre-aimed spots. Bullets thumped all around me and left little billows of dust. Then for the first time in my life, I heard the terrifying sound of shrapnel. "Boom! 'Wshhhhhhh' surround me as the exploding hot steel spread out in every direction to do its deadly work. As I tried to escape from the *desmadre* (disaster), I saw a river of wounded men, bloody and staggering soldiers everywhere, and wild-eyed and foaming horses stampeding, trying to escape that hell. After the first shells exploded, all I could hear was a high-pitched ringing in my ears. All who could, ran toward the protection of a little strand of trees several hundred yards behind us. I moved as fast as if an *alacran* (scorpion) had started crawling down my neck. But it felt as if I was carrying a bucket of water in each hand!

"In the morning light, after a hideous night filled with moans of 'Madre Sagrada and Jesu Cristo' (Holy Mother and Jesus) and cries for water from those that had not made it to the trees, there spread before me was a spectacle direct from one of the Padre's visions of *el infierno* (hell). All over the field, there were dead and dying men, horses in grotesque positions—some without limbs or heads and bloody *tripas* (guts) spilling out from their ripped bellies—shattered cannons, overturned caissons, and closest to me, where there had been that battery of artillery, a dead mule on its side, still attached to a tube, and underneath it, a man's arm protruded with frozen fingers, grasping as if for the sun.

"As the sun started to heat up the day, an unforgettable smell came from the battlefield. High above, I could see broad-winged vultures sailing serenely, almost motionless, above all this. After the night of bedlam, now in the eerie silence, my mind focused on the buzzing of flies and the chirping of crickets.

"Here and there, men gathered twigs and made little fires. Unbelievably, with a little corn meal and dirty water, they were trying to shape a tortilla. It is true, that for us that survived, 'primero los dientes que los parientes' (first your own teeth before your relatives). The firing from the other side had completely stopped.

"We put as many to a shallow rest as we could with a few shovels of dirt. But it was not enough. By late morning, we were surrounded by dirty oily smoke and the smell of burning flesh as several piles of the dead were being burned with crude oil.

"I saw Villa walking in a stunned and confused state as he asked his commanders how all this had happened. 'There were many, many more than 1500 defenders,' he said. 'And from where did that miserable little garrison get the electrical power for those enormous spotlights?' He asked everybody and nobody.

"What remained of Villa's army traveled west along the border for about fifteen miles until we got to the small *pueblito* (village) of Naco. There we rested and tried to regroup.

"Naco was ablaze with the news that Obregon had personally directed the army at Agua Prieta and that thousands of the troops that had fought in Celaya and Leon had been there.

"Slowly it became clear to us that those troops had been moved on the railroad that took the smelted copper concentrate from Douglas to the El Paso refinery! Those troops had to have been moved with the permission of the Americano's government!

"Later on, we were to learn that some of Obregon's troops entered the United States at Juarez, and some were transported from as far away as Laredo, Texas. So while we pulled the cannon through the mountains and desert with the strength of our backs and with our mules, they had been massed along the border and prepared a reinforced position and waited for our arrival, all with the approval of El Tio Samuel (Uncle Sam)!

⌒

Mounds of large heavy boulders have been laboriously positioned, one on top of the other, to a height of six feet. On top of the stacked rocks along the length of the rock pile, a twelve-by-twelve-inch-thick timber seven or eight feet long has been notched and fitted so that it lays on a number of vertical timbers of the same thickness. It is a technique that is similar to that used underground in the copper mines to shore up horizontal tunnels or vertical shafts. On the slanted side of the structure facing the expected direction of the attack, a thick layer of dirt covers most of the boulders. Nailed to the horizontal timber is a thick canvas tarp that stretches out behind the timbers. It is intended to provide protection from flying rocks for those underneath, in case of an opposing artillery attack. Behind the structure and underneath the tarp, in various stages of relaxation, can be seen uniformed Mexican Constitutionalist artillery men. Part of a spoked iron wheel, like those used in the horse-drawn rigs that haul artillery pieces, can be seen behind the structure as well as four or five similar structures all facing in the same direction.

American soldiers at a different location were also photographed digging trenches for their own safety before the Battle of Agua Prieta. They are there to observe and ensure that the battle doesn't spill over into American territory. It is now clear that the United States, having been placed in a difficult position in picking a successor after the fall of Porfirio Diaz, had made its choice between Villa and Carranza.

El General Enrabiado

"The hatred and fury that this raised in Villa cannot be described. From that moment on, he spoke only of the hatred he had for all Americanos and about his intent to get his revenge. And so it happened, even upon those who had prior to this time been his friends. It was clear to all of us that the Division del Norte was no more. I was lucky because I only had to travel the length of Sonora to return to my Yaquis, but the men from Chihuahua were hundreds of miles away from their homes. And Obregon and thousands of his soldiers stood in their paths, thirsting for more blood.

"Villa still had illusions of what were completely unrealistic possibilities. With those that were left, he would head south toward Hermosillo and start again. But Villa's ability to buy arms and ammunition in the United States was over. His printed money was worthless. His image among the people from whom he recruited was destroyed.

"Those still with him knew that Villa was a brutal man. To enforce his kind of discipline in the past, he had dozens executed, many of whom, it was said, he had personally shot. His mood and actions after the last battle were such that everybody felt threatened. One of the soldiers that had gladly followed Villa since the very beginning said loud enough for Villa to hear, 'Nothing is stupider than a herd of sheep, except for the man who herds them.'

"With the Constitutionalists on one side and Villa's angry soldiers on the other, I felt as itchy as if I had laid my blanket down on an ant hill.

"Many Villistas from Chihuahua took the most reasonable option. Some of the residents of Naco described the copper mines in Bisbee. It was said that their *mayordomos* (shift bosses) hired Mexicanos to do the dangerous and dirty work in the maze of underground tunnels. After what they had been through, this did not scare them. Many of the survivors of Agua Prieta took the seven-mile hike from Naco up the Mule Mountains to Bisbee to start a new life. When we got to Hermosillo, I also planned to slip away from Villa.

"Before I left, as he retreated south from Naco, not far from Hermosillo, Villa attacked the mining town of La Colorada, where there were engineers and other Americanos that Villa thought had supported his enemies. When they heard of his approach, to avoid being captured, some of the miners and their families hid in the network of mine shafts and tunnels that surrounded the town. Villa's men destroyed the water pumps that emptied the mines, and the lower levels of the mines were flooded. How many drowned there? Nadien sabe. (Nobody knows.)

"Villa was out of control, I saw when he had several poor Chinos hanged. Some were merchants. Some worked on the track gang for the mining company. They hung there in the public square for days with birds pecking away.

"For his journey back to Chihuahua, from any person that crossed his path, he took their horses, mules—anything of value. In his fury, he was striking out in every direction, hurting the little people, those that had been his supporters, those that didn't have any responsibility for his defeat.

"Afterwards, those Yaquis that survived the mine disaster, who had held the lowest and most dangerous jobs at the mines at La Colorada, many of them returned to the Valle de Los Yaquis (Yaqui Valley), and I too joined them. It was said that there had been just too many disasters in that unholy place—La Colorada—to be just coincidental. It had to be a place of death!"

With the last statements by Anselmo, I was stunned. Having grown up in Bisbee, I had been familiar with the history of its boom times between 1910 and 1920. In those times, the majority of miners were American-born whites. But the demand for skilled miners, because of the European war's voracious appetite for copper, attracted many others. They came from the Cumberland and Cornwall mines in England and from other mines in Scotland, Ireland, even Germany. Those experienced miners comprised the labor aristocracy.

To keep labor costs down, unskilled and semiskilled replacement workers were attracted from Southern and Eastern Europe. These were mostly Serbians, Montenegrans, Slavs, and Italians. Holding down the least-desirable and lowest-paying jobs were the Mexicans.

Bisbee, instead of being the proverbial melting pot, was instead more like a posole, the Mexican soup where white corn and brown beans retain their separate essence no matter how much you boil them together. Each ethnic group lived in a certain area and, there, interacted only with their own kind, except at work. I had experienced, as an accepted fact of life, remnants of those older times even as I was growing up. I had always wondered why the barrio, where a large number of Mexican workers had, in those days, lived and settled, was called Chihuahua hill. Until now, I had not made the apparent connection to that distant Mexican State.

I had also wondered why anybody would choose to place a small Mexican-like village, which, because of the material used on the roofs and walls of the shacks, became known as Tin Town to the Anglos. To the Mexicans, it was known as La Zorrillera (Skunkville) because of the abundance of skunks and their smell in that area halfway between Naco and Bisbee. The village was nestled in a canyon between the tailings of the mines and a boulder-strewn hill. It was in an area that had absolutely no redeeming residential qualities like water or proximity to the work areas.

Now I realized that many of the Mexicans who for decades had worked and raised families in these places were remnants of the Division del Norte who had fled north.

The railroad built and owned by Phelps Dodge, which skirted the United States–Mexico border was called, in those days, the El Paso and Southwestern. It was on the El Paso and Southwestern tracks that the troops that reinforced the Agua Prieta garrison were transported. The source of the large amounts of electricity required for the spotlights was probably, although later vigorously denied, obtained from the Phelps Dodge Douglas's smelter. Realistically, it was the only possible source of such electrical power.

After what had happened, everybody would have had a motive, be they Villa's deserting soldiers—now miners—or Phelps Dodge and the newspapers they owned, from not bringing all this to light. All risked possible retaliation, albeit for different reasons, from Villa's supporters or from Villa's enemies.

Responde el Tio Samuel

Not too long afterward, Villa took out his anger on the Americans for what he considered their treachery. In the Bisbee of my youth, it was said that the attack by Villa on Columbus, New Mexico, which I now knew occurred only four months after the fiasco at Agua Prieta, was a shameful and vicious bandit's raid on innocent people. But there was an American military garrison of six hundred men there who fought against Villa's smaller force, and as a result, Villa suffered many more casualties than the Americans.

It wasn't coincidental that Columbus, New Mexico, was the target of the raid. Columbus was a train station and critical water stop between Douglas and El Paso for the El Paso and Southwestern Railroad line's steam engines. Villa was getting his revenge.

I told Anselmo that, up to then, this had been the only time that the continental United States had been attacked by a foreign force since the War of 1812. He responded with a conspiratorial-like hiss.

"That was part of Villa's attraction. If he thought his justice required it, he would attack with two hundred men, even the United States of America. He had testicles the size of melones!"

The "bandit" who had the effrontery to respond to what many besides himself—if they had known—was treachery, now faced the wrath of the United States. General Black Jack Pershing of later World War I fame, led the pursuit into Mexico with 6,675 soldiers, many of whom were part of the famous Buffalo Soldier battalions.

For ten months, Pershing from the north and Carranza and Obregon from the south, searched for the elusive Villa.

✑

From the background to the foreground, hundreds of American infantry in a column of twos with packs on their backs and rifles slung on their shoulders wind like a serpent into Mexico.

A convoy of fifteen primitive trucks, one behind the other, forms a gently curving line from left to right on a desert road. The lead truck's front is dominated by a prominently exposed radiator with a safety valve on its top, like those used in pressure cookers, in case it becomes overheated. Behind the radiator, the vehicle's steel frame is visible. Attached with bolts are the truck's bed and sides made of thick wooden planks. Canvas is stretched over the bed in a semicircular iron frame similar to those seen on covered wagons. In front, two removable lanterns provide illumination for the trucks. Civilian drivers were hired to maneuver the trucks as the army had no trained drivers.

A squadron of airplanes with bicycle-thin landing wheels, wooden propellers, and single engines wait on the recently cleared dirt runway for their orders. Huge military observation balloons are inflated and tested over imaginary battlefields.

Motorcycles, mostly Harleys and Hendees, whose sidecars have protective iron plates with a slit in the middle instead of windshields so that a weapon can be thrust through, appear to threaten speedy destruction to any enemy they encounter.

The nation's entrepreneurs have flooded the border with products that they hope will be incorporated into the national arsenal if and when there is involvement in the European conflict. Then we were not yet the masters of war.

The photographs taken of the Mexicans during that time are strikingly different from those of the Americans. The Mexican photographs almost always focus on the faces and the relationships between men. The Americans have photographed their machines and equipment. Machines that, it would soon become clear, were not effective in the primitive conditions of Northern Mexico. Trucks that followed the decades' old narrow trails made by horse-drawn wagons and carriages bottomed out as their wheels sunk in the deep dust and mud. The motorcycles proved uncontrollable in the dirt roads full of ruts and potholes. The wooden propellers dried out in the low humidity, and their laminations separated, while the underpowered engines of the airplanes could not clear the towering Sierra Madres. Just a few of the valuable practical lessons we learned in the deserts and mountains to the south while the Germans in the Atlantic sought to extend their naval blockade and our congress vacillated.

∽

Suddenly, it all made sense; the reason Villa had attacked Columbus after Agua Prieta. Besides vengeance and the hope of obtaining dollars and weapons, he also had a more long-term strategy. He hoped to cause a conflict between the United States and Carranza. If this occurred, Villa could benefit from the fallout and perhaps regain his power. I said to the old man, "So between the hammer and the anvil, somehow the scorpion slipped by." Anselmo just cackled his now familiar, "Aha-ha-ha," as he nodded vigorously.

Soon, skirmishes between the United States cavalry and Carranza's troops occurred up to five hundred miles inside Mexico's borders. Carranza, whose primary policy was enhancing Mexico's sovereignty, couldn't accept and still have a credible position before the Mexican people of an American army of close to seven thousand, including air reconnaissance squadrons swooping all over Northern Mexico, looking for one bandit.

Things became so heated between the governments of Mexico and the US—and I say governments because it was now clear that Venustiano Carranza, *el primer jefe* (the big boss), and General Alvaro Obregon of Sonora were the revolution's victors—that President Wilson mobilized the National Guard.

Even Lieutenant George Patton, who much later during World War II would not be known as one who hid from publicity, got into the act. He decorated his vehicle with the bodies of dead Carranzista officers draped on its fenders, just like some hunters carry their trophies, as he motored across the Mexican landscape hoping to prove that his victims were in fact Villa or one of his officers.

In the meantime, the "illiterate bandit" waited in a cave somewhere in Chihuahua and wondered whether his puny attack on Columbus, New Mexico, had, had the desired effect.

"Gracias a Dios" (Thank God), I told Anselmo. "The United States had bigger fish to fry, and it withdrew the last of the punitive expedition in February 1917. Two months later, we declared war on Germany."

In Luna County, New Mexico, after the Columbus raid, there had been eleven wounded left by Villa. Excluding those who died of their wounds and a twelve-year-old whose leg was amputated at the hip because of his wound, seven were tried by the Third Judicial Court of New Mexico in Deming for the crime of first-degree murder.

The trial commenced on April 15, approximately five weeks after the raid. Twelve male citizens, all Anglo, were qualified as jurors. One other juror was excused because he stated that he couldn't sentence a man to death. All the defendants were accused of the murder of Charles Miller. The prosecutor in his opening statement said, "We don't expect to show you that either of these defendants fired the shot that killed Charles Miller or that they even were close to the place where Charles Miller was killed, but they were in the immediate vicinity assisting in the commission of the felony."

The defense's position was that the conduct of the Villistas was carried out as a semi-military plan. That defense was futile because Mexico and the United States were not at war. All the defendants claimed that they had not participated in the attack but instead stayed behind with the horses. All the defendants claimed that they had been conscripted by Villa into the Division del Norte by force. All were found guilty of murder.

On June 9, 1916, two men mounted the gallows. On June 30, the four remaining were executed. The youngest was sixteen; and the oldest, twenty-six. One of the seven's death sentence was commuted to life by the governor of New Mexico. In all probability, his mercy was influenced when he weighed the political consequences of the large number of New Mexicans of Mexican heritage.

The local paper in Deming said, "Facing death with the calmness and stoicism of Indians, the Villista bandits mounted the scaffold and were launched into eternity."

Dios tiene su razones

He pulled a little cloth bag that had a drawstring from his shirt pocket. With his gnarled hands, he carefully spread a leaf of brown tobacco paper on the thigh of his trouser. Then he meticulously spread on to it a measured amount of powdery tobacco. He picked up the little bundle, licked the paper's edge, and rolled it up. He twirled each end to hold the contents and placed the cigarette in his mouth. With a straw fired from the mesquite coals, he lit it. All this was done with the slow deliberate actions of an accomplished storyteller. Then he looked at me for so long that I felt as if I was being inspected.

Anselmo said, "You know much more of those things than I do, you and Father Reyes. You've read books. You've heard different versions of the same incidents. I don't even recognize the names of those Americanos you've mentioned and have barely heard of your war with Chermanee (Germany). I only know what I saw and what other Yaquis said after they returned from *la guerra* (war) and what happened here afterwards."

I asked, "Anslmo, what is it that happened?"

Anselmo's face unmistakably displayed his feelings. His lips appeared shapeless like a gash in the middle of his face. His good eye was like a glowing black coal deeply recessed into his skull. Even at his age, it was a face to be feared in the dark if unjustly provoked. The deft swift movement of his hands with the carving knife as he continued to shape the wood hinted of their youthful excellence.

For the first time, I noticed on the other side of the ocotillo fence two not-yet teenaged Yaqui boys. One was wearing a wide-brimmed straw hat. The other was hatless, his face cocked to one side above a strong stocky body. Although their heads were turned toward each other as if conversing, they were intently listening to what Anselmo was saying. Perhaps they sensed that this was the last recounting by one who had never put his story on paper, but a story that had to be remembered.

Anselmo immediately noticed that my focus had turned to them.

"Don't concern yourself. They don't mean to intrude. They are merely seeking instruction of how a man behaves, nothing more. Sometimes it is to us that the children teach a thing or two."

In response to a flutter outside the yard, he hobbled over and peered through a slit in the fence that the ocotillo's growth had not yet completely covered. I could see a Yaqui woman with a cloth-covered basket of woven grass. A rebozo was tied around her neck and cradled underneath the basket like a hammock. It was positioned just under her breasts to help her carry the load in the basket. She had braids of heavy black hair with strands of gray, and in each hand, she held a white long-beaked bird. She was speaking animatedly with another Yaqui woman who was squatting before two tubs, each filled with water. Underneath one, smoke rose from a mesquite fire. In the background, where a couple of men were busily about their business stacking logs of mesquite, there were wooden shacks. The crouching woman was scraping a cow's tongue with a serrated knife in preparation before boiling it.

Anselmo smiled. "Camilda has that basketful of freshly cut nopalitos. She will be able to trade the cactus and birds for what she needs. With proper preparation with red chile and other spices, it will make somebody a delicious meal. What a cook that child is." To him the woman, into her fourth decade, was a child.

He brought his thumb and fingers to his pursed lips and made a smacking sound. "A woman like that can make a man whistle, provided he is still young enough to pucker, eh señor?" Then he continued in a louder voice, which he intended that the two young boys hear.

"After the seige of Leon, several of Obregon's men were captured by Villa's Dorados. One was the officer in charge of ensuring that there had been enough ammunition for Obregon's Yaqui troops. Villa's cavalry had attacked from the rear and surprised not only the officer but also his family who he thought was safe there in the rear. As was his custom, Villa ordered that the officer be stood up before a wall and immediately shot.

"Before the execution could be carried out, a little boy no more than ten years old, who was witnessing the preparation of the firing squad for his father, ran up to Villa just as he prepared to ride away and said, 'I heard that Pancho Villa had *muchos huevos* (a lot of balls). You can't be he, shooting a man in front of his wife and children like a dog. If you have to kill someone, then shoot me!'

"There was a moment of stunned silence as Villa looked down at the boy from the height of his huge horse. He slowly got down and, with spurs making little trails in the dirt, walked over to the boy and looked in his eyes. The boy stared back without flinching, but his eyes brimmed over with tears.

"'No, *hombrecito* (little man), it is you who has muchos huevos, and you have a father who has taught you well.'

"He looked at where the boy's father awaited death and said, 'Sueltenlo' (Release him), and the boy's father was released."

Anselmo took a deep drag of his cigarette.

"Afterwards, that man became one of Villa's most valued soldiers. He helped him to keep track of ammunition and other provisions. At the time I witnessed this, I myself was but twelve years old and wondered how that small boy had the courage to do what he did.

"No, mi amigo, sometimes it is the children that teach us a thing or two."

Suddenly, having seen something, he stood up and roughly told the boys to leave as they were disturbing him. I knew that what he had to say to them was over. He stepped out of the yard beyond my vision and said something I didn't understand. Then I saw what had upset him. In the back pocket of one of the boys was a set of earphones for a Walkman, the great "homogenizer" of all people.

"See this *ojo del diablo* (devil's eye)?" He hissed at the boys and pointed to his right eye, which was covered with the cataract. "Each white hair in this old man's head is the result of each evil thought I carry up here." He struck his forehead with the heel of his palm. "But this eye is not just for evil thoughts but for the evil acts I have already done and still plan to do!" The boys vanished from our presence without knowing what they had done to trigger his fury and not waiting to find out.

He said, "*Chingados lepes, olvidalos* (Goddamn kids, ignore them), *son tan estupidos* (they are so stupid) that they couldn't even teach a *gallina* (chicken) to cluck." He hobbled out to make sure that they had left.

While he was gone, I looked up from my notebook and out into the street. There, another younger boy with a grimy, dirt-encrusted face knelt on one knee. The features of his face were pinched with concentration. With the back of his wrist on the ground, he prepared to shoot a marble with his thumb. Behind him, where the dirt road had a depression like a little arroyo that channeled rainwater into a field, an ancient woman was dumping her bucket into a large communal steel garbage drum. Meanwhile, sitting on his haunches, an emaciated black-and-white dog, whose ribs were as prominent as a greyhound's, patiently awaited her departure and his dinner.

On the other side of the street, a mother was reading a Mexican comic book to her three children as they pushed and crowded around behind her trying to see the pictures that went with the words. She was seated on a boulder next to her makeshift table made of a wooden slatted orange crate with newspaper spread on its top as a table covering. Meanwhile, a grizzled man with white hair and beard, yellowing like old newspaper, stood underneath a stall protected from the sun by a canvas held up by two long wooden poles. He carefully stacked little piles of oranges. Next to them, he had made a little mound of unshelled peanuts. When he had a customer, he would scoop them into little cone-shaped containers that he made of carefully measured pieces of newspaper. Behind him, joking and laughing with the vendor of *raspados*, were some young adolescent boys and girls. The vendor answered them good-naturedly as he vigorously scraped with his hand tool into the twenty-pound piece of ice.

I could see a number of bottles of different-hued nectar that contained all of the wonderful flavors that I remember from my youth, and my mouth watered.

How little they need to make them happy, and they seemed so appreciative of what little they had. Fortunate they are to have a connection to the past and to each other in this dusty pueblo. I think I was like that once too.

When Anselmo returned, I noticed the shallowness of his breathing and how much he labored when he moved.

"When I deal with those little cabrones, I feel just like a dog lifted a leg and pissed on my boot," he hissed.

Camilda had followed him in from the narrow alley in the rear of the house. Besides the porch where I was seated, the little house had two rooms made of adobe. Above the pine rafters, the roof rested on saguaro cactus ribs and what looked like packed earth and straw.

Camilda startled me with, "You *Yoris* (Anglos) who are so rich. Why are you here looking at the Yaquis?"

Anselmo told her, "Quiet, hija, if you are going to make a fool of yourself, make sure there are no witnesses."

Anselmo turned to me, "Camilda lived in Tucson until she was fourteen—before she returned here—to marry many years ago."

Trying to temper what he had just said to her, he looked at her with affection. "Look at her skin, the color of honey poured on a plate."

He sat down on a wooden stump, and Camilda busied herself around the wooden stove. I realized that she also lived there when he said, "Camilda is like the daughter I never had. She takes very good care of me."

He then looked at me and asked, "What about you? Do you have children or a woman?" He turned his penetrating eye on me.

"Divorced, one grown daughter studying for an advanced degree in mathematics at Boston College."

Anselmo looked properly impressed, although I knew he didn't have a clue what I was talking about.

"It is good to have children," he said.

Camilda again startled me when she unexpectedly cried out, "So you can light candles all around the little dead body and place a rosary around the baby's neck at the *velorio* (wake)?"

"What is past is past, hija," he said. "God has his reasons."

"God got what he wanted," she answered. "I made the sign of the cross and said the words, 'I baptize you, Nicolas, in the name of el Padre, Jesu Cristo y el Espiritu Santo,' over my only child's body. There wasn't even enough time to get a proper *padrino* (godfather) and a *madrina* (godmother) after he was born. I didn't even know the couple who consented to be his padrinos. They came in just as the candles around his little body were being lit. Dios me castigo! (God punished me!) After I had married in the church, Dominga was right. I shouldn't have run away."

She looked at me with eyes brimming over with tears.

"When my mother made me leave Tucson to marry in Potam, I didn't know my husband was to be three times my age. He had seen me at the Pascua ceremonies. I told her, 'I'd rather hang myself than marry him.'

"'If you don't marry Aristeo, I'll hang you myself, *mal agradecida*' (ungrateful girl), she said. As soon as I could after the wedding, I fled to Hermosillo. My poor child and I suffer the consequences for that sin to this day."

The flickering light from the stove illuminated the bottom half of her anguished face. The top half blended into the darkness.

"There I became *enamorada* (fell in love) of a young Mexican with light-brown hair, soft as silk. That baby was our only child. After that, there were no more. After a while, he looked elsewhere for a woman that could give him children so that he could show his friends and family that he was muy hombre. With me, he became more and more *corajudo* (abusive) when he had his Bacanora until I couldn't stand it—"

Before she could continue, Anselmo interrupted to save her any more embarrassment.

"Camilda's mother, as a young child, had been with the Yaqui families that had been sold like goats to work in the fields of Yucatan. I got to know her mother's older brother there and also the entire Pinuelas family. I was there when he and the other Yaqui troops who were supposed to keep order for the Federales, stripped off their black uniforms with the red braid down the trousers. They were yelling, 'Viva Carranza, Viva Obregon' because Huerta had fled the country. For weeks, I wore a high black hat with a shiny black bill that somebody had thrown away. One day, in Mexico City, after the Division del Norte had arrived, one of Villa's Dorados said that he thought the hat would look a lot better with a hole in its middle. Before he could ventilate it, I found another hat. Aha-ha-ha."

Camilda was now busy skinning and gutting a small rabbit. She then split it into four parts with a large heavy knife and dropped them into a pan of heating water. She added salt, garlic cloves, and other spices to the concoction.

"One of the boys made a lucky shot with his sling, and I traded some sugar cane for it," she told Anselmo.

"After the war, Camilda's mother and her family were some of the Yaquis that returned to Potam. I saw her mother grow and marry a man of the *rancherias* (small ranches). Over the years, they had many children. Camilda was her last. Camilda was two or three years old when she was taken by her eldest brother, Diego, and his wife, Dominga, to live in Pascua in Tucson. It is Dominga that Camilda calls her mother and who made the marriage with Aristeo."

The frothy water boiled for several minutes, tenderizing the stringy flesh while Camilda made a green sauce of tomatillo, garlic, and roasted fresh green chile. She coated the boiled pieces of rabbit with the sauce and placed them on a little grill over the coals of the wood-burning stove. Anselmo got a cup and two small glasses. He rummaged around in a burlap sack and pulled out a bottle of orange soda, popped off its cap, and served us each a few ounces of the bubbly liquid.

"*Alcawete*" (Conniver), she said to him. "Don't you see what he is doing?" She looked at me. "He is trying to find somebody for me when he is gone."

"Hija, I see how those men look at you. They can hardly wait until I'm under the ground. A different one will be at your door every night, and their women will hate you. You have no children or husband or family, except me, to protect you. You know the ways of the Americanos. I thought perhaps Tucson would be a better place for you. That's all."

El señor presidente

While we waited for the food, Anselmo sipped the soda and continued in a quiet voice, "Obregon had been well-known as a farmer and businessman in this area before the revolution. He was a respectful man, respectful of the Yaquis. He knew how to talk to the Yaquis, not like other Mexicanos. When he promised that if they fought with him against Huerta, the lands that had been taken away from them after the damning of the river would be given back; he was believed. The Yaqui generals raised thousands of men, and for many months, they followed him from battle to battle until all the others were defeated.

"But Obregon had his eyes on more than Sonora. In a country as big as Mexico, many more besides the Yaquis were needed for the war. From the big cities, Obregon recruited the workers, and they fought alongside the Yaquis. The workers were known as the Batallones Rojos (Red Battalions).

"When he continued to fight in the war, even after his right arm was blown off above the elbow by a Villista shell in the siege at Leon, even his courage was seen to be the equal of Villa's."

Anselmo looked at Camilda to see if the food was ready.

"It's still a few minutes more," she said as a delicious aroma started to fill the air.

"The victors of the revolution met in 1917 to establish the constitution for what was to be El Nuevo Mexico. It was not surprising that Obregon supported the most radical, those who wanted power to be given to the campesinos in the rural areas and the redistribution of the land that was held by the hacendados. And in the cities, power was to be given to the union workers and the Batallones Rojos, who had supported him. The radicals also proposed ownership by the nation of the entire mineral and oil wealth that lay beneath the surface, and to *hell* with the foreigners.

"Combined with all this, they proposed to suppress the Catholic Church and its clergy. The radicals considered the church as one of the major supporters of the old regime's smothering power over the ordinary Mexicano.

"So who was going to resist the man who had triumphed in the war, martyred his body to our cause, and now validated his revolutionary credentials before a world that was being swept up by these radical ideas?

"But we were to learn later that Obregon was a man around whom you wouldn't dare sleep with your mouth open, especially if you had a gold tooth.

"These radical developments at the constitutional convention were not what Carranza had anticipated. His ideas were of reform, not revolution. But the majority of delegates looked at him as if he spoke from a different century. The new constitution as proposed by the radicales was ratified. And Obregon came back to Sonora to await his turn in the presidency.

❧

Three comely young women—flowers of Mexico City's elite— each wearing a bonnet and floor-length dress look coquettishly into the camera. In the sumptuous background, there is a profusion of exotic plants and brocaded tapestries. The two who are standing have each placed a hand daintily through the crook of an arm of the man who stands between them. The blackness of his hair and of his full mustache contrast sharply with his white skin. His hands, fingers intertwined, rest on his belt as he stares with barely concealed amusement at the camera. The third woman, seated on the floor at his feet, has carefully positioned her body and long dress in a way that she considers most becoming. General Obregon, fit and handsome in his tailored military uniform, in no way detracts from the elegance of the photograph and the harmony of the setting. A widower with two children, he is sought eagerly by society matrons to attend their glittering parties.

A wet towel cools the skull and forehead of the reclining man. The bed upon which he lies is draped with white sheets as is the bottom half of his body. His body above the waist is naked, and his chest hairs are visible in the photograph. Underneath his right triceps, there is a rolled-up sheet upon which the remnants of his right arm lie. It is an unbandaged stump, severed well above the elbow. In the photograph, notwithstanding the cauterization, white bone, muscle, and tissue are visible in a neat cross section of the upper arm as is a profile of a young soldier. Perhaps he is the one who wrestled the revolver away from Obregon the instant after the explosion as he sought to end his agony and pain with a shot through the brain.

The president has been photographed in a period of repose, his eyes closed. He lies back in the canvas seat of a wooden reclining chair; his reclining position accentuates his ample paunch and the layers of fat on his neck. The hair on his head and upper lip is the color and density of an old man. The right sleeve of his coat is empty. His left hand, the one with which he constantly greets everybody in case they have overlooked his sacrifice, rests on his chest. It is five years after his mutilation; the old man is barely forty years old. The unanswered question is whether there had been a similar effect on the mind and spirit as on the ravaged body.

"For three years, we all waited for some results. But Carranza did not put into effect the revolutionary promises that the 1917 Constitution had made. At every turn, he either blocked them or ignored them. He stopped the revolution quicker than San Pedro slams the door to heaven in the face of a liar!

"Emiliano Zapata continued to press on for the redistribution of the land in Morelos. Even after Villa's defeat, he stubbornly carried on his revolution. We heard about how his guerrilla forces would disappear into the hills after lightning fast strikes on the Carranzistas. And when the government troops, with their batallones, appeared looking for the Zapatistas, the rebels had resumed their normal farming activities. Of what use is an ax against a snake if you can't find it? No es verdad, Ricardo? (Do I speak truth, Ricardo?)

"A plot was arranged to lure Zapata to a meeting with a government officer who was supposedly defecting with the arms and ammunition that Zapata desperately needed. There, where the meeting was to take place, Zapata was ambushed and murdered by Carranza's men. His body was so full of bullet holes as to make him almost unrecognizable. They feared him that much.

"Then in an attempt to stop Obregon's succession to the presidency, Carranza hoisted his charge of 'the Plague of Militarism.' He said that Mexico's curse was having its presidents rise from those that had formerly been generals. He nominated for the presidency a civilian that nobody knew with the obvious intent of using him as his puppet.

"Obregon was not to be denied his chance at the presidential sash. He responded, saying that before the old man with the goatlike white beard could steal the election, he would rise against him. Soon, the whine of Obregon's bullets was a statement that was well understood in every man's language. And once again, the revolutionaries began to fight each other.

"It was soon obvious that Obregon and his tightly knit camaradas and generales from Sonora held the real military power in Mexico. Not long afterwards, as Obregon's military supporters closed in on Mexico City, Carranza abandoned the capital and headed toward Veracruz. He took with him several railroad cars filled with his supporters and, por supesto, the entire national treasury in gold bars. But he had as much of a chance as a rabbit in a hungry dog's mouth.

"The train was intercepted by Obregon's men. Carranza escaped on horseback and continued his flight from his pursuers for several days until he was finally cornered in a small hut. In the morning, the president of Mexico was found shot, the mortal wounds in his chest. Obregon's men at the scene claimed that he had died by his own hand, pointing the revolver to his chest and pulling the trigger with his thumb, once or twice."

Camilda brought the roasted rabbit in three plates. I noticed that mine had two of the four pieces. She had also roasted some ears of corn and shelled the grains from one of the cobs with a knife. She handed the plate with shredded pieces of rabbit and shelled corn to Anslemo and said to me, "Be careful. Yaquis are extremely good at making up stories, especially that one."

"No, it is all true, Camilda, as I swear it."

Looking at him with affection, she said, "Anselmo has had few things in his life. What he has had is information. There has been no other among us as good at gathering news and gossip. That is what his role has been with the Yaqui, the seeker and teller of knowledge."

Camilda left us alone as we ate our supper, and I noticed that he barely touched a couple of kernels of corn. While he chewed and chewed on the tiny mouthful, Anselmo thought of how to respond to my question.

"And what about the presidency after Carranza's murder?" I asked.

"After Carranza's death, there was nothing to hold Obregon back. A temporary president was appointed until Obregon could be formally elected, and so he was. The first three years of Obregon's presidency were a welcome relief after ten years of killing, famine, and disease. The slogan of Obregon's administration heard and seen everywhere was 'Pan, Jabon, y Literacia' (Bread, Soap, and

Literacy). It was going to be the reconstruction of Mexico. And for a while, it was.

"Shortly after his inauguration, Obregon created a national post for the education of the poor and appointed Jose Vasconselos as its head. To this day, that man is seen as a type of savior of the Cultura Mexicana. There were soon to be rural schools, primary schools, schools for the huge number of Indian communities. It was like a beautiful spirit was sweeping the country all the way to the Yaqui towns here in Southern Sonora. Even though my interest was now turning to the *muchachas* (girls), I was not ashamed to attend the classes."

Camilda sat by the stove, separate from us with her plate of food on her lap. She seemed completely absorbed with Anselmo's words as she picked away at her food. I knew that she had to have heard all this before when the old man's thoughts turned to the past.

"To establish an identity independent of foreign influences, Vasconselos pushed for a rebirth of lo 'verdadero Mexicano,' focusing on the ancient arts of the Indians and of the mestizo arts of the colonial period. Mexicanos had, had enough of imitating the Americanos and the Europeos in their music and art.

"At the insistence of the government, the great mural paintings began to appear in public buildings. They told Mexico's story in an artistic way for the illiterate and also for those of us who could read a little," he said proudly. "So that we all could all understand about the abuses of the past and about the hopes for the future of the nation, this, after so many years of oppression and suffering.

"Some said that these larger-than-life murals of the Indian heroes and heroines were just the revolutionary government's propaganda to provide a substitute for the great assortment of saints and other holy objects that were in all the Catholic churches and that the people had venerated for centuries."

✐

Diego Rivera, a still relatively slender man in his mid-thirties, is halfway up the step ladder, and he faces the wall. In his left hand, he holds the palette for his colors. His body partially obscures his right hand with which he works his brush. He is filling in with colors the outline of an Indian woman dressed in a peasant blouse and skirt. The line formed by the curve of her shoulders and the outside of her left arm and hand, which rests on her knee, makes a graceful oval. Rivera had just returned from studying the frescoes of Rafael and Michelangelo in Italy. Vasconcelos, who had previously served at the side of Madero and Villa, had now been chosen by Obregon to supervise this new important task. Vasconcelos had disdain for Rivera, who had lived in Paris during the revolution, away from the horror and death. Vasconcelos knew that the content and artistry of the murals on the nation's most important public buildings would forever affect how Mexicans thought about themselves and their past. He submerged his feelings of resentment and judged Rivera's appropriateness for the work only on his ability and vision.

In Mexico City, the walls of the Ministry of Education, a three-story building constructed by Vasconcelos in thirteen months, contains 128 panels appropriate for the painting of murals. From the immense interior courtyard can be seen startling splashes of vivid colors on the walls of the three levels of corridors that surround the courtyard. In the wall space between and above governmental office doors, some of his most recognizable murals are located for all to see and interpret. In one of the ground-level panels, two huge arches arise above a gaping square black hole. It looks like two eyebrows over a ravenous mouth. On both sides of the hole, faceless miners move down the steps one by one as they prepare to enter the mine's opening, the mouth of the beast. The miners descending on one side of the opening each carry a heavy timber on a shoulder, upon which they can be crucified. On the other side, the descending miners carry a pick or shovel as they enter the hole so that they can dig their own graves. Diego

Rivera was not immune from the intellectual spirit of the times, and in his work, the making of public art and Marxist thought merged. This panel included a poem that urged the workers that the mined metal being used by the owners for making coins instead be forged by the miners into daggers for their use against their oppressors. Students supporting the old regime had started mutilating the murals in protest against the radical, anticlerical, and class-exploitation messages of the murals. Vasconcelos, fearing destruction of his monumental art project, succeeded in convincing Rivera to remove the poem from the mural. Rivera chiseled it out. He then made an exact copy on a small scroll, inserted the scroll in a waterproof vial, and imbedded it within the panel, hidden away with new plaster.

El Panson (the Fat One), as Frida Kahlo affectionately called him, depicted in horrible detail the pathogens of the past, and in the same murals, he included his view of the heroic Marxist symbols that he envisioned for future generations. While at home, from her bed, his Frida, almost in secret, painted about her physical agony. It was a pain that the nation's little people already shared and would continue to share with her in the future.

⤨

"Soon, the end of Obregon's presidential term was approaching, and the land in the Yaqui valley had still not been redistributed to the eight Yaqui towns. There were rumblings in our towns that other promises of the constitution were also not being carried out.

"Obregon intended to continue his influence on the Mexican nation's affairs, and he named Plutarco Elias Calles, another general from Sonora, to succeed him in the presidency. Calles had been the general directly in charge of the troops at the Battle of Agua Prieta.

"Villa, who, after Agua Prieta, was never again to be a national force, had finally voluntarily retired from his revolutionary activities, and because of this, he had received from the thankful, no longer-threatened government, a ranch and a large contingent of bodyguards.

"*Como pendejo* (Stupidly). He now made statements to newspapermen that both Carranza and Obregon had betrayed the revolution's ideals and it was his intention to support de la Huerta for the presidency. De la Huerta had been appointed the temporary president after Carranza's death, while Obregon awaited his own election. It was de la Huerta that had granted Villa amnesty and the ranch. De la Huerta announced his intention to challenge Calles for the presidency in the pending election. Villa stated that he would mobilize thousands, if necessary, to support la nueva causa.

"Shortly afterward, on July 20, 1923, a day that many of us will never forget, Villa was assassinated in an ambush of his car. Again, the finger was pointed at the government in his murder. *Por supesto* (Naturally), nothing was ever proved."

Como se pagan las deudas

The old man stood up and hobbled outside, and I heard the noise of the stream as he relieved himself. Camilda picked up the dinner's dishes and dropped them in a bucketful of heating water. She said, "He seeks as much information from you as you want from him."

"But I've said little."

"Yes, but haven't you noticed. He watched you like a hawk. What made you laugh. How you responded to his little jokes. How you accepted his gifts of food and drink. What drew the attention of your eyes. You have told him much."

In the corner of the room, she started to undo her braids. Her long loose hair with the few strands of gray now reached almost to her knees. With long strokes of a brush, she removed any tangles and quickly gathered any hair that broke off. Once she completed the brushing, she tossed the broken hair into the fire. Just then, Anselmo reentered.

"After death, a woman must collect the hair from all the places where she has left any during her lifetime. It is easier to burn them nightly than recall all the places where she has been. *Verdad, hija?* (True, my child?)"

He took a drag of his homemade cigarette.

"This is the only pleasure that is still left to me. Food and drink, except sips of water, makes me swell up like a toad. I catch only bits of sleep. Women? No pucker. Aha-ha-ha."

He closed his eyes and was silent for a long while; the corner of his mouth showed a bit of spittle.

"What I miss the most is the dancing. In my thoughts, I become the deer. Every part of my body and mind is alert to danger. Swish. Swish. Swish."

With his right hand, he picked up a dry gourd with a wooden handle then another one with his left.

"I look from left to right, from right to left. My heart beats with the drum and with the rattles in my hands. Swish. Swish. Swish. Swish."

In that smoky room, in the dark corners where the light barely penetrated, as the old man talked of the past and of his dance, I felt the presence of Villa and Obregon and of all those others who had come before and who he spoke of.

"After the Yaquis were liberated from Yucatan, we started to perform the dances again. The *chingados patrones* (damn bosses) there had forbidden us our 'heathen ceremonias,' as they described them. But we are still here."

With both hands, he shook his rattles at me.

"Swish. Swish. Swish. Swish."

He suddenly opened his eyes, looked with his ghastly white eye straight into mine, and almost shouted, "Then came the stop at Vicam switch. And the full depth of Obregon's treachery became known to us. The talking tree had been right in warning of the enormous black snake that would try to choke off the Yaquis from their land!"

Camilda, startled, stood up and started toward Anselmo after his outburst. He waved her off, having regained his composure, and now calm, he said, "It had been almost ten years since the new constitution and much more than that since Obregon had made his promises to the Yaqui troops. Calles now was safely on the presidential chair. A meeting of our tribal generals was held. It was decided to stop Obregon's train as he and his family returned to Mexico City. It was not meant to be a threat or an insult, just an opportunity to express the tribe's grievances, a chance for his former troops to regroup and remind him of our needs and his promises.

"General Matus was chosen to speak for us, and he did so in his quiet but forceful way. After the train's short stop and after photographs of Obregon's wife and his children and of the other members of his party laughing and talking were taken, as if on *un dia de campo* (picnic), the passengers reboarded the train and continued on their way.

"But Matus might as well have been talking en Chino to a mule. Not too long afterwards, a federal army of fifteen thousand men was brought from different regions of the country, and Obregon personally directed their attack on the Yaqui pueblos, and they used the full power of their modern equipment.

"Obregon had called the stopping of the train a mass uprising by the Yaquis and the first step in a racial war. He said it was time to get rid of Sonora's disgrace. We were soon to know just how heavily we had stepped into the *cagada* (sh——t).

"We had no artillery or machine guns or ammunition or any hope of resupply. Many of Obregon's *tropas de la revolucion* (revolutionary troops) were now being slaughtered at the direction of 'el general.'

✑

The photograph was taken at the instant of his death. Large puffs of dirt explode into the air behind the back of the prisoner. The bullets have penetrated and passed through his body and slammed against the pockmarked adobe wall behind him. The body that is starting to pitch forward is absent any visible evidence of any entry wounds on his chest. Instead, the storm is behind him. The executioners are five uniformed soldiers with rifles and an officer in civilian clothes and a felt hat who has brought down his sword to signal the shots. The dead man made his last statement by refusing a blindfold and by refusing to have his hands tied. His arms have been yanked up from his sides, as if a bird preparing to fly, by the force of the bullets wrenching his body. On adjacent buildings around the execution wall's edge can be seen men, women, and children—their bodies pressed against the adobes, silently observing.

✑

"Some fled to the Bacatete Mountains. Others, including me, quietly sought refuge for themselves and their families along desolate areas near the lines of the Ferocarril del Pacifico in Sonora and the Southern Pacific Railroad in the United States— in those places nobody else wanted. Of those that didn't flee, the most prosperous man in the villages, as always, was the *cajonero* (undertaker), who did the burying.

"Meanwhile, Obregon continued to control huge amounts of the Yaqui's land. Some said that with the use of the government's money and of some California banks, he became the owner of a gigantic business enterprise and his greedy fingers still sought to grab everything left in the Yaqui valley. As for his revolutionary ideals? He used to joke that Porfirio Diaz's only sin was having become too old."

He spat on the dirt floor to emphasize his disgust and, with the tip of his shoe, ground the wet spot into the soil.

"But the ambition of that man was limitless. When he returned from his term as president, he used to say that notwithstanding his age, his eyesight was so good that from his rocking chair in Southern Sonora, he could see all the way back to the presidential palace in Mexico City.

"Camilda's mother, Lupita Pinuelos, was about eight and was with the same group as my family when they fled north from Yucatan after Huerta fell. Until Obregon attacked, we all lived in Potam after the return from the jungle. When the danger was over and Obregon was gone, many again returned to the village. Years later, Camilda was just a baby, and Lupita was very sick.

Diego and Dominga took Camilda with them to Tucson, where they had made a home. When I would go to Pascua to dance, I often would see her until Dominga made the marriage to that man who already had grandchildren. In my eyes, Camilda always stuck out from all the others like a jewel, como una perla."

"Tell him about Hermosillo, where you found me. How I was a *cantinera* (bar girl), a Yaqui whore for the Yoris," she said.

"Hija, por favor, asi fue la vida. (Please, child, it was fate.) The Yoris filled you full of stories of how, if you returned, the Yaquis would kill you. What choice was left to you without a family or a husband? Obregon's attack scattered the Yaquis in so many directions that, to this day, we still suffer from the effect," he said

There was a long period of absolute silence. Trying to change the subject from Camilda and her past, I asked, "And what happened to Obregon after his attack on the Yaquis?"

"Calles's time with the presidential sash was coming to an end, so Calles and he manipulated the election process so that Obregon could again be a candidato for the presidency. The presidential term then was for four years, and reelection was forbidden by the Constitution of 1917. But they and their handpicked congress said that meant only no consecutive terms, so even Madero's original rallying call of 'no reelection' was bastardized. Obregon, *por supesto* (of course), was reelected.

"Shortly after his reelection, the *hangerons* and *lambiones* (kiss-asses) were at a fancy banquet given in Obregon's honor at the luxurious La Bombilla Restaurant in Mexico City. As the melodias of the musicos were muted by the laughing and joking at the head table, a dark young man who was drawing caricatures of the famosos y casi famosos at the fiesta asked to make one of the presidente. The presidente's bodyguards allowed him to approach, and when he got near enough to do his work, he shot Obregon several times in the face."

A cold chill spread through my body at the full force of what Father Reyes meant when he said that Madero's murder was the

Mexican people's first in a long list of lessons that they were to learn! Every revolutionary leader had been murdered, Madero, Zapata, Carranza, Villa, and now Obregon!

"And was it a Yaqui that killed him because of his treachery?" I asked, expecting that answer.

"No, *pendejo* (stupid)," he replied. "A Catholic." He took a deep drag of another homemade cigarette.

✐

The pencil drawing is of the profile of a man's face. The mustache and sideburns, unlike the rest of the drawing, is absent any penciled in lines or shading. Apparently, this blank space is intended to represent white hair. The man is wearing spectacles, and with the mustache and haircut, it just as well could be a drawing of Teddy Roosevelt as Alvaro Obregon. It is a drawing that lacks subtlety or sophistication. How was it that the thin, dark, highly nervous man who was willing to trade his life for the general's was allowed to get so close with a revolver? This shadow of a man exhibited very limited artistic gifts to receive such carte blanche, especially considering the recent prior attempt on the president-elect's life. But perhaps I too have become prey to the conspiracy-theory mania that gripped us here in the United States in the second half of the twentieth century.

Obregon knew the danger. His sleep was constantly being interrupted by the insistent barking and growling of his guard dogs. Had it been only his imagination or perhaps a nightmare brought about by his bloodshedding or that which he had caused to so many others? "Feed them," he yelled at his bodyguards. Afterward, they still continued their incessant clamor. "Give them fresh meat," he ordered. When the growling and snapping did not stop, he said, "They cannot be satisfied. It is my blood that the dogs need."

✐

When I awoke in the morning, Camilda had already stoked the fire. She had left water heating for what was to be a tea for Anselmo and me, sweetened with bits of honeycomb. Anselmo was already awake and going through a series of stretching movements. He said, "That bag of yours is a big improvement over my straw mattress. Sometimes, the Yoris get it right. Aha-ha-ha. Camilda has gone to prepare for the day's work. I tell her it is much better to work hard all day than to do nothing, except, por supuesto, if is me. Aha-ha-ha."

Camilda entered into the small structure with the same basket, and tied around her neck was the rebozo that, like a hammock, supported it. In the basket, she had freshly picked squash, several ears of corn, and a cloth bag filled with green beans. In a worn cardboard egg container, she had five little pigeon eggs. She hoped to sell or trade all this at the market.

"I have to hurry to join the other women or the old Arab's truck will leave me." She smiled and told Anselmo, "The old women have a thousand questions about why the Yori spent the night."

"What did the nosy buzzards ask?"

"Oh, important things like, 'Did he mind using the outhouse?'"

"Ahaaaa." Anselmo laughed.

Camilda came over to me and surprised me when she gave me a quick kiss on my cheek. Her hair smelled like mesquite smoke and something sweet like jasmine.

"Come back to walk a while with me if you can," were her last words as she hurried away toward the flatbed truck with the waiting women.

Part 3
Cristiada

Chihuahua Hill

I returned to Tucson with a burning curiosity about those times that Anselmo had spoken about. In my family, when I was growing up, it had been as if all our lives began in Bisbee. To a child's mind, it was as if we, and I mean parents, grandparents, uncles, aunts, everybody, had always been there, struggling mightily in the red hills and canyons to blend into pre- and post-World War II America—no different than anybody else.

I searched my memory and recalled that neither my parents nor their brothers and sisters ever went further into Mexico than Naco or Agua Prieta on the border. And then it had been only for a haircut, cheaper gas, or real vanilla.

There never were any excursions to Puerto Penasco, Bahia Kino, Guaymas, or anywhere else on the Gulf of California, which was much closer to Southern Arizona than the beaches of San Diego or Los Angeles. Yet every couple of years in July, my parents would cross the Yuma Desert at a steady forty-three miles per hour in our Ford Model A.

In the middle of the night, with the stifling heat radiating from the superheated sand, my mother would place water-soaked towels on her forehead and neck. In the clear desert air, mile after mile of sand dunes would slowly pass outside our car's open windows so her children could play in the water in the Mission Beach of San Diego for a few days.

I suppose this could be explained because of inferior roads or other difficulties of travel in Mexico at that time. But now I see that it was much more than that. It was as if they all wanted to sever themselves from their past to the south and direct their faces and lives only northward, a self-imposed amnesia of what had been left behind in Mexico. Perhaps this was a natural reaction back then to the harsher days they were living in, when a Mexican was the lowest rung on any ladder in those mining camps. It was a time when segregation was seen as perfectly normal and the question of civil rights was decades away in the future. I was discovering remnants of a past that was barely visible anymore. I realized that if those memories were plowed over again, they would be lost forever into a vacuum of nothingness.

I removed the dusty tin box from the corner of my closet. It had been placed there shortly after my mother's death, and forgotten. It contained those objects that my parents had preserved over the years. These were things that spoke to them of important matters in their present and of their hopes for the future. First communion certificates, primary-school report cards, photographs of people whom I didn't recognize, and a photograph with an endearment scribbled on the back of an adolescent with teeth too big for his young face, which I did. The tin box contained the flotsam and jetsam of their lives and also of their parents. I suspect that my mother and father too had preserved those things that others close to them valued, without really knowing why they had kept them. It was a repository of love, not information.

Included in all this was a document labeled "Declaration of Alien About to Depart for the United States." It had my grandfather's signature and was dated February 1918. The seal and official signature of the American vice-counsel were on its backside. One of the questions asked of the alien in the document was answered: "I have previously resided once in the United States as follows: 1916, Mayame, Arizona, to work." The form on its face stated that it had been prepared and submitted pursuant to the Immigration Act of 1917. The document stated that "the applicant was not accompanied by wife or children." A black-and-white photograph of a young physically powerful man, whom I recognized as my father's father and who, in the picture, sported a luxuriant black mustache, completed the document.

There was also a paper with an embossed drawing of an eagle holding a snake in its bill standing on a cactus. It was captioned: "Estados Unidos Mexicanos Servicio de Migracion." The occupation of the person authorized to cross the international border was "blacksmith." The place of his birth was "La Colorada, Sonora."

As a college student, in the crush of trying to digest American and European political and cultural history, which I had accepted as my complete heritage, as an accidental afterthought, I became vaguely aware of the Mexican Revolution. Then it was taught as a curiosity, not really a subject entitled to the rigorous intellectual inquiry of an important discipline. Even after completing the cursory course at the university, to me the story seemed to be convoluted and contradictory. Not that there was an absence of information in the material, there was an abundance of names and dates. But in the context of the world I was living in, it was as relevant to my life as the study of the Ming Dynasty. Sister Maria Luisa certainly had been right on the mark on that.

Searching my memory, I recalled that my grandfather, in one of the very few conversations we had on the subject, tersely responded to my question about what he had done in those days of the revolution. He said, "I was a blacksmith. Francisco Villa had many horses that needed shoeing. He said to me, 'Pick any horse that I have, and he is yours if you will ride with me.' I didn't accept. Instead, I chose to come to the United States."

That he had been a blacksmith was a certainty. His thick, powerful forearms and chest were the result of thousands of hours spent pounding hot metal with a sledgehammer.

He had a distinctive demeanor. He avoided the clean-shaven appearance and crew cuts of my other male relatives who had undoubtedly been influenced by the American military styles of World War II, when pride and patriotism had required that they join the marines or the Bushmasters of the Arizona National Guard. One uncle had returned a lance corporal with a glass eye and the left side of his face collapsed—the result of a Japanese bullet. There were stories of friends from the hill who had never made it home from the jungles of New Guinea. My grandfather, however, sported until his death a large handlebar mustache.

This burly man always carried a few large cigars in his shirt pocket. On each of his hands, he wore a massive ring on one of his thick sandpaper-rough fingers. The dull circular bands didn't appear to be made of gold but of some cruder metal; each had an initial stamped on it.

When I was a small child, before he lit one of those cigars, he would remove the red-and-gold-colored paper ring that encircled it. He would then place it on two or three of my extended fingers, and a laugh rumbled from deep within his chest at my proud pleasure of "having a ring like my tata." Otherwise, this quiet man, whose words about himself and his past were spare and to the point, was obviously not a man to be trifled with.

He also told me that in his youth, when the Yaquis raided his pueblo near La Colorada, Sonora, to avenge themselves for some Mexican army atrocity, everybody would flee in terror to avoid being tortured. He said the Yaquis would sometimes bury hostages up to their necks in an anthill and pour honey or some other sweet liquid in their ears and leave the ants to their work. Other times, they would skin the soles of their prisoners' feet and pull them shoeless and skinless along the hot desert sand for miles.

"Except for my family," he said to me as I listened wide-eyed with terror. "When the Yaquis came, we would stay."

Whether he was one of the ones that Anselmo described as fleeing into the United States after Villa's defeat at Agua Prieta is not clear.

By 1916, the time that my grandfather declared to the American authorities as being his prior unregistered entry into the United States, Villa was not seeking recruits in Sonora. He was fleeing for his life in Chihuahua, being pursued by Pershing from the north and Carranza and Obregon from the south.

The incident when he told me that he met Villa and had chosen to come to the United States instead of joining his Division del Norte had to have happened prior to 1916. But he couldn't have been recruited prior to 1915 because Villa had not crossed into Sonora prior to 1915. With a little fudging as to the date of his prior unrecorded entry, 1916 instead of 1915, he could have distanced himself from inquiring immigration authorities from any connection to Villa.

If he had actually lived in Miami, Arizona, or worked for Miami Consolidated as he declared, wouldn't he have spelled Miami correctly? "Mayme" is the spelling of one who has only heard the name. None of our family ever mentioned that he had lived in any other place other than the Bisbee district in those days. The exit stamps permitting him to reenter Mexico were stamped "Naco."

After Villa's defeat in 1915, the stories of his and his men's bloody atrocities in Mexico against any Mexicans or Americans who unluckily crossed his path were widely reported. After the fiasco at Agua Prieta, what had been a disciplined army degenerated into a rabble of killers and thieves. Villa and the remnants of his army struck out in every direction at those whom he considered to have contributed to his defeat at Agua Prieta. Then there followed the attack on Columbus.

In those days in the United States, to have had been allied with Villa in any way would have been very dangerous for anybody so identified.

As to the other story about not fleeing the Yaquis when they raided his pueblo, perhaps he was telling me that his family was, at least in part, Yaqui and didn't have to fear them. But all of this is circumstantial, and whether he was one of the "bola" from Sonora that joined Villa's Division del Norte before the battle of Agua Prieta is now impossible to verify.

It is just as likely that Villa, after his defeat at Agua Prieta, was seeking recruits as he moved through Sonora; and it was in La Colorada, where Villa flooded the mines, that my grandfather and Villa's paths crossed. My life's story included an important event that I knew very little about.

What cannot be disputed is that many of those others that migrated from Mexico and lived in Chihuahua Hill and Tin Town and some of the other mining camps in Southern Arizona were survivors and refugees of that battle on the border and its aftermath. They, in succeeding years, silently mingled and interwove into the fabric that is America.

How had Sister Maria Luisa described me? "Monumentally self-absorbed?" I realized that for years, I had been looking at Mexico in a superficial way. I sought out only the quaint, the picturesque, and the beautiful for my photographs. I rifled through my file of scenes I had taken in Mexico. They were of piñata makers, mariachis with their instruments at the ready, and the swirling skirts of beautiful girls and booted handsome men in mid-dance. The type of material I had sold to American travel magazines and circulated in regional art shows for years. It was the Mexico we Americans know and love. I had not been aware, except in the most superficial way, of that other part of Mexico that was slowly opening up to me.

I was reasonably well educated; Mexican by heritage on both my father and mother's side and passably fluent in Spanish. I had become so conditioned to the United States and our everyday brand of conventional culture that matters that a generation or two ago directly involved my family, or my friends' families, seemed strange and unreal. I might as well have been an Irish Catholic from Boston with a facility for Spanish or a Cuban in Florida who fled from Castro, as a Mexican who grew up seven miles from the border that separated the two sprawling countries.

Now, more than ever, my mind was tortured by the unanswered questions that Sister Maria Luisa had left with me at our last meeting. Why had Padre Reyes fled from Mexico, and why had she thought that he might have been imprisoned or executed by the Mexican authorities? The only possible source that I could think of for some answers was the testy Don Miguel.

San Pedro de Tlaquepaque

I exited Hotel Frances, walked half a block, and was at one end of the immense Plaza Tapatia. The plaza is several hundred yards in length and restricted only for pedestrian use. It is bordered on both sides by several very old three- and four-story buildings. Huge fountains of various shapes grace its entire length. The plaza is anchored on one end by the Catedral de Guadalajara. Its construction by the "faithful" took over sixty years. It was dedicated in 1618. The outer perimeter of the huge ancient building is easily the size of a football field.

Through the mist given off by the huge fountains, I could see the Greek columns of the Teatro Degollado, which mark the approximate midpoint of the plaza and where I had, on previous trips, done much of my photography.

On the other end of the plaza was El Hospico Cabañas, another imposing building. It originally was an orphanage and contained many patios and gardens. To one side of the Cathedral is the Palacio del Gobierno, a much less imposing building at least on the outside. This governmental palace, whose construction commenced in 1760, was built from taxes collected from the distillers of tequila, a booming industry not of recent vintage.

Other than being impressed by the age of the cathedral, which was dedicated 150 years before our Declaration of Independence, my focus was on the murals that, Anselmo mentioned, had sprouted up all over Mexico in the 1920s and 1930s. The murals were commissioned as a result of the revolution's leaders attempt to present an ideological counterbalance to the holy images and statuary of the Church, images that still saturate the country.

Inside the Palacio del Gobierno and the Hospico Cabañas are the magnificent murals of Jose Clemente Orozco. On the interior cupola of Cabañas are figures depicting the characters, good and evil, involved in the Spanish conquest of Mexico.

In the governmental palace, on the walls of the stairs leading to the second floor, scenes of Mexico's struggle for independence from Spain and during the conquest are represented. The church's role in these historical events is presented in the murals as horrible and hideous.

Less than a block away from the murals is the beatific statuary and the venerated image of the Virgen de Guadalupe inside the cool, incense-impregnated ambiance of the cathedral, its tranquility marred only by the occasional murmurings of black-clothed old ladies, their heads respectfully covered with black shawls. The contrast between these opposing views of the past left me with a feeling of unexpected disequilibrium.

That afternoon, I returned to the residence on Avenida Lazaro Cardenas in San Pedro de Tlaquepaque, where Sister Maria Luisa had lived. There I spoke with Geremino and Marija, the old Indian couple who were now the caretakers of the building filled with museum-quality, hand-carved furniture and colorful wall hangings and zarapes. I was invited into one of the salas whose door led from the main patio. They kept the home in impeccable condition. Marija said that after the sister's death from heart failure, Don Miguel had become so depressed that they feared for his life. When Maria Luisa's nephew, Ruben-Alfonso Marquez, the administrator of the family's remaining properties, discovered the deteriorating condition of Don Miguel and of the property, he asked the elderly couple to move in as caretakers.

"We, at first, resisted his suggestion to move from Tepatitlan to Guadalajara. Geremino and I had become gray after so many years in our pueblito, weaving the zarapes and rebozos that our neighbors seemed to value enough to trade for what we needed. Ruben-Alfonso said that in Guadalajara, there would be more customers and better prices. And for my clay pots filled with the different dyes and the looms with the half-finished rugs and zarapes? Plenty of room in the house! Every morning, we wouldn't have to move everything outside under the shade of the tree to work on and back inside at night into our crowded little house—with the crawling *nietos* (grandchildren) everywhere—to protect our work from ladrones."

"And electricity and an inside toilet, now that I have to visit it more often at night, and even a little money for our tobacco," Geremino said.

"All we had to do was take care of the house and make sure that *vagabundos* (streetpeople) didn't move in and burn the furniture in the fireplaces!"

Marija stopped the *clap, clap, clap* of the tortilla she had resumed shaping after I had entered. She walked me through a corridor to a sunny patio in the back of the house. Against one wall, hanging from the rafters, there was row after row of nopales strung with twine in long strings that almost touched the ground. I could see tiny insects that had attached themselves to the nopales. The parasitic insects looked like little white freckles on the green circular cactus pads. She called them cochineal.

She said, "It takes fifty thousand of these little ones to make a *medio* (half) kilo of red dye. Gold and silver were the only things of the New World more prized by the Spaniards than the dye made of cochineal. It is said that in the time of the Aztecas, only Montezuma could use clothes dyed with it. Dyed cotton yarn was spun with duck down or soft fur for warmth in the cold season of the Valley of Mexico. After the conquest, the robes of the European kings and queens were soon being dyed with cochineal. It was prized for its color and its permanence."

She loosened a little cloth bag's drawstring and spilled some of its contents on the table. "These, dried in the sun, are the 'negro.' 'Plata' are the ones dried over the stove. The 'negro' cochineal is of better quality but, por supuesto, also takes more time."

There were a number of clay pots that lined one wall. They contained different-colored liquids. She said that she used different materials like blackberries, alfalfa, walnut shells, and other plants found in the hills around Tepatitlan, which she insisted Geremino gather only when the moon was full, to make her dyes.

Off to the side in the corner with a cloth partially covering its top, there was another clay pot. Geremino warned, "Cuidado, no se arime, tiene miados!" (Careful, don't get close, it is urine!)

Startled by his warning that the pot, where a large number of long woolen strands were soaking, contained urine, I stopped in my tracks.

"It's my contribution to her art," Geremino said sheepishly.

"Cochino, callate!" (Quiet, you dirty man!) she said, although she couldn't help laughing. "When you soak the wool there, the *miados* (pee) bites the wool so that the dyes can penetrate the fibers. Those soaked there"—she gestured—"will never fade in the sun."

She picked up a long wooden spoon and fished out several long strands of wool from the menacing liquid. She placed the wool on a large flat wooden shingle and covered the wool with another shingle of the same size and material. She stepped on the top shingle with her huaraches and squeezed out the putrid liquid. Using the same spoon, she again picked up the wool and placed it in another pot filled with clear water, swirled it around, fished the fabric out, and repeated the wringing process. "To remove the stink," she said.

Then she hung the wool on a wooden rack. "Now it will be ready to bite the dye," she said.

With water from a tin bucket, Geremino splashed the area where the two wooden shingles were. The water, in little rivulets, flowed down the flagstone and into a little drain.

Under a tarp, I could see unprocessed wool fleece that waited, teasing and carding before the fiber could be spun with a hand spindle.

"And what of Don Miguel?" I asked. "It is he I came to see."

"Don Miguel has returned to Tepatitlan, where he was born and spent all his life, except when serving Maria required him to follow her elsewhere," Marija said, then she corrected herself.

"It's not just to use that term *serving*. There never was a person who loved as much as he did her. But it was an impossible situation with the body God gave him, poor tortured soul."

Geremino, already having eyed my rented Datsun outside, said with a straight face, "If you could wait a few weeks, Marija and I can accompany you in your car to Tepatitlan. We go every four months to visit the *borreguero* (sheepherder) and also my compadres."

In mock anger, she said, "I have to go with him. I don't like to ride the crowded dusty bus where everybody has to fight for a seat, but if I'm not there, Dios mio, the borreguero will fill him with tequila and *chistes* (jokes). Once he brought back a dirty fleece so old that the grease on the fibers was dried and hard. I had to soften it with kerosene to be able to work with it."

"I suppose also you will never let me forget the time years ago when I brought the dead skin," he said.

"Dios mio, he once brought me wool that had been yanked from a dead sheep, with the roots still attached to the fibers. He was so proud of the low price he had wrangled from some old *borracho* (old drunk)."

"Ayyy, Marija, all that is before Noah learned how to build his boat! But she never lets me forget," he said.

"Now I insist that he observes the shearing. It is the fleece from well-fed sheep, whose fibers take the dye best, that we want."

"Si, si, and to pick only the fleece shorn from the shoulders and flanks were the fibers are longest, and to avoid those shorn by the helpers who don't know how to shear close to the skin of the animal, and have to cut twice. And to stick with the viejos who know how to cut close to the skin on the first cut. And to watch out for the ladron who puts the nicest, longest hairs of the fleece, which should be the width of my palm, on top, and hides the short hairs underneath. Like a chicken, Marija, you never change your CLUCK!" The volume of his voice had continued to rise.

Before things got out of hand, I asked, "Will you wash the fleece with soap?"

"Nunca" (Never), she said in mock horror. "The soap cannot be rinsed out, and it affects the dye."

"She says she will only use yucca root, which forms a heavy lather when rubbed vigorously together in the water, by ME!"

She ignored him and continued, "And never dry the washed wool in the sun because it leaves stains."

"That even Satanas cannot remove, much less a Cristiano like me," he muttered.

Apparently, everything having been aired, Marija now reverted back to the original subject and said, "When you visit Miguel in Tepatitlan, you are in for a surprise with the Altenos." She proceeded to give me exact directions to his shack, which, of course, the feisty old man contradicted. His house was on a path, not a street, and his shack had no number. "Ask anybody and look for a goat shed next to his house." On this they both agreed and, calm having been restored, affectionately looked at and laughed with each other at some private joke.

Then their attention was back on their wool, clay pots, and looms. They had returned to the world they knew and understood. Not yet infected with the need of maximizing speed or profit, they did it their way because when they were young, that's how their *viejos* (old ones) did it, and, before that, their viejos' viejos. The elderly couple had learned early from them and imitated them for all these years. They had been happy, pleased with their skill and the beauty and order their work had provided to others.

Outside the walls of the house, the modern metropolis beckoned with a magnetism of a new and different kind. Up to now, these two had been spared, but not so many others. And these new ways subtly threatened to decompose the accumulated wisdom of generations.

La Herencia de Maximiliano

Los Altos de Jalisco, the heights of Jalisco, is north and east of Guadalajara. It is referred by some as the lean lands because it does not have the rich black soil that produces the profusion of fruits and vegetables of the other parts of the state.

It is an area that stands between 5400 and 7400 feet in elevation. It has pure air, blue skies, rolling hills of bright red clay, and, some say, the world's finest climate. This is cattle country. Ranches and dairy farms dot the landscape. Here and there, I spotted small enterprises of sheep and chickens.

The town of Tepatitlan is forty miles east of Guadalajara and serves as the region's unofficial capital and largest city. As I approached the town, I noticed acres and acres of blue maguey. It is said that this is the only area, besides the town of Tequila, where the basic component of tequila can be properly cultivated.

As I tried to orient myself at the plaza, I noticed a surprising number of blond and blue or green-eyed individuals with ruddy complexions. Notwithstanding their coloring, they were obviously Mexicans. That was the surprise that Marija had promised.

As I was to learn, Alteno heritage is Spanish, Basque, French, and Germanic. This is as a result of thirty-five thousand European troops being quartered in this region well over a hundred years ago, during Maximilian's campaign against Benito Juarez.

Since the unions between the soldiers and local women were, for the most part, irregular according to the Church's standards, the children inevitably took the mother's Mexican name. It was a little disconcerting to me to be presented to a strapping tall man with a blonde mustache and green eyes and be told his name was Chavez or Gonzales.

Unlike what the Indian couple had promised, it took quite an effort to find the general direction of where Don Miguel lived. Just before I had to go to the comandancia for help, an old woman selling tamales at the plaza overheard my inquiries and stopped me. At one time, she had worked at the Hacienda Castañeda and told me where the road leading to it could be found. She described the old buildings that were still referred to as "la hacienda" by neighbors.

As I approached the ramshackle buildings, all badly in need of repair, I could see that they had once been part of a large estate. Now, the parts of the hacienda that still had a practical use by more modern and modest enterprises had been either sold off or perhaps redistributed by the revolutionary governments. Along the road, I noticed a number of small parcels of land each with modest adobe-type homes. Each had a portioned-off section of land many with a growing crop, mostly maize. Some of the new fencing on the land incorporated the extensive old rock walls that had been laboriously constructed by campesinos and that had formerly delineated the old hacienda's boundaries.

I stopped my rented car, and as I approached the main complex, a mounted man beckoned. He expertly loped the large chestnut toward me with the easy, comfortable grace of a person who has spent most of his waking life on a horse. With a huge welcoming smile, he introduced himself, "Buenas tardes, senor, me llamo Edgardo, su servidor." (Good afternoon, I am Edgardo, your servant.)

With the courtesy and quiet demeanor that is so prevalent in rural Mexico, Edgardo carefully directed me toward a walking path that I could see was about a quarter mile away. The path led to small adobe dwelling on a green rise.

As I walked toward the white plastered adobe hut, which was, at most, large enough for two small rooms both with very low ceilings, I noticed a small wooden lean-to where an old washtub for watering the goats was kept. A number of goats were busily grazing on the slope of the hill.

At the bottom of the rise was a small shack that must have been the latrine. In the opposite direction, about fifty yards away, was the communal well that was in use at that moment by a couple of adolescent boys drawing water with buckets.

Across the rise, the orderly lines of the blue agave in various stages of maturity stretched out until the crest of the hill broke my line of sight. In the house, the door and a window opposite the entryway were open.

Don Miguel

I approached the hut with some trepidation, considering how Don Miguel had reacted when I last saw him. When he saw me, he immediately stood up from the wooden chair and table that was pushed against the wall with the open window then smiled and extended his hand. I took it, and he pumped my hand vigorously up and down.

There were papers and some books spread across the table. There was also an oil lamp on the table unlit and unneeded because of the light streaming in through the door and window. Propped up against one wall were two sets of large adobe bricks laid on their edge, about five feet apart. A wooden plank, which served as a shelf, connected the two sets of bricks. On the top edge of the shelf was another similar set of adobes, which in turn were joined by another plank. This mode of construction continued until the precarious structure topped off at my eye level. In this rickety bookcase, there was a number of well-worn and dusty books.

The floor was of packed earth. Opposite the bookcase was a small cast iron wood stove. Built into the wall was an adobe banca that served as a stationary sitting bench. On the banca, there was a human skeleton whose wired joints could be articulated so as to permit it to sit. Its grin, with several teeth missing, seemed to welcome me.

"Don't let my compadre bother you," the old man said.

In the other room, there was a steel military-type bed frame with a hodgepodge layer of interwoven wire that served as bed springs. A thick zarape was rolled up and placed at its head.

There was an elegant, elaborately carved walking stick of some dark hardwood that was entwined by a large silver rosary. The cross dangled from the walking stick's grip so that the semiround curve of the wooden handle seemed to provide a frame for the silver cross. The two objects were leaning against one edge of the bookcase.

He at once stretched out the zarape over the bedsprings, sat down there, and offered me the chair, which I took. We were at a comfortable conversational distance: he, on his bed in one room; I, on the chair in the other; and his compadre on the banca. There was no other furniture.

"I am surprised but very pleased to see you again, señor, after all this time. How is it that you have found your way from your beautiful country to such a remote humble place?" he asked.

Before I could answer, he stood up stiffly, obviously in pain, and removed the wooden cover from the clay olla in the corner. He dipped into it with a small dried half gourd and offered me a drink of water.

"Please forgive me. I've had so few guests here, and my manners have deteriorated," he said.

I took the gourd and a sip of the cool water that had the taste of clay and thanked him. He had failed to remove his reading glasses, which were perched on the end of his nose. His face had the gray stubble of several days' growth.

With the silence thick between us, I glanced at the names of the books and authors in his library. There was Lopez y Fuentes's, "Indio," Lamicq's, "Piedad para el Indio," and books by Samuel Ramos, Jesus Silva Herzog, and Octavio Paz. A large book contained photographs of murals on revolutionary and indigenous themes. With his permission, I picked up that book and leafed through it. The photographs depicted the murals painted by Diego Rivera, David Alfaro Siqueros, Jose Clemente Orozco, and Rufo Tamayo.

There was a large number of history books. Some of which I recall included works by Levy and Szekely, Jean Meyer, Enrique Krauze and even Bernal Diaz, who had accompanied Cortez in his conquest of Mexico. He didn't seem to mind and appeared flattered when I asked his permission to hastily scribble some of the names for my future reference.

It was as if I had entered the dark recesses of the stacks of a university library where an ancient searcher leafs through dusty books and jots down notes in the never-ending quest for greater understanding.

"Do my books interest you, or perhaps they surprise you?" he said and continued without waiting for my response.

"The hunger to know is not limited to those in elegant surroundings once the appetite has been whetted. I have Maria's, que Dios la bendiga (may God bless her), father, Don Alejandro, to thank for my curiosity. He knew that because of my infirmities, my life would have to be of the mind." He struggled over and dipped again into the olla for himself.

"Even as a young child, when my mother was one of his house servants, Don Alejandro made arrangements for my schooling. His compassion towards me extended even beyond his death. This land upon which these old adobes sit will have to await my burial before they too will be planted with the blue agave, of whose wine the world has such an unquenchable thirst. That was one of the few of Don Alejandro's wishes that was granted by his distant relative Ruben-Alfonso Marquez.

"Ruben-Alfonso has taken over the administration of what remained of the Hacienda Castañeda after the old man's death, when it was redistributed by the government. He was almost unknown to the family, the grandson, I believe, of Don Alejandro's sister, who had lived all his life in Mexico City. There, he was somehow involved with the politicians, but all that is behind us, and forgotten."

He motioned toward the corner of the bookcase and said, "When Don Alejandro died, Maria Luisa gave me his walking cane, and when she died much later"—he crossed himself—"I saved that rosary she had laid down so many years before. In my mind, at least, they can embrace each other symbolically after death."

I told him about the doors to the past that had unexpectedly been opened to me and that he was the only one who could explain Father Reyes's flight and estrangement from his country. He nodded his head up and down.

"I can tell you what I observed and what was told to me back then, and you judge what the truth is," he said.

He covered the water bowl, but not before he offered me more of the cool liquid with the vague taste of earth. He then cut a sliver of goat cheese, placed it on a corn tortilla, and tossed it on a heating pan. After the cheese melted, he opened a glass jar and spooned on to the quesadilla some red salsa de chile and handed it to me. He seemed to be weighing in his mind what he was going to say.

"Jalisco was relatively detached from the events of 1910 through 1920, the so-called decade of revolution. But it was the victor's constitution, the constitution of 1917, the new organic law of all of Mexico, that caused the problems in this region. This new law was intended to severely repress the Roman Catholic Church."

He then served himself a warm quesadilla and added, "You see, once the radicals seized control of the constitutional convention, they passed measures that were intended to destroy the Catholic Church all over Mexico.

"You have to understand the Mexican character when it comes to religion." He picked up the small volume written by Bernal Diaz where he described the conquest of the Aztecas. "When Cortez landed in Vera Cruz, the Europeans soon discovered that all temporal and religious power resided in the emperor, Montezuma.

"He was the Tlatoani, the personage whom the Aztecas believed provided the protective force against unpredictable natural elements. The Aztecas believed that he even had the responsibility for the sun's course of travel through the skies.

"Montezuma, as emperor, also embodied another personage, the Tezcatlipoca. As such, he was the supreme power in all temporal matters. He was best described by the Aztecas as the 'enemy of both sides.' To the Aztecas, this explained why every person, good or bad, high or low—it didn't matter—would inevitably suffer inexplicable destructive events in the course of their lives, it was all the work of the Tezcatlipoca."

All of a sudden, I heard a strange sound. I hadn't seen the birdcage in the corner. Two agitated canaries were chasing each other back and forth from a perch on one side of the cage to one on the other side. Their weight as they landed—first on one perch and then on the other—caused the cage to rock on the wire hook that attached it to the ceiling. The flutter of wings and the metronome-like metallic click of the pivoting cage were what I'd heard.

"The Aztecas had many accomplished warriors and engineers. There were men who grew and distributed the crops and men who provided all the other diverse needs of a large urban population. But they cared little for and had no experience with politics, as we know the term. Instead, they looked to those in authority for leadership. Of course, the ultimate authority in all things resided in Montezuma and before him, had resided in those all powerful emperors that had preceded him.

"When the Spaniards conquered the Aztecas, the conquistadores craftily substituted the then-existing Spanish ruling structure of two majesties for those of the emperor, both in his capacity as Tlatoani and Tezcatlipoca. After Montezuma was killed, the Spanish king and his viceroy ruled on all temporal matters. The Catholic Church controlled the spiritual realm."

The old man interrupted himself and got a third cup of water from the olla. He went over to the cage, opened its door, and filled the saucer on its floor with water.

"There, *hijitos* (my children), so that you can drink and bathe," he said.

No sooner did he remove his hand, and they were in the saucer, splashing.

"I tried bringing home the wild *jilguero* and *zenzontle* captured by the Indians. They have some of the most beautiful songs. But they flew around the cage in such desperation, trying to get out that some eventually killed themselves. So I released the others and let them fly free. It is impossible to change the spirit of some things."

He placed the gourd that had a hole drilled in the handle for a wire, back on the nail on the wall over the olla.

"For close to four hundred years, the Spanish system was in place. Over the centuries, the Spanish monarchy was replaced by Mexican elites. But through all the historical ebb and flow involving the seeking and losing of temporal power in Mexico, the brown-skinned Virgen de Guadalupe, who was said to have appeared to a humble *indito*, Juan Diego, was revered by the campesinos as the queen of Mexico. Some said that through her, the church had contrived to dominate in a permanent way the spiritual realm of the religious Mexican people.

"And after the political and military power of the old Porfirio Diaz regime was destroyed in the revolution by Carranza and Villa, it was the church's power over the minds and hearts of the people that the repressive measures of the constitution of 1917 were intended to address."

He again turned his attention to the still-agitated birds. The construction of the birdcage caught my attention. It was made entirely of small pieces of wood and wire or twine. Each hollow piece of bamboo was pierced along its length with several tiny holes where thin wires or twine were run through. They connected with a similarly pierced piece of wood and, several so joined, formed a flexible weave of wood.

At the *mercado*, I had seen rectangular wooden cages that held different kinds and colors of birds for sale. The Indians had made them using the same technique with wood and wire or twine. But Don Miguel's cage was different. Instead of a flat roof, the Indian craftsman had made an arch at each top end of the rectangle. Starting from the center point at the top brace of the rectangle, a piece of wood and twine formed the first triangle. The top side of the first triangle was the bottom side of the second triangle and so forth until all the triangles pivoting from the center formed an arch. The interior expanse of the cage between the arches on each side of the box was much greater and more pleasing to the eye than that of the simple rectangular ones. When I mentioned this to Don Miguel, he said, "The obispos and padres built their palaces to preach their European dogmas with their stories of miracles and the fires of hell. Some of the inditos learned and took what they wanted from the cathedrals and churches that they helped build, for their *pajaritos* (little birds).

He pointed to a crucifix nailed on the wall.

"The cross, the sacred symbol of Christianity, was also readily adopted by the indios, except that, for them, it had a different meaning. The cross's intersection symbolized the meeting of the natural world and the unseen mysterious spirit world that they daily experienced. I think, all in all, it was probably a fair trade off."

He looked at me over his spectacles to see my reaction.

Caridad

"It was about the time when Maria Luisa completed her novitiate and was preparing for her final vows that Calles became president. He immediately started to strongly enforce the anti-Catholic requirements of the 1917 Constitution. Carranza had ignored them during his term. Obregon? He had other matters that captured his attention. But on this matter, Calles, also from Sonora like Obregon, was a fanatic.

"But he grossly misjudged the people of this region of Jalisco. He assumed, because of their limited involvement in the *revolucion*, that they had 'no muchas ganas' (not much enthusiasm) for resistance or for fighting. He thought that they were a bunch of preening, posturing dandies."

From the outside, I heard a young boy's voice, "Don Miguel, Don Miguel, puedo pasar?" (Don Miguel, Don Miguel, can I come in?)

"Si, hijo, pase usted." (Yes, son, please come in.)

"For you and your guest, from Edgardo," the boy said and handed a liter bottle to Don Miguel.

"Gracias, hijo, and give my thanks to Edgardo." He emptied the contents into a larger bottle that he had and returned the empty one to the boy, who immediately left.

"One of my few remaining friends," he said. "He is trying to avoid any embarrassment for me by implying it is for both of us. Four or five times a week, Edgardo sends me a similar quantity.

He knows that since Maria Luisa's death, I need it. I ration it out carefully, so it will last."

Exhaling loudly, he sat down and continued, "Calles stated that the Catholicism of the Mexican people was nothing more than a veneer on ancient tribal beliefs. Calles estimated that for every week, that Catholic religious services were prohibited by the government, that 2 or 3 percent of the so-called believers would drift away from the Church. He thought that they soon would return to their ancient beliefs and rituals and away from the priest and bishop's domination.

"But in the Altos de Jalisco, the Catholic religion was not a veneer on some prior-existing tribal belief. This was where thirty-five thousand of Maximilian's troops, French and Austrian soldiers, had lived and left their offspring and traditions.

"And unlike the other areas of Mexico, there had been few marriages between the Altenos and the indigenous tribes.

"No, this Catholicism was not a shallow veneer. It was a deep, rural, European-type Catholicism. Here, there was a hatred of Protestants and a hatred of anticlerics.

"Instead of being the prissy dandies that Calles imagined, the men in this area valued physical toughness and bravery and, yes, sexual prowess. They were contemptuous of the pencil-line mustaches of the urban males of Mexico City and of their intellectual posturing.

"And the women? The Altenas? They were cut out of the same non-submissive cloth—haughty, tall, arrogant, many with light eyes. And that was Maria Luisa, mi Maria."

I was dumbfounded by the intensity of his emotions. This was a long time in the past. Yet he paused for such a long time that I thought our conversation was over. The atmosphere around us was saturated with his emotions. After a while, he coughed, pulled a handkerchief from his pocket, wiped his eyes, and continued.

"Don Alejandro chose wisely when he designated me to be Maria Luisa's *mozo* (servant). It was said that he did it in part to give me something of value to do with my life, considering that I could hardly walk and would never ride astride a horse.

"As a youngster, I would sit with Maria Luisa in the summer afternoons at the *charreadas* (rodeos). The girls were thrilled as the boys, like young pumas, would leap from one galloping horse to another while standing on the horses back, tempting death. The young men lived for danger. Broken bones and lost thumbs or fingers seemed to be a small price to pay for the adulation they received.

"Don Alejandro had seen in me, even as a child, a loyalty and affection for Maria Luisa that was beyond what I had even for my mother, Dios la bendiga (God bless her)." He made the sign of the cross.

"They would tell stories in that big house of the three-year-old toddler struggling to follow the golden six-year-old girl wherever she went, just like a dog.

"I never flinched at the comparison for it was true. Everything about her is preserved in my memory, the smell of soap in her hair when she was a little girl. I was there, nose at the window, when one morning, she first left the hacienda to go meet the nuns at the convent, wearing a dark blue skirt and a starched white blouse. Later, my heart skipped a beat when, as a young girl, I saw how she hugged her book bag against her chest as she walked, trying to hide her ripening body and trying to remain a child.

"I am carried back to the beautiful years. Those times are somehow illuminated with total lucidity from energy released somewhere in my memory.

"Of course, all was not perfect. There were rumors among the old women as to why Don Alejandro made room for me in that grand house. But the priest would chastise the gossipers and say that Don Alejandro's reward would be in heaven for having shown that act of compassion to a crippled child."

Cierren las iglesias!

The sun was beginning to set, and Don Miguel lit the oil lamp on the table. He unwrapped a cloth bag with the name "Café Combate" and placed some of its contents into a pot where water from the earthen bowl had been set to boil. After a few minutes, using a wire sieve to catch the coffee grounds, he poured each of us a cup of steaming black liquid. He warned, "Cuidado, no se queme" (Careful, don't burn yourself), as he very carefully sipped from his tin cup.

"Two incidents brought the church-state conflict to a boiling point," he said, chuckling at his little joke and inhaling mouthfuls of air as he swallowed to avoid being scalded.

"In January 1923, after the government had declared that any religious processions outside of a church were illegal, an elaborate procession of 40,000 of the faithful was held. Its purpose was to celebrate the unveiling of a monument to 'Christ, King of Mexico,' at the Cerro de Cubilete, a peak at the geographical center of the country. Accompanying the multitude carrying banners, crucifixes, and lighted candles, were eight bishops, four archbishops, and even the papal delegate all in their episcopal finery. The culmination of the ceremony was when the local bishop told the multitude that by this joint act they 'crowned Christ, king of Mexico.'"

He searched around in his collection of books and papers and found something.

"I remember that you are a photographer, Ricardo."

"Yes, but I do like to examine other's work and imagine what the photographer was thinking of at the instant he captured the image," I said.

"Perhaps what you do is more like your Americano's inkblot test?"

"Revealing my mind and not the photographers?"

Smiling, he located several photographs in a book and pushed them in my direction.

∝

In white lettering at its base, the photographer had written, "National Monument to Christ the King, Guanajuato, Mexico." The hill has a flat top and has the distinct appearance of an inactive volcano. On its sides, there are rock outcropping as if caused by ancient flowing lava streams. A road had been cut in spiral fashion through the rock from its base until it reaches the summit, where there is an immense statue of Christ. The great figure is standing on top of the sleeping volcano with arms extended, his hands ready to touch benevolently or, if threatened, to ward off.

Among the multitude, a bishop is surrounded by two priests. These two are dressed in black cassocks. The priest standing in front of the bishop is assisting him with a large book that he holds open for the celebrant. The priest to his left holds a lit three-foot long candle. The flame of the candle illuminates a pyramid-shaped metal vessel hanging on a chain from the end of a pole. It has multiple holes on its cover so that the smoke from the incense burning inside can escape. The European-looking bishop wears a thick, richly brocaded garment with a hole in the middle through which he has placed his head. The elaborately decorated fabric covers him from shoulder to knee, front and back. Over this, he also wears a long thin scarf-like garment decorated with gold thread around his neck. On his head, he wears a tall hat, and its shape is not unlike a rounded arrowhead. He is the representative of the pope.

❧

"Thirteen months before the defiant procession, Luciano Perez Carpio, associated with the presidential ministry, entered into the Basilica of Our Lady of Guadalupe and placed an arrangement of flowers before Juan Diego's ancient tilma. He quickly left with soldiers disguised as worshipers, who had entered with him. Seconds later, a bomb blast shattered windows a kilometer away. Later, church officials assured the public that the tilma and its glass covering were undamaged, reinforcing everybody's belief of its supernatural origin.

"Almost four hundred years before, Cuauhtlatoatzin, a humble indio, had been baptized and given the Christian name of Juan Diego by a Spanish priest. The baptism occurred less than five years after the Spaniard's had first conquered the Aztecas. In December 1531, Juan Diego had four apparitions of a madonna. She was not white like the Spaniards, nor dark like the indios. She was a mestiza. After her fourth apparition, Juan Diego opened his cloak to the dubious local bishop and revealed the spring flowers he had collected from her presence. Embedded on the inside of his tilma was the precious image of Our Lady of Guadalupe. Some years later, Baltazar de Echave, a Spanish artist, painted the first copy of the image on the tilma, and it has since then been reproduced countless times. That image has become the constant presence in the hearts and homes of millions of Mexicanos."

He emptied the remaining coffee in his cup on to the dirt floor and then gave the cup a couple of strong shakes to remove even the last drops before he replaced it on a shelf.

"In response to this gross provocation, young church militants recruited mainly from the urban middle classes created the League for the Defense of Religion, and in retaliation for the government's hostile actions against the church and its sacred relics, the league proposed to threaten the government with nonviolent economic boycotts.

"Ah, the league—those people, the ones that were so quick to instigate—they didn't know just what they were getting into and with whom they were dealing. Calles responded by passing laws that made unauthorized public religious services punishable in the same fashion as common crimes like theft and assault. He put it this way, 'Religion is an immoral business, and it has to be regulated, just like the practice of dentistry.' Period. End of story.

"The Church's hierarchy, hoping to cause the government to back down, responded by ordering the suspension of all public religious services throughout the nation, commencing as of July 31, 1926.

"Calles was playing with them as a cat does with a mouse. The government responded that the suspension of religious services couldn't please them more because these steps were in the exact direction that they wanted them to go. The government now would require that the churches be closed for a few days for an inventory of their property and assets. When completed, the churches would reopen under the control of neighborhood committees appointed by the municipal authorities!

"Not being satisfied with just seizing the Church's property, Calles stated that the government would now require the registration of all priests and determine if, when, and where they could function. All church schools were to be immediately closed, and foreign-born priests, expelled from the country!

"In the last days of July, there was a frantic clamor of weddings and baptisms as the faithful, throughout the country, tried to comply with the requirements of their church's liturgy before their closure.

"August 1, 1926, was a Sunday, and for the first time since the Spanish conquest, we all awoke to an eerie silence as not a single church bell tolled in Tepatitlan or in all of Mexico." The old man cupped his hand over his ear and slowly turned his head as if he was trying to hear a faint noise somewhere.

"Nada. The archbishop asked for an audience with the president and, in a conciliatory way, presented petitions signed by two million Catholics that had been collected at Sunday masses throughout the country, requesting that the constitution be somehow reformed.

"Calles responded that the church and its members had two roads available. They had to either convince the legislature in Mexico City to modify the constitution or prepare for armed conflict with the government if the church and its members didn't comply with the law. Por supesto, Calles's minions rejected the petition to reform the constitution."

Nadien se raja

The faces of the bishop of Michoacan and that of the bishop of Tobasco express incredulity and astonishment at what they've heard. They had come in the spirit of conciliation. Both are dressed in ankle-length black cassocks with small buttons fastened to the throat, where only a sliver of the Roman collar is visible. Each wears a simple skull cap. The only adornment they wear is a large plain silver cross that hangs from a chain around their neck and is fastened to their cassock's buttons at mid-chest. Both are seated at a table and have a copy of the offending constitutional provision before them. They have come to see the president for some accommodation of the enforcement of the articles, especially the one that requires the priests to register with the government. Calles has told them, without changing his expression, that he believes the Mexican clergy has always been on the side of the oppressors and that they have never sided with the poor. He further states that it is not in his character to continue to fool the ordinary people. When one of the bishops rhetorically asks him from whom a priest obtains his power, Calles answers that for the government, "that 'power' is of no consequence, nor is that 'power' going to be, in anyway, recognized." He is very clear; their options are to submit to the law or try to overthrow the government in armed conflict.

❧

"It was unbelievable. From the Hotel Frances's balcony, Don Alejandro and I observed a huge chanting crowd. Don Alejandro had insisted that we go to the convent in Guadalajara and bring Maria Luisa back to Tepatitlan no matter how strongly she objected. The entire city was at a standstill. No buses moved, and cars, barely at a crawl. The deluge of bodies in the streets blocked all traffic.

"On August 1, at the Sanctuario de Guadalupe in Downtown Guadalajara, bands of Catholic young people surrounded the church with banners and chants, proclaiming, 'Viva Cristo Rey,' and 'Viva La Virgen de Guadalupe.' The cordon around the sanctuary was never withdrawn, day or night, as the organized demonstrators periodically spelled each other.

"On the third day of the demonstration, the militants were stopping any cars that attempted to pass in front of the *sanctuario* and were forcing their occupants to remove their hats and shout 'Viva Cristo Rey' (Long live Christ the King).

"One man refused to stop his vehicle and ordered his chauffeur to drive through the smothering crowd. Rocks pelted his vehicle as his car tried to push through the jammed people. He drew his gun and fired wildly. From inside the sanctuario, others returned his fire.

"The man in the vehicle was the general in command of the city garrison, and shortly thereafter, truckloads of soldiers emptied into the square. Shots were exchanged between the soldiers and militants as men, women, and children scrambled, wild-eyed, for safety.

"Gracias a Dios." He made the sign of the cross. "Don Alejandro was able to rent a carriage with a barely breathing horse for an exorbitant price. The carriage took the three of us to the outskirts of the city. There we met some campesinos from Tepatitlan who volunteered to take us the rest of the way. It would have been impossible for me to make it even to the outskirts on foot. All the while, Maria Luisa refused to remove her nun's habit. Don Alejandro and I feared for our arrest because of her confrontational display until, thanks be to God, we were safely back at the hacienda.

"After the incidents at the sanctuario, the great bulk of the believers didn't know if and how they were to respond to the growing militancy of the league. The league had eagerly seized the leadership of the spontaneously erupting movement. Direction as to what to do next was asked of the bishops.

"In November, the bishops said that there was nothing in church doctrine prohibiting rebellion against tyranny if peaceful means had failed and if there was a reasonable chance of success.

"The league interpreted this as a mandate from the church hierarchy for war. All over the country, there were women who were disconsolate for not having a son to fight and die for Cristo Rey and the Virgen, and others who sent their only son joyfully.

"But I must step back to July of that year. Before the closing of the churches, the league had asked the episcopate committee for its approval of a general boycott that was being planned to be carried out against the government in the areas of transportation, schools, commerce, and recreation. At the time the decision was made to close the churches, the bishops also endorsed the boycotts."

He closed his eyes and, having recalled the emotions of those days, appeared exhausted.

"You look, if I may say so, Don Miguel, very tired. Perhaps I can come back another time," I suggested.

With the palms of his hands, he slowly rubbed both of his eyes.

"No, hijo, it does me good, since Maria is gone, to find anyone who is interested in what I have to say about those times. Please don't concern yourself, no se preocupe. I'm fine. Just hear me out.

"The boycotts..." He shook his head sadly. "The boycotts were when Maria Luisa first took any active part in the religious controversy and when she first met Padre Reyes.

"He had been a very active *militante* in Guadalajara. The boycotts had caused the movie houses to close because of a lack of business, and the people refused to use public transportation. Guadalajara became a city only of pedestrians. Hundreds of teachers *se resignaron* (resigned) from the state schools, and twenty-five thousand children dropped out from the government schools.

"Padre Reyes was mentioned in newspaper reports as being a courageous firebrand in the defense of Christ and his church, or as a troublemaker and incendiary hothead, depending on the politics of the publication.

"Later on, he moved on to Tepatitlan to help organize the boycotts there too. By this time, his notoriety had spread, and he could be easily identified by the federal authorities and was at great risk for his life.

"He went into hiding, and Maria Luisa became his messenger between the different boycott committee members. Maria, who had grown up in the area, caused no suspicion as she moved— no longer dressed as a nun, thank God—easily from one place to another, carrying coordinating instructions for the militantes. Communication was very difficult, and everybody had to rely on face-to-face contact as there were spies everywhere.

"The boycotts were intended to be entirely nonviolent. That was what Maria Luisa understood from the beginning and what Padre Reyes, as one of the organizers in Jalisco, insisted on. The hope was that resistance on a massive scale throughout the nation would bring Calles and his government to their senses. They hoped that the government, upon seeing the broad-based clamor del publico, would permit the people to return to their religion.

"During this time, I thought I knew Maria well enough to penetrate her innermost thoughts, and I noticed that her attitude toward me was changing, perhaps even before she herself was aware of it."

Tambien de Sonora

"But they didn't know the character of Plutarco Elias Calles. Coincidently, he had been born in Guaymas, in the same area of Sonora as Padre Reyes. Maria Luisa and he used to speculate that as a child, Antonio may even have attended the school where Calles taught as a young man, but Antonio was never able to clear that up to his satisfaction.

"Calles was the illegitimate son of a man who, little by little, squandered the wealth of the Elias family. The Eliases, for generations, had been a landowning dynasty in Sonora. The family's power and influence in the area stretched back for over one hundred years. But the president's natural father was addicted to alcohol, and his drunken rampages became legendary in those parts."

He paused and uncorked the bottle in an exaggerated, theatrical way. Then he half filled his coffee cup with the clear liquid from the bottle. With the palm of my hand over my cup, I declined his offer saying I still had some coffee. On the top of his hand, in the indentation between his pressed together thumb and index finger, he shook salt from the shaker. With an expert movement, he first downed the drink and then licked the salt from his hand. For a few moments, he savored the contrasting sensations in his mouth before he continued.

"Plutarco Elias was abandoned by his father while the old drunk pursued his river of alcohol. The young boy in a pitiful condition was taken in and raised by a man named Calles. Plutarco later took his name in his honor.

"To be the illegitimate son of such a prominent roaring alcoholic in that closed society set all the tongues wagging and must have been psychologically devastating to the boy." Again, he rummaged through his collection of papers.

∼

In Don Miguel's collection of photographs, there was an unusual number of Calles's family's photos. Perhaps these mementos that the president had taken of his family life provided a protective barrier from the reality that he had lived as a child.

The bullring is packed with thousands of aficionados. Above the crowded concrete stadium seats, there are three tiers of stands from which peer a multitude of spectators. On a separate elevated section, where the important politicians and personalities bask in the cheering and applause of the crowd, stands an attractive dark-haired woman. She is next to President Calles, who waves to the crowd with his hat. It is Natalia, his wife and mother of their five children. In a time when such scenes have become second nature with our politicians, in Mexico at that time, there were paradoxically not many such public family displays—or at least, few preserved in photographs.

At the palace at Chapultecpec, another photograph of the president and his family was taken. Calles and Natalia sat in the middle of the portrait. They were surrounded by their grown children, their spouses, and their grandchildren. Two infants sit on their mothers' laps, while assorted toddlers and school-aged children squeeze in. In total, there are seventeen in the photograph. Not too long afterward, in June 1927, before the end of his presidential term, Natalia was dead.

He was a man dedicated to and used to the comfort and peace of a wife and family. The widowed president, now in his early fifties, could not be faulted when he found a new love, the young beautiful Leonore, who filled the void that had been left by Natalia's death.

The photograph is of a proud, beaming father. He is seated on a couch and has a hand on the shoulder of each of two toddlers standing between his legs. The little boys are in traditional charro outfits. In 1932, all three were to be left without Leonore, who died of cancer. The family life that Calles had yearned for and sought since a child continued to elude him.

~

"On top of his dissolute father, young Elias Calles had to contend with the teachings of the Catholic Church. It had strict requirements for a proper Catholic wedding, before the fruit of the physical union between a man and a woman—a union barely tolerable even after marriage—could avoid the stigma of being the product of a grievous and disgusting sin. In those days, in most religious quarters, sexual desire was equated with weakness and evil and was spoken of only in the whispers of the confessional.

"Only in such a society can the true depth of the word *bastard*,"—he spat out the word with such intense vehemence that I suddenly wondered about Don Miguel's parents—"be understood.

"Years later, when Calles's presidential files were examined, they contained love letters from a prominent bishop to a Sonoran woman. He also had collected several other documents implicating priests in clandestine love affairs. He seemed to relish in their hypocrisy.

"How much all this drove him subconsciously to a blind and perhaps irrational hatred of the church and its clergy, is for others to say. Because, as you know, this was also the time when prominent revolutionaries and intellectuals throughout the world referred to religion as the 'opiate of the masses.'

"In his statements to the nation's newspapers, Calles often quoted excerpts from Upton Sinclair's book, *The Profits of Religion*.

He was fond of saying that 'the cult of the supernatural was used by the Catholic Church as a source of income, wrenched by the intimidation of the fires of hell, from the poor Mexican peasant.' When speaking of the hypocrisy of the clergy, he said, 'The privileged priests use their position of respect and trust with the poor unsuspecting *campesinos* (rural believers) as a shield for their own sordid transgressions.'

"I have often wondered if it had been another man with the presidential sash at that time in our history whether the human disaster that we were to experience would have happened. It had been close to ten years since the constitutional mandates had been in place, and nothing like what was to take place had occurred.

La familia bajo una sombra

"The Castaneda family was thrown into a terrible turmoil. On many occasions over the years, the bishop of the Los Altos diocese had asked for monetary assistance from Don Alejandro for different church projects. The bishop had also often sought the physical labor of the hundreds of campesinos and their families that worked and lived on the Castaneda Hacienda. Don Alejandro was always more than happy to 'volunteer' their sweat-stained labor 'for the greater glory of God.' But he now had a dilemma.

"The same constitution that directed the destruction of the Church's power over the campesinos also required a redistribution of the large land holdings throughout the country. Since the end of the fighting, this constitutional directive had been haphazardly enforced because of the government's need, after the economic hemorrhage caused by the revolution, for the efficiency and productivity of these large-established enterprises. They provided much of the products and wealth necessary for the country's economic survival.

"Don Alejandro had to take a stand either to protect his family's landholdings by supporting the government on the church issue, or risk the government's wrath and perhaps the hacienda by supporting the church.

"Practical considerations overrode everything else. He believed that pockets of unorganized unarmed resistance by church members would never to able to combat the power of the government. So he threw his weight on the side of the government.

"But to his surprise, this time, he couldn't automatically dictate that his workers acquiesce with his orders. Instead, he found that their loyalty to the Church was greater than their loyalty to the Castañedas, notwithstanding that Don Alejandro and his family had owned the land the campesinos and their families had worked on and lived on for decades.

☞

Outside, on the side of the whitewashed adobe wall, a large letter *A* is still visible. It is all that remains of the sign that once identified the business that was housed there. The four windows of the wall have been converted into niches for the placing of statues of the Virgin and of Christ, the King. Above the window openings, the white walls were blackened by the smoky residue of large candles that were lit to illuminate the holy images. In the open field adjacent to the wall, a couple of hundred men in white peasant clothes kneel on the ground. All have their hats removed, and all are facing in the same direction in the makeshift church. Their attention is directed toward a table under a tree that is covered by a white cloth like an altar. Many have long poles in their hands: one end of the pole is on the ground; the other end sticks out several feet above their heads. These are the poles that are used in harvesting the blue maguey.

☞

"The turmoil in the streets reached even into Don Alejandro's house. Maria Luisa's loud objection to his providing lodging, provisions, and other assistance to the federal soldiers was extreme. No amount of crying and begging by his 'guera consentida' (favorite girl) convinced him or Maria Luisa's mother, Rosanna, to change their mind. The young nun who had been so well and carefully educated at her parents insistence in the best Catholic schools and monasteries in Guadalajara and Mexico City saw her parent's support of the government's seizure of the churches as a sacrilege. 'By trying to protect your property,' she shouted at them, 'you will lose your immortal souls.'

⚜

The hard-faced mother superior wears a habit that is different from the other nuns. There is also an obvious generational difference in age between her and her charges. She stands in the middle of the other eight nuns, four on each side. Some of them are in their twenties; three are substantially older. All are clothed exactly the same, in black, from the shawl that covers their head and shoulders to the floor-length dress, and shoes. Around their necks each has a white ribbon where the golden medallion of their order hangs on their breast. There is another one, much younger, still a girl. Her head and shoulders are covered with a white shawl of the same type. She wears a floor-length white dress with black buttons fastened all the way to her neck. There is no other adornment. She is still a novice and has not yet taken her final vows.

When seen in public, she is like a white angel, silently reminding all of the eternal presence of God.

⚜

"I overheard it all with horror. She slammed out of the door and, as it turned out, never was to see them again. Don Alejandro asked me to follow her and reason with her and to do what I could to protect her.

"What he saw just as a reasonable response to the fluctuations of power, in her eyes, it was an irreconcilable betrayal of what had been instilled in her from childhood as unassailable truth. Don Alejandro expected that it would all soon be over. Then he would smooth things out with his daughter. But it was not to be.

"The tragedy of it all is that forever sacrificing the love of his daughter didn't save the hacienda as you probably noticed in your journey to Tepatitlan.

"There was another change. Maria Luisa started wearing dresses in a style used by the local girls, pinched at the waist, instead of the loose robes of her order. Her swinging undulating walk vaguely suggested gently swelling breasts and a soft pliable backside. And I thought that she looked into Antonio's eyes in a bold new way."

Los Cristeros

"It became apparent that the government would not back down from its stance. Based upon the 'go ahead' that the league believed it had received from the episcopate committee, an official call to arms was issued in very late 1926 to every league chapter in the country. The declaration was directed to the nation and declared war on the government."

He shuffled through his papers, found what he was looking for—a stained, crumpled piece of paper—and said, "I've kept a copy of it for this was the final step in the course that was to change all of our lives. The league told the people of the nation…"

He adjusted his glasses and slowly read out loud, "'The present regime is a group of men without conscience or honor. The true rebels are those who exercise power in defiance of the popular will. The hour of battle has sounded, and victory belongs to God.'

He put down the paper and his glasses and looked up at me sadly with moist, age-weakened yellow eyes.

"With this proclamation, the rebellion which would last three years, and that ultimately included at least fifty thousand armed Cristeros, engulfed Mexico."

Then his attention was on the liter bottle. He served himself a couple of ounces of the clear liquid, and this time, he slowly sipped it unlike the time before. Nor did he waste even a thought on offering me a glass.

"At this point, both Maria Luisa and Padre Reyes were way beyond their depth. Many, including themselves, had supported nonviolent economic boycotts as a valid means of impacting the government's policy. But battling with the military forces of the federal government? This appeared ludicrous.

"There was no central authority to coordinate military actions throughout the nation, nor was there any source of arms and ammunition. The government controlled the cities, the railroads, the international borders, and had the recognition of the Colossus of the North.

"But the uprising of the Cristeros was massive. Jalisco, Colima, Nayarit, and that portion of Zacatecas which adjoins Jalisco were all soon up in arms!

"But to say that, at the beginning, the government was militarily threatened is false. A federal general when describing his first battle said, 'This was not a military campaign. It is just like hunting rabbits for sport—a joke.'

"But the Cristeros, by the thousands, with their banners of Cristo Rey and the Virgin de Guadalupe as queen of Mexico, paraded around the municipal palaces of small villages and of the largest cities. They completely shut down all traffic and all of the normal governmental activities.

"Only occasionally did forays of Cristero bands of fifty or one hundred armed men attack the federal positions, not to much effect. But Calles should have been warned when, shortly after the uprising started, he received a prophetic message from one of his generals that said, 'It is very difficult to finish the rebels off because everywhere, they are protected by the people.'"

❧

It is a family portrait. In the background, an armed man with cartridge belts that cross at his chest holds a pole where an unfurled Mexican flag is visible. Superimposed on the white portion of the flag is the image of the Virgen de Guadalupe.

On one side of the flag, the father in a tan uniform with black tie stands at attention, a holster and sidearm at his hip. On the other side of the flag, his son is also at attention in the same type uniform with cartridge belt and sidearm. In his hand, the young man holds an old scabbard with a cavalry sword. The relic runs along the outside of his leg. Each wears a silver cross that is pinned to his shirt pocket, over his heart, to identify his military allegiance. They are soldiers of Christ. Seated between them is the mother, with fine features and still pretty, of obvious European ancestry. With each of her hands, she holds a hand of her other two sons: one, perhaps eight years old; the other, five. Her head is covered with a black shawl, and all three are dressed in black as if they already were in mourning.

The grizzled old Indian is wearing an enormous straw hat, whose shadow obscures his eyes, and only his white beard and unkempt mustache is visible. Around his neck, there is a knotted bandana that he uses to cover his mouth and nose from the dust of the fields when he works or perhaps to dry off perspiration. On the front part of his leg dangles a holster with an ancient handgun, placed there so that its presence would be immediately obvious. In his right hand, he holds the muzzle of a bolt-action rifle. On his dirt-encrusted feet, he wears worn huaraches. On the other side, a shoeless boy—he could be his grandson—of approximately sixteen or seventeen years, with the familiar crossed cartridge belts, and in his right hand, a bolt-action rifle. Between them, a toddler of three or four with a gun belt and holster slung over his shoulder so that the revolver is visible and hangs from his stomach. He could be a great grandson. Behind all these visible generations, nailed on the trunk of a tree, there is a cross.

The similarity between these two families is not what can be seen but what is spoken. Both say, "Go with God," when they part and "Blessed be God," when surprised. Their daily language is constantly interspersed with references to Jesus and their chosen saints as they live out their lives. It is a hard and cruel land where the just can expect their reward only in the hereafter.

❧

"Some of the federal officers, in their frustration with the lack of popular support, tried to demean the Cristeros and their religious chants of 'Viva Cristo Rey' by encouraging their soldiers to mockingly respond with, 'Viva Satanas, nuestro padre.'

"A federal soldier, still a boy, was executed by his superior officer when he was observed, while bathing in a river, to be wearing a scapular. It was without a doubt just a talisman from his mother to keep him safe. The two small squares of cloth with the sacred images were connected by a string around his neck. One square fell on his breast; the other one was on his back, next to the gaping exit wound made by the bullet.

"A definite pattern for the war was soon established. The federal troops would leave their garrisons in the cities, proceed by way of the railroad lines, and confront the Cristeros in small guerrilla-like battles. When the attacking Cristeros disappeared into the rural landscape, the soldiers would return on the trains to the protection of the city and the garrison, leaving the countryside again to the Cristeros.

"The Mexican army had studied the lessons of World War I too well. They had, for the most part, done away with mounted cavalry after the killing fields of France. But in these regions, the mounted Cristeros had a great advantage where there were no railroads or, many times, not even a road of any kind. When the federal infantry plodded ahead on foot, the Cristeros attacked and then disappeared on horse back.

"The brutality of the war was unbelievable. Any priest found in the countryside was summarily executed. Participation in any religious observance was declared a crime punishable by death. The federal army's policies of executing prisoners, killing of Cristero supporting civilians, and burning crops encouraged more and more to rebellion. The army declared that all the vacant villages and towns were to be 'free-fire zones,' in today's terms, and anybody found there would be shot. With that proclamation, any villagers that had not been belligerents before, now joined and expanded the insurrection in the countryside."

Fourteen wooden crosses stand crowded and jumbled up in a way that makes it obvious that each of the bodies contained underneath did not have an individual burial. It is a mass grave. The crosses are in a meadow that gently inclines up a small grass-covered hill. There, because of the flat perspective of the crude photograph, the trunks of the trees on the slope seem to grow out of the tops of the crosses; the crosses appear to be their exposed roots. The dark foliage at the top of each trunk in the photograph is silhouetted against a bright background. The illusion is of each trunk erupting into a spreading explosion against the sky. Off to one side, there is a lonely white cross, a sad epitaph for a child. It is one-third the size of the others. Embedded into the ground at the front of the flock of crosses, there is a rectangular granite rock where somebody has hewed out a message. The messenger wanted this place to be remembered.

"Soon it became clear, after mass defections, that the Mexican army didn't need arms. It needed men. First, they sought them in the prisons. Then several Yaqui battalions were recruited and rearmed, notwithstanding their recent defeat in the Yaqui valley. Other battalions were brought that were composed of different tribes from Oaxaca, Puebla, and Guerrero.

Tres seminarios

"Unlike Padre Reyes, who was never able to take up the gun, there were other priests who were. Two of them, Padre Aristeo Pedroza and Padre Jose Reyes Vega, who both had attended the seminary in Guadalajara with Antonio, became well-known military leaders of the Cristeros.

"Maria Luisa was not as hesitant as Padre Reyes. She was able to smuggle small guns and ammunition to some men in the hills. She also risked her life by performing missions to obtain information useable by the Cristeros.

"Padre Pedroza, who was a gifted leader of men and a military tactician, appeared to be fearless in battles. But he hated violence and limited his personal involvement in any skirmish to scanning the battlefield with his high-powered binoculars. Then he gave instructions as to the tactics to be used. His conscience permitted him to lead soldiers in the defense of Cristo Rey as long as he didn't participate in any actual killings.

"Not so Padre Vega. Although Antonio used to speak about Vega's chastity and piety as a seminarian, when he took the field with his troops, Padre Jose became truly corrupt.

"He acquired a taste for Alteñas and tequila and became a blackhearted assassin. He reveled in cruelty. Sometimes some of his soldier prisoners were stabbed to death instead of the instantaneous and more humane bullet to the brain. It seemed that his barbarity escalated in response to every federal atrocity.

"For some reason, I was drawn like a moth to a flame to these stories because they stood for something that tainted the church. This was way outside the regular role of a priest, outside the elevated position that Maria had placed Padre Reyes.

"In the spring of 1927, Padre Vega learned from secret sources that a large amount of money would be sent by train from Guadalajara to Mexico City. With a five-hundred-men force, he stopped the train carrying the *plata* (silver) at El Limon. The train had a fifty-two-man military escort that was riding in the armored car. When the firefight started, the soldiers dispersed among the passengers.

"There were many nonbelligerents—men, women, and children—cramped into the second-class wooden cars. Padre Jose ordered the wooden cars to be drenched with gasoline and burned so that those soldiers who were using them as a shield would not escape.

"Later, over fifty of the *pobrecitos* (innocent ones)—nonbelligerents, men, women, and children—were identified as having burned to death in the conflagration. Of the money that was seized, Padre Jose gave each man in his unit a twenty-peso bonus in silver. And for the unit's treasury, he earmarked five thousand silver pesos to be saved for future use.

"When the charred remains of a little child were returned for burial, I saw Antonio retching and vomiting when he heard about what had gone on at El Limon. 'Dios mio, perdonanos' (May God forgive us), was all that I understood through his sobbing. When he recovered sufficiently to be understood, he insisted that the Virgen de Guadalupe's image be wrenched from the flag that the local Cristeros now carried. On the center stripe of the Mexican flag, all the Cristeros had added the image of the Guadalupana.

"By 1928, the rebellion had expanded to thirteen states in Central Mexico from Tehuantepec to Durango. It had become clear that the Cristeros could not be defeated by the federal troops, nor could they win. The government retained control of the cities, the railroads and frontiers but the countryside belonged to the Cristeros. An equilibrium had been established.

"That was when Maria Luisa suffered her second betrayal. Some of the Cristeros saw an opportunity to gain political power by combining their number and military position with the intellectual force and political reputation of Jose Vasconcelos.

"He was widely acknowledged as being the architect of the social and educational programs that had graced the first three years of Obregon's presidency and, for that reason, was highly respected throughout the country.

"When Obregon was assassinated in 1928, just before he was to commence his second term, Calles placed Portes Gil on the presidential chair. Portes Gil sensed the threat the Cristeros and Vasconcelos presented to the government. So the new president immediately sent out overtures to the bishops. He cleverly differentiated between 'individual Catholics who dedicate themselves to acts of absolute banditry' and the 'worthy representatives of Catholicism who counsel respect for law and order.'

"He said that 'the Catholic clergy, when they wish, can resume the exercise of their rites with only one condition, that they respect the laws of the land.'"

❧

Next to President Portes Gil, there is an overweight ordinary appearing man in a three-piece black suit, tie, and polished shoes. He is indistinguishable in appearance and demeanor from the many business and governmental officials who customarily are photographed with the president. Except on closer examination, the face is familiar. It is Pascual Diaz, the bishop of Tobasco, who also served as the secretary general of the Mexican bishops. He is there to negotiate a solution to the three-year-old conflict. Because of the country's existing anticleric laws, he is without his familiar attire of a Roman collar and black cassock, which was accented by a large silver cross on his chest. Often in the past, when he had appeared at formal functions, he would add to that basic costume a skull cap of the same color and material as the wide band of silk that was bound around his waist. It was the simple elegant attire that had evolved over centuries to differentiate the princes of the Roman Catholic Church from ordinary men. Nothing could be gained and much could be lost if the bishop appeared now in such regalia. Calles had made it clear that no other authority except force would be recognized. It was on that level that the negotiators met.

⚜

"Apparently with the Vatican's approval, Archbishop Ruiz y Flores issued a similar conciliatory statement. He hailed 'the president's most important words.' He then went on to say that the decision by the Church to suspend worship in the country had been taken because the Church's hierarchy, in conscience, was not able to accept laws that were enforced in the country.

"It became immediately evident that the bishops no longer demanded a repeal of the offending constitutional sections but only that they be leniently enforced. "These efforts filled many of the militants with fury and with fear. They warned the league that the bishops should not make peace independent of the field forces. They said that to do so would be treachery. There now existed other broad issues of national values and personal rights, in addition to the rights of religion, that had to be considered before peace could be declared.

"Padre Pedroza saw the writing on the wall and wrote a letter to the archbishop stating that the higher-ranking clergy should not make a pact with the tyrant. 'The bishops had sanctioned the legitimacy of armed rebellion three years before,' he said. 'And their flocks should not be abandoned by the church to the executioner's knife.' He never received a response.

"On June 21, 1929, President Portes Gil and Archbishop Ruiz y Flores issued a joint statement. The president said, 'It was not the government's desire to destroy the identity of the Catholic Church, nor to intervene in any way in its spiritual functions.'

"The archbishop responded, 'As a consequence of the statement by the president of Mexico, the Mexican clergy will resume religious services in accordance with the laws in force.'"

❧

It is a strange marriage of the sacred and the profane. Two massive steeples rise from the main structure of the ancient cathedral. At their very top where the spires commence, a huge banner attached by ropes to the steeples is puffed out like a sail in the wind. Down the side of one steeple, a huge Mexican flag has been rolled out. On the other steeple, there appear the initials of the political party in power. On the banner, there is the name of the president in huge block letters.

Comienza la venganza

"Eight days after the cease fire, we heard that Padre Pedroza had been, without any warning, taken prisoner by the federal army. Antonio and Maria Luisa rushed to the plaza to try to find out if it was so. There they talked to some Cristeros huddled around a park bench. They reported that the old man who lived by digging graves had, with dirt on his face streaked with tears, told them about Padre Pedroza's murder. How the soldiers had smashed the butts of their rifles into his head until the ground was saturated with blood. The body was then flung into the already-prepared grave. After this, shots were fired into the body before the old gravedigger was forced to shovel dirt into the grave.

"Maria couldn't believe it had come to this. 'But how can this have happened? Haven't the bishops arrived at an agreement? I know that old *borracho* (drunk) who digs graves so he can buy more mescal. He's not all there,' she made little circles with her index finger around her temple. 'He has even seen the *llorona* (crying witch) in one of his drunken fits.'

"'No, Dios nos guarde (God protect us), it is all true,' said one of the men. 'The same story has been braggingly repeated by soldiers at the cantina.'

"Afterwards, the government and the church's hierarchy were always able to absolve themselves from any responsibility for the brutality that was carried out by 'unauthorized renegades' as individuals on both sides took their revenge.

"The often-stated prediction, that at the first tolling of the church bells, even the most militant Catholic would put down his arms, proved to be true. Just like scattering swallows, Cristeros were soon nowhere to be found.

"When the church, through the bishops, washed their hands of any responsibility for the men and women who had placed their lives in jeopardy for Christ the King, Maria Luisa went into an almost uncontrollable fury. She burned her habit and everything that represented her commitment to the church. All these items she had kept carefully hidden during the last three years. I was only able to salvage that rosary." He gestured toward the corner.

"From that point forward until the end of her life, she had nothing more to do with the Catholic Church. She even refused the last rites. After you came to see her in Guadalajara and she found out about Antonio having been in the United States all those years, her health became much worse. She had lost her desire to live.

"When it became clear that she no longer wanted to be in this world and that she would soon die, I suggested that she might want to receive the Holy Sacraments before it was too late. But to the very end, she would have none of it.

"Of the three seminarians who studied together, only two were left. Before the recommencing of religious services ordered by the archbishop, a troop of Cristeros led by the fierce Padre Vega had actually taken control of Tepatitlan.

"After its capture, el Padre Jose, as he was called, led an assault on a nearby ranch where one hundred federal soldiers were dug in refusing to surrender because they feared immediate execution.

"During the attack, Padre Jose was shot in the head. A controversy exists to this day as to which side shot him. Among Padre Jose's Cristeros, there was an older man whose wife, it was later said, had been seduced by the priest. Some said it was he who fired the bullet into the back of his skull.

"When the church bells again pealed in Los Altos, Padre Reyes was in mortal danger. He had been so visible during the boycotts that his identity was well known to many Alteños. But most of the federal soldiers were new to the area, and they needed help in identifying the Cristero leaders.

"While arrangements were being made for his escape, he hid in the house of a shopkeeper and his son. One night, federal troops surprised them and stormed the front door.

"The three had worked out a plan that if this ever happened, Antonio was to feign coming into the house through a broken window in a back room. He was to act like he was one of the Alteños that lived in the area who were accompanying the foreign soldiers, trying to identify the local Cristeros.

"They hoped that in the confusion, the attention would not focus on him. Since the man and his son were considered nonbelligerents and known not to have participated in the rebellion, it was thought that they would be safe.

"Padre Reyes was saved by the ruse, but the man and his son were executed on the spot—shot through the head as they, on their knees, vigorously denied harboring any Cristeros and as Antonio, horrified and at the same time terrified, looked them full in their pleading eyes and said nothing."

It was getting dark. Suddenly, the old man placed a piece of kindling and balled up newspaper into the old wood stove and lit a fire with a wooden match. A few minutes later, he heated some frijoles in a pan and melted into them some of the same goat cheese. With a little water and masa harina, he made four thick palm-sized tortillas and placed them on the hot metal surface of the stove. We each got two, scooped high with the bean concoction and, of course, seasoned with salsa of red chile from the jar.

He again offered me a cup of the clear liquid that he poured himself, which was followed by a second and third, from a bottle labeled "Tequila Pueblo Viejo." I indicated my preference for water from the olla and thanked him for his generosity.

After the spare dinner, because of the lateness of the hour and his natural hospitality, it became obvious that I was going to spend the night. I washed my face and hands with cold water from a basin; when finished, stepped outside with the basin; and, in a fanlike motion, sprinkled the yard. Earlier that evening, fresh water from the well had been brought to his hut in two tin buckets by the same boy who brought the tequila. I stretched out on the cot that had been designated for my use. It was too short, and my feet stuck out beyond its iron posts. The now-lit oil lamp gave off a dim yellow light. The silence after our meal felt strange considering the afternoon's lively conversation. The quiet was accented only by sounds of the last few raindrops falling from the roof, the remnants of an evening shower. Then while he sat on the chair next to the table—his head cradled in his arms— unexpectedly, in a tuneless slurring monotone, he began singing to himself.

"Some take pleasure with horses and riding. Some, from the Zenzontle as he greets the new day with his song. But I take pleasure from the juice of the agave and the swirling forgetfulness and forgiveness that it brings."

He then served himself another cupful of the water-like clear liquid and gulped it completely down. I couldn't understand any other words as he continued to mumble. I lay listening to the old man and stared at my hands on my chest so as not to have to look at his anguished face. He propped up his grinning compadre into a sitting position in the corner of the room. But for my unexpected visit, the skeleton would have kept his place of respect on the banca, always reminding Don Miguel of what lay ahead, very soon, in his future. Then Don Miguel laid down on the cotton *colchon* (mattress) that he had spread on the adobe banca. The banca was built as an extension of the wall, which served as a bench during the day, and now as his bed. He pulled a dusty blanket over himself. That was the last I remember as I fell asleep, hypnotized by the flickering light, my head on my rolled-up jacket.

Dos Viejos amigos

It must have been six a.m. when I awoke from a dreamless sleep. The old man was already up and called out the window to Edgardo. He had driven up and was now behind the steering wheel of a large open-bed truck. Men were jumping to the ground from the truck bed. Several of them had long, pole-like tools with sharpened round discs of steel on one end of their poles. These discs were wrapped in burlap rags to protect the men against getting cut by the honed steel as they jostled around. Don Miguel explained, "Those are the *jimadores* (field hands) with their *coas* (tools), sharp as razors. They are here to harvest the agave for the tequila."

I looked at one of the plants, made a comment about cactus, and was quickly corrected by the old man and told it was not a cactus but "a succulent." The ones the jimadores were working on were five to eight feet in height and had a diameter of eight to twelve feet. In the center was the pineapple or piña, a rosette-like structure, from which grew long swordlike leaves with thorns on the tips and edges.

I marveled at the speed as the jimadores would deftly reach in underneath and cut the roots, which attached the plant to the ground with the coa. Then the entire plant was pushed on its side and the individual swordlike leaves were severed evenly one by one from the base to the top. Finally, only the huge pineapple-like core was left. Two muchachos then picked the piña up; it appeared to weigh between seventy-five and one hundred pounds, and wrestled it onto the truck's flat bed.

Edgardo commented that shortly before the plant is to flower, the flower stalk is cut. "In that way, all of the growth of the plant is directed inwardly into the heart of the plant. This swollen juicy part is used for making the tequila." He invited Don Miguel and me to ride along as he made a delivery of the harvested piñas.

At the processing plant, another crew unloaded them and, with large two-faced axes, split them in half and then again into quarters. The crew then packed these sections into huge wood-fired ovens. There they would cook for thirty-six hours and then cool for another thirty-six as the heat slowly continued to cook from the inside out. Others were removing pieces of the plants from another oven; the cooking and cooling phases having been completed. Those prepared pieces of the cooked agave were being placed in the tahona to be ground up.

The tahona is a great stone wheel encased in a circular pit that is lined with cobblestones and with a pivot pole in the center. Outside of the pit, a horse attached to the pole walked continuously in a circle. The huge wheel mashed the cooked parts of the plant, and in this way, the liquid was separated from the fiber. The remaining liquid flowed to the bottom and was scooped up in buckets by the workers, ready for fermentation and distillation.

Don Miguel said, "It is still done here in the old way, without shortcuts, unlike those that use the stainless-steel vats and forced steam in those places which export much of their product outside of Mexico. I taste the difference, even if others cannot. Edgardo says it's just my imagination and my love of tradition and the past, but I think not. Quality comes from the sweat-soaked hand of the Alteños in every step of the process like in the old days. The others forget that money is just money."

With an underhanded motion, he flung a fist full of dirt into the air, and it exploded into powdery nothingness.

"Lo que cuenta, son las tradiciones y la lucha" (What is important are traditions and to struggle), he said to no one in particular.

It was time for a break. Edgardo called out and the workers, some of whom had not eaten yet dropped their tools. Two sweat-stained individuals who had been working side by side meandered toward where we had sat down in the truck's shade. The one they called La Chona, a lanky loose-limbed old man with a scrawny unshaved face and neck, started scrambling around looking for something in the dirt path. Edgardo had called the two over so that the "gringo" could meet and maybe photograph typical tequila-processing field hands. Sergio, the other one, was barely over five feet tall with a paunch that spilled over his trousers and belt. Both wore kerchiefs around their necks and sweat-stained straw hats. La Chona found and carried over a dry skillet-sized piece of cow dung. Sergio opened the truck's passenger door and pulled out a comal, a flat round piece of iron which was placed on a fire where tortillas and beans would be heated. While the dry cow dropping was burning down under the comal, Sergio broke out a scratched pint bottle that had obviously been filled and refilled many times with the clear water-like liquid. He took a gulp and passed it around to the others. While I fiddled with my camera, I was the only one that declined the offer and, an instant later, knew that had been a mistake. La Chona said he had some *guaje*—pulled from the branches of a nearby tree—in a paper bag. They are long thin pods like pea pods. He passed one to Sergio. He then broke a pod at one end and peeled it open from top to bottom, exposing the little bean-like seeds within it. Edgardo and Don Miguel declined any, while Sergio and La Chona popped some seeds into their mouths. While they were chewing them, I thought that I could redeem myself with the two and took a few. When I looked up, both Edgardo and Don Miguel were vigorously shaking their heads, warning me about not eating them, so I just slipped them into my pocket.

After the meal of reheated beans and tortillas, everybody leaned back and relaxed. The two field hands lit up hand-rolled cigarettes. A few minutes later, I heard Sergio stand up and saw him bow formally from the hip toward La Chona and say, "With your honor's most learned permission." This was followed by a strange ripping sound. A minute or two later, La Chona looked with mock respect at Sergio and addressed him with, "By the leave of your most holy worship." And a small explosion seemed to almost lift him from his seated position. It went on like that every few minutes, each in turn being more honorific and pompous in his respectful request for permission from the other, followed immediately by a clap of exploding air caused by the volatile mixture of beans and guaje in their stomachs.

Edgardo unsuccessfully tried to restrain his laughter and, in an aside, said to me, "Those *viejitos* (old men) are incorrigible. This happens all the time when we have visitors. Sergio is a strict Catholic and was a Cristero, with a wife, eight children, and God knows how many grandchildren and great-grandchildren. La Chona fancies himself more worldly, an intellectual, and an absolute anticleric not under the local priest's thumb. But their disdain for each other's beliefs hasn't kept them from being inseparable since they were youngsters running these hills. Every once in a while, though, they have a need to air out their feelings about the other's beliefs, and the beans and guaje help.

"They intended to make you part of their little joke. The only thing that irritates them more than each other's beliefs is what they see as the smugness of those who come to observe their 'colorful ways.'" He shook his head again. "*Chingados* (Damned) viejitos, they are absolutely incorrigible."

El secreto de Don Miguel

Later on that morning, armed with the half dozen corn tamales that Edgardo's wife, Elenandrea, sent to us for the afternoon meal, we escaped from the sun and returned to his small hut and Don Miguel's story.

"Padre Reyes had not been physically present during any of the bloodletting of the previous three years and now seemed to be in shock for having indirectly caused the death of the two men. We arranged for his immediate departure on a train headed north. He was never heard of again. Until you appeared.

"I knew that Maria Luisa and he had been thrown together for three years in many nonreligious circumstances. I didn't realize or maybe didn't want to acknowledge that there may have been more to their relationship than the rebellion.

"It wasn't until you brought Padre Reyes's possessions to her after his death, including her picture and even the one of her parents, Don Alejandro and Rosanna, that I came to realize that there had been more, much more.

"Since then, as I sit alone reading my books and thinking about the past, I think it is strange how Maria's life parallels what happened to Mexico. Both were betrayed by those that gave them birth, both betrayed by their church, and both betrayed by what they thought would be their future. Finally, they were left with only a stunted, twisted thing to love them and to care for them."

His eyes welled up with tears, and he gave me a strange sidelong glance and seemed to hesitate before he went on.

"So much beauty, so much promise, then it got all tangled up until there was no escape."

I didn't understand what he meant by the last statements and told him so.

He went to the table and got his quart bottle of Pueblo Viejo. He seemed to be searching for something in me as he stared into my eyes. After I declined a cup, he took one and then two, which he quickly downed. He remained silent until the liquid courage was fully circulating in his blood, then his eyes dropping to the floor, he said, "There's more, my shame, which I've kept hidden inside me for all these years." In a barely audible voice, he croaked, "While we waited for the arrangements to be completed for Padre Reyes's escape, a boy brought a note that was delivered to Maria Luisa at her door. That night, she slipped out thinking that she went alone, but I, as always, followed in the shadows. Waiting in the prearranged place, he too was alone. He took her hand and led her in the dark into a cluster of trees near a rocky stream. At the side of the arbor, there was an abandoned goat herder's hut.

"He was hatless and in shirtsleeves. Her hair, after the three-year period of growth, was tied with a ribbon near her nape.

"With light given off by the moon and the flock of stars, I could catch only glimpses of them through cracks in the boards of the dilapidated structure. They were at an arm's length speaking quietly. Her face was raised up to his. He reached and grasped her hand like she was his little sister. With her free hand, she brushed back her hair and looked deeply into his eyes. They looked so beautiful there together that a lump arose in my throat.

"I overheard her say, 'Antonio, mi amor, we have left the world we knew behind. It is all gone. We can't go back now. We have to go forward together.'

"She drew closer to him and reached up with her fingers to caress his face. He said nothing and seemed as if he had been struck dumb. For a moment, I thought of revealing my presence to stop what was happening, but I might as well have tried to stop the sap from moving in the agave or the season from changing.

"Who could have resisted her? She was like a madonna. She raised her face and kissed him softly, full on the lips. He had dropped her hand, and his arms remained clumsily at his side as he teetered in his mind with uncertainty. She bent down and invitingly spread her *mantilla* (shawl) on a patch of grass. Finally, with both arms, he drew her hard towards him. Then she was fully pressed against him, and her words of love were smothered against his lips. Their thighs pressed flat against each other's in the overpowering neurobiological reaction that was a new experience for her.

"Before me, the priest had become just a man, and Maria Luisa, a woman.

"I was in a jumbled panic of jealousy and fear. Jealousy that I was losing Maria Luisa forever to the priest, and fear that I was losing my priest, my church, to her. All I wanted was that it remain like it had always been, she and her Miguelito. She was everything to me, my sister, my daughter, my mother, my friend. Now, all that was over. It would be Maria and Antonio, with me left out.

"That night, once and for all, she rejected as being hypocritical and false all that had been drummed into her mind by the church and her parents. Now, that sublime love and passion that she had felt for them had suddenly been shifted to the priest who was to be the love of her life.

"All of a sudden, I was full of revulsion and disgust. I was there not to protect her as her father had asked of me so many years before, but for my own selfish purposes. I scurried away like the rodent that I am before I intruded any more. Even I who had lived my life as an observer had my limits.

"The next day, que Dios me perdone, I slipped an anonymous note to the federal authorities, identifying a house where it was rumored that a priest was hiding. That night, the two men were executed in front of Antonio's face. Two days later, he left on the train heading north, drunk with guilt that his forbidden meeting with Maria Luisa had somehow disclosed his hiding place to the government. For all the following decades, Maria Luisa withered away, waiting for him to return as did I with guilt eating away at me with the enormity of what I had done. My soul, like my body, was stunted.

"For Antonio, there wasn't enough time before he left on the train going north to sort out all the emotions dealing with his meeting with Maria Luisa and the execution of his two friends. Before, in our conversations, I remember that he liked to say that God had a way of punishing a sin without the need of using a cane or a whip. Antonio now carried the death of two innocents on his conscience.

"It was as if Maria Luisa's life was suspended when the train carrying Antonio pulled away. Later on, I realized that only she was able to break away from the past, from the church. But when he left, she was left untethered. I never really got her back. She kept going over and over what had happened without disclosing to me what I had seen, what I knew.

"I heard rumors at the church that he had made his escape and crossed the border. Maria never knew, and after the funeral for the two men, she didn't step into a church again in her life.

"As for me, it took me years to become aware that my unrealistic love for her was not even logical, nor, God knows, was my vanity logical. And for years, I carried around my own tailor-made blindness that was to warp our two lives.

"Shhhhh." He placed his index finger to his lips. "And I never told her a thing. She would have followed after him.

"It would have been much better if she had never known that he had been alive all those years. That was the cruelest cut of all.

She discovered that he had chosen the church and not her. The church that she thought had betrayed them all. The church that she had rejected and come to hate.

"Apparently, Antonio, unlike Maria, was able to differentiate between the Holy Church and the bishops who were, in the end, subject to evil just like the rest of us. But in her eyes, they were all one and the same.

"After the bombshell that you left with your visit, she would wring her hands and speak only of a life that was wasted. Dedicating herself to the memory of a lover that had been executed before he could return to her was much different from the picture that was now burned into her mind. He had been a busy parish priest living the full life that he had chosen.

"In what must have sounded like an altar boy's logic to her, and not the flesh and blood torment that she suffered, I tried to convince her that his love for her was so strong that because of his priestly vows, he feared having any contact with her ever again and that was the reason he never returned to Mexico. We both knew that after the troubles were over, he could have come back at any time. But she would not be consoled. She said all this had been just a casual incident in his life.

"What you brought was like a dagger right into her heart. Only I knew the truth. What had happened to the two men was not divine justice to punish the priest and the nun. Instead, their deaths were the result of my baser emotions of fear, and jealousy. Isn't it peculiar how the same incident is given such different interpretations by those that were actually there, if they don't know all the facts?

"Or perhaps God used me as an instrument to punish us all for what we did. That is what a priest would say. Ricardo, it is all too deep for me.

"But it still feels like it all happened just yesterday, and like they say, only our outside gets old. The most important emotions and memories are still fresh, hidden deep somewhere in our brains, awaiting something or someone to pull them up and wring the tears from our eyes.

"Both Maria Luisa and I went to the funeral at the reopened church for the two executed men. Everybody from the village was there at the services. They had known the family for decades. Our presence was the least thing that could be done. But fear was in every person's face. Everybody wondered, 'Was this only the first of the reprisals?' Most didn't know the circumstances of what had happened to cause their deaths. Maria Luisa thought that she knew, but only I knew.

"Slowly, we became the two irritable and impatient old people that you saw, surrounded by the tension that develops from too close a proximity for too long a time. Even so, I remembered her like she had been. To me, she became like a dried flower still retaining the beautiful essence of her former self.

"But what kind of mask did we each wear? All those years we kept from the other what we each secretly thought—that, that house harbored a murderer.

"Afterwards, when I was alone, I would cover my ears with both hands to try to stop the screaming of the wives and the children resounding in my mind, as they lowered the two bodies into the ground.

"Edgardo was one of the little boys whose father and grandfather were buried that morning. And I am reminded every day. Those youngsters that bring me my water and tequila? They are Edgardo's sons.

"I needed to tell somebody after all these years, but not him. No soy tan valiente, I'm not that brave.

"May it please God, and now you, that he never finds out what I did."

After I assured him that his secret was safe, he said, "Nothing helps until my brain is numb with alcohol. Then I get peace."

There was a very long pause in his story, and again I thought he was through talking. But it was as if telling someone after all these years what had really happened had given him a type of absolution. After a while, he resumed relating the historical events as he had experienced them, as if he had not just opened his heart for another to see the burning pain that was hidden there.

"At the war's end, there were 70,000 dead, and over the years of the Cristiada, 450,000 men, women, and children, mostly from Central Mexico, fled to the United States. This was in addition to the 300,000 Mexicans that sought refuge mostly in the border states of Texas, New Mexico, and Arizona between 1910 and 1920 as a result of the Mexican Revolution.

"It was said that not even a pin would fit in the second-class coaches during the religious war as the trains headed north." He paused then said, "I've been told that many of those refugees settled in the gentle climate of Southern California.

"The rest could have been predicted. With the end of the Cristiada, Portes Gil had served the purpose of the jefe maximo, Elias Calles. Fourteen months after he had placed him on the presidency, Calles replaced him with Ortiz Rubio. Two years later, Ortiz Rubio was replaced by Abelardo Rodriguez as Calles maneuvered his marionettes.

"As for Jose Vasconselos, it was widely said that he won the popular election against Ortiz Rubio in November of 1929, but the government declared otherwise. Vasconselos fled the country when there was no popular uprising protesting the stealing of the election as he had hoped.

"The Mexican people were exhausted by all the fighting and killing and had no energy for more conflict."

When Don Miguel mentioned all those people fleeing Mexico, I thought about my grandfather, Padre Reyes, Anselmo, of all those faceless miners who had lived on Chihuahua Hill, and of all the other people who had migrated to other forgotten places in Southern Arizona and California, all with their own personal reasons for leaving Mexico and what had happened there.

Yet they had been but a drop in the flood of fleeing Mexicans that slowly spread throughout the length and breadth of our land.

Part 4
Pesadilla

Otro camino con Tata Lazaro

In Mexico City, a soft rain washed the streets surrounding the house where many said the source of all political power in Mexico resided and which had been so since the assassination of Obregon. It was three o'clock in the morning, and only one room in the building was still lit. It appeared to be on the floor where the bedrooms were.

A servant answered the insistent knocking on the front door and was instantly overpowered as several men pushed themselves into the residence. Some of the intruders seemed to have an intimate knowledge of the building and knew exactly where to go, as if it had been rehearsed. They quickly bounded up the stairs to the third floor. Light could be seen streaming from the space between the floor and a door.

It was that door that was suddenly pushed open and entered. A still powerfully built, squared-jawed man was illuminated by a lamp that cast strange shadows on his face. Plutarco Elias Calles, in his robe, thought his life was over.

Instead, the ceiling lights were turned on, and he was instructed to dress himself immediately for traveling. While he was doing so, one of the intruders closed the book that he had been reading. The name on the cover was *Mein Kampf*.

He put on a three-piece suit and carelessly tied the tie. The vest was adorned with the gold chain and watch he always carried, which he nervously placed in its special vest pocket.

With few, if any, words, he was hustled into a vehicle among the several that were parked outside the residence. The entourage drove directly to the airport where an airplane with engines warming waited.

Three intimidating men accompanied the old general into the airplane's cabin so that he wouldn't even consider the possibility of resistance. Within minutes, the airplane was airborne and headed for the United States. In its flight's path, the airplane passed over several ancient churches, now schools, that bore his name. The jefe maximo of Mexico was being exiled. It was April 9, 1936.

✑

In the front of the photograph, there is a big square vehicle like a Ford Model A, but much larger. Along its black exterior, which has five side windows, there is a running board so passengers can step inside or out of the bus's elevated interior. On the top of the bus, there is a steel frame that holds a number of suitcases and a spare tire. Two American tourists, a smiling woman smartly dressed with a fashionable purse under her arm and a man in a dark blazer with a flat-brimmed straw hat set at a jaunty angle on his head, smile at the camera. In the distance, there is a snow-capped mountain range. Between the couple and the mountain range, the side of a cathedral with stained glass windows is visible. A sign painted in Spanish underneath the stained glass windows proclaims, "Plutarco Elias-Calles High School, Number 1." Just as if it was written in Chinese, the tourists appear oblivious to its significance. Instead, the Americans' focus on bartering with the ragged Indians so that they can squeeze out the very best price from the vendors for their trinkets. Apparently, not a thought is given by the pair to the peculiarity of an ancient church being used by the government as a school.

✑

By the act of exile, President Lazaro Cardenas, Tata Lazaro, as he would come to be known by the poor natives, gave notice to the Mexican people and to the world that the series of hideous assassinations of Mexico's leaders was coming to an end.

It was not a coincidence that the great national figures of the Mexican Revolution came from the northern states. Madero, Carranza, Villa, Obregon, and Calles all came from Mexican states that are pushed up against the United States. Zapata is not included in this group because his military impact, not his status as a revolutionary icon, was limited mostly to the state of Morelos.

One of the reasons for the northern clustering of the revolution's leaders was the availability of weapons across the border and the ready market in the United States for the booty seized by the revolutionaries from the Federales and their supporters. The United States was also seen as a place of refuge for the revolutionaries until their weakened positions strengthened. Both Madero and Villa fled north into the United States early in their careers. The scattered communities in Mexico's north— hundreds of miles away from the control of Mexico City and with a much-smaller Indian population—developed a characteristic independence from the central authority.

Now that the armed military period of the revolution was truly over, a different kind of man emerged from what has been called "Mexico profundo, the eternal Mexico."

Lazaro Cardenas was born and raised in the state of Michoacan. Michoacan, with its vast orchards, was a place where, for centuries, first the Spaniards and then the hacendados had forced, by one method or another, the indios and then the poor mestizos to work for them. Besides being an ancient land, it was also a patient land where change occurred with imperceptible slowness. Its society has been compared to a stream that has always been there. In that world of endlessly similar days and seasons, it is not known where the stream starts or where it will end.

The only thing that is clear is the importance of the family and the importance of the Church. It is a place where first Holy Communion has been celebrated by devout families for generations. Every year, young girls in veils and little boys in immaculate white shirts and pants prostrate themselves before the altars and, not as obviously, also before their families. They are obedient to God and subservient to the wisdom of their ancestors. Michoacan is in the heart of the nation, and it is snarled with its past.

Cardenas was the eldest boy in a very large family and early on, he was called upon to shoulder the support of his widowed mother and younger brothers and sisters. At a very young age, he joined the revolution and immediately came to a general's attention because of his elegant left-handed script, a very useful skill at a time where typewriters were not easily available on the march.

～

He has the thin shoulders and a gangly long-boned appearance of a boy just entering into his adolescence. Seated on a square wooden chair, he has a hairless face with ears still too prominent for his boyish face. Perhaps to give himself the appearance of more heft, around his calves, his pants are stuffed into leather riding sheaths, which are held in place by leather straps. His skinny ankles, visible above the scuffed half boots, dispense with the illusion of weight. The crossed cartridge belts reveal how thin his chest is. Thrust to the front on his belt, which appears as if it could make another turn around his waist, is a small Derringer with a bone-white grip. Across his knees, there is a heavy Mauser rifle that seems beyond his strength to lift and fire. Cardenas, of the prominent revolutionaries, was the only one who actually grew up while participating in the revolution. Unlike Madero, Villa, Carranza, Obregon, and Calles, he was the only one that had not followed a different occupation, such as butcher, businessman, or teacher before the revolt. Perhaps it was his involvement with other poor young soldiers who owned nothing like he that explains why he remained, throughout his career, the one most dedicated to social change so as to help the poorest of that society.

⚬⁊

His career was dotted with other incidents of good luck. Being the commander of the first line of defense against Pancho Villa in the battle of Agua Prieta was one. Then when Obregon sent troops in pursuit of Carranza fleeing Mexico City, Cardenas was stopped by a swollen river from being the commander of the troops that captured the president. Thus he was spared the taint of being accused of some complicity in Carranza's murder.

There was also the personal affection that Calles had for "the kid," who, over the years, he rewarded with a variety of governmental posts, including the governorship of Michoacan.

Upon completion of the short terms of the three presidents who Calles placed on the presidential chair, Calles chose Lazaro Cardenas to be the candidate for the six-year term that was to commence in 1934. Unlike his predecessors, once he had been chosen by Calles, Cardenas went directly to the people and campaigned throughout the country for months, as if the people's votes would actually determine the presidency.

He spent endless hours under trees in town and village plazas and listened. He would sit in a straight back chair in front of a simple wooden table while the nation's poor and forgotten poured out their petitions and described their needs.

"Bring us the fire that doesn't burn, Tata."

And many times, electricity did arrive not too much later in that village. He struggled incessantly through the primitive roads of the country to go to where the little people lived.

⚬⁊

Photographs in the country's newspapers and periodicals showed him attired in a coat, tie, and large-brimmed felt hat. Casually, he wears trousers of a different color and fabric than the coat, and the pant legs are stuffed into knee-length boots. Above the ankle on the boots, tiny spurs are visible. The horse he rides is almost up to its belly in the running stream. Cardenas has rolled back on his saddle so that his extended legs, which he holds stiffly locked at the knee, comfortably clears the water. His hands effortlessly grasp the reins, and his face is in repose. He looks as comfortable as if he was sitting back on his old rocking chair. Behind him, a worried-appearing local politician in a matching suit, tie, and large-brimmed hat is leaning forward on his horse as he accompanies the president-select into uncharted political territory. He has bent his legs at the knee, but his boots cannot escape the water that they are being dipped into up to the ankle. He has much to learn from Tata Lazaro about riding and politics.

Calles consolidated his power by making it beneficial for the regional strongmen and powerful interests throughout the country to unify under him and to prosper with a central government. Now Cardenas would try to extend access to the government's power to the masses. Always sensitive to their poverty, he would arrive unannounced at a village so that the poor wouldn't sacrifice their chickens for a feast in his honor.

I thought back to the periodical that Maria Luisa had so carefully unwrapped that afternoon in Guadalajara. That residence had been on Avenida Lazaro Cardenas, which meant next to nothing to me then. I now knew that instead of being one of many insignificant roads in the metropolis, it was a major boulevard named in his honor, and it cut across the entire metropolitan area of Guadalajara.

Her description of the self-absorption of Americans, at least this one, was right on the mark. I had been oblivious at that time to the man who is recognized by many as being the only true Mexican revolutionary or, at least, the moral conscience of the revolution.

Before I left Los Altos, Don Miguel had given me Maria Luisa's copy of the *Revista Illustrada*. He had salvaged it from Maria Luisa's possessions, which, after her death, were being disposed of as having no value. I unwrapped the carefully packaged magazine that was now several decades old and, for the first time, minutely examined it.

Besides the likeness of Villa with his usual odd facial expression combining fierceness and mirth, the magazine also had photographs of Generals Alvaro Obregon and Plutarco Elias Calles and of the twenty-year-old Colonel Lazaro Cardenas.

The magazine's lead article gave a description of "the admirable defense of Agua Prieta." It stated that Colonel Cardenas commanded the first line of resistance, which emplacement Villa himself had stormed. The report went on to state that Colonel Cardenas had played a critical role in General Calles's victorious defense.

I had begun to appreciate the extraordinary coincidence of the four—Villa, Obregon, Calles, and Cardenas—being on that remote battlefield in Agua Prieta near the foot of the Mule Mountains of Southern Arizona. Each of these men, all for different reasons, were to become an icon of good or a symbol of evil for the Mexican people, although at the time Father Reyes gave her the periodical, Cardenas had not yet had—and no one could have guessed—the historical effect he would have on Mexico and on the United States.

Contra el jefe maximo

When Calles revealed Cardenas as his presidential designee, it had been common knowledge that since Agua Prieta, Calles had treated the younger man almost as a son. But notwithstanding his personal affection for him, Calles immediately started to destabilize the Mexican political scene once he had designated Cardenas as his presidential choice.

That had been the successful ploy that Calles had used with the other short-term presidents so that he could retain the political control of the country.

Each prior designee, upon being chosen by El Jefe Maximo, had no independent national political strength except through Calles. When a crisis arose, the new president had to seek the help of Calles with the military, the labor unions, or the other entrenched sources of power in Mexico to survive.

He had refined the process. Calles would provoke the crises immediately before or immediately after the inauguration. Before the new president could establish any independent source of power, he was left floundering and grasping for help from Calles.

Following the now-familiar tactic, in July 1934, the day after Cardenas was elected president, Calles made a proclamation to the Mexican nation that was widely disseminated and said, "The revolution is not over. The nation should direct the education of its young in the same way as is occurring in Russia, Germany, and Italy. Although the adult generation is profoundly infected by the religious cancer, every effort should be made to convert the young to a rational view of the world."

This declaration by the jefe maximo generated a new series of violent attacks against the church and in some regions, encouraged the local authorities to again attempt to limit the number of priests in their communities.

The Catholic Cristero guerrillas retaliated with a campaign of terror against what they called Atheistic socialistic education. During the new crises, over one hundred public school teachers throughout the country were assassinated, and numerous government schools were sacked.

❧

The beak of the bird is just an inch away from touching the sporty felt hat of the marching demonstrator. The dead buzzard has been strung up by its feet and is hanging upside down from the pole that the marcher holds. The weight of the inverted wings has, because of gravity, opened them up so that they spread down and out to each side. It looks as if the buzzard is inviting all to share its putrid feathery embrace. Above the dead carcass, a sign attached to the same pole declares, "Here comes the Archbishop of Mexico." The marchers are well dressed in coats, ties, and fashionable felt hats with contrasting bands. They are, perhaps, urban union organizers or teachers who have not made their peace with the church.

❧

Cardenas's goal was social revolution. He made it clear to the gathering storm of Cristeros that, provided the church didn't obstruct his overall political plans, he had no intention of being sucked into the same ideological swamp the country had just extricated itself from.

Tata Lazaro had correctly sensed the country's abhorrence of another religious war. He also was sensitive to the ordinary

Mexican's fear of the proposed countrywide socialistic education. This awareness, sharpened during his countrywide campaign, allowed him to sidestep El Jefe Maximo's trap.

Cardenas was also busy elsewhere. He publicly supported the epidemic of labor strikes that paralyzed the country between his assuming the presidency and June of 1935. During that period, over 1,200 labor strikes flashed across the country.

New leaders of labor were grasping for the power that had been held by Calles's labor supporters. Calles, not sensing the urban worker's dissatisfaction with the rapacious self-serving status quo of his labor allies, made a statement that was widely circulated in the nation's press. "These savage strikes are placing the country's development in jeopardy." Calles's statement spread like wildfire with the workers.

Overnight, Cardenas was now seen by the urban working classes as their representative. He now had the broad-based support of the newly emerging labor leaders who had replaced Calles's friends in the labor movement.

❧

The hammer and sickle are prominently displayed on the banner that states, "Communist Party of Mexico, Affiliated with the International Communists." Immediately to its left, there is another banner: "Cardenas and Mexican Oil Workers Join Together to Crush Nazi-Fascism." Underneath the banners, there are crowds of men and boys who watch as workers in lines of nine or ten march by.

❧

Cardenas also obtained the support of old friends whom he had cultivated for years in the military. Many were fed up with the imperious ways of El Jefe Maximo. He also sought the political influence and support of former President Portes Gil with the bureaucrats and politicians.

Portes Gil was still held in high esteem by many for having been instrumental in ending the religious war, and he was smarting from the way Calles had treated him after his success.

Within a period of a few months, the jefe maximo had been defanged by the adroit Tata Lazaro and was headed toward involuntary retirement in San Diego, California.

Cardenas recognized the injustice that the Yaquis had suffered at the hands of the Mexican elite. He ceded the land back to them on the right bank of the Yaqui River. With the land, there was to be the necessary water from Angostura Dam and permanent access to their beloved Bacatete Mountains that fed the river. What Cardenas did not foresee, as had the talking tree that Ansemlo had spoken about, was the enormous black snake that in the future would again put the Yaquis in danger.

Mexican Highway 15 now connected the fertile Yaqui Valley to the lucrative markets in the United States, and these hundreds of miles of black tar and pavement soon would again threaten the Yaquis's land that "God gave only to them."

Esto le pertenece ha Mexico

I have taken to using buses when traveling in Mexico. They are reliable and reasonably comfortable, and they don't have the culturally shocking effect on me that traveling by air has. One hour after departing from the hustle and efficiency of the Tucson or Phoenix International Airports, with their multiple airlines and routes, you will land on the relatively vacant tarmac of the airport of a medium-sized Mexican city.

The last one hundred yards or so to the terminal is through exhaust fumes and hot winds generated by the jet's motors. The wealth disparity between the two nations immediately strikes you. Here, the public facility doesn't provide each airline with an individual space for picking up or leaving passengers.

In the terminal, there are no crowds because a very large segment of the population has been priced out. The pretty ticket sellers, mostly college students, disappear as soon as the airplane takes off again. They were there only for the planes arrival and departure. It is obvious that this is not how the great majority of Mexicans travel.

The action in Mexico is in the crowded bus terminals, where rows of differently hued bus lines heading in every direction await their passengers. Here, each bus line has its designated area for arrivals and departures; and unlike the US, where Greyhound usually dominates in interstate travel, the passengers here, many times, have several choices.

The higher-end buses are usually driven by pairs of uniformed men. They are similar in age and uniformed appearance as those who pilot our airplanes. The use of two drivers is for purposes of safety on long overnight trips. The co-driver sits alongside his partner, chatting with and observing the driver during the mind-numbing midnight hours.

On the Mexican highways, only the Pemex sign signals to the motorist about the availability of gasoline or diesel. The proliferation of different private companies hawking their petroleum products that is so common in the United States doesn't exist here. Pemex is a result of Cardenas's actions.

Article 27 of the Mexican Constitution of 1917 declared that all subsoil wealth belonged to the nation and not to the owners of the surface land. Foreign companies that had obtained oil concessions during the regime of Porfirio Diaz fought vigorously against its implementation. The government had been slow to implement Article 27 because of its desperate need for hard currency after the financial bleeding it suffered during the Revolution. In 1937, a confrontation arose between the oil workers' union and the foreign oil companies. Mexican law required that a special committee of experts be chosen to arbitrate the controversy.

The committee studied the case and issued a massive document that arrived at several conclusions unfavorable to the oil companies.

In November 1937, Standard Oil curtly responded to the arbitrators' decision, "We cannot, and we will not pay."

Cardenas then raised the stakes between Mexico and the foreign oil companies by canceling the 1909 oil concessions that had been granted during the last years of Porfirio Diaz's regime. He refused to reduce the arbitration award. But in an effort to be conciliatory, Cardenas did offer to guarantee that if the amount awarded by the arbitrator was paid, no further labor problems would arise with the oil workers. It was during this negotiation that the famous exchange between the company representatives and the president of Mexico occurred.

"And who will guarantee that the increase will not be more than twenty-six million pesos?" asked a company representative.

"I will guarantee it," Cardenas replied.

"You?" said a company spokesman while the other companies' representatives exchanged derisive smirks.

The president of Mexico responded, "Our negotiations are finished."

Ten days after the meeting, on March 18, 1938, the arbitration commission found the oil companies "in contempt" of their decision. The oil companies finally agreed to pay the twenty-six million pesos, but it was too late.

Cardenas, following the lead of Franklin Roosevelt with his fireside chats, went to the nation with a radio address. He asked for the nation's support not only for the recovery of the nation's subsurface wealth but also for "the dignity of Mexico that foreign companies think they can ridicule. They offer this insult after having obtained such great benefits from Mexico's natural resources."

ༀ

The reed-thin British ambassador is impeccably dressed in a linen three-piece suit. Ramrod straight, he walks agitatedly toward the government offices. He wears no hat on his gray elegantly cropped hair. The expression on his bespectacled face and the position of his hands and feet imply great anger and haste. He, as his majesty's representative, is not used to being confronted. Behind him is the highly polished fender and bumper of his Rolls Royce. Across the two-lane street, in the background, there is a modest-sized, heavy-walled building with thick wooden doors. The windows are also protected in the Mexican style by thick wrought iron. Not too long afterward, Mexico broke diplomatic relations with Great Britain, and the ambassador was asked to leave Mexico City. It was a city that, in that decade, had become a bohemian mecca for socialists and expatriated communists like Leon Trotsky, for intellectuals and artists, and for unorthodox lovers like Diego and Frida.

⁊

In response to the radio transmission, two hundred thousand people flooded the Zocalo, the huge governmental plaza in Mexico City. Ordinary Mexicans offered personal things that had value—from jewels to chickens—to help uphold the country's honor by compensating the oil companies for the investments they had made in their country. The Catholic Church supported the government in its decision and thus continued to reduce the state-Church conflict.

The expropriation of the oil caused grave international repercussions between Mexico and the English, Dutch, and American governments. But a British-led embargo that closed off the traditional oil markets available to Mexico for its oil had unexpected consequences. Suddenly, Nazi Germany became Mexico's major petroleum customer, followed by Fascist Italy and Japan. Cardenas's gamble that the Roosevelt administration with its Good Neighbor Policy was much more concerned about national security than the interests of expropriated American oil companies was correct. The American government did not want German and Japanese "geologists" and "technicians" prowling over Northern Mexico and exploring to the south toward the Panama Canal, nor did it want Nazi submarines refueling in Mexican ports.

⁊

In front of the ornate national cathedral in the Zocalo, there is a multitude of celebrating faces. A profusion of signs and banners are being thrust skyward. Many signs block each other so that their messages cannot be completely read. One sign partly proclaims, "Autonomy!" Another urges, "Support the Independence of Our..." It is not necessary to read the entire statements to understand the joy of the people for their country's economic independence from the foreign oil merchants after so many years.

Tlataoni moderno

As I journeyed on the bus through the towns and cities of Mexico, I constantly saw the red, white, and green initials PRI on walls and boulders and sometimes even delineated with colored rocks on hills adjacent to the highways. This was the final legacy that Cardenas left to Mexico.

When he supported a new union movement in his first months as president, he planned to establish something akin to a "company union." The company would be the government of Mexico. He envisioned no less than establishing a new relationship between capital, labor, and the government.

Cardenas intended to transform the conclave of generals and regional elites that Calles had formed, into a party of the masses. In his mind, there was room for all within the new political party—campesinos, organized labor, governmental bureaucrats, the military, and the emerging middle classes.

If they chose, they all could be affiliated with the new political regime through their respective organizations. All influence and political benefits would flow through the party. Those who chose not to join the party's organizations would find themselves outside looking in.

It was Cardenas's intention to permit the Mexican people to choose between the large all-encompassing organization that he formed and any other competing organizations that might arise to contest for political power. He was attempting to open the political process in Mexico in a way that it had not been before, and at the end of his six-year term, he revealed Avila Camacho as his choice to be his successor.

The opposition to Camacho coalesced around General Juan Almazan. His support came from a bizarre grouping of former supporters of Porfirio Diaz, including his widow, and Zapatistas; old Marxists like Diego Rivera and the Catholic Cristeros; dissatisfied new members of the middle-class and deposed generals regrasping for power; sons and supporters of former presidents; and those who resented the government and union rackets and the always-enlarging political gravy train.

The election was not peaceful. The newspapers were full of photographs of bloody encounters by those involved in the election. Chaos threatened to break out once again in Mexico.

The Electoral College published the final absurd tally of the vote:

> Almazan: 15,101 votes
> Avila Camacho: 2,476,641 votes

It became obvious that Cardenas and the party, which later would be renamed the PRI, had chosen the political stability of the country over any possible contrary political voice of voters.

When Cardenas saw Mexico again threatening to explode in armed conflict—this time on a global stage where the forces of fascism, communism, and capitalism were in a mortal struggle—he chose to postpone the democratization of the country.

For the next fifty-plus years, what could have been originally excused and understood in 1940 as a reasonable response to an emerging national crises because of the political conditions in the world, became entrenched as the Mexican system of national politics.

For the following nine presidential elections, a similar procedure became the destiny of the Mexican nation. Each president, upon approaching the completion of his six-year term, would reveal his choice for a successor.

The untouchable dogma of this system was that there could be no reelection of the outgoing president. This was supposed to protect against a single man remaining in power or retaining any prolonged or dominating influence over the reins of the Mexican government.

After the revelation, the candidate traveled across the country, supposedly seeking the peoples' votes. In reality, he was acting to legitimize the revelation. The new president would then appoint, from top to bottom, the new officials throughout the country who were chosen to carry out his policies. The outgoing president was given a type of immunity for any political or financial misdeeds that may have occurred during his presidential term.

Over the expanse of more than four hundred years, the PRI had resurrected the concept of the Tlataoni of the Aztecas. Through a mysterious process, the emperor would choose his successor; and upon his revelation, the chosen one appeared before the masses of assembled Aztecas, and they gazed at the new Tlataoni in wonder.

His power was absolute. But the source of the power was in the act of investiture by the retiring Tlatoani and not in the individual characteristics or policies of the chosen man. The transfer of majesty was institutional, impersonal, and sacerdotal. Thus they were able to avoid the murderous conflicts between those who lusted for power.

In modern Mexico, the revelation had also become institutionalized, and it disclosed to the nation who would be "el senor presidente." In all ways, the new president would act as the chairman of the board and the CEO of the nation, the uncontestable source of power in Mexico for the next six years.

Reconciliacion

Tata Lazaro had chosen his successor well. Upon his inauguration, Avila Camacho declared to the nation, "I am a believer." And by this simple act, he put an end to the Church-state conflict.

But Mexico was caught in the maelstrom that was sweeping Europe. The Mexican sympathizers of the Spanish dictator Francisco Franco supported an organization called the Spanish Falange. Its purpose was to tie South America and Mexico to the Fascist movement. It was to be organized as a peasant league centered around the old Cristeros with a blend of Nazi and Franco slogans. The attitudes of the Diaz era appeared to threaten to sweep the country.

⨏

The building is about fifteen stories in height. It appears to be cut out of a single piece of granite. The building's design has five rectangular sections like five loaves of bread placed on their ends that form the bulk of the structure. The building is tapered visually by having the two outside rectangles end at the eighth floor. The next two rectangles end at the tenth floor. The longest rectangle is the middle one, and on its roof, there is an undecorated tower that is completely flat on top. The tower continues the visual tapering line set by the rectangles. It is a steeper and longer version of the Mexican pyramids to the south. It is a building unlike any that had been seen before in Mexico City. All the windows throughout the building are square, and there is no adornment or frills of any kind on the walls or windows. It conveys the visual impression of order and power if not beauty. It would fit more comfortably with the powerful building designs and style of the 1930s and early 1940s in Germany or Italy. On the wall at street level, next to a window protected with thick iron bars, there is a large circular emblem with a silver eagle in the middle. Its wings are spread an equal distance to each side, and the bird's face turns to its right. The bird holds in its claws a leafy circular silver bough that contains within it a black swastika.

In Mexico City of that time, this building was in great contrast to the graceful buildings of three and four stories with arched tiled openings for windows and awnings that graced the tree-lined boulevards. Many of these had adopted French-style mansard roofs or window-doors that opened up to elaborate wrought-iron balconies that overlooked the streets that they faced.

✑

In June 1942, the Mexican government of Avila Camacho declared war against the Fascist Axis to the dismay of many Mexicans.

"Why is Mexico fighting on the same side as the Americanos?"

"Why will our guns not point at the Yanquis (Yankees)?" many asked.

On September 16, 1942, at a celebration of Mexican Independence Day before the reviewing stand of the national palace, all the living ex-presidents of Mexico—Cardenas, Portes Gil, Rodriguez, Ortiz Rubio, and even Calles, back from exile— stood with Avila Camacho.

Tata Lazaro and El Jefe Maximo, after years of exile, met once again on the reviewing stand. Cardenas spoke first and addressed Calles with, "How are you, mi general?"

Calles responded, "Very well, mi general."

After that, there was silence. Only they knew what thoughts crossed their minds about the association that extended back to Agua Prieta in 1915.

All the former presidents on the reviewing stand stood together with Avila Camacho and asked for the support of all loyal Mexicanos in the declaration of war against the Fascists. With that symbolic act, Mexico passed into its modern era.

Pesadilla

The Elite bus from Guadalajara stopped in the Hermosillo station in the middle of the night. I buttoned my jacket to keep the January chill out and jumped out to get some coffee.

To my great surprise, the terminal was bursting with hundreds of men. Several buses from different bus lines belched diesel smoke and awaited the return of their passengers. Some of the men were very young; some, in the full strength of their manhood; and a few grizzled and well past their prime.

They all appeared to be traveling light without any except the most rudimentary of luggage. They bantered back and forth in a cheerful manner. All of a sudden, it hit me; these men were all heading back north to the United States to their work.

They had returned from the United States to the cities and villages all over Mexico to be with their families for the Christmas season. Now it was time to go back.

I thought about Padre Reyes and Anselmo, who had used the railroads to flee from Mexico. Now it was the highways that served as the route for thousands and thousands to go north to sell their labor.

I returned to my seat shaken, not having expected to see that multitude in a bus station at 2 a.m., two hundred miles from the international border. My mind turned to a visit I made to Chicago the previous fall, when the icy winds were starting to blow off the lake.

In front of the Lincoln Park Zoo, I heard Spanish being spoken. A man of obvious Mexican-Indian descent was on his knees shaping a paver with a little handpick. He was trying to size it so that it would fit snuggly with the other pavers that adorned the sidewalk. He was chatting amiably in Spanish with his partner, who brought sand and stacked the pavers that awaited to be worked on.

The man's dark hands were chapped, and his skin weathered and cracked. The man expertly chipped away with his little handpick and then fitted the stone. Both were dressed in overalls and heavy flannel shirts to protect against the invading cold. Both were probably three thousand miles away from their homes.

As the bus headed north from Hermosillo toward Nogales and the border, I kept falling in and out of sleep. I couldn't tell if I was dreaming or imagining. I saw the hands with the little handpick chipping away; then other hands appeared, picking fruit; others, washing dishes and digging holes; hands with picks; hands with clippers; hands with shovels and brushes and sledge hammers; on and on.

Then two of those hands were attached to my grandfather wielding an ax, chopping a mesquite that he could sell for firewood. My other grandfather was on his knees, and in his hands, he had a rosebush. He was planting it in a public park. They were all doing those things we Americans can't or won't do but which contribute to our good life.

Then I thought of my encounter on the street in Guadalajara of those who are unable, or are too young, to care for themselves and of the grotesque fire-breathing man selling his health and his life for a few cents. They were the ones who are left behind.

For an instant, I had something akin to a schizoid reaction—I, who had always considered myself after persistent, if not intentional, indoctrination by my family, my schools, my culture as being 100 percent American.

Suddenly, I started to identify with these brave hardworking men who left their homes, their loved ones, and their country. Sometimes, they are small dark Indian men who barely speak Spanish and who journey on foot across deserts and mountains and end up in Chicago doing what needs to be done but which we won't do. Sometimes, they are barely indistinguishable in appearance from most of us.

Still, they have to hide from unscrupulous predatory Mexican bandits who seek to rob them of the little they have and from the American authorities who hunt them down like criminals or animals. They come to this country in the dead of night, almost on their knees, and in a desperate attempt of survival, many have to deny who they are. They endure this all for the possibility of earning an hourly minimum wage while the employers here in the north eagerly await their appearance. Back home, their families anxiously check weekly with the telegraph office to see if they have been lucky.

These are the people who are too strong to give up. They are the ones who are willing to search in the magnet of the north without any promises or guarantees. They risk everything, and they have come here not just to give up.

The Super Bowl and the Internet awaited me as did my increasingly confused feelings about the migration. To my surprise, my heart, if not my head, remained with the men at the Hermosillo bus station as they made their desperate plans of survival.

Mariposa

It had been a few months since I had spoken to my daughter, Emma Lily. When I returned from Mexico, there was a Christmas card from her. She was taking a semester break from her studies at Boston College and was spending time with her mother, Consuelo, in New York. She left no telephone number or address. "I am enjoying the sights. Mom is looking into the Sephardic connection," was all her scrawl said.

I met Consuelo during my first semester at the university where she was already working on a masters degree in biochemistry and was developing a reputation in her university circle as being one to keep an eye on. For generations, her family had, had its roots in Northern New Mexico. She considered herself "Hispano" long before the popularization of the now-familiar "Hispanic." She liked to say that her ancestors were Spaniards, never Mexican. If you saw her, who could tell?

Both my daughter and her mother were raven-haired beauties with dark eyes and radiant olive-colored skin. Consuelo carried herself with a pride of heritage that bordered on arrogance. In me, perhaps she saw the blossoming artist, the Bisbee turquoise waiting to be chiseled out of crude copper ore and polished.

Not long after we met—not believing my good fortune that she had accepted—over a long weekend, we eloped to the red cliffs of Sedona. There, we spent three passionate nights in a motel room next to the creek. We made a pact to always preserve the splendor that, at that time, at least I thought, happened only once in a lifetime. The promise was sealed by the uncontrollable physical madness of our first few couplings. For a young miner who had never even dreamed of the "opening of doors" that being with Consuelo provided me with her friends, who were all grad students at the university and young professors, my life then was perfection.

After our wedding, I continued to work the underground mines at San Manuel, and we lived the life of part-time students, and not too long afterward, Emma Liliana was born.

After I completed my studies, Consuelo expected that we would move east to New York or north to Santa Fe or San Francisco. "Places where new Hispano talent is appreciated," she said. But by then, my mind was directed only toward the south.

For a long time, I didn't fully recognize the fundamentally different views of the world that we had. I used to tease her with, "Come on, Consuelo. We all basically look the same, depending on how much indio is in each of us," or "The food we eat? Lo mismo, except for slight regional variations in the chile," or "You can't argue that all our parents and abuelos, here and from over there, weren't Catolicos?" She never even smiled at my weak attempts to be funny.

One Sunday afternoon, while we waited for news regarding her fellowship application, we stopped for a quick cup of coffee at Burger King alongside the interstate near the university. With a "Buenos dias," I greeted a dusty Mexican couple carrying woven straw bags, waiting outside for a ride, while the teenaged boy with them went inside and ordered two one-dollar hamburgers. Before paying, he returned outside and huddled with the man and woman. The woman fished around in a small pinch coin purse and, under her rosary, found a few pennies and handed them to him.

In the drive-through lane, two young men with shaved heads and wearing basketball jerseys waited in a new truck with enormous tires. They were causing a scene because their Whoppers were supposed to be without onions. Two new Whoppers were quickly produced and handed to the driver who had three little tears tattooed on his cheek by his eye. The clerk, a petite blond teenager adorned with four earrings on one ear and a ring on every finger, including her thumbs, quickly tossed the rejected food into the boy's bag and looked around carefully before she pitched in a pint of milk that had been sitting on the counter.

"Did you see that?" I asked my wife.

"Yes, it is disgraceful. They are grimy and dirty, nothing but trash! You have to stop encouraging them."

I looked at her in astonishment. Viewing the same occurrence, we had seen two completely different things—an act of unexpected compassion, and something to be ashamed of.

Consuelo had grown up in a time and place when many wanted to differentiate themselves from the sweaty migrants from the south. Hadn't my cousin, Rafael, the first grandson of my mother's parents, gone to Northern Spain on several occasions to pursue his Basque heritage? Not once did he set foot in Mexico where his parents and grandparents had come from. It was a time when Quintana became Quinn and Rivera was transformed to Rivers as fast as a county judge could sign the order for a name change.

Consuelo had heard about the Sephardic Jews who had been expelled from Spain in 1492. It was said that they hid their identity in the New World because of fear of the powerful Spanish Catholic Church and the Inquisition that might follow them. Five hundred years later, the impoverished migrants from the south continued to bring their traditional Mexican culture and the Catholic Church with them. Many times, the ragged newcomers were no different in appearance than those who had been here for generations. It was when the migration was becoming a flood that Consuelo began to search for Jewish ancestors and symbols among the gravestones of her family, and in vague stories, she remembered having been told by a maiden great-aunt. That old woman had, nonetheless, attended mass and taken communion at the cathedral in Santa Fe every day of her life until she died in her nineties.

Before I left on another photographic assignment, I contacted my niece, Vanessa, who I knew kept in touch with Emma Lily and indirectly with my ex-wife. I hoped that she might have the current phone number or address of my daughter. I must have blanched when she said, "Emma Lily is down in Miami to attend her mother's wedding at the synagogue. I thought you knew."

Since I always had held the hope that Consuelo and I would get together again after everything got sorted out, the shock of hearing that she had married a wealthy Jewish business man whose family, in the sixties, had fled Castro's Cuba must have shown on my face.

Quickly changing the subject, Vanessa asked, "What are you doing this weekend, Unk?"

"Nothing in particular."

"How about using that magical camera of yours and taking a short trip with me?"

"For you, anything," I said and kissed her on the top of her head so that she couldn't see my eyes brimming over.

The church was nothing more than a large rectangular room that was of a size and height that, on a different occasion, could have been easily converted to some other use, like a bingo hall. The construction was of unplastered block with a concrete floor that had been sealed and polished many times. The steel-sashed windows had different-colored pieces of plastic glued on to the clear glass of the pane. The plastic pieces had been arranged in an artistic way, forming pleasing designs and religious images. Still, they were a pale imitation of the stained glass majesty of other, more prosperous Catholic churches.

On the wall above the center of the simple altar, there was a statue of the crucified Christ. To its right against the sidewall were two rows of four folding wooden chairs. To its left, there was the familiar painting of the Virgen de Guadalupe. Surrounding the painting's border was a lit multicolored string of tiny Christmas lights.

Vanessa had asked me to photograph her friend's "quincianera." It is a traditional Mexican celebration that is becoming increasingly popular with Mexican-Americans. On the girl's fifteenth birthday, her family celebrates her leaving childhood and becoming a young woman, and she dedicates herself to the virgin and to Jesus. After the church service, there was to be a coming-out party with food and a dance. In a much more modest fashion and with a religious component, it was like the cotillions that the socially prominent here in the north lavish on their young girls when they are blossoming from adolescence into young womanhood.

Before anything could start, we had to wait for the arrival of Father Mulvihill, and he was not expected for at least twenty minutes. The elderly Irish priest was a type of circuit rider. He traveled to those slowly disappearing mining towns that are on the northeast side of the Catalina Mountains and down the barely flowing San Pedro in Southern Arizona.

There was to be six couples, part of the girl's dance troupe, that would serve as attendants. The boys were in an adjacent room getting dressed. I helped Vanessa carry her costume bag from the van and started to excuse myself from the girls' dressing room.

"You don't have to leave yet, Unk," she said. "Let's talk."

Each girl had a cosmetic case with a mirror. She peered into hers while she put her long hair in a ponytail. She said, "I know you want to ask because everybody does. Each one of the group is in high school or college."

While they all were concentrating on preparing their faces, she braided the ponytail and wrapped it into a bun, which was held in place on the back of her head with bobby pins. Her conversation came to an abrupt halt because she was giving her full attention to putting on long black eyelashes, liner, shading, and lipstick.

"Is that you?" I asked. She laughed then said, "Just wait. The miracle isn't over yet. We all practice three evenings a week with the maestro. Did you know that he was the director of a famous Ballet Folklorico in Guadalajara before he came to Tucson? We have to thank his wife, a former dancer, for the exotic makeup and the design of the costumes. The dancers' mothers are the seamstresses."

She slipped on her black high-heeled shoes, bent her ankle to show me the nails on the shoe's heels, and said, "So that the *zapateado* (heel stomping) can be heard."

Under her street dress, I could see what looked like bloomers that were held snuggly at the knee with a purple ribbon.

"We never know where we are going to dress, so we always have to be prepared. The maestro says it is all part of our discipline."

Again I started to leave, but by this time, one of the other girls had picked up the dress that she would later wear and, with her arms fully extended at shoulder level, let the fabric drape down to the floor like a beautiful inverted fan. Vanessa got her costume and stood behind the other girl's screen and said, "We take turn. First me, and then I'll help her. When we go to perform at schools or parks or fiestas at people's homes, sometimes there is only a small corner to change from one costume to another. We'd rather have people see us dance than worry about where and if we are going to be able to change."

A few moments later, she stepped out from behind the fan a spectacular symphony of colors, fabrics, and ribbons.

"This is our *traje de gala* (festival dress)," she said, and while the other girls helped each other, she completed the costume.

"We all expect you to take a photograph of each of us in the way that only you can, Unk. I know how you like to get to the nitty-gritty. So I thought you might like to know how the great transformation takes place." She laughed.

On her neck, she placed a double strand of beads. Two large golden earrings and heavy black yarn braids with ribbons of a matching color as those on the bloomers completed the costume. The braids were attached to the hair bun with a comb and bobby pins, and they formed two ovals on each side of her face.

A couple of minutes later, all six were ready. It had taken less than ten minutes. They had all been changed into head-turning beauties.

In the next room, a similar transformation had taken place, and six skinny young men now emerged as manly charros.

Father Mulvihill was ready. After all these years, he had never lost his Irish brogue and spoke in a colorful mishmash of English and Spanish. For years, the Mexican-American communities in Southern Arizona had been ministered to by Irish priests like he—I suppose because a generation of potential Mexican priests had not gone to a seminary in Mexico because of the Cristiada.

When I reentered the church, the two rows of folding wooden chairs were now occupied by a mariachi in elegant-tailored outfits. The musical group was also composed of young men and girls of similar age as the dancers. The ceremony started when the mariachi started to play. The six male dancers in rows of two came down the aisle, large traditional sombreros in hand. At the front of the church, they stopped and faced each other so that each of the girls, in dresses the color of the rainbow, could walk down the aisle between them. A girl in a white bridal dress followed and was accompanied by her mother, father, and brother. She knelt before the altar.

The only one more amazed at the proceedings than I was Father Mulvihill as he stood facing the group with an open mouth. I thought to myself, *These young people are changing the church and its rituals in a way that is relevant to them just like the Yaquis did with their deer dance.* The understanding old priest only smiled wisely and said nothing.

After the mass, the families and friends waited for the fiesta to start in the parish hall. The dancers, the young girl, and her family entered in couples to the music of a familiar Mexican march played by the musicians while I took photographs of everything and everybody. I moved over to the priest, who was standing near the kitchen, intending to take his photograph. The delicious smell of barbacoa, tamales, and frijoles, all made by the girl's *tias*, saturated the air.

"By the way, me boy, what is the name of that lively march?" the priest asked as he munched on a tortilla chip piled high with guacamole. At the first opportunity, I called Vanessa and, over the tumult, asked her.

"Why, Unk, don't you know? That's Zacatecas. That was the march they played when Villa and his Dorados entered Mexico City. You really should study up on your Mexican history." She laughed.

The priest's eyebrows rose at the comment. He said, "Does me heart good to see the pride in those kids. It wasn't always like that, you know."

"Father, sometimes it's the youngsters that teach the old crows a thing or two." I said, "I heard that before, somewhere."

I thought to myself, *That's my girl. You kids get them while they're still young. Before they need to go to Northern Spain or back to 1492 to find something to be proud of.*

Father Mulvihill said, "Richard, what say you if we step over there and have ourselves a wee brew. Our job with this crew is over, me boy."

"Ricardo, Father," I said. "The name is Ricardo."

The ballet completed one of their dances to loud applause, and little kids attempting to imitate what they had just seen stomped around the hall, grateful to be able to expend some of their excess energy.

"And what song is that? I've heard it before," asked the priest.

"You should have. That's La Negra (the Dark One). Some Mexican-Americans like to say that it is Mexico's real national anthem." I laughed.

The dancers, in their beautiful costumes, circled the dance floor, acknowledging the crowd's applause before they exited. I yelled at my niece, "Hey, Vaness, do you know what Vanessa means?"

"You got me there, Unk."

"Butterfly," I said. "Vanessa means butterfly."

Part 5
No nos dimos cuenta

La invasion de los mineros

There was one final surprise. As a small child in Bisbee, I had visited my other grandfather, my mother's father, in his small second-story bedroom in a house that was built on the side of a hill. Because of its construction on the slope, each story of the house had a ground-level entrance. Through the eyes of a child, I remembered that the walls of the bedroom were painted gray and they had a shiny antiseptic enamel-like finish.

My grandfather was bedridden and in the last stages of cancer. He always greeted me with a smile despite his agony, and he would weakly place his wasted arm around my shoulders. An image of the Virgen de Guadalupe hung on one wall in a wood picture frame. Underneath it on a small table, a votive candle with a waxed-filled saucer was always lit.

The only other adornment in the sad room was on his nightstand. There was a framed picture of an elderly, robust-looking man with a large white mustache. On the man's chest was a profusion of ribbons and medals. He had a silver sash around his waist and matching silver epaulets on his shoulders. I never knew who he was.

Many years later, I asked his eldest grandson, Rafael—himself now well up in years—who the man was.

"Don't you know? That was Porfirio Diaz. Your Papapa thought he was the greatest man in the world. He used to say that Don Porfirio brought Mexico into the modern world when it had been nothing but a backward backwater, a country of men leading burros carrying water bags. He said that he built the railroads and developed the mines and oilfields. That Mexico City became like Paris—Paris with a Spanish accent and with houses covered with bougainvillea.

"Your Papapa was one of his Rurales who served under Coronel Kosterlitzky. He used to tell me how in 1906 and 1907, when the copper miners struck in Cananea, Sonora, first the Rurales and then the federal army, using bayonets and bullets, moved in to break the strike and restore order."

I had heard about the miner's strike in Cananea. Some said it was the first uprising in what was to become the Mexican Revolution.

Cananea, Sonora, is approximately forty miles south of the international border at Naco. In Cananea, Col. William Greene with money from Wall Street investors had developed one of the biggest copper mines in northern Mexico. On Friday morning, June 1, 1906, Mexican miners appeared at the Oversight mine of the Cananea Consolidated Copper Company and prevented the seven o'clock shift from entering the mine.

The miners had congregated at Calle Principal of Ronquillo, the nearby Mexican pueblo, where most of the miners lived. Soon there were over two thousand miners crowded around the road blocking the passage that led into the mine. Some waved red, and some waved white flags. They were there to protest the wage rate—three pesos for a ten-hour shift—paid by Cananea Consolidated to the Mexican workers. Americanos for a similar day's work were paid five dollars. At that time, a dollar was worth two pesos.

"I loved that old man," Rafael, who was now older than our grandfather had been at the time of his death, said. A huge tear fell on an old newspaper as he sat reading it hunched over, and it slowly spread as the paper absorbed the moisture.

"Ocho horas, cinco pesos...ocho horas, cinco pesos" (Eight hours for five pesos), the strikers chanted. The strike was intended to be peaceful. There were no plans for violence. Many of the strikers, laughing and joking, were in their Sunday Mass finery. There was to be no arms, nor had any dynamite been stolen from the mine. The leaders of the walkout believed that pressure on the company to grant the demands would come from the solidarity of the large number of striking miners and the justness of their cause.

Handbills that reflected the growing discontent with Porfirio Diaz's regime circulated from miner to miner.

> Mexican Workers,
>
> Cananea, Sonora
>
> June 1, 1906
>
> Curse the thought that a Mexicano is worth less than a Yanqui. That this is a fact is the result of a very bad government that gives the advantage to the exploiters rather than the true owners of this unfortunate land. Awaken! Our country and our dignity demand it!

Colonel Greene came down from the big house on the mesa to meet with the mob. He stood on the front seat of his roofless automobile imported from the United States, which since its arrival on Greene's flatbed railroad car had been an object of great curiosity and admiration in that northern Sonoran outpost. He was a popular figure. Whenever and wherever he was seen by the miners, "Viva el Coronel Greene, Viva!" often accompanied him in his inspections. Hadn't he brought jobs and wages where there had been none?

"By the time I learned and understood about the incident at Cananea, it was too late to ask my Papapa about it," said my heavyset cousin with the thick, close-cropped, snow-white hair.

In explanation for the wage disparity, Greene, standing over them from the height provided by his automobile's seat, first spoke about his need for experienced American underground miners, which statement didn't go down well with the grizzled Mexican workers.

"But there was another consideration," he told them. His wage scale was so favorable for the Mexican miners he employed that the month before, the president of Mexico, Don Porfirio Diaz, had ordered that there be a reduction in the scale of wages that Greene paid them by fifty centavos per day.

Greene addressed the assembled miners with a megaphone.

"I've been told that my wages are so favorable that the Mexican economy is being upset. Campesinos are leaving the cultivation of the land and other types of work in surrounding pueblos to seek employment here. After consulting with Governor Izabel, he has urged me to start following the government's new regulation. So you see, amigos, there are other things that I have to consider. Go home, muchachos. Go home to your familias."

What he didn't mention was that the night before, Greene had gotten wind of the impending strike. He sent an engine and his finely appointed traveling coach—which he often used in his travels back to New York—to Bisbee to prepare just in case reinforcements and firearms had to be mustered. This was the same coach where he had lavishly hosted many American investors and captains of industry and, of course, Mexican politicians when he was assembling his vast Sonoran holdings.

Despite the colonel's urging, the strikers did not disperse. They continued their march and approached the lumberyard. One of the loyal Americans at the yard, one of the ones who had been armed and deputized by the company, felt threatened by the mob. A four-inch fire hose was turned on the demonstrators. Then shots were fired, and there were several dead and wounded strikers on the sidewalk. The enraged mob of strikers rushed and overpowered the armed "Americanos" and then set fire to the lumberyard. Two Americans were stabbed and killed with the long, pointed steel shafts that the miners used to drive into crevices in the mine wall where they placed their candles to light up their work area. These foot-long implements were driven into the Americano's chests.

With flames threatening the mine buildings as smoke billowed from the fire, Greene sent a frantic telegraphic message pleading that the Copper Queen Store in Bisbee be kept open for some emergency purchases. As a result, close to a hundred rifles and shotguns and a large number of pistols, plus thousands of rounds of ammunition were prepared and waited to be picked up by Greene's men. He also sent an underling to Hermosillo to transport Governor Izabel. Greene had also sent the governor a curt telegraphic message:

"Urgent bring troops. Forty killed. Don't stop at Imuris. I will wait at Naco and train you here to Cananea."

The United States consul, upon hearing of the conflict from the governor of Sonora, communicated with his secretary of state.

"Americans are being murdered and property dynamited." As a result of this exchange of messages, there was official contact by American authorities with the Mexican government in Mexico City. Porfirio Diaz eager to placate the "Americanos," immediately responded that the Mexican government would handle the crises.

But Greene was not so sure. The nearest military infantry unit was located at Magdalena, and there was no direct railway line from there to his mine. The Mexican infantry would require a forty-mile cross-country march to Cananea. And the mounted Rurales, who had been successfully controlling the campesinos for the Porfiristas for such a long time, were also quartered at Magdalena. They would require almost two days of mustering and of hard riding to get to Cananea.

In desperation, Greene called Walter Douglas, the general manager of the Copper Queen mine in Bisbee, and told him of the striking miners and of his loss of control of the situation. Douglas told the Bisbee Town Marshal to call for volunteers.

Drafted from the bars and whorehouses of Brewery Gulch in Bisbee, considerably more than two hundred miners and gamblers assembled at the Copper Queen store where the weapons awaited. Most of the volunteers were already well fortified with alcohol and eager to confront the "Messicans."

In flatbed cars, they were transported the seven miles to the border at Naco. There, Governor Izabel and Colonel Greene nervously paced back and forth, looking north for the reinforcements. The governor, sensitive to the political situation, said that they could not cross the border as an armed group. That could be interpreted as an invasion of Mexico. After quick consultation among themselves, Mexican border officials came up with a scheme. Instead of permitting the mob into Mexico as a unit, they would be allowed to cross, one at a time, as individuals. On the Mexican side of the border, as soon as they had all reassembled, General Torres swore them into the Mexican army.

Then the armed mob from Bisbee, now Mexican soldiers, climbed on flatbed railroad cars and were transported toward Cananea.

Some credit the Mexican train engineer with having avoided a bloodbath by first slowing and then stopping the train a couple of miles outside of Cananea where the miners were still demonstrating. The newly mustered soldiers would have to cover the remaining distance on foot.

✐

A long column of at least one hundred armed men, two abreast, can be seen snaking underneath a railway trestle. The view of the front of the formation is lost around the corner. Above the bridge can be seen the two smoke stacks where the concentrator and the smelter are located as well as other company buildings. They are on their way to join the company men, American employees who await these reinforcements, their rifles at the ready.

✐

On June 2, before the striking miners and this newly assembled irregular force could face off against each other, Colonel Kosterlitzky, whom the Sonorans had nicknamed "the Butcher," rode into Ronquillo. With units of his heavily armed Rurales and their exhausted horses, they took up strategic positions surrounding the strikers and declared that the Bisbee miners were no longer needed. The action by the train engineer had kept the strikers and the Bisbee miners apart long enough to permit the deployment of the Rurales and, although later hotly disputed, no shots had been exchanged between them.

❧

Two squads of mounted men, approximately twenty Rurales, are visible in the photograph. They all wear large matching hats, which provide protection from the Northern Sonoran desert when on a forced march, and matching ponchos that cover their shoulders, thighs, and parts of their saddles. The heavily armed men are passing in front of a store with a four-foot high-concrete loading dock. Behind it, plate glass windows display the goods that are for sale to the miners at the company store.

❧

Martial law was proclaimed by Governor Izabel, and he authorized that anybody found on the street after dark was to be shot. Nobody doubted that Kosterlitzky and his men who patrolled the streets would carry out the order. Meanwhile, the *carcel* (jail) de Cananea became packed with known, or suspected, *huelgistas* (strikers) as the Rurales combed the streets of Ronquillo looking for strikers.

Those strikers who were not jailed were told that lists of those workers not returning to work immediately were being prepared. Those on the list would be drafted into the army and would go to Southern Sonora to fight the Yaquis.

The Bisbee miners were reassembled on the track, and the direction of travel of the flat cars waiting outside of Cananea was reversed. The miners and gamblers were soon back in their drinking establishments and brothels in the Gulch in Bisbee. There, the incident was soon forgotten as an evening's insignificant alcoholic escapade.

But in Mexico, in the minds of many Mexicanos, the incident festered as one of the prerevolution horror stories, as to what the government of Porfirio Diaz had become. The dead strikers became known as the "Martires de 1906" (Martyrs of 1906).

Reports in Mexican opposition newspapers screamed, "The first volley was terrible. Almost a hundred corpses and several hundred others fell to the earth while they tried to defend themselves with knives and stones."

The truth of how many were killed is lost to history as both the workers and the government manipulated the figures. Three months later, this latest outrage was still on the tongues of many Mexicanos. They screamed that Porfirio Diaz's government had imported foreign arms and foreign men to put down what was said to have been a peaceful work stoppage by Mexican workers.

Shortly thereafter, the Flores Magon brothers, the publishers of *Regeneracion*, a magazine that pressed for the overthrow of Porfirio Diaz, crossed the Rio Grande near El Paso and headed south from their sanctuary in the United States. They and their followers were the first to try to overthrow the government of Don Porfirio Diaz although their premature attempt ended in failure.

Some of the Cananea strikers had learned a valuable lesson. There was great strength if they all acted together. Two of the timekeepers who worked for Cananea Consolidated and who had participated in the planning of the work stoppage were, later on, to become revolutionary generals in Sonora.

"Didn't you wonder why the three oldest, your two aunts and your mother, who were all born before 1910, were born in

Mexico, in Guaymas and Cananea, and all your uncles, who were born after 1911, were born here in Bisbee?" asked Rafael.

"Your Papapa had to leave Mexico when Don Porfirio was overthrown and fled to France. I didn't know enough back then to ask him how it was that he had gotten work tending the roses and grass outside the general offices in Bisbee instead of going underground like every other Mexicano? Or whether there were other Rurales that had settled in Bisbee?

"And much later, why was he warned, on that predawn morning in 1917, to immediately leave his wife and six children in the house on Chihuahua Hill and temporarily flee from Bisbee? Only a very few knew that company bigwigs like Walter Douglas and local authorities had secretly hired some goons and gunmen to go from house to house and collect over one thousand miners, union sympathizers, and Wobblies, and deport them permanently from Bisbee.

"The local sheriff later testified at a court trial involving the Bisbee deportation of all those men that some of the deported Bisbee miners were ex-Villa soldiers who had arms and ammunition cached in the nearby mountains, which they intended to use in a planned Bisbee strike, something like what had occurred years before in Cananea. And that is why they had to be rounded up and deported.

"Having been warned by somebody, my Papapa was not there when the roundup was carried out, and when things cooled down, he was able to return to work with the company and to his family."

I had heard stories from my mother about the deportation, when as a child she had seen hundreds of men being herded down the Bisbee canyon by rough-looking men with rifles and bats.

The arrested men were identified ,and their names placed on company lists of those who were not to return to Bisbee. They were then loaded on the El Paso and Southwestern in cattle cars and dumped without food or water in the desert outside of Columbus, New Mexico, where the mine owners knew a company of US Cavalry was stationed, just in case trouble broke out. Before the locomotive left Bisbee, the arrestees were warned by the authorities and employers that they no longer would be welcome in the Bisbee district.

So the image I had about my heritage being with the revolutionaries was not true. My grandfathers had been on different sides in the revolution, all of which became irrelevant in their new country.

Mientras no nos dimos cuenta

I have come to understand that we are still in the middle of a vast historical migration. Not counting those migrants who left Mexico for unique personal reasons, the first trickle of Mexican immigrants to this country in the last hundred years started when Porfirio Diaz's supporters fled Mexico. This was followed by the larger wave of refugees that occurred as a result of the Mexican Revolution. An even larger swell of religious refugees followed because of the Cristiada. Since then, it has become a tsunami caused by the economic disparity between the two nations.

All the while during the same time period, in the United States, there also were great changes. In 1902, congress passed the National Reclamation Act. Under this law, the federal government wanted to concentrate "reclamation efforts" in the west, on land that was held in the public domain. The idea was that after a small farmer made a claim of no more than 160 acres of the public domain and resided on and worked the land for five years, he would then receive title to the land from the government. In this way, it was hoped, the deserts of the west would bloom with crops like they had in the mid-west and east in the hands of small farmers. But in the arid west, because of the absence of dependable rainfall, water would have to be collected and delivered to distant fields so that the claims would be of value.

In Arizona in 1905, Roosevelt Dam, a gracefully designed structure with stone turrets and with the elegance of a medieval castle rose 280 feet above bedrock. But there were no eager hordes of landless Americans who headed to that irrigation project to stake their claims. There were few farmers who had experience with this type of agriculture and fewer still who could hold out until the life-giving water arrived. Instead, in a process that was to be repeated over and over again, when engineers, surveyors, and construction crews appeared to start a project, speculators and farmers descended on to the desert to stake their claims, intending to hold on to them until water gurgled in the ditches and concrete canals. Then they could sell for a large profit.

The Salt River Project, which now serves the Phoenix metropolitan area, had precious few acres in the public domain. As a result, much of the Salt River Valley's farmlands remained in the same hands, except that the land had vastly increased in value because of the availability of water. Before, to become the owner of land had only required an investment in "keep out" signs, barbed wire, time, and labor. Now the collection and distribution of water in the desert required a huge investment of money and planning, which was provided by the United States government.

The 160-acre rule was soon being interpreted by the Reclamation Bureau as permitting 160 acres each for a husband and a wife, and with time, the concentration of farmlands in a few hands seemed to be limited only by the ingenuity of the farmers and their lawyers. In California, the concentration of land ownership was to be repeated.

Hoover Dam on the Colorado River followed, and it was accompanied by a system of less spectacular dams that helped to distribute the water. The All American Canal soon made the Imperial Valley in the southern deserts of California, one of the garden spots of the continent. Not surprisingly, many complained that water was being managed more for private than for the public's interest.

There was a complete absence of grassroots communal tradition with this type of farming, unlike the small farming communities that had developed over decades in the Mid-west and the East. Instead of family farmers working and living on their land as had been the original intent of the law, the focus of many of the new absentee owners and investors was to rely on technical expertise distributing water to distant desert acres and to use the advanced business practices of agribusiness.

The first projects, although huge by then-existing standards, were small in comparison to what occurred in the Great Central Valley of California. That vast arid region lay between the Sierras to the east and the coastal ranges to the west and stretched from Los Angeles to San Francisco, a distance of five hundred miles. By 1920, the southern parts of the San Juaquin Valley were running dry. Although the King's River project irrigated over one million acres, if the hope was to make California the "world's greatest garden," the Sacramento River would have to be tapped. To that end, the Central Valley Project was conceived. From Shasta Dam, the Contra Costa Canal ran westward toward San Francisco; and the Delta-Mendota Canal ran southward, paralleling the San Juaquin River, which had dried up because of the upriver withdrawals for irrigation. There was also the Friant Dam, northwest of Fresno, which fed the Friant Kern Canal that ran toward Delano and Bakersfield, and that, for 150 miles, irrigated the entire desert in between.

The golden faucets had been turned on, and the desert valleys bloomed like no other in the world, creating vast wealth for California and, indirectly, for the rest of the country.

But a huge army of farm workers was needed to toil in the ditches and the fields to reap the golden harvest. Not surprisingly, the farmers and investors who benefited from the vast subsidized projects specialized in crops, which left the greatest profit. It was reported that, at one time, a single acre of tomatoes required one thousand man-hours to plant, cultivate, and harvest. More often, irrigation farming required large numbers of workers only during the harvest to bring in the crop, and then the workers were expected to leave before they became an unproductive burden.

During the early years, Japanese, Filipinos, workers from India with their white turbans, along with Mexicanos were seen toiling in the fields as the labor source. But as the irrigation system matured in the Roaring Twenties, it was the Mexicanos who became the most reliable and accessible recruits.

Then during the Depression, desperate people fleeing Oklahoma and the Dust Bowl provided willing workers. Under these new conditions in Los Angeles and elsewhere in the valley, signs were seen everywhere, stating, "Employ no Mexicans, while a White Man is unemployed." Thousands of Mexicanos, many of them American citizens born in the United States, were deported first by the federal government and, when that stopped because of President Franklin Roosevelt's order, by state and municipal authorities.

These labor conditions continued until the defense industries, because of the war looming in Europe and Asia, cranked up their factories. As war threatened, more lucrative and less physically depleting work in the defense industries became available to the Americans who had, in desperation, trudged to California's farmlands during the Depression.

The growers again sent recruiters into Mexico to bring thousands of men and women to do the temporary work that no one else would do. The migrants lived in squalor in hovels made of cardboard and flattened tin cans. Different families were separated only by chicken wire in the shacks. Men and women were sought to pick the hated small boll Pima cotton that grew only in tall plants where breezes couldn't penetrate the heat and humidity.

Those who complained about the conditions risked being deported and dumped back into Mexico without their pay. Agribusiness, with its subsidized water, had found a never-ending source of compliant workers. It was the Mexican campesino that had been tied down for generations in almost involuntary servitude in the great haciendas to the south and for whom the revolution had provided no permanent relief.

With their quiet, persistent presence in the vineyards, orchards, and fields, they became the dominated class. The rootless people who moved with the crops and who it was said, cared not for the education of their children or of other dearly held American values. When they tried to band together to improve their lot, those already here were pitted against the thousand of desperate newcomers who arrived every year. In the great valleys, there was tear gas and bats and vicious dogs. But it was this despised race in these fields of plenty who made the vast agribusiness of the new hydraulic society the envy of the world.

California had become America's El Dorado; and the San Juaquin Valley, California's crown jewel. But the Golden State, the home of so many of the country's new social and economic trends, had collided head on with the iron law of unintended consequences. The structure it had built, relying on cheap labor to serve and support its privileged society, slowly spread throughout our country.

It is as if a fabric had been woven, joining our two countries along the two-thousand-mile border. The Mexican people continually go back and forth between the two countries like a shuttle through a loom, constantly strengthening the fabric. Dreams of wealth and economic opportunity beckon them north. Traditions, culture, and family draw them back south. After each back-and-forth process, more and more of their economically deprived young become aware of the wonders that are to be found here in the north.

Each year, the fabric's pull becomes stronger, and many have just begun to focus on this phenomenon that is slowly changing the United States, starting in California and the Southwest and spreading northward and eastward.

Quin Qon

"Ricardo, can you believe it? After all this time, I saw Evangelina," said Don David.

I had picked him up at a Downtown Tucson bus stop after receiving an urgent call at my home.

"She was kneeling, head bowed, praying the rosary as I pushed the big dust mop down the aisle of St. Patrick's. After having made it clear so long ago that she would see me no more under the selfish conditions that I had wanted, there she was, her face still lovely. But because of some infirmity of age, when she stood to talk to me, her head was in a permanent rigid position as if she was looking down, inspecting her shoes. After my wife, of all the women, she, most of all, touched my heart."

His hands trembled as he lit a cigarette, then he continued, "I was almost as startled when I saw her at the church as when I first met her, way back when I was still trying to adjust to the end of what had been my world. It was an early evening in late October, already pitch-black at the cemetery, I had lost track of time and that the next day was 'El Dia de los Muertos.' What had started with me kneeling, saying the rosary, ended with me face down, spread eagle on the ground that covered my wife's fresh grave. Evangelina was on her way, using a dim flashlight, looking for the nicho of her sister's grave. The nicho turned out to be an old bathtub, sawed in half, and the severed end stood up in cement. It made a perfect symmetrical enclosure for the statue of the virgin and for candles and the picture of her sister. Evangelina was there to clean the tomb and repaint the grave marker, and she gave out a squeal at our unexpected meeting. I was so startled *que se me salio el caldito* (peed on myself)," he chuckled, recalling the squirt of pee that had escaped him in his fright.

"While the thumping of my heart raced uncontrollably, she curiously looked on without a word at what she had found there in the dark. Later, she told me that she thought that my pose, face down on the ground, was an imitation of Christ on the cross, a touching symbol of my Christian devotion. She was wrong. In my insane grief, I had sought to have my pores pressed against the dirt of my wife's tomb and somehow absorb the soft, lush, physical essence of the woman I had loved and lost overnight to what the doctor said was an 'embolism.' And that was to be the first of our many secret encounters.

"Although she said that she had seen me before around the sacristy trying to be of service to Padre Reyes, I had never noticed her and her husband, who sat in the back pews. In every way, she was the opposite of my wife, mi morenita, who had been so beautifully and enticingly fleshed out like soft summer melones.

"Evangelina was tall and *guerra* (fair) and so thin you could swear that only the bones of her shoulders held up the elegant dresses she liked to wear, with breasts so small I would tenderly cup them in a way you hold a sparrow to prevent it from flying away, and with the face of an angel.

"In our lovemaking, she was so different. I had to learn to accept that, that extraordinary experience that I had loved, now lay buried.

"With Evangelina, it was as if she was fighting off something that she strongly resisted, something that had to be dragged into existence, something that was so odd that when it finally arrived, it was like a rainstorm freakishly exploding the heat of July in the Bisbee canyons and as I lay exhausted.

"As the years passed, I asked her many times to marry, to fill the hole that had been left in my world with my wife's death.

"'David, it cannot be. I'm already married in the church,' she said.

"'So is it better that you go every month to Douglas, where the priest doesn't know you and me, to confess?' I asked.

"Without telling her, I went to the only source I trusted and asked Padre Antonio, man-to-man, if it would be wrong for us to marry.

"'If she does this thing, she will be lost, and she will never find herself again,' he answered, strangely avoiding my eyes.

"But I didn't give up so easy. For an unspoken reason, she had no children, and so I dangled the thought of our having a child to try to convince her to change her mind.

"'I already have a little one that I'm close to, very close to, in Michoacan,' she answered.

"Still, she wanted me to be faithful only to her. She wanted me to be monogamous outside of marriage while she was adulterous inside of her marriage. I told her, 'What is fair for one is fair for the other.'

"In that small community, there arose rumors about me and another woman, and she heard them, and so that was that. She saw me no more."

After the death of Padre Antonio, the small church used by the Mexicanos in old Bisbee had been sold and became somebody's residence. The space on the second floor, where the small organ had been and which overlooked the pews below, had become a sleeping loft for artists and free spirits. The bishop had decided that in contemporary, donation-shrinking times, it would not do for there to be two churches within three blocks of each other—one for the Mexicanos and the other for everybody else. As the town contracted after the closure of the mines, the two congregations merged, and now everybody went to mass at the much-grander St. Patrick's.

Completed in 1917, it was the crowning example of the exuberant expansion of the Bisbee community when the demand for copper was at its zenith. The church was modeled on one in Whales, in the British Isles, and was of a majestic Gothic-revival design made with special yellow brick and with magnificent stained-glass windows reputedly the finest in the entire state. Don David marveled that in his old age, he had been given a hand, admittedly a small one, in preserving its beauty and utility.

"There I stood with my mouth open. After all these years of stubbornly not wanting to see me, Evangelina had sought me out. She had come to ask me to help find her 'nephew' from Michoacan.

"He has not appeared in Sedona, where a job was waiting for him at a resort. It has been months since he left with plans to cross the desert, but not a word. We are frantic,' she said.

He looked at me through shot-glass thick spectacles, and his pupils appeared like two dark plums.

"I thought of you, Ricardito. Can you help? It is important to me.'"

I understood just how important. The old man had taken a van that transports passengers back and forth from South Tucson to Douglas and places in between. This was the first time he had left Bisbee and his little miner's cabin perched three flights up from Tombstone Canyon, the town's main street, since he had driven Padre Antonio around in the old Dodge years ago.

"I haven't been to Tucson since mucho antes que murio Antonio, el trafico esta terrible" (I haven't been to Tucson since long before Antonio's death—the traffic is terrible), he said, and he crossed himself. We arrived at my Tucson mountain home just in time to drive into a cloud-encrusted dark-pink–and-orange sunset sinking in the west.

The next morning, we were the first "customers" downtown at the Consulado de Mexico. The pretty clerk, who spoke with a pronounced Mexican accent, listened to our story and then directed us to a small separate building behind the consulate to "El Departamento de Proteccion a Mexicanos." There we met the director who, as a representative of his country, was impeccably groomed and mannered and who took down as much information as we could provide about name, height, weight, and other identifying marks like tattoos and scars, dental information, where and when the crossing had occurred, and the clothes worn.

He checked a computer database that he said was shared with other consulates along the border and found no obvious match. He responded to our spoken curiosity as to why he sought the physically identifying information from us by saying, "This year, we've already had 170 bodies reported and recovered, of which we have identified all but sixteen, which we assume were also undocumented workers. But only Dios sabe how many others are still out there."

He looked up at us with the quiet solemnity that a search for a lost family member required.

"I'm sorry. There is nothing here of any help in your quest. But many times, 'undocumented crossers' are arrested by the authorities of the Estados Unidos and either deported or charged with a federal crime. I suggest that you try the federal court, three blocks from here, *quien sabe* (who knows), he might be in their custody." He pointed in its direction.

Assembled outside of the locked courtroom, thirty or so lawyers attired in compulsory suits and ties awaited entrance. Inside, deputy US marshals could be seen through a small window on the door, leading rows of manacled men and women in orange jumpsuits. First, they were filed into the jury box then on to the seats around the courtroom normally reserved for lawyers, law clerks, and law enforcement personnel. Then they were led into the several rows of spectator seats until the courtroom was packed with these strangers in orange. Once permitted to enter, in a cacophony of shouted names, the lawyers attempted to identify and locate their clients. Awaiting a decent time so as to permit them to locate each other, the court clerk finally buzzed the judge. Fifteen or twenty cases were called by the clerk, and using an interpreter, those illegal entrants, en masse, entered pleas of "not guilty." Not much thought was given that all these individual cases were being set to be tried on the same day by the same judge. Because only a fool will reject the plea bargain offered by the US attorney. Harsh as the sentence for illegal reentry can be with a plea bargain, if one insists on a trial, the Federal Sentencing Guidelines expose those convicted to sentences of up to twenty years in prison. The clerk called twenty more cases and assigned them in the same way to another judge. This process continued until the room was cleared.

We then went into the court clerk's office, where a computer search of all of their hundreds and hundreds of cases, pending and completed, provided no match.

"There is only one other place I can think of," I told Don David.

A few miles away, the county morgue is located just two or three lush practice fields away from the stadium where in the spring, the White Sox, Diamondbacks, and Rockies had practiced in preparation for their seasons. The office of the county examiner is located in a red brick building that is surrounded on three sides by a twelve-foot-high block wall. On the fourth side, in the back, under an airport-like hangar roof, sat an 18-wheeler trailer with its refrigeration motor on at full blast.

I knocked on the locked front door of the building, and a matronly middle-aged woman behind a glass window electronically opened it. Behind her, I could see two tan-uniformed Tohona O'odham police officers with their distinct arm patches. One was completing some paperwork; the other, at a sink, was vigorously washing and scrubbing his hands, trying to remove the smell of death that had emanated from the body they had recovered that day in the desert.

Along the two-thousand-mile Mexican border, the border patrol had clamped down on "illegal aliens" entering through the urban areas between the two countries. Instead, in an attempt to discourage their entry, they funneled the undocumented into the potentially deadly passage way that was Arizona's remote deserts, including the one on the O'odham reservation. Between the Tucson and Yuma sectors, the border patrol reported detaining more than five hundred thousand crossers in one year, the very great majority being job seekers or those seeking to reunite with their families, some of these attempted to cross multiple times.

Most of the undocumented have no experience in the massive desert and its 115-degree–and-higher temperatures. "Pollos" or little chicks is what they are called by the "coyotes." The nickname *Coyote*, in turn, is given to those individuals who, for a substantial fee, show the pollos the way to cross the border. The pollos, traveling light, carry almost nothing, perhaps a small knapsack, plastic milk cartons with water, and trash bags to sleep on and to protect against the ants. Under dim starlight, they follow zigzag trails where they stumble into cholla and other cactus and thorny scrub brush. During the blistering heat of the day, the lucky ones hunker beneath Palo Verdes or squeeze against the sides of arroyos for slivers of shade. If their body temperature reaches 107 degrees, vital organs fail.

The refrigerated trailer is needed to handle all the overflow bodies found in the desert. Pima County had recently built the modern facility that, at that time, was thought would be large enough to store all corpses that might require forensic studies for a population of one million. They had not anticipated all these extra dead bodies. And now there even was talk of the need for another refrigerated 18-wheeler.

The woman who had let us in and seemed extraordinary cheerful, considering her macabre function, said, "Typically, if they've been out in the desert for any time, we just get body parts. Otherwise, even with the trailer, we wouldn't have room. The vultures and the coyotes scatter the bones all over out there.

"We always try to reunite bones and possessions for future possible ID. Many times, on a bone, all that is found is leathery mummified tissue. But realistically, nobody is interested in conducting an extensive forensic study because it is clear what caused their death. We store them for a decent time, and if they are not ID and claimed, we bury them as a "John" or "Jane Doe" in a pauper's grave. I say we should call them "Pancho" or "Panchita," but who the hell listens to me? Now, there are whispers of cremation. It's cheaper."

"What about the remains of the sixteen individuals that have not been identified?" I asked.

"Sometimes there was not much left, maybe part of a skull or maybe the bones of a wrist, hand, and forearm. We know when they are from different corpses because, even though they may be found close to known trails, when they could no longer go on or where they were abandoned by their 'coyotes,' if the body parts are found miles apart from each other and at different times, well, it doesn't take a Dr. Quincy or the CSI."

The officer who had just completed scrubbing his hands overheard us and put in his two cents. "Out there everywhere, we find shallow graves and crosses without names, and we know we aren't finding the graves that have no crosses.

"The easy ones to ID are the ones whose companions turned themselves in, asking to be rescued from certain death, and then report a body left somewhere back there in the desert. Most were dropped off at the border, arriving in dilapidated flatbed trucks or rusty cars where coyotes waited to guide them through the maze of paths. With my binoculars, I've seen fifteen or more board a stolen Chevy Suburban, its backseats removed, squeezed in like sardines one on top of the other, with truck-bed-size pieces of plywood separating the layers. They are the lucky ones because they surely will be caught before they get lost and die in the heat like the ones on foot. Everybody wins. The coyotes have already got most of their money, the unsuspecting driver received a very reduced price with a map, the stolen truck will be returned to its owner, a little worse for wear, and we have our statistics, which the politicians and the law enforcement apparatus can use for their own purposes. It's all a big game.

"As to the ones on foot, most are caught, but some will only be discovered by our reservation's law and order, weeks or months after their deaths."

The clerk gave the talkative tribal officer an annoyed look and continued, "Anything found near the remains is photographed and preserved, hopefully for later identification." She paused, looked up, and asked, "Would you like to see the photographs? They are not pretty."

The old man nodded. She went to a file cabinet and brought out some large, numbered manila envelopes. One by one, we started the ghastly process. The first ten-by-twelve photograph was of a skull with pink-and-white dentures locked in a mad grin. The empty sockets stared back at us for having invaded its privacy. The stomach-turning review of the photographs continued. One was of an intact swollen body with a large quantity of a black substance leaking out of its mouth and fouling the desert sand surrounding it. Most were only remnants, bones, and desiccated flesh of what once had been a living person. On the fifth file, along with the photographs of a hip and a long thigh bone and of pieces of what appeared to be flesh attached to a hand, there was a pair of crusty denim trousers and a separate close-up photograph of a man's ring with what appeared to be the initials "QQ."

Don David's face blanched.

"Is there anything else on that ring?" he asked. The custodian carefully checked the computer file whose numbers matched those on the envelope.

"It says here that on the inside of the ring, the name *Gabriela* is engraved."

"That's him. That's QuinQon—Medardo Rodolfo Cervantes. Evangelina told me that he carried that nickname all of his adult life, appropriate for a six-foot-five giant who towered over everybody in his village. They say his head was the size of a watermelon and his hands were like hams. His wife's name is Gabriela."

Nobody rejoiced that we had found him.

The next day, at the store front van stand, I parked my car, and we awaited the arrival of the vehicle for Don David's return trip to Bisbee. He passed me a brown bag with a bottle. After what we had seen the day before and what he was going to report when he got back, we both needed fortifying.

"What is happening, Ricardito?" the old man asked with a perplexed look. I signaled with my face and hands that I didn't understand his question, so he continued. "On the way to Tucson, the van was stopped twice by the migra. One time, this side of tombstone, everybody had to get out, and we were asked to produce our green cards or border *permisos* (permits). For the first time, I felt real fear, Ricardo. After over fifty years here, I have never gotten a permisso, never felt a need to, *quien es mas Americano que yo?* (who is more American than me?)"

He tossed the now-empty half pint of Seagrams into a dumpster, and as I reached into the backseat to get his canvas satchel, he said, "It wasn't just me, you know. Both your *abuelos* (grandfathers) and Padre Reyes and *muchos otros* (many others) who lived close to the border, once we got a job in the mines or settled a bit, not a thought was given to the then-imaginary line that separated the two countries."

He suddenly stopped what he was saying as if he knew something that I didn't, something that was too personal for him to bring up. My mind flashed on my own mother and father, but I left that question unasked.

"Gracias a Dios, one of the border patrolmen knew me from seeing me on Sundays at St. Patrick's, passing the collection plate, and, before they questioned me, said, 'He's okay.' And they went on to the next man.

"To pass the time on the trip to Tucson, I had been talking to a man seated next to me in the van about his situation. He had reentered near Naco after having recently been released from the federal prison outside Florence and deported. Three daughters, all born in the Estados Unidos, and his wife were waiting for him in Modesto, California. He said his oldest daughter was just starting junior high school, and he had such hopes for her, she was a smart one. He showed me her picture. He had lived there for eighteen years and most recently had been managing a car wash. He said that they often washed the border patrol vehicles. There, he had never even been questioned about his status in California when he joked with the officers in Spanish or broken English while putting the finishing touches on their cars.

"But after so many years of living in Modesto, he had to return to Mexico one more time because of word from his brother that his mother was gravely ill in Guadalajara. Unfortunately, she died before he could see her one last time. After they buried her, he tried to cross back to join his family in California but was caught at the border.

"He told me that *mucho antes* (much before), before my girls were born,' he had a minor squabble over some *celos* (jealousy) with the woman who was to become his wife and was charged with 'domestic violence.' This was during the time after the O. J. Simpson acquittal, when even a slap or a push between spouses in California was treated as a felony. In turn, considering the small nature of the infraction, he got a slap on the wrist from the court and was sentenced to community service, counseling, and the one day he had served the day he had been arrested. Afterwards, he and his *novia* (girlfriend) married and continued living together.

"Three little girls were to be born to them there in Modesto. When he was caught at the border after his mother's funeral, trying to return to Modesto, the federal authorities checked his FBI record, and they classified the family squabble so many years before as a prior conviction for a 'crime of violence.' Depicted by definition, if not fact, as a 'dangerous felon,' he received a thirty-six-month prison sentence from the federal court for his illegal reentry after the funeral. When that sentence was completed, he was picked up at the prison and deported back to Mexico, and now he is caught again trying to get back to his familia. Who knows how much time this crossing is going to cost him?

"'What about my wife and three little girls? Who will take care of them?' he asked as the border patrolman placed the handcuffs on him.

"Ricardo, que esta pasando? People say that a new state law will require even the Bisbee City police to check for my papers if I get a ticket for my dog messing the city park at the 'grassy green.' *No entiendo* (I don't understand)."

I didn't answer. I could only think of the tiny casket, one normally used for a baby, that would be met by Medardo Rodolfo Cervantes's family at the airport in Michoacan when what was left of him was returned home.

In 2005, Walmart, the world's largest retailer, whose business model is studied and admired by many businesses, agreed to pay 11 million dollars for having, from 1998 to 2003, used contractors who hired undocumented workers to clean their stores. These contractors had hired workers to clean more than a thousand stores—stores located in Massachusetts, Connecticut, New Jersey, Pennsylvania, Michigan, Alabama, and Texas.

Walmart's fine was less than one-half of 1 percent of its 2004 profit, and a much-smaller percentage of their profit if divided into the five-year period covered by the investigation.

Meanwhile, back in Tucson, daily, weekly, month after month, the orange clad and the families they support are just the collateral damage in the elaborate ruse of enforcement that, for years, focused only on the supply side of the business equation. Below the enforcement radar, politically powerful business interests have benefited from those lucky Mexicanos who completed the arduous journey to the awaiting jobs. Nobody seemed to notice that the fine imposed on Walmart would fund not even one day of the costs of the courts, government lawyers and appointed defense attorneys, border patrols, and prisons, the apparatus needed to process those who are caught.

Strung along the border, fearful, angry veterans of America's recent wars face southward and scan the horizon with binoculars. They hunker down under blue plastic tarps with lawn chairs and picnic paraphernalia—all made in China and purchased at Walmart. These people are there to protect their world from foreign encroachment. The dreadful menace is the "illegal alien" seeking work.

This great disabling fantasy of fear corrodes everything moderate in them. Instead of a reasoned, fair solution, they propose to make us all safer by declaring, carte blanche, that 10 or 15 million undocumented be designated as felons and deported without even discriminating between those that have been here a day or a lifetime.

Not a thought is given to the fact that most of them have come as a result of decades' old enticements by many of our most respected businesses who sought their cheap labor, nor of the benefits of lower prices in goods and services that have been passed on to all of us. Ensnarled in this mélange of the undocumented are their children born in the United States, who, because of the location of their birth and the law, are now American citizens.

A new line was being drawn in the sand, one that I had not anticipated or looked for. Suddenly, for me, the flow of history was being scaled down and personalized. Circumstances were placing the pride and respect for the fairness and justice of my America, this great land of immigrants, in potential conflict with the love of my family and friends and of my history and culture.

The deadly threat to our country, many say, are these people who stoop and haul and scrub and sweat all the while singing their songs and laughing and dreaming that they can somehow also be Americans by sheer striving. Nor are they seen as to what they have been and are, a gift to America.

It has come full circle; the self-appointed "minutemen" patrol the same border between Agua Prieta and Naco—where the survivors of Villa's Division del Norte crossed the border, trudged up the Mule Mountains of Southeastern Arizona to begin their new life more than ninety years ago, and started it all.

Part 6
Camilda

Dos pochos

After completing an assignment in Colorado, Rueben Kay, a publisher of books of photographic art, whom I had met casually at a photographer's workshop and who had his offices in Chicago called unexpectedly. He had recently seen some of my photographs in magazines and wanted to see the complete collection that I had taken over the years in my trips into Mexico. I hoped but didn't mention, fearing that he might laugh, that he might be interested in publishing a collection of my work.

At his small cluttered office, instead of asking to see what I had brought, he showed me and asked my opinion of some striking black-and-white portraits and other photographs of working-class Mexicanos, most of who had been taken in the 1940s, '50s, and early '60s. I looked at them with a critical eye. Many of the subjects of the photographer had been posed in the corner of a room, apparently to give the photograph depth. The edges of the ceiling and the sides of the wall on either side of the photograph formed a shallow *V*. The closed side of the *V* focused the viewer's eye on the subject of the portrait. After looking and pointing out a number of different individual portraits, the portly bald man gestured toward a large print and said, "That's him. That's the photographer."

Underneath the shallow *V* of the ceiling, a nut-brown old man held his head rigidly and stared into the camera in a pose that dripped of pride and dignity. He was seated in a stuffed easy chair. His right arm rested on the worn plaid fabric of the chair's armrest. Sparse hair, splotchy skin, and a skinny sagging body hinted of a lifetime of alcohol and cigarettes. Ripples of the inevitable excess skin of the old on his collapsing face were scrunched under his buttoned collar. He wore a long-sleeved white shirt and a tie of some thick material with a knot too large for the unstarched collar. From innumerable pressings, there was a shine at the creases of his cuffed cotton gabardine pants. His high-top work shoes with steel rivets had been buffed so often and so long that the rough black leather had a dull luster.

Along the left side wall of the photograph, I saw that there was a team photograph of the old Chicago Bears. The players wore tight-fitting leather helmets of a bygone era, and the absence of any face masks on the helmets helped to emphasize the size and broadness of their skulls. Absent also were any black faces on this team. There were also framed individual photographs of two athletes.

Underneath the one of the football player who was in an old-fashioned uniform was the name *Rick Cazares* in large block letters cut from a magazine or a newspaper. There was also a much more recent photograph of Sammy Soza in mid-swing over the word *Ositos* (Cubs) in carefully drawn block letters.

Along the right side wall of the photograph, there was a large Aztec calendar in the familiar circular pattern. Recently, I had seen more and more of these wooden calendars displayed in the homes of Mexican Americans. The calendars are usually intricately constructed of hundreds of pieces of different tropical woods that, when dry, leave muted colors in an orange, brown, and tan palette. On that wall, there was also an old photograph of a pretty Mexican woman in a starched dress with flowers woven into the fabric, and beneath her crossed ankles, the brand-new leather sole of one of her shoes was visible. On her lap, she held an infant. There was also another photograph, of two little boys, visible on the wall. The toddler had his arms around an infant who was seated between his legs.

Ruben looked at the photograph through the bottom part of his bifocals and said, "That old man is Casimiro Cazares. See why I like his work? In that self portrait, he tells so much. Long ago, he assimilated into the life of Chicago, but he remains with his heart still firmly planted in the past.

"Originally from somewhere in Southern Mexico, he now is a man caught between two cultures. Some would call him a *pocho*, bleached by the ways of the Americanos."

He turned his gaze on me, his head tilted back, still looking through the bottom part of his lenses, and minutely examined my face.

"You, Ricardo, are just the opposite, and most would say, you are the real pocho—American born and bred, now trying to add a little color to your life by digging around in Mexico, but also caught between two cultures.

"My idea is to publish a collection of both of your work— his photographs taken here in the States, and yours taken in Mexico. 'Dos Pochos,' caught between two cultures, but in opposite directions."

He tried to relight a partially chewed up cigar and said, "Just think about it a few days, Ricardo. Let the idea digest in your belly before you give me your answer. In the meantime, maybe you would like to meet Casimiro?"

He looked back at the photograph. "He used a timer on his camera for that shot. I've seen several of his close-ups, always in black and white. He takes ordinary objects, like this one." He handed me the print, and the smoke from his now-lit cigar curled around his face as he bent over his desk.

"Look at the textures. It's an ordinary brick wall as light filtering through the trees strikes it. Somehow, he brought out beauty and strength that would have escaped me. Look at that one—extraordinary detail."

"Same thing as to the faces he's captured—deeply weathered by the sun or by unrelenting toil, always of Mexican workers—or of their dark-eyed children, full of life, and of the promise of their hope shining through their eyes.

"To interpret what you see, both you and he sometimes use a telescopic lens and at other times, a microscopic one. You both see reality in a succession of different images, simple and stark, but I try not to read too much into either of your images."

He tossed the smoldering remnants of his wet cigar into an ashtray.

"Have you heard of the photographer from Manhattan who, anxious to understand the culture in Oaxaca, spent a whole week—can you imagine?—taking photographs of tribal dancers? In their dances, they wore heavy-carved wooden masks and large head decorations. He noticed, as he worked, that there always was a young boy—an apprentice, he thought—who was there at every performance.

"To more accurately understand their 'culture,' he provided the dancers with a cheap disposable camera and suggested that they bring him photographs depicting, in their eyes, things like joy, fear, dignity—for an appropriate fee, of course.

"When his guide had the film developed at the camera shop of the four-star hotel, the photographer thought, 'There is a mistake. The poor, uneducated dancers didn't understand the word *exploitation*. That frame on the roll of film was only of five evenly spaced nails, nailed horizontally on a shed's wall.'"

He found a new cigar, lit it, and a cloud of smoke partially obscured his face.

"It seems that every night, after the evening's last performance, the dancers walked home to their village in the hills several miles away. The next day, at dawn, they would start the walk back for another day of dancing. For their efforts, they received a few coins that tourists sometimes tossed.

"The owner of the nearby hut had hammered nails on his wall so that each could hang his gear and leave it overnight in the empty shed—to avoid carrying it all back and forth. For the rent of the nails, he charged one half of what was collected each day by the dancers. He was a busy man, so he hired a small boy to keep track of the take of the dancers so he wouldn't be cheated.

"Ricardo, I don't want glossy photographs taken by some Madison Avenue hot shot who one week is working for Vogue or Vanity Fair with cadaverous young nymphs and the next week has gone back to nature with the *primitivos*. I want the real thing."

Casimiro

Casimiro made the money to support his passion for photography as a dishwasher and janitor at Frida y Diego's, a trendy Chicago restaurant that serves dishes from the recipes that, they claim, Frida Kahlo made for Diego Rivera in their Casa Azul in Mexico City. The restaurant, besides having the walls painted in an incandescent blue color, was covered by prints of her paintings, but only those prints that were not so graphic or surrealistic as to affect a diner's appetite. Tunas, the purple fruit of the cactus, and different-colored pitahayas, mangos, calabazas, and watermelons had been painted by an artist on the blue wall between the prints, making a kaleidoscope of forms and colors.

The owner of the restaurant, a striking blond young woman with a very short haircut and a stylish masculine-cut suit, told me that Casimiro lived alone and liked nothing better than to show and sometimes sell a print of his work. He welcomed visitors to view his collection or to hire him for special projects, if the proposed project interested him. His walk-up apartment was only a short block away from the restaurant.

"It will be especially so if the visitor is a colleague photographer," she said as she dialed her cell phone to assure that he was there.

The old man in a blue terry cloth bathrobe and slippers greeted me as if I was an old friend. His eyes baggy from sleep and his wrinkled pajamas and grey stubble hinted that he didn't stand much on formalities. Other than for his unmade bunk and a tiny kitchen with a hot plate and a small refrigerator under the counter, the entire space was dedicated to his passion. There was a variety of photographic equipment, lenses, and cameras on a table. Envelopes crammed with prints of photographs catalogued in some unknown way were in cardboard boxes strewn here and there around the floor or piled one on top of the other all over the apartment.

"Ricardo, verdad? Bienvenido y pase" (Ricardo, right? Welcome, come in), he said with a broad smile.

I was surprised that on his walls, instead of his own favorite photographs, he had two large prints of Frida Kahlo's paintings. Two mugs were immediately produced, and he filled them with *orchata* from his tiny refrigerator.

"This is as good as any in Mexico, and it is from a *tiendita* (little store) just down the street. Mateo and his wife, Nina, know just how to combine the rice water, sugar, and cinnamon. That's what I love about Sheecago. If you know where to look, it is just like home. *But, ay Dios, los inviernos son infiernos.* (My God, winters are hellish.)

"I spoke to el senor Kay. He comes over at least once a week to the restaurant to sample the type of food that Frida supposedly made for El Panzon (her Fat One). He loves anything Mexican, authentic or not," he said, chuckling to himself.

Without further aimless conversation, the old man got to the point of our meeting. "He told me about his idea. 'Dos Pochos.' A Mexicano bleached by decades of life in America. The other, a 100 percent American that changes a little into the color of bronze as he discovers his past in Mexico's history and culture—all seen through their eyes and their photographs. What do *you* think, Ricardo?" He emphasized the *you* as he wiped his mouth with the sleeve of his bathrobe.

Refilling my mug without waiting for my response, he continued, "Did he tell you that I first came to Sheecago over fifty years ago during World War II as a Brasero? Thousands of us had congregated at the soccer stadium close to mi pueblo to sign up for work in the United States. It was like a fiesta. With so many Americanos in uniform, el Tio Samuel looked south for workers. We looked north—adventure, *dinero, muchas gringas* (money, many blondes). Ha-ha-ha! At least that's what we thought.

"The two governments agreed that those *pelados* (penniless individuals) who were accepted into the program, they would be transported by Mexican trains to the border. The group that I was with was checked out by the Americanos at the border in Nogales. There was photographs and *formas, muchas formas* (forms, many forms), and then we switched to an American train. Not long afterwards, we started scattering to all corners of Los Estados Unidos.

"I was just a boy of seventeen with a young wife, not yet a father. I liked working outside in the sun. My bones didn't complain much back then. I first worked on the track gang of the railroad. Then with others, I soon learned como se hace el pastel. I left the railroad and the pick and shovel, and picked algodon in the south and moved north as the seasons warmed—all the way to Illinois, Wisconsin, Minnesota to the Canadian border. I picked *melones, tomates,* carrots, apples, *peras*—anything that grew in the soil.

"They say that there was almost a half-million braseros sponsored by the two governments. Nobody knows how many factories and farms, desperate for laborers, found a way around the government program and its regulations. Once here, it was easy to find unregulated work that paid better.

"Even if my pay was small, somehow if I was willing to double and triple up in my accommodations—how's that for a five-dollar word, Ricardo?—there was always enough left to send back to Amelia and the son that she had given me. *Mas tarde* (Later), there was to be another *muchachito* (little boy)."

He paused for a long moment then continued, "*Desgraciadamente* (To my great shame), without realizing, I slowly started to lose my family. Being apart all year, except for a couple of weeks during Navidad y el Ano Nuevo (Christmas and New Year), became the normal. There were no telephones in our pueblo like there is today, except at the *commandancia* (police station), and their messages only brought bad news.

"What could pencil and paper tell of my life in the north, of what I saw with my eyes? When I first got here, I could hardly read or write. How many times could I write "te quiero" before it became just two words scribbled with a pencil on paper?

"I did the next best thing. I bought a cheap Brownie camera and photographed what I saw, *en ves en cuando* (once in a while), I would send a photograph with the money order so Amelia and mi hijitos could also see.

"I missed my familia, which I hardly knew anymore, and in the cold winters, I missed the warmth of the sun of the Valle de Teohuacan.

"Desgraciadamente, I turned to drowning my loneliness with alcohol. Anyway that was what my excuse was. There were fights at bars and trouble with the law and arrests.

"Soon, the brasero program was no more. And more and more, I started to fear returning every year to mi Mexico because of the risk of jail or prison if I was caught when I tried to reenter into the United States. And truthfully, maybe because I was afraid of what I might find when I returned home. It wasn't just the poverty. There were rumors, and Amelia was still a beautiful woman.

"But what would my family do without the little I continued to send. They had become accustomed to better things.

"'Coyotes' and the desert were for young men. All the years of working in the fields with the short hoe had taken their toll on me.

"Then one month, my letter with the pictures and the money order was returned undelivered. Mi *primo* (cousin) later told me, when I asked my cousin to investigate, that she had moved away from the village with the boys. There had to be somebody else. The separations had been too much for her, for us.

"Years later, when there was talk of amnesty for those illegals that had been here for many years, it was too late for me. I feared that my prior arrests would condemn me, and if I applied, I would be found out and the government would return me to Mexico. To what? Of what use is an old broken man?

"Over the years in Sheecago, word spread among my friends, mostly other illegals from Mexico, about my photographs and how I sent them home, and that's what I did to pass the time. I photographed men that were here working. They would choose the backgrounds that they wanted for their photographs. The Sears Tower or when the Mexican National Soccer Team played at the Soldier Field or wherever was their choice. They wanted to show their familias back home that they were now Norte Americanos. And over the years, I accumulated, from pawnshops and police sales, the equipment which I needed to take a decent photograph.

"Rigid envelopes, so that the photographs within wouldn't bend, with my return address here in Sheecago went all over Mexico. To the Districto Federal, to Queretaro, to Campeche, to Tamaulipas, Nayarit, north and south, east and west, even to the Valle de Teohuacan, where I was from, the place where, now, only in my dreams I can return.

"*Mi pueblito lindo* (My little village) is in the valle south of Mexico City and north of Oaxaca, where they say corn has been cultivated for 5000 years. You add *frijol negro* (black beans) and the great variety of wild chiles from the hills, and is it any wonder that the Zapotecas, five hundred years before Jesu Cristo"—he crossed himself—"created their great civilization there?"

Monte Alban

"Oaxaca and Monte Alban are not far from where I grew from a child to a man. Can you believe it? Monte Alban was a magnificent city for a thousand years, and it was abandoned five hundred years before the conquistadores landed in Mexico.

"When I was nine or ten, two or three times a week, my father and I would lead our burro with the *chicole* lashed to it, out into the surrounding hills to where there are groves of very tall cactus. My father made the chicole from a long center shoot of an agave. To its end, he had attached a little basket made of some type of very flexible cane. From the very top of the cactus, we would harvest the fruit of the plant—red, yellow, crimson, different sizes, different flavors—in the late summer when the fruit had ripened, the aroma around the groves era fantastica.

"He would always let me eat the first ripened one, which we captured in the basket from the top of the cactus. They were at least fifteen, maybe twenty, feet high, but they seemed so much higher than that to me back then.

"The spines would easily fall away from the pitahaya without hard scraping. That's how we knew it was ready to eat."

The old man stood up and, from the corner of the room, picked up a hollowed-out gourd that, on one end, had a long gooselike neck and a round bulbous bowl on the other.

"I have kept this to help me to never forget those days."

He proceeded to demonstrate how the long thin end of the gourd was thrust—between the long arms of the maguey and the inch-long thorns at the tip of each arm, and into the cavity that had been cut out from the plant's core. Like a straw, he sucked the hole at the bulbous end and showed how the liquid that had accumulated in the maguey's cavity was harvested.

"Then when the gourd is full"—he used his index finger on his extended arm to close the hole on the end of the gooselike neck—"we would deposit the *agua miel* (sweet liquid) into a container. We would drink a little of the liquid to refresh ourselves after our long walk, and the rest would be saved to ferment and make pulque.

"Mi Papi also showed me about the *guzanos* (worms) de maguey and the small *chapulines* (grasshoppers) that could be roasted and added to our beans, tortillas, and chile.

"Did you know that some scientificos say that there have been people living in that valle for eleven thousand years? Long before the Zapotecas and Monte Alban.

"Hundreds of years after the Zapotecas were gone, the Aztecas moved south from the nearby Valle de Mexico. The Aztecas were just 'the new keeds in the barrio,' que no, Ricardo? Ha-ha-ha!" he laughed heartily.

"I knew nothing of this back then. If I had, I probably wouldn't have cared. It has been the distance in space and time that has made me hungry for what was all around me back then, when I was blind.

"Instead, in those early years here in el norte, I spent too much time trying to blend in. Practicing, trying to say Sheecago and Sheeken so that my *cuates* (buddies) wouldn't laugh and say, 'se le escapo un frijol a casimiro,'" he chuckled at his little joke.

"But all that practice, it has been of no use, as you can tell. I have been to Monte Alban several times. When I first saw it, to my young eyes, it appeared abandoned, desolate. But even then I could see that it was a place of great architecture and great vistas.

At the museums here in Sheecago, where I like to spend my time, I heard it said that once it had been a city of God, like Jerusalem, Mecca, or Lourdes.

"At Monte Alban, the mountaintop had been leveled and raised platforms of rock placed there. These platforms served as the base for the pyramids. To the naked, untrained eye, it was a civilization of architecture and engineering. But what was not so obvious was that it was also a civilization of matematica y astronomia. The Zapotecas had a profound understanding of the movements of the sun, the moon, the stars. And this knowledge, they incorporated into their rituals.

"This was a civilization that did not know the use of the wheel or know how to make iron with heat. But they had calculated the solar calendar as being 365 days in length. The Indians later refined the calculation of the earth's yearly journey around the sun to a precision that was considerably beyond what Europeans or other civilizations had yet done, or would do, for many years.

"The Zapotecas had another calendario, el calendario sagrado. This calendar was 260 days in length. For the Zapotecas, each of these days had a specific sacred significance. Gods, both kind and evil, presided over each and every day. And every 52 years, as measured by the solar calendar, the beginning day of each of the calendars coincided.

"The Zapotecan priests and rulers awaited that day *con mucho miedo y mucha anxiedad* (great fear and anxiety). On that day, ordered by the gods as the start of the new era, they feared that the sun might not rise again. And these intricate calendarios dobles, in one form or another, spread throughout Southern Mexico and what we now call Central America.

"Believe it or not, Ricardo, Monte Alban, in all its magnificence, had a special area reserved for la cancha de pelota—a ball court— something that was unheard of then in Europe. Having seen my Sheecago Bears play and with the roar of the spectators in my ears, I imagined the entire population of Monte Alban observing the game or, more correctly, the sacred ritual. The ritual was performed with a ball-like object made of an elastic substance that magically bounced off—poof—of the performers.

"Only their most graceful and gifted athletes were permitted to strike the ball, which they did only with their shoulders, hips, chests, or *nalgas* (butts). They jostled each other with desperate intensity, trying to keep the bouncing pelota moving constantly between them and, at the same time, to keep it from crashing to the ground.

"No matter how great their abilities and no matter how great their effort, they could not do so for long. This ritual mirrored the lack of control that their rulers, no matter how powerful, had over their own daily lives and over the forces of the earth and sky. And this was in obvious contrast to the immense power of the gods who had so synchronized the movements of the sun, the moon, and the stars.

"I believe the performance by the Zapotecas was not a game. It was a rite of subservience and humility toward the gods who had such power over the sky and over the destiny of the people. Such was the power of their gods that only once every 52 years, they permitted with unfailing accuracy that their calendars converge.

"Of course, the purpose of the ball courts cannot be proven with complete certainty, but it is based upon interpretations by scientificos who studied the ball courts themselves and who studied the carvings on stones found at Monte Alban.

"What I do know, there is no evidence that the Zapotecas suffered from the blood madness that later would infect the Aztecas.

"The fragility of their records and the fanaticism of the *españoles* when they arrived centuries later and who, in the name of Jesu Cristo, burned and reduced to rubble everything that deviated from what they understood to be 'the one true way,' led to the destruction of everything but the most durable. Thousands, perhaps tens of thousands, of artifacts made of gold were melted down as the conquistadores lusted greedily for the substance of which the artifacts were made.

"Only a comment in one of the conquistadores notes was made of the peculiar objects that, when thrown on the ground, bounced back into the air with great speed. A thousand years before Mr. Goodyear and his experiments, the Zapotecas had discovered that boiling the morning glory with the gum of a certain tree produced a pliable elastic substance that would bounce. All that knowledge, and who knows what else, was lost.

"And you and I carry the blood of the ones who, so certain of their beliefs, joyfully destroyed the newfound heathen and their world and, in their 'righteous anger,' destroyed their barbarian art and just incidentally, so they said, satisfied their lust for the pagan's gold.

Casimiro carefully replaced the gourd in its special place on a top shelf.

"We, you and I, Ricardo, also carry the blood of those 'barbarians' that, for centuries, studied the heavens and built the pyramids.

"And now, Ricardo, the new *raza* (people) that arose four hundred years ago as a result of the mixing the blood of these two great civilizations has run headlong into another one that is technologically much more powerful and much more grasping."

Las Dos Fridas

Casimiro turned on the light of the table lamp in the tiny hall and directed its light toward the framed print that hung there.

"Look at that painting on my wall—Las Dos Fridas. It was painted way back in '39. But she already saw things clearly, important things, things that did not become clear to me until much, much later."

✐

Seated on a long wicker bench, there is a double image of the artist, as if she had painted it in front of a mirror. Although the faces are identical, the clothes that each Frida wears are completely different from each other.

One wears an elegant white ankle-length dress. The lace dress has a high neck that extends to her jawline and frames her face, and ruffled sleeves that extend below her elbow. It is an evening gown that, even now, would be stylish in Washington or New York ballrooms. The other Frida wears a simple Mexican-Indian collarless and sleeveless blue blouse decorated with a single yellow ribbon and a skirt the color of earth. In her right hand, the Mexican woman lovingly holds the left hand of the woman in the beautiful white dress. In addition to their hands, there is one other connection. A single artery from the heart of the Indian Frida winds out from her heart and behind the neck and shoulder of her sister and into her exposed damaged heart. The Mexican is giving her sister her life's blood. The return artery, the one that is supposed to give back the life-giving blood to the Mexican, winds around the shoulders of the white lace dress. But the return of the fluid is not possible because that artery has been severed, and the woman in white holds a pair of scissors in her right hand. The blood dripping from the broken connection has pooled twice on her lap as it cascades down her otherwise immaculate white dress. The Mexican Frida, deprived of the return of the lifeblood she has just given, holds in her hand the useless end of the artery severed by her sister.

༝

"When Cuervacio was still a boy, during my last trip home, we went to Oaxaca. I wanted to see Monte Alban once again. I told him about the wonders that had been there more than two thousand years before. And that was the last time I heard from my son, until two years ago.

"I was surprised when I got the long-distance phone call at the restaurant. Who could be looking for me there? It was Cuervacio. It didn't seem possible, but he was now a man with a family of his own. He had come in illegally and had worked his way north by working first in a sheeken farm in Arkansas. His job there was to catch the sheekens as they ran, *como locas* (like crazy), and flapped and scratched and sheet all over him in the sheeken house, just like a movie of Cantinflas, but not so funny for him. Then in the slaughter houses in Nebraska. He told me of the long rubber boots as high as his huevos, which he wore to keep himself clean from the blood and the gore of the slaughtered cows, but nothing could be done about the smell except putting a little Vicks menthol in his nostrils.

"We talked about the last time that we had been together and of our trip to Monte Alban. Now mi hijo wanted to see the great beautiful city that he had heard of and only imagined in his mind and which was built two thousand years after Monte Alban. La

Gran Manzana, the Big Apple, was the *sobrenombre* he heard given to it in the television news reports from Mexico City, and so after so many years, that was the end of our conversation.

"A few weeks later, Cuervacio called once again. He was in awe and total amazement to be in 'el capital del mundo.' He described the Manhattan buildings and the subways and the crowds.

"He said he had made friends with a Dominicano, who told him there was work at the very top of the world, en las Torres Gemelas (Twin Towers), for one who was willing to do whatever was needed and who wasn't too choosey or demanding."

Casimiro paused for a long time before he continued. "It has been some months now, and he hasn't called again. I'm sure I'll hear from him soon, and maybe he'll come here to Sheecago to visit me, and we will talk after all these years about what is past. I will always have room here for mi muchacho."

The old man's eyes—which saw beauty in the smallest, most insignificant things, things that are solid and endure—suddenly brimmed over with tears. Somehow, I felt he was wrong and that his son would not call again. Instead, he had become another of the faceless multitude, uncounted in life and uncounted in death, who had journeyed from the south with hearts full of hope. And if they were not caught so as to be treated like loafers, like outlaws, or thieves, many disappeared and left only their spirit that, like an arrow, pierced deeply into the heart of those who loved them.

Camilda

A few days after Rafael had identified the photograph of Porfirio Diaz as being the picture of the mystery man in my grandfather's room, he handed me a large manila envelope.

"Here," he said gruffly. "Maybe you can find something. It's been in the upper shelf of my closet for years. I guess nobody ever got around to putting them in an album."

I took the stack of old photographs and suddenly saw him with new eyes. My seventy-five-year-old cousin was making plans to return once again to Spain, to the Basque country.

"My last trip, I'll probably not be back. I would be positive of not returning if it wasn't for my grandkids being here in the States," he said.

Still an imposing man, he carried 280 pounds ramrod straight on a frame well over six feet tall. Light-skinned with dense white hair that he kept cut very short, in the military way, he could pass anywhere as a Northern European or Irishman.

In the early 1950s, Rafael proudly wore the emblem with the anchor and globe with other guys from all over America. In those days, just out of high school, he had little hope of further education. So he joined Swedes, Italians, Jews, and others—black and white—from all over our country. Mexicanos running away from the underground copper mines and the orchards and fields too had become part of the mix. And the greeting "Semper Fi" was drummed into all of their heads as only the marines can do.

He was one of the ones that faced the hordes of Chinese communists on the Korean peninsula. Afterward, when he returned an NCO, he found that the life he had left behind still waited for him. This was before "Brown v. Board of Education" and "Black is Beautiful" and "Si Se Puede." It was a time very different in outlook and perspective from today. This was before the movie and musical icons of World War II and the Korean War, Sinatra and Crosby, were suddenly rooted out and replaced in the collective consciousness of a new generation by a gyrating Elvis one Sunday evening on the *Ed Sullivan show*. The counterculture's Summer of Love in San Francisco, Woodstock on the East Coast, and the purgatory of Vietnam were still in the future.

Drummed into his child's mind in that mining town was that denial of his Mexican roots was the passport to successful inclusion in the dream and promise that was America. Fifty years later, he still struggled with that virus, and until recently, I had not noticed how much I too had been infected with a less-virulent strain in the spectrum of shame of those days. But I had opened that door and now saw things that I hadn't understood before about myself. Hopefully, the new generation will show us another way, unless a new unexpected wave of forced shame and denial will be thrust upon them too.

The paradox was that this proud man was the one who had preserved the photographs, and he was the one who remembered the stories of the family in Mexico. Consciously or subconsciously, he wanted to be sure that it was all preserved and remembered in case he didn't return from Bilbao.

Back home, on my patio table facing the Tucson Mountains to the west, I spread them out. There were old photographs of fresh-faced young people some of whom I recognized as aunts and uncles, in their teens and early twenties, taken in different settings and on different occasions. There was even one of my parents before they married. Ordinary photographs that, for me now, were made extraordinary because of my knowledge of what was to happen to them as they lived out their lives. All the dead were there, leaving so many unanswerable questions, things about which I was never going to be sure.

There was one group photograph that especially caught my attention. It was of a picnic at, what must have been, the shallow San Pedro River, a popular area for summer outings not far from Bisbee. The young men have their pants rolled up to their knees; and the girl's skirts, barely clearing the water, have been modestly hitched up to the same length.

They are laughing and scattering in different directions from a bending man with a short-sleeved collarless black shirt. He is shoeless with his trousers' legs in the water. Both of his hands grip the brim of a soaked felt hat with which he is scooping up water. He has a huge open-mouthed grin, and his wire-rimmed glasses teeter on his nose; it is as if Father Reyes is joyously baptizing them all with the bounty of this country.

Among the revelers, they are all there—my mother and her two sisters, all born in Mexico, and her three brothers, all born here. All of them scattering from the priest's watery blessing.

In the background, in the shadow of an enormous cottonwood tree, among the less rambunctious, there are a number of men and women observing the shenanigans. I recognize two men. One, with a handlebar mustache and a cigar in his hand; the other one is taller, an erect slim man with a high receding hairline and a broad smile. They are my grandfathers.

In the midst of all this activity are several toddlers seated in the water. One little girl is splashing water on another one who is crying. A boy, a two- or three-year-old, also seated up to his waist in the clear water, is looking with black shiny eyes directly into the camera. He has a startled quizzical expression as if wondering just what it was that has just happened behind him. That little boy without his trunks is me.

I carefully slipped the photograph back into the old envelope. The desert night was suddenly all around us. It was no longer a time of color in the desert. There were only silvery shadows and silhouettes of the wondrous life around us. As we walked along the trail, she suddenly pointed, and I caught only a glimpse of a flapping bat.

"If we wait a bit, as it gets cooler, we might see the three-legged coyote that occasionally comes to visit, or perhaps the family of javelinas that push over my plantings to get to their roots," I said.

"They are like sentinels overlooking the city," Camilda whispered as she looked up the mountain.

I looked up in the bright moonlight and saw the army of saguaros spaced out like in a military formation up the mountain's incline.

"Or the spirits of those already gone," she said.

"They grow only about an inch each year."

She remained silent for a minute in the advancing darkness.

"Maybe, Ricardo, we will walk together long enough to see them grow a foot."

"Perhaps even two feet," I replied.

We remained there without speaking for a long time, watching the city's lights begin to light up like diamonds, each with our own thoughts.

"Ricardo, do you ever feel that maybe you don't belong here?" she asked.

Not answering, I looked down into the valley that bisected urban Tucson and across to its most prominent mountain range, the Santa Catalinas. And as the curtain of darkness intensified, the twinkling lights creeping up their foothills became clearer. They mark the sumptuous homes of wealthy migrants moved from Iowa, Chicago, and other areas north and east of here, to retire or to just enjoy the good life and beauty of the Sonoran Desert. And I thought about my daughter and ex-wife who had moved so far away from everything I thought was important without as much as a glance backward.

I knew there was an intermittent ribbon of green down there not visible now in the dark, mostly mesquite and hardy palo verde, which, like me, had thrust their roots deep into the parched sandy soil. The trees and bushes marked what was left of the Santa Cruz. Years ago, wells had pulled the surface water's flow underground from what had once been a south-to-north stream.

I knew that, in 1775, Juan Bautista de Anza, the commander of the presidio at Tubac, had followed that stream. He had received an order from Commandante-Inspector Hugo O'Conor, who was inspecting the presidios on the Sonoran frontier for Carlos III, the Spanish king. Anza was told by O'Conor to move the then-northernmost Sonoran presidio, which was located at Tubac, an additional sixty miles further north to what is now the present site of Tucson.

The missions of Tumacacori, outside of Tubac, and San Xavier, sixty miles to its north, had almost been destroyed when, eight years before, because of some royal squabble, Spain's King Carlos III had ordered his military to expel all the black-robed Jesuits from his lands. After their expulsion, the missionary work with the O'odham started seventy years before by Father Kino had been placed in great jeopardy without their European caretakers.

Soon, the missions along the Santa Cruz came under attack by the Apaches, and San Xavier was burned. Fearing that the physical deterioration of the missions was just the least of their problems, considering the Spaniard's dependence on the O'odham's labor; one of the Franciscan friars, the Order sent to replace the Jesuits, wrote to his fellow brothers and, when speaking of the O'odham, said, "For God's sake, don't let those people lose their spiritual submission to the missionaries."

Then, as now, there were two Catholic churches. The hierarchal male-dominated church obsessed with dogma and rules that is focused in extending the Church's reach and, therefore, the

Vatican's power. And the truly noble church, one composed of lowly priests and nuns and laypeople who toil entire lives to care for the poor and needy, and who will even cross deserts in search of souls trying to pass on the Lord's admonition of "love thy neighbor as thyself," and who never, in their lives, will even encounter an archbishop or a cardinal.

But Anza couldn't carry out O'Conor's order to move the presidio immediately. Almost at the same time as the expulsion of the Jesuits from Northern Sonora, Padre Junipero Sera had arrived on the continent's Pacific Coast after a torturous journey from Mexico's interior. There he dedicated his first mission, made out of crude logs, and named it San Diego. This was the first European mission on the coast of what was then known as Alta California.

Padre Junipero Sera had reached Alta California from Guadalajara by crossing el Golfo de California from San Blas on the mainland, to Cabo San Lucas in Baja California. He then sailed to Puerto Escondido by following the Baja California coast. There he continued north up the arid Baja California peninsula.

There was considerable anxiety among the Spaniards because rumors were rampant among the friars and military men that Russia and England were poised to threaten Spain's territorial claim to Alta California. The total Spanish population in Alta California was then only about seventy.

Permanent settlements were critical to cement Spain's territorial claim. Padre Sera, after his arduous journey, reported a desperate need for a more practical land route from the interior of Mexico through Sonora, to Alta California.

Reports by Indians of an encounter with a white man who wore long clothing that reached to his ankles had filtered eastward from the Pacific Coast. The report of this encounter was passed eastward from tribe to tribe until the Sonorans too heard about it. The Spanish viceroy decided to seek a land route by retracing those reports westward across the desert toward the coast.

Juan Bautista de Anza, commander of the Tubac presidio, was given the duty of leading that expedition. He first conducted an exploratory trip to verify the viability of the venture. In the autumn of 1775, Juan Bautista led a group of settlers that followed the Santa Cruz, the trickle of water going north from the Tubac presidio. Of the 240 in the group who would make the journey, there were 200 settlers—men, women, and children— who herded 1000 heads of livestock. The rest were soldiers.

The settlers had been recruited in Sonora and Sinaloa from the dirt-poor mestizos who had nothing to lose, except their lives, in risking such a journey. The women each were given six yards of colorful ribbon as an incentive. The gray-robed Franciscans promised them that only in heaven could such a good life exist as in Alta California.

The settlers came from Culiacan, in the province of Sinaloa, and from San Miguel de Horcasitas, which was then Sonora's provincial capital. The presidio of Horcasitas was located near the Rio Sonora and was on the western edge of the land where the Yaquis had lived since ancient times.

Horcasitas was placed in the center of three missions—Ures, Populo, and Los Angeles—whose locations formed a triangle around Horcasitas. In this way, the presidio could provide the missions with protection against raiding Indians.

But the friars soon discovered that this arrangement was a double-edged sword. The presidio's soldiers and camp followers provided an ungodly example of drinking, gambling, and wenching to the residents of the missions. The missions were where the faithful commonly greeted each other with a "Hail Mary," which was responded to with a "conceived in grace."

When the Jesuits first arrived in the area decades before, they had devised a strategy of convincing the Yaquis to move from the more-than-eighty rancherias they had scattered to, to the vicinity of what the Jesuits hoped would become eight missions. There, their harvest for souls and for the labor to construct the mission's buildings, gardens, and orchards could be more fruitful. Later on, these missions were to become the Yaqui towns on the Rio Yaqui.

The priests also tried to lure the Yaquis to move to the three missions that surrounded Horcasitas. The priests first convinced a few families to settle within the mission's boundaries. Then those families would establish a ceremonial kinship with other Indians as a compadre or a comadre. The kinship of any newcomers, as a sponsor or as being sponsored, was based upon the priest's baptisms, confirmations, or wedding. In this way, the family circle by blood or ritual grew, and the population of the missions did also.

The officials and priests who normally governed and explored for the king and the Church were called Peninsulares and were born in Spain. Individuals like Anza, who was born in New Spain of Spanish parents, were called Criollos. The settlers who accompanied Anza, however, were mixed-blood mestizos, mostly of Indian women and Spanish men, and a few *mulatos*.

The five hundred fresh horses expected by Anza at Tubac for use by his expedition had been stolen by an Apache raid and scattered to the four winds a few days before his arrival. To Anza's fury, El Capitan Colorado, Hugo O'Conor, had taken the soldiers from Tubac to reconnoiter sites for another possible presidio and left Tubac unprotected. The settlers would have to do with what they had brought with them and the few nags the Apaches left behind.

One day, north of Tubac, Manuela Pinuelos, one of the settlers, gave birth to a son. Probably the first child of mixed European and Indian blood born in what, many years later, would be known as the territory of Arizona. Manuela did not survive the birth.

At San Xavier del Bac, they observed the repair work being done by the Franciscans and the O'odham, the desert people, on what was left of the mission building. Later, it was to become a much more ambitious project, and the beautiful "Dove of the Desert" of San Xavier would not be completed until 1797. Since, it, along with the majestic saguaros, has become the icon of our community.

I thought of the recent pageant I had attended at San Xavier. A community choir made up of singers of many nonnative Christian denominations sang the soaring, magnificent music of the Christmas story, which has inspired composers for so many centuries. Not surprisingly, the O'odham's role in the pageant was limited to providing little brown-faced children in native dress with lighted candles, carrying a banner of the Virgen de Guadalupe down the aisle that their ancestors had built.

For that hour within the church's walls, the listeners were transported from their humdrum lives into the sublime. In the golden luminescence of hundreds of luminarias placed in the niches of the altar and the tops of the side walls, for just a fleeting moment, I experienced something similar to the religious fervor and joy of those Spanish priests and native people who had built this labor of love so many years before—the faith which, when it blossomed, has been such a critical part of the character of the Mexican people.

Seven miles downstream at Chuk Son, the name given to the settlement at the base of the mountain that dominates modern Tucson, the settlers rested at the casita de San Agustin. A mission of adobe was being constructed there. The structure the Franciscans built first after personal shelter was the rock walls surrounding the small mission's garden. The walls were there to keep foraging animals out. When sentinels posted on the peak observed the dust of what could be approaching Apaches, the same rock walls served as protection for their animals, and they were herded inside to avoid being scattered and stolen by the raiders.

After a short rest, the settlers followed the Santa Cruz to where the stream emptied into the Gila River. Near there, some of Anza's party visited what was, even then, an ancient Indian ruin called by some as La Casa Grande de Moctezuma. The four-story building had been constructed centuries before of mud made from caliche, a substance found in the desert floor a few inches below the surface. When water was added to crushed caliche, it became as hard and solid as rock. It was a building technique not known to the desert's more-modern inhabitants. The great house located about a mile from the Gila was at the end of what had been a large canal downstream from the river. Much later, it was determined that floods had deepened the river's channel, so the Indians could no longer fill the canals that led from the river and watered their fields. The Hohokam, for their survival, reverted to scattered rancherias along the desert rivers. The O'odham are just some of their descendents.

High up on the upper west wall of the casa grande, a circular hole aligns with the setting sun during the summer solstice and, for two or three days, casts a perfect circle of light on an interior wall. For the Hohokam, that marked the end of one season and the birth of another. Large shallow oval pits constructed of caliche and small round river rocks that were covered with a rubberlike substance from Guayule have been found, and people suggest that there may have been ball games similar to those that the indios played almost two thousand miles to the south.

Where the Gila emptied into the Colorado River, a Yuma tribal chief showed Juan Bautista and the settlers where to safely cross the river. He also revealed the secret of traversing the desert and the miles of sand dunes that lay before them. And so, Juan Bautista divided the group into three. Each traveled with their animals a day apart so as to permit underground springs to refill the desert water holes.

In January, the settlers arrived with their pack animals and herds of livestock at San Gabriel Arcangel—Padre Sera's first in the string of missions up the Pacific Coast. Then they followed the trails used by the Indians since time immemorial, along the coast to the newly named San Luis, Obispo de Toledo. The intrepid group continued north toward the Mission San Carlos Borromeo de Carmelo.

When he heard of their approach, Padre Sera left that mission with three other priests to greet and celebrate a solemn Mass of Thanksgiving for the successful arrival of the settlers from Horcasitas and Culiacan. Only Manuela Pinuelos had died, while giving birth, on the journey. Two more mestizo children had been born to the settlers during their journey to Alta California.

Finally at their destination, Anza explored the Rio de San Francisco and the enormous bay that it emptied into. There, sites were chosen for the presidio and for the mission that would be constructed at the Arroyo de Dolores.

Upon his return from Alta California, Juan Bautista couldn't finish the task that had been assigned to him by Comandante Inspector O'Conor. Having navigated the Sonoran route to Alta California, other much more pressing matters now awaited him in Mexico City. Instead, the task of moving the garrison from Tubac to Tucson fell to Teniente Olivas, who completed the move in 1777.

A continent away along the Atlantic coast, men from a different world and with a different kind of strength and courage were declaring their independence. Thirty years later, Lewis and Clarke made their celebrated exploratory trip from the Mississippi River to the Pacific Coast. Forty years after that, the Mormon battalion, on their way to San Diego, stopped in Tucson, by then a Mexican town, for reprovision and rest. They were graciously welcomed by the Mexicanos, and the Mormons traded buttons and cloth for grain and other life-sustaining provisions. No mention was made that the battalion was going to join the United States Army of the West in its planned war against an infant Mexico.

We had remained there, under the sprinkling of stars, without speaking for a long time, each with our own thoughts.

Speaking louder, making sure that I'd hear her after my long silence, she asked again, "Ricardo, don't you sometimes feel that we may not belong here with the Americanos?"

From somewhere, I heard, "Ahooooaaa," and an unexpected laugh that startled both of us. The sounds had come out of my throat! Having just made the unexpected connection in my mind, I looked at her lovely chiseled bronze face and said in mock exasperation, "Ha que mi Camilda Pinuelos. That's going to have to wait for another day's conversation."

She looked at me quizzically after my outburst, as if asking, "What's with you?"

I said, "Vamos mi pochita. We best go back. We have to get up early tomorrow."

"I will prepare us the carne seca that I have been drying on the roof and *huevos* (eggs) for our *desayuno* (breakfast). Tomorrow is when you will photograph the birds?" she asked.

"Yes, it's not far, just down I-10, about fifty miles, a little past Texas Canyon near Wilcox. They are sand cranes—all the way from Siberia, they say."

"Is it true that their outstretched wings are over five feet wide?"

"Si."

"Why are they here?"

"Only to visit while the days are short where they come from."

"Like the *papalotl*, the monarch butterflies from the north that visit Michoacan?"

"Yes, something like that," I said. I got her hand, and she held on tightly to mine. Then with the thumb of my other hand, I flicked on the flashlight that would help us find our way back to our home.

Time Line of Novel's Historical Events in Mexico

1903–1907: Flores Magon brothers publish a magazine, *Regeneracion*, with headlines, "The Constitution Is Dead." They condemn the Mexican feudal system of the haciendas, lack of legislative protection for factory and mine workers, and the prevalence of child labor. Members of a new clandestine political party organize the miners in Cananea, Sonora, and go on strike against the American-owned Cananea Copper Company. After a brief period, Porfirio Diaz breaks the strike using the bullets and bayonets of the Rurales and the federal army.

July 8, 1910: Porfirio Diaz is reelected president of Mexico, a post he has controlled since 1876.

November: Francisco Madero, leader of the rebellion against President Diaz returns to Mexico after having sought refuge in San Antonio, Texas.

May 10, 1911: Juarez, Chihuahua, falls to Madero's forces led by Francisco [Pancho] Villa.

May 25: Porfirio Diaz resigns and flees to Paris, France.

October: Madero is elected president and inaugurated in November.

April 3, 1912: Villa joins Victoriano Huerta, Madero's field commander, at Torreon. Because of Villa's alleged insubordination, Huerta sentences Villa to be executed.

June 3: Madero intercedes and saves Villa's life and instead imposes a prison sentence. Later, Villa escapes from prison and flees to El Paso, Texas.

February 9–18, 1913: Huerta and Felix Diaz, nephew of deposed Porfirio Diaz, lead a counterrevolution and arrests President Madero and Vice President Pino Suarez.

February 22: Both the president and the vice president are assassinated.

March 23: After learning of the assassination, Villa returns to Mexico and starts to raise an army.

March 28: Venustiano Carranza, governor of a northern state, declares himself "primer jefe," the successor of Madero, and the first chief of the constitutionalist army.

August 26: Villa's new army, the Division del Norte, routs the federal forces at San Andres and captures three locomotives and boxcars.

October 2: Villa's Division del Norte captures Torreon.

October 10: In a rigged election, Huerta is elected president.

October 17: Carranza establishes a provisional government in Hermosillo, Sonora.

November 15: Villa captures Juarez and takes three thousand prisoners.

November 19: Villa wins the Battle of Tierra Blanca.

December 8: Villa's Division del Norte captures Chihuahua, the capital of the northern state of Chihuahua.

January 1914: Villa defeats the federal forces at Ojinaga. General John Pershing crosses the Rio Grande to call on Villa and pays his respects to him.

March: As the revolutionary forces are closing in on Mexico City, Villa learns that Carranza has sent another general to take Zacatecas, the doorway to Mexico City, which had been Villa's objective.

June 23: Villa takes Zacatecas without Carranza's approval. To stop Villa's entry into Mexico City, Carranza withholds ammunition and coal for Villa's locomotives.

July 8: Obregon captures Guadalajara.

July 15: Huerta resigns and flees to Spain.

August 15: Obregon, with Yaqui troops, occupies Mexico City on behalf of the constitutionalists. Carranza joins him.

October to November 12: Convention at Aguascalientes establishes a new entity—the conventionalists—claiming to be Mexico's legitimate source of power. The attendees are the generals of the successful revolutionary forces.

November 28: Villa and Zapata, as part of the conventionalists, enter Mexico City and are photographed together in the presidential palace.

1915: Obregon sides with Carranza, and Zapata with Villa as war breaks out between the victorious revolutionaries.

April 6–15: Villa is defeated at Celaya in two battles against Obegon.

June–September: Siege at Leon. Villa is again defeated and seeks refuge in Chihuahua. Obregon losses an arm to an artillery shell from Villa's forces.

November 1: Villa is defeated at Agua Prieta, Sonora. The constitutionalists are led by General Plutaraco Elias Calles. Colonel Lazaro Cardenas is decorated for his role in the battle. Before the battle, thousands of constitutionalist troops are transported through the United States on the El Paso and Southwestern. This was a railroad line used by Phelps Dodge to move copper ore from its Douglas smelter to the refinery in El Paso. The garrison awaiting Villa's attack is swollen to over six thousand men. The use of large spotlights to light up the battlefield during Villa's night attack leads to Villa's troops being decimated.

March 9, 1916: Villa attacks the town and military garrison located at Columbus, New Mexico. Columbus is a water and refueling station on the El Paso and Southwestern railroad line between Douglas, Arizona, and El Paso, Texas.

April 8: General John Pershing's Punitive Expedition involving 6,675 men reaches three hundred miles into Mexico searching for Villa.

June: Skirmishes occur between Mexican troops and the Punitive Expedition. Bitter communications are exchanged between President Carranza and President Wilson. Wilson mobilizes the National Guard.

June 27, 1916 to February 5, 1917: The Punitive Expedition withdraws from Mexico.

February 5: The new radical constitution gives birth to twentieth-century Mexico.

April 6: United States declares war on Germany.

April 10, 1919: Emiliano Zapata is assassinated by order of Carranza.

June 1: Obregon declares himself a candidate for the presidency. Carranza raises the issue of "the plague of militarism" and offers, instead, his own candidate, Ignacio Bonillas.

April 1920: Carranza summons Obregon to Mexico City to face trumped-up charges.

April 20: Obregon declares a rebellion against Carranza.

May 7: Carranza flees Mexico City.

May 21: Carranza is assassinated.

June 1 to October 31: Adolfo de la Huerta is inaugurated provisional president. He obtains an agreement from Villa to cease his revolutionary activities. Villa is rewarded with a ranch and a large group of bodyguards. Jose Vasconcelos is given an important position as rector of the National University in Mexico City and will become Obregon's minister of education and culture.

September 5: Obregon is elected president to a term that is to end in 1924.

1923: Obregon designates Plutarco Elias Calles to succeed him as president.

July 20: Pancho Villa is assassinated after declaring his support for De la Huerta for the presidency in the pending election.

1924: Plutarco Elias Calles begins the presidential term, which is to end in 1928.

1925: Tension between the "two majesties," the state and the Catholic Church heats up. Calles vows to carry out the 1917 Constitution's mandates directed against the Catholic Church.

January–July 1926: Calles passes legislation requiring priests to register with the government and declares the teaching of religion and the conducting of worship services to be crimes.

July: Bishops declare July 31 as the last day that Masses will be celebrated in Mexico.

August 21: Calles meets with the archbishop and refuses to make concessions to the church.

October: The senate makes the reelection of Obregon possible upon Calles completing his term.

October 1926 to April 1927: Obregon, with fifteen thousand federal soldiers, attacks the Yaquis whom he had led in several critical battles of the Mexican Revolution. For their loyalty in the Revolution, Obregon had promised the Yaquis "freedom in their own lands."

January 1927: The Cristeros rebel against the government in its attempt to destroy the Church. By that war's end, there were 50,000 Cristeros in arms and 25,000 deaths caused during the uprising.

July 1928: Obregon, the president-elect, is assassinated by a Catholic fanatic at La Bombilla restaurant in Mexico City. Calles places Portes Gil in the presidential chair to commence Obregon's term. Portes Gil serves from December 1928 until February 1930.

June 1929: Portes Gil negotiates a peace agreement between the government and the Catholic Church. Calles names Ortiz

Rubio to succeed Portes Gil. Calles creates the National Revolutionary Party, the precursor of the PRI. Jose Vasconcelos's candidacy for the presidency unites university students, middle-class intellectuals, workers in the northeast, and the Cristeros. It is his declared intention of returning to the original roots of the Revolution and opening the door to democracy.

November: Calles declares Ortiz Rubio the winner of the election. Vasconcelos goes into exile.

September 1932: Ortiz Rubio resigns, complaining bitterly of Calles's thinly veiled dictatorship. Calles chooses Ablelardo Rodriguez to complete the final two years of the now-six-year term.

1933: Calles designates Lazaro Cardenas as his choice for the new six-year term.

1934: Cardenas assumes the presidency for a six-year term.

April 1936: Calles is exiled to the United States by Cardenas.

March 1938: Cardenas orders the expropriation of all subsurface resources in the hands of foreigners to be returned to the Mexican nation. Cardenas attempts to open the political process to the masses through their participation in an expanded political party and its component parts.

1939: Cardenas designates Avila Camacho as the party's choice for the presidency. Opposition to his choice coalesces around General Juan Almazan. The only unifying position of Almazan's supporters is their opposition to the party in power. Bloody encounters throughout the nation between the contending parties threaten Mexico with renewed chaos. Avila Camacho is declared to be the winner of the election by the government.

1940: Avila Camacho puts an end to the church-state conflict by declaring that he was a believer.

June 1942: Mexico declares war on the Axis powers.

September 16: All of the living former presidents of Mexico join together and ask for the country's support in the declaration of war against the Fascists.

1946: Miguel Aleman is revealed by Avila Camacho to be his choice for the presidency. Aleman assumes the presidential sash. Every six years, the outgoing president reveals who will succeed him as Mexico's new president.

2000: President Ernesto Zedillo presides over the first democratically conducted election in over sixty years. His party, the PRI, is defeated. Vicente Fox Quesada, the candidate of the center right PAN, is elected as the president of Mexico.

Summary

The epic story of the extraordinary migration into the US of millions of Mexican people. A migration that began with a trickle of refugees fleeing the Mexican Revolution and became a torrent as the Revolution intensified and the new revolutionary government attempted to destroy the Catholic Church in Mexico.

Ricardo, a Mexican-American born in a mining town in Southern Arizona, only has fragmented images of those times based on old photographs and whispered stories.

In his journey of discovery, he slowly peels away page after page of the past and discovers unexpected things about himself and his family when he encounters an elegant old woman from another era, a wrinkled Yaqui deer dancer who had fought in the Revolution, and a hermit with an ugly secret hiding away in a field of blue maguey in Jalisco. It is a chance encounter with a group of vibrant young people celebrating their culture that opens the door to his heart and his future.

The story includes figures familiar to Americans like Pancho Villa and Emiliano Zapata, and also includes Alvaro Obregon, Elias Calles, and Lazaro Cardenas—presidents who were instrumental in molding modern Mexico. A time line of significant historical events in Mexico is included.

In 1915, immediately south of the Arizona-Sonora border, the two armies of the successful revolutionaries, whose leaders had become rivals for power, clashed. Three of the victors of that battle against Pancho Villa's Division del Norte were later to become presidents of Mexico. This is the story of forces on both sides of the border that helped weave the human fabric that more and more unites the two countries.

About the Author

The author's parents and grandparents migrated from Mexico into the mining camps of Southern Arizona in the early years of the last century. A graduate of the University of Arizona, he served as a judge in Tucson for twenty-five years.